Francis

The Saint of Assisi

8-9

Francis
The Saint of Assisi

A Novel

Joan Mueller

New City Press
Hyde Park, New York

Published in the United States by New City Press
202 Cardinal Rd., Hyde Park, NY 12538
www.newcitypress.com
©2010 Joan Mueller

Cover design by Durva Correia

Library of Congress Cataloging-in-Publication Data:

Mueller, Joan, 1956-
  Francis : the Saint of Assisi : a novel / Joan Mueller.
    p. cm.
  Includes bibliographical references and index.
  ISBN 978-1-56548-332-3 (pbk. : alk. paper) 1. Francis, of Assisi, Saint, 1182-1226—
Fiction. 2. Italy—History—476-1268—Fiction. 3. Christian saints—Fiction. 4. Assisi
(Italy)—Fiction. I. Title.
  PS3563.U3455F73 2010
  813'.54—dc22
                                                        2009039016

Printed in the United States of America

Contents

1
As Good As It Gets

In the sun-streaked late August silence, a skylark trilled its joyous aria, but Francis, exhausted by a late night of partying, lay asleep. In the corner, his elegant blue satin mantle lay crumpled on the floor where he had dropped it early in the morning before collapsing into bed. His imported ivory silk tunic was stained and hopelessly tangled around his contorted, limp body.

He was twenty years old, of medium height, with black hair and a low forehead. His eyebrows were straight, and his nose was narrow and perfectly proportioned for his handsome face. One delicately shaped ear was visible just above the top of the bed covers.

"Francis," Pica hollered from the bottom of the stairs.

Francis turned over, still asleep, and smiled, dreaming about the music and the laughter at the party that had ended only a few hours ago. His smile revealed even, white teeth behind his slightly parted, thin, well-shaped lips. His trim black beard and hair, cut to suit the latest fashion, emphasized the slenderness of his neck, which flowed into a lean, compact body with arms that were rather short for his height and ended in hands with long slender fingers.

"Francis," his mother cried out again, with a note of anxiety bordering on panic in her voice. It pierced the fog of his inebriated brain. One leg kicked the covers away in a reflex that sent a spike of pain through his head, which felt like it was being gripped in a vise. Through partially opened eyes he could see a few narrow rays of light streaming in through the shutters cover-

ing the single narrow window of his room, but his mind refused
to believe that morning had come, and he drifted back to sleep.

Standing at the foot of the stairs and looking through the
door of the shop, Pica could see her husband, Pietro, fast
approaching from the direction of the central piazza. She called
out once again, trying to awaken her son, but also kept her voice
low enough so her husband would not hear her. She had been
relieved when she heard Francis come home in the early hours,
and even more relieved that her husband had remained sound
asleep. When Pietro had left the house that morning to meet
with the other commune merchants in the town's central piazza,
she had hoped that she would have sufficient time to get Francis
out of bed. Unfortunately, Pietro had returned much sooner
than she had anticipated.

Only when Francis heard his mother frantically running up
the long flight of stairs did he manage to become minimally
conscious and sit up, swinging his feet over the edge of the bed
and moaning as another jolt of pain hit him. It wasn't just his
head; his whole body ached. He tried to focus his eyes, but the
pain was so insistent that he let his head fall back on the pillow.
When he opened his eyes again, Pica was leaning over him,
her slender face flushed with an all-too-familiar combination
of anger, fear, and determination.

It was too late — Pietro Bernardone was furiously thun-
dering his way up the narrow, wooden steps, his deep, rough
voice making even more noise than his heavy leather boots.
"Francis," Pietro shouted, "where the devil are you?"

Francis's mouth was stale and dry with the fuzzy aftertaste
of last night's wine, and his tongue was too thick to blurt out
an alibi. Pica slammed open the wooden shutters, picked up
the blue mantle with disgust, and threw it on the bed.

The morning sun brought with it the sounds of the bells
throughout the town tolling the hour of Sext, one of the
canonical hours that divided the day for layman and clergy
alike. Francis winced at this fresh assault on his aching head.
Pica shook him roughly by the shoulder and shouted. "Francis,

move!" She slapped her son sharply on his cheek. "Here, you will need a new tunic. Wash up! You smell like sewage!"

Pietro angrily shoved open the door at the top of the stairs. "You no-good, worthless dog!" His face was scarlet with rage and his hands curled into fists. "I trust you to open the shop and here you lay in bed like a damn beggar! Everyone is open and ready for business but Pietro Bernardone. Why? 'Oh, our dear Francis is sleeping this morning,'" Pietro whined mockingly, his voice cracking, unable to sustain the tension of the pitch under the force of his anger. "Even the monks laugh at me. They laugh at you, too, you who are so free with my money. Money comes only from work. You are a grown man, and I still cannot trust you! A father has the right to expect an honest day's work from his son. You know how to spend money and how to waste money, but where are you when it's time to work?"

Pietro's rage and frustration had been brewing for a long time. His son's behavior was annoyingly cyclic. Just when Pietro thought he could trust Francis, Francis abused his trust. Francis had talent and intelligence — and charm. He could sell cloth to the most reluctant customer, he could predict the next fashion trends better than Pietro, he could please and flatter the ladies, but could he open the store on time? No! Pietro was beside himself. He simply did not know what to do to make his son take life — and business — seriously.

Francis tried to wiggle into clean clothes while shielding his head from the blows he knew would follow. Pica's bottom lip quivered; she stood between her son and Pietro, ambivalent, half trying to protect her son, but vigilant also to protect herself. Pietro lashed out to strike Francis but his blow glanced off the top of his son's head and hit his wife full in the face. Francis moaned as he stumbled, arms only half into his tunic. Pica cried out in pain and fear, while Pietro ignored her and continued to shout at Francis. "Get up or I'll beat the hell out of you."

As Francis stumbled down the stairs, Pietro's anger escalated, his pointed boots falling hard upon his son's buttocks and legs. Alone, Pica gently fingered her swelling face and tried to compose herself. The skin around her eye was puffing out a bit, but was not broken. On the street, Pietro gave his son one last kick with his tooled boots. The inevitable chorus of gossips who had gathered when they heard the commotion smiled and whispered as Pietro, muttering angrily, stomped toward the square. Once again his son had brought him public dishonor.

Still dazed, and feeling his bruises, Francis tried to face another day of following Pietro Bernardone in his trade. At twenty, Francis had worked in the family business for six years and was respected as a skilled merchant. He had attended the international trade fairs in southern France with his father ever since his early youth and, thanks to his natural flair and love for fashion, understood the evolving trends so important to the Bernardone business. His knowledge of and taste for French fashion was the best in the region, and his opinions on style and elegance were considered authoritative.

As he stood next to the display in front of the shop and squinted in the intense sunlight, Francis felt a despondency that was due to more than overindulgence in wine. He was completely frustrated, bored, and tired with his miserable life. For all these long years, he had made his way down the narrow steps from the family residence located on the top floors to work in his father's shop. There were occasional trips and fairs, but even these were becoming routine. He enjoyed the customers and knew how to court them, but the game of commerce was fast becoming old.

"Yes, dear Lady, this is truly your color," Francis reassured a noble woman who needed more help with her breath than with her wardrobe. "Yes, this is a lovely brocade, but surely your wife deserves an even more luxurious design," Francis murmured, nudging a cheapskate husband as his wife blushed at his side. "Yes, the pattern is stunning. The silver threads bring out the beautiful brown in your eyes," Francis said, as he exercised his charm on a young lady whose natural inclinations seemed more suited to the outdoors rather than to a life walled up in her father's palazzo.

There was still a part of him that enjoyed dealing with the customers, keeping abreast of constantly changing styles and tastes, and amusing himself with the sheer entertainment of the human comedy acted out in the shop every day. Yet the hours, especially the morning hours, were long. The fabrics blended into variations on the same theme; the customers dissolved into variations on the all-too-familiar themes.

"How do I look?" Lady Marangone would shyly ask. The Marangone family lived two doors away from the Bernardones. Lady Marangone was a lovely, kind, and discreet woman who, because of her intelligence and prudence, was trusted with many of the secrets of the commune women. But her demure modesty was the exception. "Will I impress?" This was always the unspoken concern of someone like Lord Marescotto di Bernardo Dodici. Lord Marescotto had vast properties in the valley between Perugia and Assisi. A tall, stately, shrewd man, he was forever anxious that his appearance accentuate his unassailable right to power and privilege.

"Will the ladies notice me in this?" the young knight Matteo della Rocca would wonder, fingering a fine piece of brocade which he was considering having made up as a mantle. Matteo was a good friend of Francis. His father, Simone, had three sons, Matteo, Giovanni, and a young child named Pietro, and was lord of Rocca Paida on Mount Subasio. Giovanni della Rocca was a sensitive man who had his father's love of the wildness and freedom of life in the mountains, and little taste for the gossip and pettiness of the town. Matteo didn't seem to care all that much about anything. He had a simple goodness, a basic innocence, but he was easily tempted by good wine, women, gambling, and song. All of that could be found only in town. He was a man without deep convictions or a sense of direction, one who improvised rather than planned his life. He had found, he was sure, a sympathetic spirit in his good friend Francis.

The idlers who had gathered up the street from the Bernardone storefront had heard Francis and his friends singing in the streets the night before. "The man is a fool, he'll never amount to anything," Canon Silvester, a bitter and cynical cleric, remarked in a voice just loud enough for Francis to hear him. His fat stomach bulged over a wide leather belt that was stretched to the breaking point and fastened in the very last hole. Silvester clutched and fingered his purse, which was firmly tied to his belt and worn to a soft sheen. He checked it frequently, always wary of the predatory fingers of the lay people who lived outside the San Rufino gate.

"He is not selfish like his father. He is a good-hearted man," said Giovanni di Sasso, Francis' old schoolmaster. Giovanni's closely cropped gray hair almost gleamed in the sunlight; his beard was tidy and well kept. The boys had kept his spirit young, and the years spent teaching had made him wise. He was a refined, delicate man, strong in character but with little taste for argument.

"He is a fool and a spendthrift. If he had to earn his own way, then he'd be able to get up in the morning. He's had it too easy. Pietro should give him the boot more often." Tancredi di Ugone, the great noble lord of Parlascio in the upper section of the city, had little use for such a delinquent son. "Do you hear that, Francis?" Tancredi bellowed. His dark, penetrating eyes, noble breeding, and his capacity to take advantage of the new money economy made him one of the most powerful men in Assisi. "If you were my son, you would have the boot more often." Several of the bystanders nodded, eager to show their agreement with the influential town father.

Giovanni glanced compassionately at Francis, who was carefully arranging the display in front of the shop and pretending to ignore the remarks so pointedly directed at him. "Just as well he pays no heed to them," di Sasso thought. The old schoolmaster knew that it was useless to attempt to change the opinions held about Francis. There was one thing that was certainly true about the outgoing and fun-loving Francis Bernardone. Everyone in the commune had strong opinions about him. Unwilling to waste any more time listening to Silvester and Tancredi's attacks on his former and beloved student, Giovanni excused himself and walked toward the church of San Giorgio.

"Have a little bit of a headache this morning, Francis?" Lady Peppone's high twanging voice plucked at Francis's nerves like a claw. Francis summoned his courage and focused on her enormous breasts, which boldly asserted themselves through the far-too-thin and revealing fabric of her dress. She insisted on buying such sheer, inappropriate material despite discreet efforts by Francis to recommend other, more suitable choices. The woman had a mean streak, always the first to spread malicious gossip and critical of everyone who did the same, while remaining oblivious to the fact that others made fun of her behind her back.

"Good morning, Lady Peppone," Francis said. "A most beautiful morning." He turned away from her, trying to appear busy rearranging the top layers of fabric on the display. But Lady Peppone would not be dismissed so easily. "The store is opening a bit late this morning. It must be difficult for your father to put up with such an irresponsible son. Oh well, old man Bernardone has cheated so many people, I guess it serves him right too ... "

Francis had long ago learned to ignore Lady Peppone's nonsense. He tried to avoid staring at her massive breasts and repressed an impulse to laugh at her outlandish style of dress. Then Francis saw Lady Marescotto di Bernardo Dodici approaching the store from the central piazza. "Lady Marescotto, please come in," he said, offering his hand to the thin and somewhat reserved woman, who gave Lady Peppone an unfriendly glance. Seeing that Francis was suffering from the after-effects of the party that had kept all of Assisi awake the night before, she glared at Francis with an expression of disapproval. The reproach was momentary, for Lady Marescotto badly needed advice from him. She was lost when it came to the world of fashion.

Francis ushered Lady Marescotto inside and, with graceful flourishes, presented bolt after bolt of precious fabrics from the store's tallest cupboard, mounting a stool to reach the scarlets and silks found on the top shelf. "Francis, does this color accent the green in my eyes? You know, green eyes are difficult to work with," Lady Marescotto fretted. Matching the green in Lady Marescotto's eyes was serious business, as Francis knew only too well.

"Is this a new bolt of silk, Francis? I don't want to appear in public wearing cloth from the same bolt as someone else,"

Lady Marescotto said firmly. Francis paused. The bolt was new, and the imported cloth was very expensive. He knew that Lady Marescotto was a bit strapped financially at the moment and would not be able to purchase the entire bolt. "I assure you, Lady Marescotto, that I will take whatever you do not wish to purchase on my next trip to Foligno. I promise you that I will sell this particular fabric to no one else in Assisi. I give you my word." Francis put on his most serious, businesslike expression.

Lady Marescotto was relieved, but was also anxious to avoid giving the impression that a lady of her high station would be unduly concerned about money. "Now," she said decisively, "I will need a silk or linen to complement this fabric and perhaps a brocade to use as a covering."

Francis's eyes darted from one bolt of fabric to the next, as he tried to conjure up a mental image of the sort of dress that would suit her conservative taste yet not be too dull and unfashionable. He made several suggestions and then paused when he noticed Lady Marescotto hesitate. In his excitement he had suggested combinations that were too new and extravagant — and expensive. He realized his error and adjusted his strategy.

"That brocade is beautiful, but perhaps a bit too heavy," he suggested. "Here, look at this one. Its weave is thinner, more delicate, and its embroidery more subtle. Ah, and the colors are right for you, my Lady."

Lady Marescotto readily agreed with his recommendation.

"I will speak with the dressmaker about the pattern, my Lady. Do not worry, it will be cut to rival the most exquisite of French fashions," Francis reassured his very satisfied customer.

Lady Marescotto left, arms tightly clasping her stomach. "She is such a nice woman," Francis thought, "but she always seems to be in pain." Happy that he had already made one good sale, Francis was grateful to be alone as Assisi paused for the midday meal. He did not dare go upstairs and join his family for dinner today. His father would still be angry, and Francis felt nauseated by the very thought of food. He walked to the front door of the shop and leaned against one side of it, absentmindedly rubbing his still aching head and looking out at the empty street, baking in the warmth of the midday sun.

*A*ssisi, perched on the steep slope of Mount Subasio, was surrounded by walls that formed a rough oval. The city was guarded by the imposing stone towers of the Rocca Maggiore, a well-fortified castle occupied by a German count who, as the agent of the German emperor, was attempting to reestablish feudal order in Assisi. The newly emerging commune of Assisi included not only the walled city but also vast areas of the mountainous terrain surrounding it and great portions of the valley of Spoleto, with its fertile, rich soil below. In addition to the Germans who occupied the fortress, and the many monks and nuns living in the monasteries, there were about twenty-two thousand inhabitants within the commune's boundaries.

Some twenty noble families dominated it, but businessmen and landowners like Pietro Bernardone, one of the wealthiest merchants in Assisi, were gradually challenging the power of the aristocracy and undermining it through their accumulation of wealth in an increasingly monetized economy. Bernardone's wealth was his power; the same nobility who were forced by ruinous spending to turn to him for loans were the ones selling him pieces of their hereditary lands to pay off these loans.

Although usury was technically forbidden by law, men like Francis's father manipulated every legal loophole to their advantage, often charging exorbitant interest and forcing desperate nobles either to capitulate to their scheming and frequently fraudulent business practices, or to engage in expensive and prolonged litigation. Lawsuits were a growth industry in Assisi.

Bernardone was ambitious for status as well as money. He overcame his innate tendency to conserve his wealth and allowed his son to spend lavishly, for it was his intention that Francis should marry above his station, thereby uniting the Bernardone fortune with an illustrious noble name. That he was despised by the nobility was of little matter to this self-made man who had risen from hardy peasant stock. Shrewd but not complex, he was direct in speech and aggressive in behavior. His muscular, stout physique was suited more to field labor than to the confines of a merchant's shop. While he presented himself with bravado, he had the habit of nervously chewing the inside of his cheek, something that betrayed his ever-present anxiety to the more observant.

It was a wonder to the citizens of Assisi that this crude and grasping man had produced such a handsome and naturally graceful son. Most ascribed Francis's innate charm and gentility to his mother, the refined and pious Pica. It was true that he had her delicate features, beautiful dark eyes, and radiant smile. Not that Pica Bernardone had many occasions to smile. Both mother and son were frequent victims of Pietro Bernardone's volcanic anger — Francis because he did so well at play and so poorly at work, and his mother because she attempted to defend him. It was all very well for Francis to employ his charm to persuade women to buy the best, most expensive, luxurious fabrics when he waited on them in the family shop, which was stuffed with imported silk, wool, and linen. It was also fine, up to a point, for Francis to spend his time drinking and eating and roistering with the golden youth of the commune. But that Francis displayed none of the grasping acquisitiveness of his father — that was not acceptable. Bernardone was a realist; he lived above the shop that made the money that paid for his son's luxurious lifestyle. Francis might well one day live in a castle, but that day had not yet arrived. Until such time, he expected his son to be as diligent and cunning in business as he was, but these expectations had not been fulfilled.

While the family did indeed live over the shop and not in a castle, it was a substantial building, constructed of thick stone and standing between the small church of San Nicolo and the Benedictine monastery of San Paolo. As one faced the ancient Temple of Minerva and turned left down the Via Portica, one came upon the imposing Bernardone establishment, next to the other shops that sold the most luxurious and expensive goods available in the town. Outside Bernardone's shop at the street level, there was a colorful display of fabric, less expensively priced and serving as an inducement to enter the dim interior, reached through an anteroom with one door leading to a steep flight of wooden stairs and the other into the shop itself, divided into two rooms. A display area of shelves held bolts of less expensive fabrics and, beyond that, a large cutting table behind which was a sturdy locked cabinet containing the most precious items in stock. Bernardone sold Italian woolen material but also the more desirable and expensive imported English woolens and a fine selection of Burgundian wool, acquired during regular trips to the great mercantile fairs in France. Bernardone also offered linens and silk, both the imported material from the distant East and the less expensive domestic variety.

Behind the main display room was the counting room, where there was a large table, splotched with the wax from candles, on which sat a calculating board with bone counters, and wax tablets on which records and tallies were kept. The accounts of Bernardone's high-interest loans were also kept here, loans that were either repaid promptly or were the cause of frequent vigorous legal actions when overdue. Parchment, the Bernardone seal, a jar full of quill pens, ink, and binding cord were also neatly arranged on the table. While working there, Francis or his father would perch on a high wooden stool. Behind this table, in a corner of the room, stood a tall, finely crafted chest made of thick oak. It held the magnificent full suit of armor that Bernardone had purchased for his son. It was an emblem of Bernardone's dream — that Francis would become a knight and a member of the nobility. But in the turbulent days of A.D. 1202, the shining metal also had a grim, utilitarian purpose.

Alone in the store, Francis wandered into the stuffy back room. A large lantern cast yellowish light on the wax tablet, the quill, and the calculating board, ready for the making up of accounts. Francis counted out Lady Marescotto's coins and adjusted the bone counters. He pushed the calculating board carefully to one side and, as if in a trance, walked over and unlocked the cupboard. Its heavy oak door creaked open to reveal the magnificent suit of armor. The hauberk with its long sleeves, hood, and mail gauntlets was the latest design from Milan. The nobles of Assisi envied Francis's embroidered linen surcoat, his protective cuirass, his golden shield, his custom-made helmet, and his Florentine sword etched with fine threads of gold. Francis put one hand on the hilt of his precious sword. He would fight for the honor of a noble woman, he would impress her noble father with his prowess, he would ...

A noise coming from the inside of the store brought Francis back to reality. He thought he had locked the front door. Quickly shutting the cabinet and peering out of the counting room, Francis spotted a shadow of a man. Francis recognized him. It was Albert, a beggar in clothes that were worn to rags. His fingernails were long and crusted with dirt, his hair hung long in greasy strands, and his feet were bare and crippled. "In the name of Jesus Christ, I beg you, kind sir, for alms," the beggar pleaded.

"Albert, has no one fed you today?" Francis asked. There were many beggars in Assisi, but Francis had a special feeling of compassion for this one. He was a kind, mind-your-own-business sort of fellow, who begged only when it was necessary. A simple soul, Albert had a light in his eye, a kind of gleam of faith and hope which, despite his deformity and filthy appearance, made him oddly attractive, a more sympathetic figure than most of his companions in misery.

Francis quickly glanced around the store wanting to find some cloth to give the man so he could wear something less degrading than the tattered garments in which he appeared day after day, but there was nothing suitable — silks, brocades, and fine wool were not appropriate clothing for a beggar. Had he been seen wearing such fine stuff, he would be accused of robbery, and his second fate would be worse than the first. The beggar coughed weakly, trying to hide a respiratory difficulty. Albert was a good man. He was a person who was not greedy enough to make it in this world — a man who had been left behind. The town fathers said that he had been imprisoned and tortured in Perugia as a young man and had never recovered from the experience.

Francis raised one finger and gestured for Albert to remain, then went into the counting room. He emerged with several of the coins Lady Marescotto had paid that morning and pressed them into Albert's grimy hand. Grateful, the beggar bowed, in a way that was quietly dignified. Concerned only with being able to get enough to eat that day, he did not even look at the coins.

"God reward you," Albert said quietly, and he limped quickly out of the shop. The beggar was anxious not to be seen by Pietro, who had kicked him out of the shop many times. Albert's hunger had overcome his prudence — and on this day he blessed God when he saw the face of the son, rather than that of the father.

*L*ocking the shop's front door so as not to be further bothered while Assisi was enjoying its siesta, Francis returned to the counting room and again opened the cabinet, revealing the glimmering armor's helmet, coat of mail, cuirass, breastplate, shield, and sword.

"This is my destiny," he thought. "I cannot keep selling cloth day after day. I must prove myself in battle. I must fight with honor. I am born a merchant's son, but I will die a noble knight. I will be a knight not by blood, but by valor; a knight not by pedigree, but by glory." Stretching out on the floor and resting his pounding head upon a piece of folded wool that he had placed near the open cabinet, Francis closed his eyes and allowed his imagination to recall the memories that his armor conjured up of his participation in the peoples' revolt against the Rocca Maggiore.

"Francis!" Who was shouting?

"Francis!" Where was the voice coming from? "Francis!" Who was it?

Despite his aching and dizzy head, Francis could recall every detail of the staggering chaos, the sweat, the dust, the heat, and the frenzy of his time in the skirmish, when he felt, truly for the first time, that he was born to be a knight. Conrad of Urslingen, duke of the imperial castle that hung like a dark cloud over Assisi, had left his fortress to join forces with Pope Innocent III. The people of Assisi, who had suffered greatly under the cruelty and excesses of German rule, were scandalized. How could the pope associate himself with such a criminal? By the time the pope heard the protests of the people and thought better of the alliance, it was too late. The people trusted neither pope nor emperor. They took their destiny into their own hands.

"Francis!" the voice in his memory shrieked.

Marescotto di Bernardo Dodici, the husband of Lady Marescotto, a superb horseman and an able commune leader, rode toward him on his large, black stallion. Francis, who had momentarily been dazed by the sight of a torrent of people rushing up the mountain with swords, pickaxes, and clubs, tried to focus on the apparition emerging through clouds of dust.

"Francis, watch out!" Marescotto shouted.

Francis turned and saw a German knight riding toward him preparing to hack him down. People were fighting desperately all around him on the blood-soaked ground, yet he felt somehow removed from the general skirmish and caught up in quite another one in which there remained only the German knight and himself. "Holy Virgin Mary ..." Francis cried out in supplication, and instinctively swung his sword.

The tip of the German's sword touched his face and then, for a moment, it was suspended in the air. The knight's horse bolted past and Francis looked down to see the German collapsed on the ground, blood gushing from a massive wound in his neck. Then he felt strong hands grasp his shoulder and push him into the line of attack. He turned around, thinking he would see Marescotto, but he had vanished in the fray.

At that moment, papal legates arrived and pleaded for the citizens of Assisi to adhere to the cause of the Holy See. Their pleas were drowned by howls of rage. The people had vanquished the hated Germans; they wanted no part of the pope's tainted cause. Why would they submit to another who tottered between loyalty to them and to the German crown?

There was to be no mercy from the men of Assisi that day. The Germans received no quarter; the men were cut down, the women of the imperial castle were raped and then killed, and the bodies of all, including young children and the old, were thrown down the back of the steep mountain cliff. The stones of the fortress were ripped out of the walls and carted downhill to enlarge the walls fortifying Assisi. Having turned against both emperor and pope, the people of Assisi revolted against the full weight of feudal authority that had oppressed them — and they had given no thought to the consequences. The task of enlarging their commune walls brought relief from guilt and from the fear of reprisal. Francis found that his spirit enjoyed the building more than the fury of the raid.

In the end, however, Assisi's dream of autonomy was frustrated by the shifting allegiances of feudal Europe. The pope, who favored the rights and exemptions of the ancient nobility, allied himself with the cruel and deeply hated Perugia, Assisi's neighbor. The canons of the Cathedral of San Rufino in Assisi, who were for the most part the sons of the urban nobles, fought openly against the bishop, who was in league with the papacy and the rural nobles. The merchants of the commune emboldened by their ever-increasing fortunes continued to arm themselves against the noble classes who by feudal right controlled the roads and exacted heavy tolls on goods that moved over them, as they tried to get what they regarded as their fair share of the wealth being created through the rise of the money economy. In this time when the old feudal ties were being sundered and long accepted authority ignored or challenged, neighbor fought against neighbor, brother against brother.

It was the force of the rising money economy that was turning the feudal order inside out. Drunk with the power of new money, the people continued to revolt, moving next against their own nobility.

The nobles fled Assisi to their ancient castles on Mount Subasio. The rugged cliffs, sheer precipices, and the slippery, narrow, acorn-strewn paths up the sides of the mountains made attacks on these fortresses difficult. The nobles, who preferred the comforts of the commune to these frigid and wind-blasted strongholds, took up arms and reverted to the warlike ferocity of their ancestors. Some of the more adaptable nobles had managed to establish themselves in profitable mercantile activities in Assisi and were leaders in the government of the commune and its emerging money-driven, lucrative economy. Others angrily insisted upon their ancient rights and attempted to force the citizens of Assisi to support the twenty local noble families with age-old tributes of labor and goods. They waved time-worn documents stamped with the imperial seal in the faces of the people of the commune, demanding that they defer to the traditional supremacy of the nobility. They ranted and litigated, failing to understand that the ransacked stones of the imperial castle were being built into the walls of the thriving, new commune.

As he lay in a kind of semi-consciousness, Francis's body occasionally jerked and shuddered as he remembered joining the others from Assisi who had stormed the castle of Sasso Rosso. The nobles of this castle controlled the road spanning the short distance between Assisi and Spello. Nobility who had joined the new trade economy and rich merchants who arrogantly presumed to ride horses into battle and bear arms, as well as masses of blood-thirsty commoners, surprised and overwhelmed the nobility entrenched behind their fortified walls. Hardly able to comprehend this transformation of once docile citizens of Assisi into arrogant enemies, the proud Sasso Rosso knights Alberico, Conte, Ugone, Fortebraccio, Gislerio, Girardo, Leonardo, Oddo, Monaldo, Paolo, and Rinaldo fled, leaving their fortress and their possessions to be plundered and burned by these outlaw commoners and their turncoat noble allies.

Montemoro, the "cursed castle" as it was called, was next. Its sister castle, Poggio San Damiano, which levied heavy tolls on merchants crossing the mountains, was destroyed. The castle of Morico was leveled. Lord Celino's fortress of the Poggio was fiercely attacked and destroyed. San Savino — reduced to dust. Bassano — ruined. Francis remembered well the ferocity of his relatives and his father in these attacks. He relived the moments of battle — the sound of his own rasping breath, the pounding of his heart as he witnessed the raping of women, the killing of children, and inhaled the smell of burning flesh. He had taken part in this merciless revenge; the blood on his sword had born witness to that.

By night, arsonists set fire to the city palazzos of the aristocracy. In January of 1200, many families escaped to Perugia including the powerful Offreduccio family. In this family, Favarone and his wife, Lady Ortolana, escaped with their six-year-old daughter Clare and her younger sister Catherine. Clare had come into the Bernardone store many times with her mother. Francis smiled as he remembered the little girl with dark sparkling eyes, quick intelligence, and thick blonde curls. Lady Ortolana was a woman of reputable virtue whose piety and courage had taken her on pilgrimages to Rome, St. James of Compostella in Spain, St. Michael on Monte Gargano, and even to the Holy Land. Her daughter Clare had her mother's determined spirit and integrity.

The Offreduccios were the lucky ones. Many members of noble families died, their screams lost in the fires consuming them. Those who survived the wrath were reduced to poverty. Their hunger forced them to beg from those they had once oppressed, groveling before illiterate and uncultured men who had the audacity to arm themselves against the defenders of the old order.

The commune consuls were intoxicated by their newly won power. The nobles either accepted and led the cause of the rebellious in Assisi or joined forces with the Perugian nobility and, within the fortifications of Perugia, plotted revenge.

The door of the shop rattled, jarring Francis out of his reverie. Jumping to his feet, he rolled up the wool he had been using to pillow his head and quickly checked his hair and clothes, brushing off the dust from the floor. Smiling, he entered the salesroom and opened the door to his afternoon customers. Soon the store filled with those enriched by new money, eager to impress. Knowing that these arrivistes would spare no expense, Francis showed them the finest cloth in stock. The coins poured into the cash box as a river of luxurious goods flowed out of the Bernardone establishment.

"This cloth is typical of Brabant. It was purchased at the May fair in Provins. I assure you, Lady, that this is the only piece like it in all of Umbria," Francis promised.

"You yourself traveled the Via Francesca to purchase this fabric?" asked the potential buyer.

"Yes, I can assure you that there is not another like it. I bought the piece you see lying before you, myself," the merchant's son smiled. "And the fair, the fair is wonderful?" his customer inquired.

"Yes," replied Francis, "the fair flaunts the riches of the world. One shops for cloth in booths lined with velvet and silk. There are embroidered brocades, leathers, black velvets, and silk so thin as to capture the eyes of those who behold one draped in it. Pearls, ivory, gold, and silver flow out of every street. The smells of cinnamon, cloves, ginger, indigo, pepper, and saffron mix in the cosmopolitan air. There are exotic drugs that free inhibitions and encourage all to buy liberally for the sake of profit. Rich and exquisite wines are in abundance. Money is everywhere. One hears languages from even the most distant regions of the world. During the evenings, men drink and impress beautiful women with their adventures, how they evaded the grasp of predatory nobles and the treachery of sea pirates, withstood the rigors of beating a trail through the snow in high mountain passes, safely passed over treacherous glaciers, and fought off bands of marauders and thieves. And there is such a variety of women," Francis explained, "women, free and enslaved, black, white, and brown, are everywhere."

Francis loved entertaining his customers with stories of the fairs. His feet danced as he described unimaginable luxury and wealth flowing from every corner and every street, and his customers never grew tired of listening to him. Overcome and fascinated by the images of abundant gold, luxurious cloth, and the splendors of cosmopolitan culture, the women in the Bernardone store begged Francis to tell them more.

"Wondrous works of art are everywhere, and troubadours, trouveres, and minstrels sing of faraway lands and adventures," Francis continued. The mention of trouveres and the awe of his customers inspired him to sing one of his favorite ballads. His voice, his beautiful voice, serenaded the women, while his sparkling eyes, expressive hands, and agile, joyful feet brought the words to glowing life.

A dragon ugly and bold emerged from the sea
And came into the town eating all in its path

The citizens panicked and armed themselves
With forks and hoes, and knives and arrows, and spears.

Oh now what will become of us?
And who will save us from this great trouble?
For all of hell's fire and fury and fear
Are punishment for our dreadful sins.
En masse they rushed to free themselves of the curse
From lives now burdened with terror and crushing fear
The dragon's horror and might alarmed
All knights and archers, and soldiers and peasants,
   and slaves.

Oh now what will become of us?
And who will save us from this great trouble?
For all of hell's fire and fury and fear
Are punishment for our dreadful sins.

Then two thousand knights ...

The shop door opened again and Francis stopped his singing, smiled at the ladies, and refocused his attention on the selling of cloth. He did not need to finish the ballad. His purpose had been to entertain, and his customers all knew the end of the story. The king decides that a maiden, whose fate is chosen by lot, will be sacrificed to appease the dragon. The lot falls on the king's own beautiful daughter who is sent alone to the island of the dragon. The knight, George, finds the maiden and kills the dragon.

"The Bernardones, Lady, are at your service to bring you the world. I not only have this Brabant, but a piece of silk that would complement the etching," Francis suggested. He continued to tempt the neighboring merchant's wife who gave in and bought bolt after bolt of imported fabrics. One by one the customers came through the door to purchase the world.

The afternoon always passed more quickly than the morning. Closing the shop, Francis dismantled the outdoor display and bolted the shutters for the evening. Tired and hungry, he strolled up Via Portica into the Piazza della Minerva, the central square in Assisi. The humble parish church of San Nicolo stood to his left as he passed, while the large and impressive Roman Temple of Minerva with its ancient steps and Corinthian columns towered in front of him. Farmers who had brought their crops into the city gathered the little that was left of their goods. Merchants of wine and food prepared for the evening's revelries. Amidst all of the activity and noise, a lone, terribly deformed humpbacked woman hobbled slowly through the square.

"Francis!" a voice called out.

"Bernard," Francis greeted his friend. A young noble lawyer, Bernard, and a small gang of companions had been waiting for Francis to emerge into the square. The highly intelligent, well-respected, and good-looking Bernard frequently sought relief from the futility of Assisi's endless litigation by joining in the spontaneous celebration of life, song, and wine that filled so many of Francis's nights. Bernard was lanky and shy, but had a willing, almost contagious smile and a quiet, yet ready sense of humor.

"I heard you singing to the ladies in your store today, Francis. Did they put a coin in your pocket?" Bernard laughed.

"Oh now what will become of us? And who will save us from this great trouble?" the young men teased, singing in high, affected voices.

Undaunted by their laughter, the good-natured Francis picked up the song again and sang and danced with the others as they made their way into the smoke-filled hall of the largest tavern in Assisi. They were immediately seated at the most prominent table.

"Now let us dine and drink on the profits of singing to the ladies!" Francis jested.

Servants brought wine and food to the table and offered it first to Francis. If, after tasting a glass of wine or a particular dish of food, he found that what was offered did not measure up to his epicurean standards, Francis politely waved it away. Only the best was good enough. Everyone knew that the merchant's son would, as usual, pay the entire bill. One could eat and drink liberally on his tab without fear of overstepping his generosity. After all, Francis was rich, very rich, filthy rich. Even if one's family had suffered the cruelty of Bernardone's predatory financial dealings, a nobleman could always take advantage of the son's bountiful spending. Handsomely dressed in the latest French styles, Francis was a model of success and fortune, and he shared his fortune with others of and above his class. "Eat, eat!" Francis encouraged. "Drink, drink!" he urged his guests.

One of the men motioned to a waiter and whispered into his ear. Within seconds, a small group of beautiful, young, and seductively dressed women appeared. The men eagerly shared the ever-flowing wine with the ladies and vied with each other to charm the loveliest ones by an impromptu composition of songs that, of course, featured the names of those they wished to impress. As the flirting continued, no cup was allowed to remain unfilled, even for a moment. The odors of roast meat, delicate cheeses, and pastries fresh from the oven blended with the sweet scents worn by the women. Gradually one couple after the other slipped away into dark corners and alcoves off the main hall, embracing and exchanging kisses and intimate touches. Francis resisted the attempts of one particularly attractive young woman with golden hair and a flashing smile to lure him away from the table. Pouting in disappointment, she turned her attention to the eager Matteo who sat to the right of Francis. Matteo returned her smile and slipped his arm around her waist, pulling her close to him.

As the evening wore on, the party spilled out into the street with Francis leading the songs and the storytelling. Having memorized verse after verse, and adept at improvising, Francis was a master entertainer. He stood on the top step of Minerva's ancient temple and sang in a voice that was clear, sonorous, and beautiful. Once he had secured the full attention of all the merrymakers, Francis, who was regarded as one of the most graceful dancers in the commune, led his party in a line of sway-ing figures through the narrow Assisi streets, the walls echoing with song, laughter, and footsteps. Old ladies hearing his voice smiled as they lay awake remembering the dreams of their youth. Lovers were inspired; children were lulled to sleep by the familiar sounds of revelry. The golden youth of the city, led by the son of one of Assisi's most prosperous merchants, celebrated the freedom of the night, ignoring the cares that would come with the morning. While there were always detractors, the vast majority of the people in Assisi genuinely enjoyed the spontane-ity, generosity, and joyfulness of Bernardone's son.

2
Blood

The afternoon hours dragged endlessly as Francis leaned against the cold stone wall outside the Bernardone store. He smiled courteously to those ambling down the narrow street, but his smile camouflaged his real purpose. Echoing off the ancient walls of the Temple of Minerva were low but impassioned voices in the town's square. The prominent commune citizens were engaged in an argument about the future and their collective fate and fortunes.

Francis attempted to make out what the town fathers were saying, though he knew well the common sentiment. Nearly two years ago, after the raid on the castle of Sasso Rosso, Girardo di Gislerio, son of Alberico, asked for citizenship from the consuls of Perugia. Other lords, exiled from Assisi during the civil unrest, had joined him, pledging their revenge on the commune. Assisi's access to roads and trade was continually challenged. The contest threatened Marescotto's and Bernardone's property in Collestrada, a fertile field between Assisi and Perugia.

"Gisler ..." Pietro Bernardone was raging and cursing.

"Collestrada properties," Marescotto di Bernardo Dodici stated firmly. "Our land is at risk. This is what really matters, not just one traitor." Even when he was angry, Marescotto spoke with exacting clarity. He knew how to cut through the most complex political arguments and always come out ahead.

"War," Simone della Rocca decreed. Della Rocca spoke like a man of the mountains. He was strong and tough, skilled in battle and always prepared to wage war and not at all suited to the subtleties and refinements of city life.

Francis's heart thudded like a caged beast anxious for release. Had he heard the word "war"? A twisting wind swept from the rugged Subasio mountain down the shop-lined street momentarily carrying with it the words of anger and defiance. Francis shivered both from the damp cold and from excitement.

Turning his ear in the direction of the piazza, Francis continued to hear only snippets of the almost inaudible conversation. Again he heard his father's gruff voice.

"Taxes ... tolls ... Perugini ... Campagna ... no more tolls ..." Pietro shouted.

Had he heard a call for war? Gislerio's Perugian citizenship had deprived the commune of Assisi the right to tax his Collestrada properties. The argument was about money, access, trade, and now, the consequence of betrayal — war.

Was war a threat or a definite plan? Francis's disquiet intensified, although his pleasant smile never left his face. He had grown used to duplicity. The one who sells cloth, can also don armor.

The thought of armor drew Francis away from the few snatches of conversation he could overhear and back into the store. A hired servant was busy with a customer, and neither servant nor customer paid attention to Francis as he entered the shop. Wandering into the counting room, Francis's hand automatically reached for the key to open the large cabinet protecting his store of armor.

Whenever Francis twisted the heavy iron lock, the smell and sound of raids and death came back to him. He could feel hot winds of blazing fires and hear the awful, terrified screams of those being burned alive, some screams coming from those to whom he had once sold cloth. He remembered the bloodcurdling shrieks of warriors readying themselves for the plunder. His gut twisted as he recalled the chaos of violence, and the starvation and destitution that came in its wake. His heart leapt at the thought of the power and plunder of war. The riches to be made in time of peace paled in comparison to the fortunes that could be gained in war.

Yes, he loved wealth. Yet his itch for money was different than his father's. The one who had been given everything felt little terror at the thought of being stripped and impoverished. Pietro Bernardone had started with little and had amassed a fortune, but since the fear of failure and destitution always lurked beneath his greed, there would never be a limit to his rapacious appetite for more, and more, and more.

Francis remembered the leaner times. Although the Bernardones always had sufficient food and adequate clothing and shelter, his father's appetite for accumulating wealth and his drive for success grew exponentially with each passing year. As the years passed, the relationship between father and son became progressively strained. A hardened, indifferent heart was the price of Bernardone's achievements. When he pondered his father's successes, Francis felt both lucky and angry.

The Bernardone family interrelationships had always been awkward for Pietro. Pica had married him after the death of her first husband, and from this first marriage had a son, Angelo, who was about four years older than Francis. Although Angelo lived outside of the Bernardone household, he posed a threat to Pietro's fortune. Pica had brought to her marriage with Pietro a large dowry as well as a considerable amount of property. If Francis did not fulfill his duties as Bernardone's heir, Pica's properties that were under Bernardone's control but designated for Francis would go to Angelo.

Francis had never been close to his half-brother, and felt caught between the enjoyment of easy money and his discouragement concerning his progressively disintegrating relationship with his father. Even when he was a young man, this conflict had manifested itself. He gave generously to the poor, something always encouraged by his mother, but often a source of anger for his father. He devoted great care to his manner of dress, yet he occasionally explored alternative fashion statements insisting that his clothes be designed from sewing together the most elegant cloth with common peasant rags. At such times, Francis used clothing to react against his father's almost obscene wealth and his infatuation with all that it could buy.

*O*pening the large cupboard and staring at the gleaming, beautifully wrought armor had become a daily ritual for Francis during the long afternoons in the store. In a kind of trance, he picked up the treasured pieces.

From the top shelf, Francis took the shining flat-topped helmet that was slightly flared out in the front in order to give added protection to the throat. A steel crossbar reinforced the eye slits as well as the length of the helmet. Small holes punctured the front section below the eyes to encourage circulation. Francis placed the helmet over his head and peered around the room. The helmet sat on his head awkwardly. Chuckling a bit, Francis held the helmet in place with his left hand and adjusted it to compensate for the absence of both the mail coif and the quilted arming cap that gave additional protection to the head and cushioned it from the weight of the mail and helmet. He stared at the leather cuirass reinforced by steel-lined plates to protect his breast and back. Finally, he lifted the heavy hauberk, with long sleeves and attached mail gauntlets and coif. The hauberk was to be fastened around his head with a lace of leather and latched with a small buckle. It was beautiful. It was brilliant. It was all his.

As if defending himself, Francis drew his prized Florentine sword that his father had given him — shining, long, sharply pointed, with a slightly beveled edge. In his head, he could still hear the cries of those impaled by this sword, but its glittering, sophisticated beauty quickly muffled them. His standard and shield bore the insignia of the contrada of L'Abbadia, the section of Assisi surrounding the San Paolo monastery where the Bernardone family lived, whose insignia bore the sword that severed the head of Saint Paul the apostle. This biblical sword too had blood on it — the blood of a silent scream.

While he was still trying to adjust the uncomfortable helmet, Francis heard his father's voice coming up the street.

"Damn Perugians. Damn tolls. Damn them all!" Pietro yelled.

Francis quickly, but carefully, laid down his sword and removed the helmet from his head, but it was too late. His father's heavy, determined footsteps passed rapidly through the shop and pounded onto the floor of the counting room. He spotted Francis as he was removing the helmet.

"Now that's my son," Pietro said with pride.

Francis was relieved to hear a compliment rather than a reprimand or a sarcastic, hurtful remark. He smiled, put the helmet in its proper place, and fumbled with the latch. As his father outlined the escalating preparations for war against Perugia, Francis hung onto his every word.

"The brigade from Fabriano will arrive tomorrow afternoon," Pietro reported. "The bishop will swear them in tomorrow evening at the cathedral of San Rufino. They are bringing twenty-five archers and six cavaliers — Alberto Guelfo, Raniero di Offreduccio, Giunta, Todino, Raniero di Bonifacio, and Rinaldo Dera. Cavaliers from Gubbio, Trevi, Sassoferrato, Narni, and Apulia are on their way."

News of war rang true as a coin in the counting room. Perugia had to be defeated. Assisi was smaller, but it had money; it could hire soldiers. Francis's head was spinning as he imagined knights coming from as far as Apulia to battle for the freedom and wealth of Assisi. His heart began to pound — so many knights, so many horses, so many men, so little time.

"We are ready, Francis," Bernardone said confidently, noticing the apprehensive expression on his son's face. "We have negotiated and planned for two years. You, my son, will make Bernardone proud, eh?"

Even in this case when he felt sympathy with his father's passion, Francis found himself unable to respond. He would make his father proud. He would make Assisi proud. He would prove himself noble. He would distinguish himself above others in battle. All of this he felt, but as he stood before his father, he could not bring himself to articulate it.

He was intimidated by his father's power. Francis, the one who imagined himself as the bravest of all knights, could only muster a meek nod in answer to his father's question. It wasn't enough, and Francis knew this. His father wanted to see some bravado. Francis had it in him; he found no difficulty when it came to displaying it before others. Yet, when confronted by Pietro, his spirit was subdued. Once again he felt like a child, one who could never measure up to the expectations of his powerful and ruthless father. For a moment Francis doubted whether he was truly ready, but he quickly rejected this thought. His armor was strong and beautiful; his bravery would distinguish him on the field of battle. He was ready for any challenge that came his way.

Bernardone peered at the calculating board.

"Business was slow this afternoon," he muttered. "There is too much going on in Assisi for people to think about buying cloth."

"I'll close down the counter," Francis responded dutifully.

Bernardone nodded. He seemed disappointed in his son. Francis stumbled past him and went through the main room into the anteroom and out the door. The air was cool, but welcome after the damp atmosphere of the counting room with its heavy odors of candle grease and sweat.

"Francis," a voice called out from somewhere in the twilight. Francis straightened. He did not immediately recognize the voice. "Francis, it's Matteo, Matteo della Rocca." "Ah, Matteo," Francis brightened. "How's it going?" The tall, robust form of his friend emerged from the gathering darkness. "Francis, a bit of drink tonight, yes? Can we count on you to come?" Matteo asked shyly. He wanted to party, but needed Francis to pay the bill.

"Yes," replied Francis. "But first, I must eat. I'll meet you in the square later."

"Until later! Eat your mama's cooking first," Matteo teased.

As he walked away, Matteo looked over his shoulder and shouted, "Bring a friend, bring a bottle, bring your money. Bring it all tonight, for soon we will be dead."

Francis smiled at Matteo's characteristic pessimism. This was a time for thoughts of glory, not death; victory, not defeat.

He carefully gathered up the pieces of cloth that stood on the display rack beside the door. In the distance he could hear Matteo's lugubrious chant fading away.

"Soon we will be dead."

"Soon we will be dead."

Arms loaded down with fabric, Francis readily accepted the servant's help with placing the goods back into the cupboard. Leaving the worker to lock down the shutters of the storefront, father and son silently mounted the wooden stairs leading to the family's living quarters.

After weeks of preparation, planning, and training, the day came when Francis woke to don his precious armor. He had worn it many times before, but this November morning was different. The wealth and freedom of Assisi were at stake. Its shops remained silent and shuttered against the early morning light as the town was filled with the peal of bells summoning its citizens to take up arms.

In the family stables, Francis kissed his mother good-bye. As if to protect Francis's heart from any weakening of martial spirit at the sight of his mother's tears, Pietro cuffed his big hand around his son's neck in a gesture intended to remind him of what lay ahead of him on this day of battle. Even the mail covering did not protect Francis from the choking effects of his father's grasp. Pica was shaking with fear. She had seen and known the terror of Perugia's fury. Everyone knew the fierceness of the enemy, but only the women were permitted to show their fear.

"Be careful, Francis," she pleaded, trying to speak through the sobs stuck in her throat.

A mother raises her son for this moment, the moment when he must be brave for something beyond himself, beyond his family, and certainly beyond his mother. Yet Pica, like most women sending their sons to war, was not convinced. She wished that she could hold her son as a baby again, play with him as she could when he was a little boy. He had grown up so fast and the thought of sacrificing him to the cruelties of Perugia was more than her heart could bear. She would not allow herself to imagine the events of this day. She would remember Francis's tiny fingers and bumbling first steps. She looked into her son's eyes and whispered again.

"Be careful, my son. Let the others be brave. Come back to your mother," she pleaded.

Bernardone inserted his leg and foot between Francis and his mother, his large hand still around Francis's neck. "It's time to move, son. You will be fine. You will be brave. You will bring your family honor."

Francis nodded. Why must he always be rendered speechless by the words of his father? It wasn't the words exactly. Then what was it? Francis kept pace with his father as they walked away, Pietro retaining his fierce grip on his son's mail-covered neck. He could not let himself be distracted by thinking about his mother. It was time to be a man. It was time to move on to his noble destiny.

Once mounted on his horse, Francis regained some sense of authority and prowess. A cool mist pierced by fitful sunshine surrounded the gathering of the men of Assisi and their hired mercenaries. Their destination was Collestrada. Francis knew the territory well. His father owned land in the fertile and coveted valley fed by the Tiber River in Campagna near the Collestrada castle. The right to this property had been fought over by Assisi and Perugia for years. The territory was essential to Assisi's trade and revenues; it was worth the price of blood. He was armed well, he reassured himself. It would turn out all right.

The consuls' plan was straightforward. Assisi's army would advance down the lower slope of Subasio onto the plain. They would pass through the territory of Campagna and would proceed up the Collestrada hill. The strategy was to challenge the ancient resources of wealth and privilege with the arrogance and power of new money. The consuls felt that they had invested well in both arms and in the mercenaries who would fight for their cause. Assisi would be protected. Its sons would fight bravely, and if their skill was wanting, the hired mercenaries would fill in the gaps.

The names of these hired warriors suggested the fierce and invincible image the mercenaries used to intimidate their enemies: Ruggero di Malcavalca — "Roger the Evil Rider," Saraceno di Campodonico — Saracen of Campodonico," Vadovinco — "I Come, I Conquer," and Vadovinco's brother, Deusteadiuvet, meaning "God Help You." Surely such men would give Assisi the necessary edge in battle — or so the leaders of Assisi hoped.

Francis's heart pounded as he rode amid the fluttering standards of the martial procession passing from the cathedral to the main city gate. All remaining behind in Assisi turned out, praying and waving handkerchiefs at the mounted knights, the highly skilled archers, and the amorphous mob of foot soldiers. Francis, characteristically caught in the glory of it all, breathed deeply and searched the crowds for ladies of influence who might be impressed by the splendor and craftsmanship of his armor. He loved the way the gold-accented details of his suit glittered in the sparkling sunlight. For Francis, life was indeed more like a fashion show than a battlefield. He was the son of a luxury cloth merchant, not the son of a mountain knight. Francis knew this truth in his heart. Yet, if he wanted to accomplish more than his father, he needed to fight bravely. His father had brought the family great wealth; Francis would bring it nobility.

During the four hours that it took to move equipment, animals, and men across the short distance to Collestrada, Francis found himself thinking less about the glories of victory and distracted by the beauty of his native countryside. Once the Collestrada hill was in view, Francis, concealed by the high reeds of the Tiber, took his place among other horsemen who were assigned to spy on the movements of the enemy. Small winter birds dove in and out of the canebrakes. The sunlight danced on the winter browns, golds, and dull, muted greens.

Francis wondered how nature could remain in peace in the midst of such human fury. Sunlight danced, birds flittered, the hues of colors shifted in subtle nuances as clouds passed and broke around the sun.

Archers overwhelmed and occupied the Collestrada castle in the early afternoon, while the Perugians gathered on the Tiber's other side. The distance of about one-half mile between the armies was spanned by age-old feuds, vendettas, and bad blood. Perugia had always won. Today Assisi hoped that it would be its turn; Francis prayed for luck — and survival.

*H*e wasn't sure who attacked first. The sides rushed together with the energy of pure lust for power and money on one side, and a confidence bred from a long-standing superiority on the other. The Assisians, organized and disciplined like never before, stayed with their companies. Francis was in the mix, using his skill, remembering his training, maneuvering his spirited horse, and following the commands of the more experienced. He was determined to stomach the carnage, heavy sweat, terrified screams, and human tragedy of the battlefield in order to obtain for Assisi the privileges of power, freedom, glory, and wealth.

Matteo and his brother, Giovanni, fought alongside Francis, forming with others an inner ring of defiance against the stronger Perugian cavalry, but the Assisi horsemen were driven back up the hill. Francis hoped that the archers would provide them some respite. His arm lifted his Florentine sword to stab and slay. The November air cooled the sweat forming and dripping from his brow through the small ringlets of the mail coif underneath his helmet. As the battle raged, Francis's company fought with a ferocity that came from their certain knowledge that the fate of Assisi rested with them on that field, on that day.

In the periphery of his vision, Francis saw it happen. He knew the emblem well. It was that of Monaldo Offreduccio, a noble of Assisi turned Perugian traitor. The traitor suddenly appeared from nowhere and slashed his way into the Assisi company. The circles of the mounted knights were broken, and the riders were plunged into confusion and disarray. Monaldo's horse thundered through and in an instant, Matteo fell, twisting his hip as he landed with a pounding thud. Screaming in pain, the wounded knight tore off his helmet to examine his injury. Matteo's father, Simone della Rocca, never lost his focus on the battle but knew, in an instant, that Matteo did not have a chance. Giovanni, his other son, was also at risk. He would mourn the fallen later.

Francis, however, was distracted. He began to dismount in order to give his friend Matteo assistance, setting himself up as a slow, cumbersome target trapped in heavy armor and ill-protected from the weapons of the common foot soldiers. Simone's experienced eyes immediately spotted the imminent danger Francis posed to all.

"No!" Simone shouted.

Veterans of generations of fighting, and no stranger to the tactics of the Perugians, Simone and his son Giovanni rode in closer to Francis to stop him from dismounting. Meanwhile, a Perugian foot soldier distinguished himself by lifting Matteo's cuirass and mail and splitting the knight's abdomen lengthwise with a crude sword. Matteo let out an eerie shriek, more in horror than in pain, and Francis froze, again making himself an easy target. An enraged Giovanni swiftly hacked open the head of the Perugian commoner who had despicably taken cowardly advantage of a fallen knight.

The Perugian cavalry had penetrated the ranks of the Assisi cavaliers. Seeing that they had lost control of the situation, the commanders sounded the retreat. Simone signaled Giovanni to ride out with Francis, while he turned to finish business with Monaldo.

"Go!" shouted Giovanni to the still bewildered and grief-stricken Francis.

"Go!" Giovanni slapped Francis's horse on the rump and joined the charge of other frantic Assisians all trying to save themselves from the one thing they dreaded far more than death — capture.

In his terror, Francis instinctively followed Giovanni. His heart raced as he heard the screams of both vengeance and victory following close behind. Foot soldiers, having little chance among the charging cavalry, ran screaming in all directions. Some hid in reeds, others in nearby fields and woodlands, but it was no use. The Perugians were not interested merely in defeating the enemy. The arrogance of the men of Assisi demanded their annihilation. The commoners were viciously slashed and harried, dismembered, ridiculed, hunted, and slaughtered like animals. There was no mercy; the Tiber flowed with Assisi's blood.

Francis rode frantically, urged on by the more experienced Giovanni. His eyes were fixed on his companion in arms, but they still automatically recorded the images of horror that would later haunt his every quiet moment. The fields were littered with the bodies of Assisian nobles, merchants, and commoners. Heads were hacked from bodies; some bodies had been slashed open. Entrails taken from these bodies were strung from trees or stuffed into the mouths of the dead or the almost dead. Genitals were hacked off, leaving victims writhing in pools of gushing blood. Hands and feet littered the fields. Heads were hung up on pikes as trophies. Eyes were gouged out. Blood was everywhere. Nature's browns, golds, and greens were replaced with red, only red.

Bloodthirsty flies and brazen vultures immediately descended, feasting on the bounty of the battlefield. Francis would remember the smell later. For now, he had all he could do to dodge the flies threatening to invade the eyeholes of his helmet.

"So much blood," he kept muttering, but he could not comprehend it.

He tried to remember faces as he raced by, but they were mangled, broken, disfigured, and twisted in the grimaces of agony and death. He spotted no one he knew.

"How can I recognize no one?" Francis's heart pounded in his throat. "These are Assisians. Matteo, did I see Matteo?" He could not remember.

Francis's head was swelling with confusion and heat under the increasing burden of his heavy helmet. The Perugians were all around him, with many more gaining in the pursuit. Francis tried to prepare himself for death, but could not. His mind was overcome by the massacre, by the stench, by the hordes of flies, by the brazenness of the vultures, by the blood, by the oncoming darkness. He tried to focus, but his mind resisted. His legs were numb; his mind knew only panic.

"Where is Giovanni? What happened to Giovanni?" Francis shouted.

The strong legs of Francis's fine stallion continued to carry the terrorized rider away from his pursuers. He knew the Perugians were close behind. He knew there were Assisians ahead and beside him. Who they were, he could not tell. It wasn't that he was afraid of death. His terror resulted from his inability to see the collective face of Assisi. It had vanished; there was only blood and maimed bodies. Massacre, there was only massacre. Assisi was dead, vanquished in an afternoon. There was blood, blood, endless blood ...

"Marescotto, where is Lord Marescotto?" Francis's mind raced, remembering the paternal protection that the Lord of Collestrada had once given him.

"Giovanni?" He couldn't see his friend.

Simone. Had Simone saved his life? He couldn't remember. Matteo. No, he couldn't allow himself to weep. Francis swallowed hard and tried to concentrate on self-preservation.

"Ride, ride, ride," his now whirling mind commanded.

*T*he battle shriek of the Perugian knight hit him first. Francis landed hard, but hardly remembered being felled. Once down, he saw only the horror on Matteo's face. His mind went numb. He had no plans for this. He had fought bravely. He had not imagined his fate at the hands of the Perugians.

The Perugian knight continued in pursuit of other men from Assisi leaving underlings to round up Francis and the other fallen cavaliers. Perugian foot soldiers stripped Francis of his treasured armor, while three Perugian knights guarded the precious booty. Unlike the Assisian commoners, the knights were chained together: naked to be humiliated, not killed. Assisi had money to ransom its noble and merchant sons. Perugia would win the war, humiliate the fallen, demand even stiffer tolls, and require extravagant ransoms for the horsemen — who they would make sure would never fight again. Assisi's arrogance in confronting the obvious superiority of Perugia's military machine had earned them this fate. Perugia, the victors promised themselves, would not be forced to fight against these detestable and foolhardy neighbors again.

The road to prison seemed endless. Commoners were casually murdered on the way. Their pleas for mercy went unheeded. There was a young peasant boy, a child, perhaps only twelve or thirteen. Francis saw his face as he cried, pleaded for his life, and then died, hacked through.

"It wasn't his battle," Francis wanted to cry out.

"It wasn't his fault. He had to come. He was forced. We were all forced," Francis's heart protested.

Francis looked at the dead, mangled boy and saw himself. He hated his father, he hated war, he hated money.

The muscles of the young boy's legs and arms still twitched in a macabre spasm of death.

"It wasn't worth it," Francis thought. "He's only a boy, a poor boy, an innocent boy."

Francis, stripped, roped, and chained together with the other Assisi nobles and merchants, was forced to drag his contrada's standard, the standard of the area of Assisi, around the monastery of San Paolo, in the dirt behind him. Old noble warriors, proud and fierce, were spat on by arrogant peasants. Prominent men like Francis were pelted with mud. Young men, boys, stifled tears as they were herded toward the jeering crowds in the enemy town.

Once in Perugia, Francis attempted to wall his mind off from the humiliations inflicted on him, and to close his ears to the howl of the mob. He could see no faces — ah, yes, he saw one, the face of Matteo. Francis blinked hard; was Matteo dead? A cold wind blew across his naked, shivering body as if it too was mocking the arrogance of Bernardone's son. He remembered Matteo. Then he remembered the boy, and after the boy, he remembered nothing.

The first night in the squalid and overcrowded dungeon brought no relief from the nightmare. Francis had all he could do not to vomit at the putrid stench of sweat, blood, and urine. The stone dampness invaded every crevice of his bones with chilly hopelessness. Men once united in battle wrestled with each other over the right to lie down. Sleep came in fits between shouting, tears, and cries of despair.

Those who faced the first few days with reason and fortitude were slowly demoralized by endless monotony in the damp, cramped darkness. Men accustomed to woods, fields, and rugged mountain passes were ill-suited to enclosure. Here in prison, one's new and intimately hated enemy was the man who one just yesterday called "comrade."

During the day, Perugian life went on as though the prisoners below the town's square did not exist. In exile, Lady Ortolana and her young daughter Clare prayed for the Assisians whenever they entered the central Perugian piazza and thought of the unfortunate men of Assisi, languishing in the dungeon of a building at the edge of the piazza called the Campo di Battaglia. Without her uncle Monaldo's knowledge, Clare helped her mother prepare food that a servant delivered to the Assisian inmates. Francis recognized the Offreduccio's servant and remembered the little girl with thick, blonde curls and dark eyes. Although Francis had been one of those who had set fire to the Offreduccio palazzo, he had not intended that his acts directly harm Clare and her refined, gentle mother, Ortolana. Francis placed his head in his hands and pulled a clump of hair on each side of his head until he could feel the pain.

During the long nights, the men of Perugia could be heard in the square above the dungeon enjoying life and savoring victory.

Deprived of all their accustomed comforts and usual pursuits, the prisoners below improvised games of chance, quarreled over the meager rations given out each day, and fought to defend the miserable spaces that they claimed as their own. Demoralization spread like the diseases and infections that slowly attacked almost every inmate in the God-forsaken quarters.

Since he was a merchant's son, Francis did not feel the same depths of disgrace and dishonor that plagued the members of Assisi's nobility. As winter turned to spring with no hope of release, it became clear that Perugia was willing and able to extend the sentence, taking ransom payments, but delaying release of prisoners in order to undermine their health and morale and thus ensure that Assisi's power to take revenge would be crippled for many years to come. The men of Assisi were watched carefully, and released only when they were at death's door. Assisi was paying Perugia for the right to bury its sons.

Francis had a fever like all the others. During the summer months, the cold of the damp quarters was replaced by fetid heat which brought out swarms of vermin and insects and made the already miserable food rotten. Most painful to Francis's soul was the lack of love. There were no women in the prison. No women to clean the dirt, warm the body, or whisper to the soul. Assisians were just commodities to the Perugians. The guards, mere commoners, saw the prisoners as despicable and expendable outlaws. Their lives were worth no more than the price of their eventual ransoms.

The spirit of the proud Simone della Rocco nearly broke, not under physical hardship, but under the inhumane disgrace and humiliation of living in such confining quarters. His hatred for Perugia had intensified over decades and could find no outlet in this cramped hole filled mostly with men younger than himself. His frustration slowly turned into a pervasive anger that colored his every word and move. At one point, it even turned violently against his own son, Giovanni. He lashed out, breaking his nose.

The others had little patience for Simone's bad temper. They isolated him and made him the butt of jokes.

"Old man Simone is feeling cheated today. His dinner had only three worms instead of the regular five!" taunted a young knight from Orsara of Apulia. The Apulian knight had hired himself out as a mercenary and only hoped that Assisi would pay him well for his troubles.

"Damn fool to put himself and all his sons in this battle. If his relatives don't pay, we'll never get rid of him," Elias di Bonbarone lamented. Elias was a superb leader who found it difficult to put up with Simone della Rocca's abrasive mountain ways and temper.

"He acts as if della Rocco shit doesn't stink," the knight Angelo di Tancredi sneered. Tall and muscular, Angelo was a patient man who had paced himself for a long wait. Elias admired his psychological stamina. Angelo was usually quite courteous in speech, but the sight of Giovanni's broken nose had pushed him over the edge.

"The man doesn't have the money to keep enough land to pee on," the Apulian knight jeered.

"Asshole," Angelo snarled. "Oh, excuse me, Lord Asshole," he said, bowing in mock respect and then kicking Simone's foot in disgust. Angelo had inherited a disposition for harsh and uncompromising views from Tancredi, his father, but he was usually able to keep this tendency in check.

"Better call him 'Lord' or he'll break your face too," Elias egged on Angelo's disgust.

Overcome by the humiliation of his imprisonment, tormented by his responsibility for besmirching his reputation and the honor of his noble family, and brokenhearted by the loss of Matteo, Simone retreated ever more deeply into dangerous depths of silent anger. The younger men all stood vigilant against him. Once Simone had led these men, had been respected, and had seen his orders obeyed. Now he was just a sick old man, who had revealed his vile character and lack of courage.

Francis regarded Simone with compassion; this was the man who had saved his life. This was the man who cared for him even as his own son was being dismembered. This was the man who kept his focus, who did not sacrifice his goal. Francis respected Simone. He even liked him. Simone had shown a kind of care for Francis that Pietro Bernardone had never displayed.

Simone had not sent his sons off to fight alone. He had gone to war with them. Simone had fought not for money and trade routes, but for Assisi's honor.

Trying to divert the anger and contempt directed at Simone, Francis stood up and began pounding his foot and clicking his fingers, imitating as best he could the music of the tavern. What the dungeon needed was women, and love, Francis sang. He would change the atmosphere by summoning up memories of love.

The distraction seemed to have the desired effect.

"How can you be happy in this hell hole, Francis?" Elias asked, astonished by Francis's joyful energy.

"How can you think about singing?" inquired the hurting Giovanni.

"You are a fool, Francis!" Elias grinned. "A madman!"

Francis laughed with the others, happy to play the role of fool in order to defuse the growing anger directed at poor Simone. As he hid his embarrassed and woeful face in a dark corner, Simone understood what Francis was doing and why.

"A fool. A madman. Is this what you think of me? Is this how you appreciate my performance?" Francis chuckled. "The day will come when I will be honored by the entire world."

The prisoners laughed and groaned. Simone's eyes turned toward his son Giovanni. With the other prisoners' attention fixed on Francis, Giovanni could risk giving his agonized father a loving glance. Simone coughed; it was becoming harder for him to breathe. Francis also coughed and struggled to catch his breath. The performance was taking a great deal of his slender reserve of strength.

In the months that followed the battle of that single November day, summer came and went. Francis became more ill with each passing day, as had so many before him who had been sent back to Assisi to die. As the months dragged on, he saw his life progressively slip away. He looked at the men remaining around him. No longer was there the bravado so confidently displayed before Collestrada. There was little energy for arguments, games, or songs. Francis looked around blankly at the living corpses that remained in the foul prison and coughed weakly, his lungs wheezing as he took in each breath. He felt like he was burning up.

Francis's mind replayed moments from his past, like a man preparing for death. He remembered the tenderness of his mother's hands. He remembered her care for him during a childhood illness. Days of school at San Giorgio returned with memories of the old canon, Giovanni di Sasso, who even then was gray-headed, teaching the boys the song of Saint George while peering at the fresco painted on the church wall. Francis loved that fresco of Saint George. As a child he dreamt of riding his horse and of saving a helpless lady from the evil dragon. Francis smiled sadly. It had been a child's dream.

Between the recollected moments of his childhood, searing memories of Collestrada intruded even into the few hours each day that Francis tossed and turned in his feverish sleep.

"Matteo!"

"The boy ... what was his name?" "The heads, the limbs ..."

"Who were they   those faces?" "Red, red everywhere."

"Blood."

Francis's mind was tormented by these frightful images. He was burning up, dying.

3
Shock

The Perugians accepted Bernardone's ransom at the end of November, 1203. It had been about a year since the fateful battle of Collestrada. They dumped Francis in the Collestrada field and left him to fend for himself. Hardly strong enough to walk and nearly delirious with fever, Francis stumbled upon a kind peasant who placed him on his cart and carried him back to Assisi. Pietro Bernardone paid the peasant farmer for his trouble, while Pica put her dying son to bed.

Francis spent Christmas day of 1203 in bed, weak with fever. On December 28, the Feast of the Holy Innocents, the long, gray, winter afternoon was broken with shouts from the town's square, followed by the exclamations of Pietro.

"The deal has been finalized. Bulgarello of Fossato and Albertino are putting the castle of Serpigliano under the protection of Assisi. The Nocera road is open to us," Pietro announced.

Bernardone's excited words fell on Francis's fevered brain like a weighted anchor lugged into a boat too small and weak to hold it.

"Shhh, Pietro," Pica whispered. "Francis."

"Oh, damn him. He needs to shake this off. It's been long enough now. Others have recovered, but he ..."

"And others have died," Pica interjected. "Pietro, please. He is burning up."

Francis turned in his bed, eyes away from his father. He was tired of the arguing. He was tired of his father's news of deals and alliances and skirmishes.

"Francis!" Pietro demanded his son's attention.

Francis closed his weary eyes. The game had cost him too much.

It all seemed so trivial now. Merchants and nobles fought over this castle and that property as though they were empires, risking life and limb, as well as sons and grandsons, for the right to use roads and to cross over streams. The sons and grandsons were the innocents, innocents slaughtered to protect the selfish interests of their fathers.

There was a grace in being sick; it was a legitimate excuse for inaction. Yet, at the same time, the sickness wore him down. The Perugians had released him, but his fever held him prisoner. It had been their plan all along. Sickness was the weapon of the enemy, yet, here in his own house, Francis used it to protect himself from the intrigues of his father, of the town fathers. Francis turned in his bed, confused, sweating profusely. He did not know who the real enemy was.

"Let him be," Pica demanded.

Bernardone, exasperated by his son's long convalescence and also a bit suspicious of it, was losing patience. "What kind of man cannot get out of bed? What kind of grown man relies on his mother to take care of him?" he shouted. "He is a coward. He was a coward in battle, a coward in prison, and now a coward in his own home."

"Francis fought bravely in battle," Pica said defiantly. "He was a hero."

"Hero? They say he completely lost his head when Matteo died. People die. That's the way it is. Many more could have been killed because Francis did not keep his wits." Pietro's voice was full of scorn.

"You were not there. You do not know what happened," Pica insisted. "Francis was a hero. He fought your battle for you. He deserves your respect. He is your son."

"They tell me that Francis entertained them in prison. They laugh at me on the street. They say, 'Francis is a troubadour, not a knight. Bernardone has no knightly blood. Bernardone has worked for nothing. His son cannot defend his land. He dresses like a knight, but inside the metal there is only a fool.' " Bernardone was furious. "Pietro," Pica responded angrily, "your son lies here burning up, sick from fighting your war and instead of thanking him — instead of blaming yourself, you push him down even as he struggles to get well. What kind of man are you? Leave us."

"He is a loser." Pietro's face was scarlet with rage and embarrassment. "I gave my son everything and he cannot succeed. He could not save the Collestrada property that belongs to his father. Now we are reduced to making deals with the Perugians."

Pica was white with anger. Pietro, frustrated that his efforts to celebrate good news had only caused additional friction between him and his wife and son, turned abruptly and stomped downstairs.

Francis was obviously aware of Bernardone's mood, if not his every word. He tossed, wet with perspiration. At times he shook with chills, while his fever continued to rage. Seldom leaving his side, Pica attended Francis constantly. Pietro, with little patience for Francis's extended sickness, scowled in frustration while keeping his anxiousness to himself. Pica knew her husband. She did her best to set limits on his anger, and Pietro, although always testing these limits, knew that it was best to obey her.

Safe for the time being from the demands of his father, Francis sighed and distracted himself from his fever by listening to the birds singing outside the window. Pica took his head in her lap. It was love that would cure Francis; she would persevere until he was well again. She also heard the birds. In the midst of their happy tune, her heart thanked God for the life of her son.

It was not until February 1204 that Francis showed signs of recovery. His fever came and went. Some days he had strength to walk with a cane around the house, and other days his fever would force him to return to bed. He began to long for the day when he would be strong enough to go downstairs into the square. He began to dream again of fields and streams and the Subasio mountain. Although his continued absence from work in the shop meant that his father had to put in long and tedious hours waiting on customers and doing the books, he did not regret his delinquency. Pietro had paid heavily for his son's ransom, and a return for his money in terms of practical help with the store was slow in coming. Francis did not seem to care. His son's lack of gratitude drove Bernardone crazy.

One day when the fever seemed to have subsided, Francis haltingly made his way down the steps into the town's square. He tried to delight in the sun and the life of the piazza without focusing upon the interpersonal and political complexities of those standing and gossiping there. Knowing that he would be the subject of many of those conversations, Francis tried to stand straight without leaning too heavily on his cane. The four Assisi consuls who had been arguing on the ancient steps of the Temple of Minerva paused when they saw him.

"Is that Francis?" Alduccio asked. His small squinting eyes seemed to miss nothing that happened in the Assisi piazza.

"Francis Bernardone? No, it couldn't be him," replied Muzio. "Yes, that's how thin he is. He has the fever," the kind and sympathetic Giacomo remarked.

"Well, he survived Perugia. That's more than can be said for others," Alduccio replied.

"He is so thin, but it is good to see him back. Pietro is lucky to have his son," said Carlo, who had lost his son on the field of Collestrada.

"Pietro, oh yes. But Francis is Pica's boy," Muzio remarked smugly, giving the impression that he understood the goings-on of the Bernardone household.

The four consuls proceeded on their way without greeting Francis. His happiness to be out in the square again was replaced by a feeling of strangeness. Many of his friends and companions were no longer alive. He could almost see them milling around the square, laughing, and determined to be strong. With those memories came the face of Matteo. No, he must quit thinking about Matteo. He could not get well if he allowed himself to think about the blood and horror of Collestrada.

His knees shook, and he began what seemed to be a terribly long journey back upstairs to his bed. His fever returned, making him sick, unable to sleep and unable to think. The bells of Vespers rang and he could hear the monks gathering to sing the evening's praises of God in the monastery of San Paolo next door.

"O God, come to my assistance," the Abbot began.

"O Lord, make haste to help me," the monks responded.

Francis closed his eyes. The singing of the monk's prayers comforted his tormented soul. Without thinking, he found himself praying with them. He had heard their rough chanting since early childhood.

"With all my heart I cried out to the Lord, and the Lord stooped to hear my prayer," the monks chanted.

Just when the sounds of the monks' prayer began to dissolve into sleep, Francis was suddenly confronted again by the anguished face of Matteo. Was it Matteo's face? Matteo and the young peasant boy were constantly in his dreams; their faces tended to blend into a single mask of agony. He had nightmares about their fates, about his sufferings, and about the sufferings of his comrades in the Perugian dungeon. Often he woke, shaken with fever and horror with only one memory — blood, red blood. He had blocked most of the terror of the torture inflicted upon him by the Perugians out of his mind. He could deal with the memory of Matteo's death better than he could those months of his own suffering.

As the days passed, Francis made several attempts to walk around the town's central piazza. Physically he was able to move his legs and body, but mentally he found it difficult to manage even a simple greeting. Noticing his reticence, people began to talk; they wondered if his mind had been affected by his ordeal and illness.

Everything seemed so empty to him now. People worried about such unimportant things. They hurried about as if everything they were doing was important. The consuls continued to devise strategies to restore Assisi's power, honor, and glory, but in truth they were greedy only for profit, roads, rights, and money. It was this greed that had led to the death or imprisonment of their sons. His own father had, in effect, sold his son, betrayed him for a handful of coins as Judas had betrayed Christ.

Francis, driven by fever-inspired anger, finally allowed his mind to consider it — his father was not a father, he was a Judas. Did the consuls not understand what was happening to Assisi's sons? His father knew the risks of sending him off to fight against Perugia. He felt himself weaken and become lightheaded again. He tried to dismiss these bitter thoughts and headed home. It was enough for today.

Weeks later, the white and red roses of spring were in full bloom when Francis at last felt well enough to venture beyond the town's square. His heart longed to see again the fields, the olive trees, the golds, greens, and browns of the budding vineyards. The natural beauty of his father's properties had always soothed his spirit. He could not find this consolation in the people, noise, and selfish business affairs of the town's square. Perhaps after the long months of winter's dark and cold, beauty would cure his soul of the anger and despair that was slowly poisoning it.

Francis went out around 8:00 A.M., after the bells sounded for the monks to begin chanting the canonical hour of Terce. The morning sky was glorious and the air was warm. Feeling that his legs were strong enough, his soul drove him past the merchants in the square in front of San Nicolo and through the San Giorgio gate. The guards greeted him, and he managed to offer them a smile.

Leaning on his cane for support, he wandered pensively through the vines and the gnarled trunks of olive trees with their blue-tinted leaves. Starved for beauty and serenity, he used the full power of his senses to capture the exquisite

beauty of the landscape. He closed his eyes and listened atten-
tively, attempting to immerse himself in the subtle rhythms
and melodies of birds and wind. He breathed deeply, inviting the fresh spring air to clear his mind of the memories of
blood and slaughter.

Opening his eyes, Francis saw a flock of small brown birds
twittering, chirping, and announcing the arrival of spring.
Francis looked at them, studied them hard, but remained
untouched. He felt suddenly angry at the carefree birds flitter-
ing from vine to vine. Were they, like all nature, indifferent to
his suffering? Did they not care? Did God not care?

"Peace, even here I can find no peace," Francis cried in
desperation.

He tried hard not to panic. Francis had waited for the day
when he could return to these fields and to the serenity that
they had always offered him. If he could not find peace here,
would he find it anywhere? Would he ever find peace again?
Would his mind always be tormented by images of blood and
death? Was there to be any hope, any life for him beyond the
narrow confines of his father's shop?

His mind was confused and his body trembling as he made
his way back to Assisi. He crossed the square and went up the
stairs of the Bernardone home. Pica, who had hoped that the
open air of fields and vineyards would do her son good, immediately saw that he was distressed and quietly prepared his bed.
Francis, sweating from fever, lay down without saying a word.

"What will become of my son?" Pica wondered, trying not
to let her face show her anguish.

Instinctively she began to sing softly. It was an old lullaby
— one she had sung to Francis when he was a baby. Perhaps it
would help Francis recover some of his innocence; perhaps it
would calm his anguished soul so that his body could heal.

Francis closed his eyes, and tried hard to escape the darkness that would invariably turn into images of blood. He tried
to retain the healing images of the day, the smells, sounds, and
colors of natural beauty in which his soul sought to immerse

and cleanse itself. But everything was different now. He was different. He feared that life no longer held a place for him, and that he would never again find beauty in Assisi. He dreamt of leaving home so that he could get away from it all, and do something bigger — something noble.

*H*is friends tried in vain to help Francis become his old and joyful self. Those who had returned after spending time with him in the Perugian prison understood his struggle. Many of those imprisoned had gone mad after being tortured in the Perugian dungeons. Some survived the ordeal, and some didn't. It was hard to predict who would fully recover. The town consuls worried that Francis might become a victim — perhaps not to death, but to madness.

"Francis is not the same," Alduccio observed, his small eyes squinting in the morning sun.

"He just can't get well. He always was a bit delicate," Giacomo added kindly.

"I blame it on Pica, she coddled him too much," Muzio stated in his customary critical manner. "Francis was never cut out to be a knight. He is a businessman like his father."

"Like his father! Like Pietro Bernardone! Never!"Giacomo objected.

"If he doesn't mind his father's shop, what will he do?" Alduccio asked.

The consuls feared that Pietro Bernardone's son might become a victim of his father's ambition and of his mother's tenderness. Would Bernardone send his son into battle again? Francis would never survive. He was a casualty of the demon of mind and spirit that was punishing the greed of Assisi. Every family was mourning a son, a grandson.

Every family had its living dead.

Francis began to realize that his biggest fear was not death, but living out the rest of his life as an invalid. He could escape his father's shop only if he could recover his health. Once well, he would again be able to pursue dreams of glory.

Now it was not the Perugians, but illness that imprisoned him. His recurring fever was becoming a living death. Sickness would confine him to the shop, keep him in Assisi, and sentence him to perpetual subservience to his father. The sickness was becoming Francis's enemy. He wanted to become well and to get on with life.

By late spring, he was back in his father's shop. The young man who Pietro had hired to help out had taken on many of his responsibilities, and Francis was eager to have him continue doing so. He frequently took refuge in the back counting room. Often, when the fever returned, he simply laid down in the corner near the cabinet that had once held his magnificent armor. Francis felt a strange sense of peace with the hollow emptiness of the cabinet. His father had the keys now. It was used to guard a few of Pietro's most valuable bolts of cloth.

As the months wore on, Francis wondered how he would survive the tedium, the smallness of his father's world. Nothing seemed to rouse his spirit, neither the luxurious quality of the new fabrics Pietro had brought back from his last trip to the great fair in France, nor spending evenings with his friends and dancing and flirting with the women who joined their parties. Night after night, Francis sought to drown his emptiness with wine, women, gambling, and song. His friends were concerned about his melancholy, but continued to encourage him. He was, after all, quite generous. When Francis felt better, he stayed up carousing with his friends, only to have the fever return the following day, along with the wrath of his father. It was an endless cycle. Francis's body could not sustain his carousing, erratic lifestyle. It could not tolerate the rich foods, the abundant wine, and the late hours. But he was indifferent to the toll that his nightlife was taking on him and ignored the protests of his mother.

"Francis, the drinking does not help you. You are the son of a merchant, not the son of a prince!" Pica warned him one morning when she came into his room to change the perspiration-soaked bedding.

Francis turned over, head heavy, his eyelids hot. He was so weary, so tired. He had everything, but having everything had become bitter. The Perugian dungeon had taken away his dreams. He did not want the life of his father. While he still enjoyed what pleasure his father's wealth could provide, he despised the shop and the values of his father, and he hated the grasping selfishness of those who would do anything to become influential and rich.

"Francis," Pica pleaded, stroking her son's hair gently.

"Francis, you must stop going out every night. It is making you ill. Your father is right. You are too generous with his money."

Francis turned his face away from his mother and escaped into the tormented dreams brought on by his fever. He could not bear being a disappointment to his mother, but the heaviness of last night's wine submerged him in sleep, even as the golden light of day filled his room.

*T*hat night, Francis went to the tavern looking for one of his friends, an Assisi nobleman.

"Francis, over here," Angelo di Tancredi called. He bowed in his usual courteous manner. He had recovered from the Perugian prison with no obvious ill effects.

Francis's tall, thin, and shy friend, Bernard, caught up with Francis as he sat down next to Angelo. "You weren't in the shop today. I came over looking for you, but the shopkeeper said that you were under the weather."

"Under the weather for work, but not for play. Francis knows how to do it right. Perhaps his sickness is more about wine than about fever," Angelo grinned. His dark hair coiled in tight curls around his head. He was almost as tall as Bernard, but was stronger and more robust.

"Then let there be wine for all," Francis exclaimed.

As wine was poured, all were grateful as usual to Francis for picking up the tab. With the wine flowed the stories.

"They say that Gautier de Brienne has defeated Diopoldo at Salerno," Giovanni della Rocca explained. "Brienne now attacks Diopoldo at the castle of Sarno." .

"They say that nowhere are women as beautiful as they are at Brienne's court," Bernard interrupted, raising his eyebrows and smiling broadly at the group.

"Perhaps there is a woman for you there, Francis," Angelo suggested, playfully ruffling Francis's hair and grinning.

Giovanni was hoping to tempt Francis to join a group of knights from Assisi who were going to Apulia as paid mercenaries to fight under the command of Brienne. He stirred a primitive impulse in Francis — an excitement that he had not felt since that fateful day of battle with Perugia. The music of drums, a reed instrument called the shawm, and a stringed vielle grew louder, to compete with the shouts of laughter from the customers in the tavern.

"At the court of Brienne, there are beautiful women, the noblest of knights, the greatest luxury, playful tournaments, interrupted only by bloody battles for the good of God and the poor," della Rocca promised.

Francis felt his spirit lighten. He imagined himself at the court of Brienne. He imagined fighting bravely and winning the attention of Brienne himself. He imagined the women at the court of Brienne vying for his attention and admiring his armor, his elegance, and his bravery. No more would he drink and gamble in the small taverns of Assisi. His acquaintances would no longer be limited to the merchants and nobility of commune; nor would his life revolve around the endless struggles between Assisi and Perugia. No, in the court of Brienne he would become a master of the sophisticated courtship of noble love. He would love purely and with complete generosity. He would be the most courteous of knights and his magnanimity would encounter others cultured in the art of chivalry. He would enter battle only for God and for the poor.

Buying another round to distract his friends, Francis left the tavern with Giovanni. Brienne was the epitome of chivalry and was searching for knights to enlist in his service. Francis's spirit revived after this meeting, and he continued to meet with Giovanni to make plans. He paid attention to every detail of his armor and wardrobe. At night, he and others whom Giovanni had recruited practiced courting the fair women they would meet by singing songs of love to them in French. In the end, Francis's enthusiasm outdid that of his noble friend.

Always ready to encourage Francis's ambition to enter into a noble marriage, Pietro supported his son's plan. He gladly commissioned craftsmen to produce a complete new suit of the most exquisitely decorated armor. Bernardone was merely a merchant, but his son would be knighted by the great Gautier de Brienne.

Francis would be strong and valiant in battle, his deeds would be celebrated in song, and he would marry a noble woman. Bernardone would provide a wedding worthy of his son's station, thereby enhancing his family's honor. The marriage would be, above all, good for business.

Pica's objections were ignored.

"Francis, your fever," Pica pleaded. "Francis, you do not yet have the strength. Here in Assisi you have everything you need to lead a happy life."

Excited by the prospect of serving Brienne, Francis felt vigor and health returning to his wasted, abused body.

"You see, Mama, the fever has not returned for days," Francis contended. "I am better all the time. Because of your patience, my health has returned. I will do great things. I will make you proud. I will bring home a noble bride."

Pica was not persuaded by her son's grandiose plans and feared for his health and safety. She did not feel it was necessary for Francis to be knighted by Brienne. He was still ill and weak. Her heart was filled with anguish and with premonitions of disaster.

The work of craftsmen began to pour into the Bernardone home, armor intricately etched and gold-plated, an outer mantle crafted from exquisite silk with an ermine collar. Pieces of his wardrobe were made of linen and silk with delicate patterns embroidered with gold thread. Sword and shield were fashioned with the greatest skill and gilded with gold.

All in Assisi knew of Francis's plans; and many were making good money from them. Francis, on his white stallion, regularly strutted through Assisi's central piazza wearing various pieces of his splendid armor and wardrobe, awing the bystanders. He was the talk of Assisi.

The glories of fields and mountain began to give him some pleasure again. One day after delivering fabric to a customer, Francis's thoughts of love persuaded him to dismount his horse. He began singing to the streams, to the birds, to the trees, to the vines, and to all creation the love songs he was composing for his fair and true lady. The mountain trees seemed to sway in time with his melody.

"Am I disturbing you and your lady, Francis?" a voice asked that came from somewhere behind the trees.

Francis recognized the voice, and responded in good humor. "Ah, my good Lord Celino, you are interrupting my courtship of a fair lady."

"I see that, Francis, and I am so sorry," Celino chuckled. A knight from the fortress of Poggio, Celino was amused by the spectacle of a young man dressed in an ermine-collared silk mantle and waving his sword at the birds and trees. "I thought perhaps that God had blessed our mountain with a new bird that was singing so beautifully. It seems that we have here a new love bird."

Francis smiled, but then saw the pitiful figure of a man coming from behind the trees. The noble, Celino, who once had great wealth, was reduced to wearing pathetic rags. His hair hung in greasy strands, the shoes on his feet were worn thin, and he had no cloak to protect him from the mountain winds. Francis tried not to gasp in surprise.

"Celino," Francis said sympathetically.

The nobleman waved his hand dismissively; he seemed to be oblivious to his wretched state. Francis looked into his eyes. They were empty. Francis, along with others from Assisi, had long ago sacked his castle. Now facing his former friend, Francis's pity was unbounded. The knight, seeing Francis's shock, was now clearly embarrassed by his condition and turned away. When he had heard Francis sing, he had forgotten his miserable appearance.

Instinctively, Francis took off his ermine-collared mantle and ran to cover the shivering man. Celino looked at the mantle and then stared into Francis's eyes. He could take such a mantle from Francis as a true gift. Francis offered him the food that he had brought with him from Assisi. Grateful, but too embarrassed, confused, and disheartened to say much, Celino thanked Francis and took the food with him into the woods. Francis paused, knowing that he had seen in Celino's vacuous eyes a mirror of his own soul.

Without any warning, the fever returned. Francis first felt the chills and then the dreaded lightheadedness. He turned his horse back toward Assisi. His horse knew the way.

His mother heard the faltering steps of her son as he slowly climbed the stairs, and she prepared his bed. Francis collapsed into it, wet with perspiration.

Dusk turned to night and Francis continued to sleep. In his dream, he saw a man who called him by name. "Francis," the man whispered.

He was the very image of a rich and powerful prince, and Francis readily followed him into a great palace. Its walls were covered with displays of glittering coats of mail, shining bucklers, gilded weapons, jeweled helmets, saddles, caparisons, and the shields of noble families. Francis had never seen anything like it.

"Whose palace and arms are these?" Francis inquired.

"The palace and the arms are for you and for your knights," the man replied.

Francis, half awake and half asleep, tried to make sense of his dream. When he opened his eyes, it was a glorious sunny morning. The song of the birds of Assisi seemed to echo the happiness he knew he should feel within his heart. He spoke of the dream to his mother and reassured her. "I will go to Apulia," he said. "I am destined to become a great prince. I will bring to the Bernardone family great wealth and even greater honor. I will bring home a treasure of armor and weapons."

After a day's work in the shop, and still heartened by his dream, Francis was in good spirits when he reached the town's square. He saw poor Albert sitting on the steps of the Minerva Temple and leaning against one of the tall and mighty Corinthian columns as he slept. Francis woke him up and gave him some money. Albert was not at all pleased to be awakened from his nap.

Undaunted by Albert's less than enthusiastic response, Francis made his way to the tavern, ordered a round of drinks, and shared what he thought was the meaning of his dream with Giovanni della Rocca. "The palace and arms are mine. I shall become a great prince, and I shall remember you, my friend, who opened my eyes to my future destiny," he promised. The two talked for hours that night, agreeing on the final details of their plan and setting a date for departure to Apulia.

When the fateful day arrived, Francis, Giovanni, and a few others received the blessings of their families and the cheers of a large crowd of citizens who watched them depart though the town gate. Francis tried to seem steady and confident as he rode on his beautiful white charger, but the fever still gripped him. He was occasionally made dizzy by chills and bouts of nausea. The situation was not helped by the fact that the men wore full armor as they made their ceremonial departure. Only by a sheer act of will could Francis manage to stay on his mount.

Accompanied by their squires, the men took the road to Spoleto, passing through places so dear to Francis's soul — the twisted olive trees of San Damiano, the humble but pure and clean stream of Rivotorto, the dilapidated church of San Pietro della Spina, the serenity of Fontanelle. He looked up toward the imposing monastery of San Benedetto and the ruined castle of Sasso Rosso.

During the journey, Francis became more and more ill. His fever was raging, and the perspiration ran off his forehead and poured down his back. When they reached Spoleto at the end of the day, Francis, animated more by desire than by physical strength, stopped with the others at the Basilica of Saint Sabinus, a gathering place for those who were preparing for battle. They offered their obsequies and invoked the protection of the saintly Bishop Sabinus, who, according to legend, often came to the aid of worthy knights endangered in battle. Francis sank to his knees, petitioning the good bishop. He was glad for the rest and for the coolness of the basilica.

The Duke of Spoleto was subject to Pope Innocent III, and since Brienne's efforts against the Germans were advantageous to papal authority, those joining Brienne were granted the same indulgence as those participating in the Crusades. Francis would be fighting not only for knighthood and nobility, he would be fighting in the name of God. Francis crossed himself and looked up at the large crucifix hanging over the altar. God would protect him.

As the men prepared to depart the next morning, Francis, completely exhausted by fever, had to give in. He had slept poorly and was plagued by a deep ache in his bones. He promised Giovanni that he would meet him at the castle of Lecce. His faithful squire, accustomed to dealing with Francis's intermittent fever, attended him. Again Francis slipped in and out of consciousness and lay, wracked with chills, in his room at the inn. He feared that, despite his best efforts and meticulous preparations, he would not be able to continue on his journey to Apulia. Then late in the afternoon, when he had finally managed to fall into a deep sleep, Francis heard a voice calling him.

"Where are you going, Francis?" the voice asked. It seemed to come from some vast, indeterminate distance.

"I am going to Apulia, to join Gautier de Brienne. I am going to fight bravely and to win the honor of knighthood. I will win the favor of a most beautiful lady and bring honor to myself, my family, and to God," Francis boasted.

"Who do you think can best reward you, the Master or the servant?" the strong yet gentle voice inquired.

"The Master," Francis replied.

"Then why do you leave the Master for the servant, the rich Lord for the poor man?" asked the voice.

Francis opened his eyes and saw the banner of his contrada standing against the wall. He had grown up under the banner of Saint Paul and knew well the story of the great knight of the Gospel whose dedication to the wrong cause was mercifully intercepted by Christ. Francis wanted with all his heart to be a knight dedicated to a just, noble, and godly cause. He closed his fevered eyes and responded without resistance, "O Lord, what do you wish me to do?"

The response of the Lord of his vision was similar to that given to Saint Paul after the Lord had blinded him on his way to Damascus. "Return to your own place and you will be told what to do," the voice commanded. "You must interpret your vision in a different way. The arms and palace you saw are intended for knights other than those you had in mind; and your principality too will be of another order."

That night, Francis pondered the message of his vision. He had been inspired by the first vision, encouraged in his belief that his destiny first lay in Apulia and then in a world far beyond Assisi. This second vision, however, was difficult to interpret. What is a principality of another order? What was the Lord of his vision talking about? Was his fever making him hallucinate? Was he going mad? Unable to sleep, he tossed and turned trying to understand the message of his dream.

What were his choices? It was obvious he was not going to Apulia. He had given his best to this effort, and struggled to regain his health, but the fever was unrelenting. He could, of course, go home and bury himself in his father's shop, but the thought of accepting his fate as a merchant turned his stomach sour. He did not want to turn into his father; he wanted to be something more. In his dream, the Lord had promised him that the arms and palace of his vision would be for him and for his knights. Francis would be a great prince; this was a good dream, not a feverish illusion. For Francis, it was the only dream left. He would obey the Master of his dream and believe that his vision would put him on the path of power and glory.

He rose at daybreak determined to trust the Master in his dream. God had given Saint Paul the message to wait in the city, and Saint Paul became a great man, a man of honor. Francis would also be a great man. God would make something out of his sickness. God would make him rich, and would make him a prince. God would bring him a noble wife. He only had to wait until he was shown the way.

The gossips of Assisi were shocked when they saw Francis come through the town's square.

"Francis is back" Lady Peppone announced. Her giant breasts bobbed furiously as she rushed through the steep, narrow streets above and below Via Portica, trying to be the first one to break the news.

"What's the matter with him? I thought he was on his way to Apulia," the old knight Tancredi exclaimed.

"He is a good-for-nothing who only likes to spend his father's money," Canon Silvester bitterly retorted, chewing on a handful of olives with one hand and clutching his money bag with the other.

"He goes through the square as if he were some kind of prince. The man has no sense of honor." Tancredi was thoroughly disgusted. He was proud of his sons. He had raised them to respect the obligations that came with nobility and privilege.

"Bernardone will beat the hell out of him." Muzio spoke loudly enough so that there was a distinct possibility that Pietro Bernardone might hear him in the cloth store.

Many in the crowd in the town's square drifted over to the Bernardone shop. The episode would be too good to miss; they wanted to see Pietro's reaction to Francis's return.

Francis simply climbed the stairs and got into bed, avoiding the shop. Pietro was busy with a customer and had not
heard Muzio's remark. Muzio knew better than to repeat it.
Pica could be seen closing the shutters of the windows upstairs.
She knew that the tirades would come later. For now, Francis
needed to sleep.

"Francis," she asked softly. "What happened?"

"I had a dream," Francis replied quietly. "I will be told what
to do here in Assisi." His pious mother was sure that her son,
who left with the banner of the contrada of Saint Paul, had
received the same guidance that the Lord had given to Saint
Paul. Even throughout the days of Francis's carousing, she
knew that her prayers for her son would be answered.

"Francis seems to lack direction," Lady Marangone had suggested one day. She had often seen Pica's bruises and wanted
to offer her an opportunity to talk about the problems between
Pietro and her son.

Pica, always loyal to Francis, looked her friend straight in
the eye. "What do you think my son will become? Through
grace he will be a son of God."

Lady Marangone knew that she had hurt her friend. She
assured Pica that she had been mistaken; Francis had great
potential. He was smart; he was charming and entertaining.
Yet, Francis did have the fever. He would never again have the
stamina he had in his youth. He did not have the health to fight
battles. Lady Marangone had been on the verge of suggesting
to Pica that perhaps she could persuade her son to be content
working in his father's shop. It would save his health.

Pica, obviously quite hurt, turned again toward her friend.
"Through grace he will be a son of God," she insisted vehe-
mently.

Lady Marangone smiled gently. She knew her friend well,
and should have known better than to speak against Francis.
She had not intended to be derogatory, and realized now that
there was no more that she could do other than to keep silence.
She never should have intruded into the Bernardone's affairs.
She climbed the stairs of her family's upstairs apartment with

deep regrets. She knew that Pica would never forget her criticism of Francis, and she could do nothing about that now.

Word that Francis was back in Assisi spread instantly, but Pietro was the last to know. By the time he thudded up the stairs to find his son, Francis had gotten out of bed and was already on the streets. He had had a little rest, and the fever seemed to have subsided a bit. His friends were glad to have him back.

"Francis, did you get sick?" Bernard asked.

"Francis, why are you back?" Peter di Catanio wondered. Both Peter and Bernard were lawyers, always full of questions, although Peter had much less wealth than the noble Bernard.

"I came back to do great things in my own land," Francis replied in his usual confident yet endearing manner. "You will see, I shall become a great prince."

"A great prince?" Francis's married half-brother, the child of Pica's first marriage, Angelo, glared at Francis. Angelo looked a little like Francis, but was taller and also had Pica's thin nose and brown hair. The seemingly irrational behavior of Bernardone's son was affecting his mother, and this irritated Angelo.

Francis's friends were puzzled, but accustomed to Francis's tendency to make abrupt shifts in his thinking and attitudes, and they were glad that he had returned. The feast day of Saint Vittorino, one of Assisi's bishop martyrs, was fast approaching. Francis was the leader of the Company of the Baton, a society dedicated to reenacting annually the martyrdom of Saint Vittorino. As the elected leader of this Company, Francis was given a bishop's staff and those belonging to the Company swore obedience to him. The Company also met for elaborate banquets that often ended with singing and dancing in the streets. Such a banquet had been planned for the coming evening. Now that Francis, the leader of the Company, was home, they would not need to worry about paying the bill. The merchant's son would plan a wonderful party and pick up the tab.

Francis avoided his father by spending long hours making preparations for the party all of Assisi was talking about.

"He came back to be a prince in his own land," Bernard whispered.

"He is already a prince here." Celino spoke with authority on this point. Francis had quietly given financial help to Celino and enabled him to resume something of his former life. He was able to hold his head up again and join members of the nobility in the town's square.

"Only because of his father's money, not because he has noble blood," Tancredi objected. Tancredi was a supporter of the commune, but still had a difficult time letting go of old attitudes.

"He did the right thing coming home," Lady Marangone asserted.

"A man has to know his place; Francis belongs here," Alduccio agreed.

"His money belongs here in Assisi," Celino added.

Francis saw to it that the evening's table was elegantly prepared. There were trays full of varieties of fruit, glasses of wine, and platters of choice meats. Trying to compensate for a certain lack of enthusiasm about preparing this party, Francis had outdone himself. There were more delicacies than ever before. The wine was of a superb quality and was ordered in great abundance.

Men and women sat on scarlet cushions picking away at the delicacies and becoming more and more convivial as glass after glass of wine was poured. Francis appeared in a magnificent purple brocaded mantle and a dazzling silk ivory shirt. He used this grand occasion to announce formally to the people of Assisi that he had returned to his native city for good. His friends were pleased; they had not really wanted him to leave and become a knight of Gautier de Brienne. They valued Francis's taste and depended on his generosity. Here, he would always be a leader. Wherever Francis was there was more wine, more elegance, and more glorious song.

The would-be prince, dressed in his royal purple mantle, held the staff of Saint Vittorino while the party goers respectfully swore obedience to the man who had the honor of representing the saint — and the honor of paying for the celebration. Francis tried hard to play the part. He had been the signore of the Company many times and was able and happy to pay its expenses. Yet, tonight he took little pleasure in his role. He still did not feel well, and the spiraling events of the past few days were catching up with him.

Observing some of the nobles enjoying the party, he seriously considered for the first time the contrast between his wealth, or at least his father's wealth, and the economic vulnerability of the noble class.

"I am already prince of Assisi," he thought, but it was not something that he could take pride in.

His attention wandered as the party became noisier; the crowd followed the musicians who played lutes and mandolins out into the streets. Men and women sang love song after love song. Gradually, some noticed that Francis did not come forward as usual to lead the evening's entertainment. Others' lesser talents were happy to fill in, but the party was not the same. Old ladies accustomed to Francis's voice peaked through their bedroom shutters hoping to spot Francis in the crowd without being seen themselves. They had looked forward to hearing Francis sing tonight. Maybe he was hoarse. They hoped not; a voice as beautiful as Francis's had to be protected, needed to be nursed.

"Is this all there is for me?" Francis wondered as he stood in a doorway watching the celebrants dance in the streets. "Is this what my life will be? Will I live and die for this?"

The pledges of support and obedience that he received from his willing followers seemed so empty tonight. Yes, they were willing to follow him, but tonight it was not because he was fun or entertaining. It was simply because he was paying the bill. He was distracted by the Master of his dream and was lulled by his words.

"Why do you leave the Master for the servant, the rich Lord for the poor man?" Francis repeated to himself. "Return to your own place and you will be told what to do."

In the darkness, he fell out of step with the crowd, sat on the stairs of the Temple of Minerva, and again pondered the words. "Why do you leave the Master for the servant, the rich Lord for the poor man?"

Bernard and Peter noticed Francis's absence and they left the crowd to look for him. Seeing Bernard and Peter, the crowd followed them up Via Portica. There on the Minerva steps sat Francis, beautiful in his purple, looking up at the sky. He was completely absorbed in his thoughts, happy to neither speak nor move. The wine had mellowed him; it had cleared his head.

"Then why do you leave the Master for the servant, the rich Lord for the poor man?" he continued to mutter.

The question both haunted and consoled Francis. He pondered it over and over. It filled him with an inexplicable sweetness. Later he would tell his friends that if he had been cut to pieces that night on the steps of the Minerva, he would not have moved. The voice was a direction for his spirit.

Some broke away from the crowd and ran to Francis, overtaking Bernard and Peter. Francis, startled by the noise, snapped out of his trance.

"What were you thinking about, Francis?" asked Peter. The young lawyer found Francis interesting, and respected him as a leader. "Why didn't you follow us?" wondered Bernard.

"Are you thinking about getting married?" Peter questioned, trying to offer Francis an explanation for his unusual behavior.

Francis smiled, grateful for the suggestion.

"Yes, you are right. I was thinking about wooing the noblest, richest, and most beautiful bride ever seen!" he replied.

Francis's eyes twinkled. His natural delight at playing to the crowd had returned. The message was a direction for him. He needed only to ponder it, to stay with it.

"You are a fool, Francis," Peter mused.

"You are a romantic, Francis." Bernard slapped his friend on the shoulder.

"You are our bishop, Francis. To you we owe obedience and submission!" Angelo jested.

"And our bill!" the crowd cried in an almost hysterical unison. Many spent the last hour of the party trying to guess the identity of the bride Francis had in mind.

"She must have been at the party. Why else would Francis have been so preoccupied?" Bernard's keen, legal mind was sorting through the possibilities. He was trying to work out Peter's theory.

"He must have seen her in Spoleto. This is why he returned. He will need time to woo her properly," Peter said, pleased that Bernard took his suggestion seriously.

"If he is to be a great prince, he must be planning to marry a noble woman," Celino stated, joining in Bernard and Peter's conversation.

Francis did his best to respond to the talk and jests of the crowd, but his soul was pulling him back into his dream. He wanted to hear the voice again, and he wished that the party would end.

Eventually the revelers slipped away into the waning darkness. The first streaks of dawn would soon appear. Alone, Francis made his way pensively through the quiet streets.

4
The Bitter
Becomes Sweet

Taking leave of his associates, Francis pretended to go home after the party, but later emerged from the shadows and wandered alone in the dark and quiet Assisi streets. He knew that he would not be able to sleep. His mind was restless, struggling not so much with questions as with sheer confusion and frustration. How long had he walked? Would morning never come? The drinks and the evening's party left him strangely frustrated, sad, and empty.

He had everything. He had money, land, and power. He had friends. He was a popular and respected businessman. He could have more. He could become richer and richer, but to what end?

In Perugia, his life had meant nothing. In Perugia, he was cursed and mocked. To the enemy, his life was worth only ransom. "One must expect abuse and scorn from the enemy," Francis reasoned. "I must keep before me a noble dream, a noble desire."

They were all empty words now. The dream had died. It would be no more. Donning his glorious armor once more would only earn him contempt. He was not going to be a knight; he was going to be a merchant. The predestined goals of his life were money and power, not heroism and chivalry. Francis looked into the future and saw himself turning into a version of his father. He wanted to scream. This is not what he had wanted. Perugia had taken away the dreams of his youth.

Francis mulled the biblical line over and over in his mind. "Vanity of vanities, all is vanity." The words of Ecclesiastes suddenly hit home. He thought about himself as a merchant laden with an oversized moneybag and being dragged into hell.

"I am already in hell. All of this money does not bring happiness," Francis thought.

"It is all vanity — worthless."

Francis continued to walk the streets of Assisi silently, oblivious to his surroundings. A rooster crowed, and Francis greeted the guards just as they were opening the town gate. He did not even think about taking his horse. He did not have to go far; he just needed to get away.

Assisi was struggling to wake up after its all-night revelry. Francis left town without turning back. The countryside had always been more of a home to him than the town. Many times he had sought comfort in the shadow of the Subasio mountain. He hoped that Subasio would soothe his soul once more.

Leaving the gate behind, he could see the dilapidated church of San Damiano and headed for it. He had visited the tiny church since he was a child and had always liked the old priest there, a holy man who was content to live in poverty and to maintain the crumbling structure as best as he could.

"The priest has been old forever," Francis thought.

Francis remembered the many times when his mother took him to San Damiano. They would observe a morning fast and then wander from church to church begging God to protect Pietro on his journeys and thanking God for the family's many blessings. By mid-morning, Pica's pockets always produced a bit of bread for the hungry child who delighted in accompanying her on these pilgrimage mornings. As Francis approached San Damiano, the refreshing innocence of this childhood piety returned. He exchanged friendly words with the old priest and humbly knelt for a blessing. Then he rose, entered the tiny church, and knelt before the ancient crucifix. Instinctively, he prayed the prayer his mother had taught him.

"We adore you, Lord Jesus Christ. Here and in all your churches throughout the whole world and we bless you. Because by your holy cross you have redeemed the world."

He gazed with tired eyes at the old Byzantine crucifix on the painted panel hanging above him. The figure of the crucified Christ showed no anguish, but looked serene in the midst of his sufferings. Rather than a crown of thorns, his head bore a golden halo. At the top of the crucifix was a beautifully painted scene of a victorious Christ entering heaven accompanied by angels and welcomed by the hand of God the Father raised in blessing. Those depicted below the cross obviously knew the resurrection secret, for they smiled, rather than wept, and conversed with each other. The angels surrounding the cross also smiled and spoke with each other in joyful wonder.

What always held Francis's attention were Jesus's eyes. They seemed to follow him, lovingly inviting him to accept his peace. They did not threaten Francis with more pain; instead, they consoled him. The crucified Christ before him knew the experience of suffering and he knew the joy of peace found after suffering. Francis looked at the Lord's eyes again. He wondered if he would ever know Christ's peace.

He prayed, looking directly into the Lord's eyes: "We adore you Lord Jesus Christ. Here and in all your churches throughout the whole world and we bless you. Because by your holy cross you have redeemed the world." Then he slowly got up off his knees and left.

Father Pietro met him outside the door of the church with a piece of bread. Francis smiled, knowing that the kind priest had meant the bread to remind him of the days when his mother had brought him to this church and fed him, bringing enough also to share with the good priest. Assuming that the priest was sharing with him his own meager ration, Francis divided the bread in two, keeping one small piece for himself and returning the larger to the old man. The priest nodded in gratitude and promised Francis that he would remember him in his prayers.

*L*eaving San Damiano behind, Francis took the road toward the small women's monastery of Sant'Angelo di Panzo. The branches of the holm oaks swayed in the wind, shading Francis from the sun and making lovely shadows on the narrow dirt path. As Francis approached the church of Sant'Angelo, he could hear the women chanting the canonical hour of Terce.

"These women have little," he thought, "but because they have nothing of worth to protect, they have peace."

The sun was already hot, and Francis was hungry. He ate the priest's bread. Although it was poor fare, it actually tasted good. He picked up his pace; he needed to get away from Assisi, and to be completely alone.

Francis's heart delighted in this landscape of ancient olives, rugged precipices, and secluded caves that he knew so well. Breathing deeply of the morning air, his tired eyes fixed themselves on the dew-laden leaves of the olive trees. He paused for a moment to wash at the little spring that bubbled up near the monastery.

The water was cold, but refreshing. The birds were dancing, hopping in and out of the tangled mass of thistles. Francis fancied that their calls joined the chant of the women of Sant'Angelo in their morning praise. He closed his eyes and carefully listened to the prayerful melodies. The prayers, the birds, ah yes, and the spring. The spring, bubbling quietly, was praising the morning. Francis sat on a log that was warmed by the sun, and listened to the prayers, the birds, and the spring.

He was tired, so tired. He couldn't sleep here — it was too open. He needed to go further.

Past Sant'Angelo, Francis left the well-worn path that eventually turned toward the steep mountain road leading to the monastery of San Benedetto and forged his way through thick brambles into a nearly inaccessible hollow. A tiny brown and white bird scampered ahead of him, leading the way. The back edge of the thicket was dominated by a giant, steep cliff whose base formed the caves that were Francis's destination. With the bird as his guide, Francis reached the sunlit slope of the cliff and settled into one of the caves. He was finally alone.

Francis spent the next hours meditating on the significance of his disturbing but powerful dream. He played it through over and over again in his mind, line by line. He knew now that it was God who was calling him. He did not know what God meant by promising him that he would be a great prince, but it seemed to Francis that the Master of his dream could be trusted. Francis would never again be healthy enough to pursue dreams of knighthood. He did not want to spend the rest of his life in his father's store. He was ready to listen to an alternative plan; he was desperate for an alternative.

"Francis," he remembered the voice calling out to him.

No one had ever said his name in quite that way. Francis prostrated himself in the cave and played the memory of the voice saying his name over and over again in his mind. The entire morning passed, but Francis remained lost in thought.

"The palace and the arms are for you and for your knights," he repeated.

In the presence of this Master, Francis's troubled soul knew a consolation that he had not felt for a long time — the consolation of unconditional love. After the wounds of Perugia, he needed to spend time being healed by this love. He needed to make decisions that were responsive to this love. He needed to find some kind of meaning for life that would help him survive.

During the weeks that followed, Francis continued to spend evenings in the tavern with his friends, but during the day, apart from doing various short business trips, he hid in the caves on Mount Subasio and meditated. The progressively bizarre behavior of Assisi's beloved son was the subject of speculation and gossip.

"He never recovered from the war. He isn't quite right in the head," Muzio asserted.

"He is becoming pious like his mother," said Galbasia di Peccio, a young woman who always enjoyed an engaging, spirited controversy. Galbasia's family had only recently successfully litigated for its freedom from serfdom and won its case against the canons of San Rufino.

"Francis! Pious? I don't think so. He parties too much. He likes the good life," snorted the judgmental Canon Silvester. He certainly was not going to take his cue from a former serf, who thought she now had the right to spout off her mouth in the town's square.

"Francis is pious in a man's way. He never swears. He is always courteous," Galbasia insisted. The newfound freedom of her family was making her bold.

"He might be pious, but he certainly is no monk," Silvester retorted. Galbasia blushed, remembering the good times that she had enjoyed in the tavern with Francis. Francis was never indiscreet, but he did know how to show a woman a good time.

"Monk! No. But he is a good man," Lady Marangone took Galbasia's side.

"He is generous, especially lately. He is giving the beggars more and more. If he keeps it up, the beggars will be eating better than we do," Galbasia, taking advantage of Lady Marangone's assistance, pressed her point further.

"He is guided by God. How did he know that Gautier de Brienne would die before he ever joined him in Apulia?" Francis's friend, the lawyer Peter di Catania asked.

Silvester refused to listen to such foolish talk from lay persons who understood nothing about God or sanctity. Muttering about their ignorance, he went off in a huff.

"I agree, Peter," Lady Marangone continued, ignoring Silvester. "Bernard said that no one knew about Brienne's death until days after Francis came back to Assisi. He thinks that Francis was guided by God."

"Bernard, the lawyer, said that? Well, Bernard is no fool," Lady Bona di Guelfuccio edged her way into the conversation. The noble Guelfuccio and Offreduccio families had returned from Perugia after negotiating a tentative peace with the people of Assisi and were working on the reconstruction of their palazzos.

"Francis also said that he will be a great prince. How will he do that in Assisi? Francis is a dreamer, not a saint," Tancredi asserted. "His father lets him get away with too much foolishness."

"His mother says that he will become a son of God," Lady Marangone insisted, glaring coldly at Tancredi. She knew that underneath Tancredi's gruffness was a warm, kind heart.

"His mother is his mother," Tancredi retorted. He was not about to be publicly contradicted by a woman, not even a woman of Lady Marangone's stature. "A mother has to say crazy things about her son. Wait until Pietro comes home and finds that his son is spending half of his time in caves."

"Pietro will blow up," Muzio shouted as if he were looking forward to the confrontation between father and son.

"I wouldn't want to be any place close," Lady Bona admitted, her dark brown eyes opened wide to reveal her playful spirit.

The gossips agreed. Francis's mysterious return to Assisi before the news of Brienne's death had to be explained in some way. Francis's friend Giovanni had not returned from the aborted expedition to Apulia until days later. He swore that no one knew of Brienne's death when Francis had decided to return. Francis's squire claimed that Francis was told to return in a dream. Maybe Pica was right. She had always said that God had a special destiny in mind for her son.

Whenever he could leave his duties in the store to the hired hand, Francis continued to spend much of his days in various caves all over the Subasio mountain. He became more and more quiet, withdrawn, and pensive, and he continued to meditate on his vision.

"Who do you think can best reward you, the Master or the servant?" Francis tried to understand the meaning that Brienne's death had for him. He had thought Brienne would make him a knight, but Brienne was a mere man, a mortal man. With his death, Francis's well-laid plans for knighthood had vanished in an instant.

Francis's eyes filled with tears as the thought of the shortness of life brought to mind the face of Matteo. For the first time he was able to contemplate Matteo's terrified eyes and to weep over the loss of his friend. They were peaceful tears, deep tears, needed tears. As he wept, his fever returned, and Francis stretched out on the ground just at the edge of the cave where the sun could gently warm him. His friends, the little brown and white brush birds, sang and scampered about joyously. As Francis mourned Matteo, he again heard the loving voice of his Master soothing his soul.

"Who do you think can best reward you, the Master or the servant?" the voice asked.

"The Master," Francis was convinced. "The Master."

He repeated the words "the Master" over and over again even as the warm sun lulled him to sleep. His fever raged, but his anger was quieted. He was able to understand now how much he had loved Matteo.

The thought made Francis wake with a start. His dead, frustrated, confused, and cold heart was able to ponder love. He felt the Master smiling at him.

"What do you wish me to do?" Francis asked.

"Return to your own place and you will be told what to do," the Master said.

The Lord was right. Francis's soul was healing. He was finding peace again. He would love again.

Suddenly, a small, thin voice startled Francis. "For the love of Jesus Christ, I beg you ..." the voice whimpered.

It took Francis a moment to break away from his train of thought.

"For the love of Jesus Christ ..." the voice pleaded again.

Opening his eyes, Francis saw a crippled man, emaciated and starving. The beggar said nothing more, but looked at Francis with hopeful eyes, holding out his hands. Francis didn't recognize him. There were many beggars outside of Assisi wandering on the Subasio mountain. Francis had always had a reputation for generosity, but today he gave more abundantly than ever before, offering the beggar everything in his purse. The beggar was astonished; he didn't know what to make of this strange man who dressed as a merchant but behaved like a hermit.

"God reward you," the beggar murmured, risking a slight smile.

News of Francis's generosity spread quickly over the mountain. Soon beggars found Francis no matter how secluded his cave. If a poor person begged from him when he was far from Assisi, he gladly gave all the money that he had. When he had no more money, he gave them a piece of his clothing, taking off even his shirt to give to a beggar for the love of God.

He prayed also in the many poor and dilapidated small churches that dotted the commune countryside. He bought vases and other objects for the service and adornment of these churches. He would often commission exquisite things like chalices for worship and send them secretly to poor priests.

When his father was away on business, Francis would heap the Bernardone table both for the afternoon and evening meals with loaves of bread as though for the entire family. When his mother asked him why he had bought so much bread, he replied that he wished to distribute the loaves to those in need. He confided to his mother that he had promised God that he would always give alms to anyone who begged in God's name. His mother simply smiled, proud of her son, and blessed him in her heart.

But Francis wanted to be more than a benefactor of Christ, he wanted to be Christ on this earth. After all, when the Lord Jesus Christ came to earth, he came as a poor baby wrapped in cheap and rough swaddling clothes. The image of the Son of God dressed so humbly impressed the luxury cloth merchant. He realized that if he wanted to follow Jesus Christ, he would need to change the way he dressed. Francis longed to leave Assisi in order to go someplace where he could put on the clothes of a beggar. He wanted to look more like his beloved Master. If he tried this in Assisi, people would howl with laughter. He needed to get away from them and their idea of who and what the son of Pietro Bernardone was supposed to be.

He needed to get away, and yet, at the same time, he had been told to stay in his own place. He pondered again the journey of Saint Paul. Paul was told to wait in the city, but Ananias was sent to advise him. Who would play the role of Ananias for him? Who could he turn to for advice? As soon as he asked himself the question, Francis understood what he was to do. He would open his heart and soul to the old priest at the church of San Damiano.

*T*here is a moment in the struggle when one knows that one has discovered direction. Springing to his feet, Francis nearly ran down the mountain. Halfway down he slipped, his feet losing traction on the rolling acorns that lay everywhere on the steep mountain path. He fell backwards and landed hard, hitting his head. Francis brushed himself off and went on. He would tell the story of his struggle to the old priest of San Damiano. Father Pietro already knew him well, and he would know what to do.

It was early afternoon when Francis, winded but energetic, arrived at the dilapidated church. The priest was watering his small vegetable garden. Begging for his blessing, Francis asked the priest for spiritual guidance. The priest took Francis into the empty, silent church and sat down within view of the crucifix that he knew Francis loved. Francis told the priest everything — the war, Matteo, the horrors of the prison, his father, his dream, the blood, and his sins.

The old priest listened, but knew that someone more powerful would be needed to guide Francis. Next to Bishop Guido, Pietro Bernardone was the most important landowner in Assisi, and it did not take much discernment for the old priest to realize that Pietro Bernardone would not approve of Francis's ideas. There was potential for trouble here. The old priest was holy, but he was also no fool.

Assuring Francis that his dream sounded as though it bore the fruits of God, the old priest waited. Francis asked the question.

"Tell me, Father, what should I do?" Francis asked.

The old priest did not hesitate, for the next step was clear to him. "You must present yourself to Bishop Guido," the old priest suggested. "Obey whatever he tells you, and you will find peace. Reveal your soul only to him."

Francis's heart puzzled for a moment and then realized the wisdom of the old cleric. He would present himself to the bishop. There was still plenty of sun. There was still time.

Francis left San Damiano and hurried along the short distance back into Assisi. On the way, he met Lady Ortolana and her daughters Clare and Catherine, and paused to greet them. Clare carried a small basket that bulged with provisions for Father Pietro.

"Good morning, ladies," Francis said, bowing his head in respect. The women smiled politely. Lady Ortolana had grayed during her exile in Perugia, and Clare and young Catherine had become beautiful young women. Ortolana noticed Francis admiring the exquisite embroidery that decorated Clare's linen collar.

"Clare embroidered the collar herself," Ortolana said proudly, knowing that Clare's artistry would not be lost on the luxury cloth merchant.

"It is beautifully done, Clare," Francis smiled at the twelve-year-old.

"Thank you," Clare smiled graciously. Her straight teeth and heavy blonde curls complemented her obvious inner beauty. Francis was impressed by her radiant self-possession, rare in someone so young.

Arriving in Assisi, Francis knocked at the gate of the bishop's palace next to the church of Santa Maria Maggiore. The porter, recognizing Bernardone's son, quickly obtained permission from the bishop for an audience and then escorted Francis into the bishop's office. Guido offered Francis a drink, but Francis declined.

"Lord Bishop," Francis said meekly, "I have come for spiritual advice."

The bishop paused. He had heard talk about the odd behavior of Francis Bernardone. He knew that he had returned from Spoleto before the news of Brienne's death was known. He was very willing to listen to the heart of this prominent Assisi son. He wanted to know first-hand what was going on.

Francis looked confidently at Bishop Guido. He was aware that Guido was not known for his spiritual astuteness. The bishop was a powerful, litigious, and ornery man who owned half of the property in the commune of Assisi. As a powerful feudal lord, he insisted upon his ancient rights, often angering commune leaders, the Benedictine monks, and even the canons of his own cathedral. He had a violent temper. Once, fuming with anger, he went into the piazza and physically attacked an antagonist. On another day, he had an argument with the clerics of the hospital of San Salvatore over the ownership of a few bottles of wine. Even at funerals, his greed drove him to quarrel loudly and inappropriately concerning the proper payment due him for the obsequies.

The imprudence of Bishop Guido was so notorious that Pope Innocent III himself saw fit on several occasions to admonish him. Proper use of papal sanctions would have spared the bishop's office from the ignominy of Guido's temper, but Guido's hunger for revenue was insatiable. The pope, although appreciating Guido's unswerving loyalty, constantly urged him to be more discreet.

Francis was wise in the world's ways; he was well aware of the bishop's greed and his temper. He also knew that Bishop Guido was a good and true pastor. Francis, as one of his flock, could trust him in this role. Heeding the advice of the old priest at San Damiano, Francis told the bishop of his dilemma.

The powerful Bishop Guido was a bit disconcerted, but quickly recovered. He had plenty of experience caring for the souls of rich people who had suddenly found religion. This newfound piety was good for Francis Bernardone. Guido was happy to be able to help him.

"You must do penance, Francis. You have led a sinful life. There is a pilgrimage to Rome leaving on Friday. Make your preparations and come back Thursday afternoon before Vespers to receive your blessing. I will provide you with a letter certifying that you are a true pilgrim."

Francis felt joy like he had not felt in a long time. Rome was only a few days' journey from Assisi, and yet it was far enough and big enough to preserve Francis's anonymity. In Rome, Francis would pray at the tombs of Peter and Paul. There he would ask for further direction.

Over the next two days, Francis prepared his wardrobe and his heart for the pilgrimage. On Friday morning, clothed in a pilgrim's tunic and staff, he left Assisi just as the guards were opening the gates.

Francis proceeded to the small church of San Damiano where Father Pietro was waiting for him and gave him a blessing. He paused before the beautiful crucifix that seemed to hold up the old church.

"We adore you, most holy Lord Jesus Christ. Here and in all the churches that are in the whole world and we bless you. Because by your holy cross you have redeemed the world," Francis prayed.

Pressing a coin into the hand of the old priest, Francis proceeded toward Foligno. He found himself walking in haste, anxious to get to Rome, but the sun, the birds, and the warm breeze gradually calmed him. Now, in the troubled spring of 1205, Francis pondered the words echoing in his dream.

"The arms and the palace you saw are intended for other knights than those you had in mind and your principality too will be of another order," the Master had told him.

"Other knights," Francis wondered. "Of another order?"

As he continued walking, Francis reflected on the stories that the canon of San Giorgio had told him when he was a child. Saint Peter was a fisherman; and when the Lord called him, he promised that Peter would be a "fisher of men." Francis, who wanted to be a knight, was promised that his "principality would be of another order." The tactic was the same, Francis reasoned. Peter the fisherman became a fisher of souls. Francis would become a knight, a knight of God.

The crowded streets and bustle of Rome always filled Francis's soul with excitement. He went at once to the basilica of Saint Peter in order to visit the tomb of the apostle. As he was making his way through the crowds pressing around the tomb, Francis noticed that many people left what seemed to be very inadequate offerings.

"Surely, the greatest honor is due to the Prince of the Apostles. How can some people leave such meager alms in the church where Saint Peter's body rests?" Francis wondered.

Somewhat taken aback by the apparent lack of reverence of the crowd, Francis, full of fervor, took a handful of money from his purse and threw it in though the grating before the altar of the saint. The coins made such a clatter that those mulling around the tomb turned to identify the generous bene-factor. Francis smiled a bit impishly, hoping that he was able to inspire similar generosity in his fellow pilgrims.

The steps to the basilica were filled with beggars asking for coins from the pilgrims who came and went. Francis began speaking to those who were willing to talk with him. Among the beggars he found a young man with crippled feet who was very amiable. Francis took out a handful of coins and asked if the beggar would trade clothes with him until sundown. Used to the idiosyncrasies of pilgrims, the beggar agreed, and Francis quickly took off his own tunic and replaced it with the beggar's miserable rags. Feeling a little out of place in his new tunic, the beggar told Francis that he would be inside the basilica. The merchant's son nodded and promised him extra coins at sundown.

Francis felt comfortable in his ragged clothes. In Rome, no one knew him. He was alone, a mere beggar among beggars. He stood on the steps with the other beggars and asked for alms in the French he had learned from his trips to the international cloth fairs in Champagne. He loved to speak French, even though he did not know it very well. The other beggars were both amused and irritated by the exuberance of the stranger. They had seen this sort of piety before and tolerated it as an annoyance that would soon pass. Francis tried to make con-versation, but to no avail. The beggars were not interested in making him feel welcome. In their eyes, he was a nuisance and an imposter.

Francis continued to ask for alms, knowing that in the end he would give what he collected to the beggars with whom he shared the steps. He would not cheat them of their daily earnings. He wanted only to understand their experience, and to be recognized as another Christ.

As the sun was setting, Francis distributed the modest amount of money he had been given in alms to the other beggars, who were glad to see him leave. He entered the basilica and found his friend sleeping in a corner. Gently nudging the beggar, Francis exchanged clothes with him for the price of a few extra coins. Purchasing his pilgrim's badge from a vendor on the steps of Saint Peter's, Francis felt ready to go home. He peered at the lead badge that bore the image of Saint Peter holding a key, and of Saint Paul holding the sword that had severed his head.

*O*nce home, Francis gave a report of his pilgrimage to Bishop Guido, and continued to frequent the caves of Subasio. One day while praying, he spent his time asking the Master of his dream, "O Lord, what do you wish me to do?"

Over and over, Francis begged for guidance. The hours passed quickly, and morning turned to evening. During the weeks that followed, Francis often did not go home, but spent entire days and nights in the caves waiting for the voice of his dream to give him further direction. After months of persevering in prayer, Francis received an answer. He recognized immediately the voice of his Master speaking to his soul.

"Francis, if you want to know my will, you must despise all that your body has formerly loved and desired to possess," the voice explained. "Once you begin to do this, all that formerly seemed sweet and pleasant to you will become bitter and unbearable; and the things that formerly made you shudder will bring you sweetness and contentment of body and soul."

Francis paused, trying to understand.

"What I now experience as sweet, I must despise. When I do this, the bitter will become sweet; it will bring me peace," Francis repeated.

"I must despise that which I have loved and wanted to possess. Then the bitter will become sweet; and the sweet will become bitter," Francis repeated again.

He did not know what the words meant. He had already changed his life, was spending much less time carousing with his friends, and was spending most of his time alone. He was happy in the solitude of the caves. He had needed the time and found that the mountain was healing his wounds.

The next day, Francis took his horse and rode out to the family property in San Pietro della Spina. He left through the Moiano gate near the bishop's house, took the road that passed near the monastery of San Masseo, and turned toward the leper hospital of San Lazzaro d'Arce near the small church of Saint Mary of the Angels. Francis loved the small church of Saint Mary's, but found it difficult to pass by the leper hospital. He willingly gave large amounts of money and even his own clothes to the poor, but the contamination of the lepers filled him with horror.

Francis continued to ponder the words of his Master. "I must despise that which I formerly loved and desired to possess. Then the bitter will become sweet; and the sweet will become bitter."

Leprosy does not respect class or culture. Francis could indulge himself with romantic notions of being poor like the poor Christ, but the stench and living death of leprosy terrorized him. San Lazzaro d'Arce was a place even more horrible than the Perugian prison. It consisted of a number of rude huts built of sticks and mud clustered around a chapel. Here the lepers lived together, rich and poor, cultured and illiterate, sentenced by virtue of their disease to the wretched colony of suffering. After their clothes were taken away, each was dressed in a gray uniform made of coarse, cheap cloth of cotton and wool. They were given a bell to ring to warn others of their presence. San Lazzaro was the living hell of those abandoned to a slow, cruel death.

"The bitter will become sweet; the sweet will become bitter," Francis repeated over and over.

His horse stopped short and reared, interrupting Francis's thoughts.

He had not heard the bell or the voice. Directly in front of him on the road was a weak, hideous, sore-infested creature. The bandages covering the stumps of his hands were yellowed and blood-stained. He walked on stubs for legs and leaned heavily upon his crutch. His face was horribly disfigured and dripped with heavy, putrid pus. He reeked of urine and of dead, rotting flesh.

Francis had all he could do not to gag. The stench of the leper's disintegrating body permeated the humid, still air.

"The bitter will become sweet; the sweet will become bitter," the words of his prayer kept echoing through his horror.

Tempted to hold his hand over his nose and mouth and avert his face as he had always done, Francis found himself unable to move, confused by the words of his prayer.

Holding his cup out in petition and shivering despite the heat, the leper stood in ghostly silence. His gray sackcloth was covered with flies, but he did not seem to notice. Francis swallowed hard as he observed the pus seeping down from the leper's deformed nose and settling upon a crusty patch on his chin. Again he feared that he would vomit.

"Despise that which you loved and formerly desired to possess. The bitter will become sweet; the sweet will become bitter," Francis continued to remind himself.

Taking some coins from his pocket, Francis, determined to be fearless in the service of his Master, dismounted his horse, ran up to the startled leper, gave the leper the coin, and kissed his bandaged hand. Startled, the leper instinctively responded as in days long past and gave Francis the kiss of peace. The shock of encountering a human person behind the overwhelming stench melted Francis's heart. He gazed into the eyes of the leper for a long time and then mounted his horse. When he looked back, the leper was gone.

That night in the tavern with his friends, Francis chose less expensive foods and drink. He also wore a simple, unpretentious tunic. When his friends commented on his appearance, Francis had a ready reply.

"When one is in love," he smiled, "the bitter becomes sweet; and the sweet becomes bitter."

Jesting, Francis wove an outrageous ballad incorporating the words of his prayer into a tale of a bumbling knight. The tavern exploded with laughter. Francis Bernardone was a strange character, but he was an entertaining companion — and he would invariably pick up the tab.

Despite the usual revelry, Francis felt strangely empty. "There has to be more to my life than this," Francis admitted to himself as he ambled home.

A few days later, he took a large sum of money and rode to the leper hospital. Francis wandered among the wretched huts gathering the hospital inmates together. The stench was horrid, but today Francis was prepared. As a reputable Assisi merchant, Francis had always been a generous benefactor of the leper hospital, but had previously relied on servants to deliver his alms.

"Francis Bernardone is here!" the word spread from hut to hut.

Once assembled, Francis gave the lepers alms and kissed their hands. The lepers were astonished. Many cried and thanked Francis over and over for his generosity. The priest at the hospital embraced Francis and thanked him profusely.

"Today you have sought out and found Christ, who prefers to take his place among the poor," the priest exhorted Francis. "The Son of God became human, was placed in a manger, was wrapped in common rags, and died naked and despised. He came as a poor man, but the world did not recognize him. You have recognized him today, Francis. Now go, with God's peace, but come back to us soon."

Mounting his horse, Francis waved to the lepers and the priest, and sauntered back toward Assisi. His heart overflowed with deep, peaceful consolation.

The words of his Master could be trusted. He would despise his former life so that he could truly know the sweetness of joy and peace. Like Paul, he knew that the scales were falling from his eyes. There was an alternative to becoming a greedy, gluttonous, and murderous merchant. Francis would choose the alternative; he would embrace the bitter for the sake of the sweet.

5
Construction

The party goers were finishing the main course, while the evening's musicians took a break, knowing that they would soon be caught up in a much more intense round of singing and playing upon the completion of the meal.

Two of the musicians, a harpist and a dulcimer player, covered the absence of the others by playing a soothing, plaintive French melody. The lonely dulcimer spun its long, slow, modal phrases to the chordal accompaniment of the small harp. The dulcimer melody mesmerized Francis. There were no words to the tune. It quieted the crowd already lulled by a surfeit of wine and food. Francis closed his eyes.

Here, in the midst of his businessman's life, he found a moment of peace. Opening his eyes for a moment and noticing that his comrades were also listening raptly to the haunting lament, Francis allowed himself to become lost in the music again. Just as he did this, the musicians, all too abruptly, ended the melody. Francis wanted to rush out to them and offer them money to play the song again and again.

He could not resist the temptation. He handed the dulcimer player some coins and asked him to keep playing. The crowd applauded, not only because they loved the song, but also because they were eager to encourage Francis's generosity.

The dulcimer player, happy for the money, but even more encouraged by the fact that his art was respected by such a prominent businessman as the son of Pietro Bernardone, began to play. Francis raised his arms to the crowd.

"Good music should be rewarded. The song is beautiful. Let him play on!" Francis exclaimed.

The crowd cheered and then fell silent to listen to the music. It almost seemed that, in the midst of the banquet, the crowd had paused for a moment of prayer.

The dulcimer player, accompanied by the harpist, improvised on the simple tune, expanding it not by variations but by pulling out the rhythms freely and taking advantage of the flattened notes to express more fully the melody's beauty. Truly a master of his art, he wove his lines attentive to both the power of the melody and the receptivity of his audience. At the first sign of restlessness, he proceeded toward the cadence.

"Better to end early while they still hunger for more," the experienced dulcimer player reasoned.

He signaled to the other musicians who were also caught up in the power of the melody. The stringed rebec and pipe players joined the dulcimer and harp in a lively dance tune. The waiters brought out trays of fruits and delicacies. Francis made the rounds, greeting and toasting his guests and wishing them a good time. The lovely music had revived his spirits, and he was actually enjoying himself.

The party spilled out into the streets. "Francis, sing us a song," the crowd demanded.

Francis hesitated, but the crowd insisted.

"Francis, Francis, Francis, Francis," the instrumentalists accompanied the chant of the crowd. "Francis, Francis, Francis!"

Pressured by their enthusiasm, Francis edged his way into the piazza and took his place on the top step of the Temple of Minerva. He motioned to the rebec player who began a French trouvere song accompanied by flute and vielle. Francis spun out the lyrics, telling about sad days long ago when knights, worn out by incessant battles, laid down their arms, unwilling to fight. The noble women, realizing that the knights' weariness would make them less than ardent lovers, held a tournament in order to understand more fully the hardships their knights had suffered for them. Maybe, if they understood manly pain, they would be able to inflame the hearts of the knights again with passion for a just cause. The women fight, Yolenz de Cailli, Margerite d'Oysi, and Amisse, all for the cause of love.

As the musicians increased the tempo, the crowd demanded that Francis improvise more and more verses. The women in the crowd pretended to fight with each other as the men cheered them on. Francis laughed, and delegated the responsibility for spinning out further lyrics to his noble friend, Bernard, who did his best. Unable to improvise fast enough to keep pace with the frantic beat, Bernard faltered. Seeing Bernard's embarrassment, Francis rushed to his side, filling in whenever Bernard missed a beat. The crowd loved Francis. The party would be the talk of Assisi for days to come.

The next day, Francis opened the shop and then rode out to Spello to deliver cloth to a nobleman. He started early, eager to finish the short trip so that he would have time to spend alone on the mountain. He passed the little church of San Damiano.

"We adore you, most holy Lord Jesus Christ. Here and in all your churches which are in the world and we bless you. Because by your holy cross you have redeemed the world," he recited.

Francis meditated on the meaning of this simple, childhood prayer. He truly believed that Jesus Christ was present within the tiny, dilapidated church.

"God needs a better house," Francis said to himself. "I, who am not even a nobleman, would not live in such a house."

Francis began to imagine how he might fix this tiny church that he loved so much. He looked at the cloth that he was carrying.

"It would not take too much to fix it," he figured. "The receipts from the sale of a few bolts of imported cloth and, perhaps, the price I would get from selling my horse."

Francis petted his stallion.

"Don't worry," he assured his horse, "I would leave you in good hands."

Finishing his work in Spello, Francis returned to the forests of his beloved mountain. Settling himself in the entrance to a cave, he recalled again the plaintive tune of the dulcimer player. Tiny brown and white brush birds sang around him. Francis was more relaxed, more peaceful than he had been in a long time.

He sat on a stone, head in his hands, and began to think about God's poverty. A traveling preacher had once come through Assisi, a happy, jovial man, who talked about the poverty of God. Francis smiled as he remembered how the man danced and sang the wonder of Jesus coming to earth as a baby. Yes, Jesus was a baby who was born without shelter. His mother had to wrap him in rags. There was no place for him to lay his head. He pictured the dilapidated church of San Damiano.

"Even now we welcome you so poorly," Francis exclaimed.

He stretched out and relaxed, allowing the light of God's sun to warm him. He pondered the words over and over. "The bitter is sweet; the sweet is bitter. What does this mean?" he asked.

The sun lulled him into a kind of semi-consciousness. As he became deeply relaxed, the face of his Master returned to him.

"The bitter will be sweet; the sweet will be bitter," the Master gently assured him.

Francis repeated the line with his Master. Suddenly, into his consciousness, the kind and good face of his Master changed into that of the old, humpbacked woman from Assisi. The transformation was startling, and Francis was jolted back into an awareness of his surroundings. He could not shake off the fear he experienced when he pictured this woman's horrible deformity. In his heart, the fear was put into words.

"If you serve Jesus Christ, I will heal this woman's deformity and cast it upon you," the demonic voice hissed.

Francis's peace evaporated in an instant. He wanted to be good. He wanted to be generous with God and others. If he wasn't to become a knight, he at least wanted to have a noble spirit.

"What if I say 'yes' to God and God takes everything from me?" Francis worried.

Somehow he knew that the question was wrong, but Francis continued to wrestle with it.

"God should be given God's due," he thought. "Yet, one cannot be imprudent."

Francis remembered the town's gossip about other people who had taken their religion to the extreme.

"I don't want to go crazy over religion," he thought.

The very thought made him want to laugh. "I don't think there is too much of a danger that the son of Pietro Bernardone will end up a religious fanatic," he concluded and chuckled out loud.

Yet, Francis was not sure. He no longer felt safe in the cave. He could bear being regarded as a religious fanatic, but the ugly deformity of the humpbacked woman struck terror in his soul.

"God, please don't take away my health, my appearance," he begged.

Francis understood what he had to do. He had to focus again on the face of his Master. His Master's eyes, his words, would bring peace. Francis repeated the Master's words. "The bitter will be sweet; the sweet will be bitter," he whispered. "The bitter will be sweet; the sweet will be bitter."

A few days later, Francis was walking again near the church of San Damiano. He went inside, looked at the image of the crucifix he loved so well, and knelt down.

"We adore you, O Most Holy Lord Jesus Christ," he started. "Here and in all your churches which are throughout the whole world ..."

Francis looked up. The eyes of the crucified yet risen Savior were the eyes of the Master in his dream. Francis had known this for a long time. He was at home with these eyes. He began the prayer he had said over and over again in the caves. He said the words looking right into Christ's eyes. The eyes gave him courage. He wished to pray as a true knight; he wished to serve his Lord without fear; he prayed to serve his Lord with total generosity. Francis began:

Most high,
glorious God,
Illumine the darkness of my heart.
Give me a right faith,
certain hope,
and perfect charity.
Lord, give me sense and knowledge
so I might always do your holy and true command.

Over and over again, Francis said this prayer, pausing on one phrase and then another, all the while focusing his eyes on the image of the Crucified hanging in the dilapidated San Damiano church. The old priest had seen him enter, and, from time to time, he peered into the back entrance. He did not want to disturb Francis while he was at prayer yet, at the same time, he wanted to be attentive to any pastoral need that Francis might have. The priest of San Damiano had grown old caring for this son of Pietro Bernardone. He hoped, along with Pica, that Francis would become a good and holy man.

Pausing from the words of his prayer, Francis looked at the eyes of the crucified image and remained captivated. Simply and gently the eyes cut through his confusion. Within himself he heard again the tender and compassionate voice of the Master.

"Francis, do you not see that my house is falling into ruin? Go and repair it for me."

Relieved that his Master was suggesting that he undertake this project and not threatening him with a crippling deformity, Francis jumped to his feet.

"I will be happy to do this, Lord," he answered.

Almost dancing with relief, Francis exited the tiny church. The priest, who was sitting outside the entrance, approached Francis intending to engage him in conversation and thereby get some sense of Francis's state of mind. Before he could say a word, Francis took a handful of coins from his purse.

"I beg you, Father, to buy oil and to keep the lamp before the image of the Crucified constantly lit," he asked.

Although Francis usually gave the good priest a fair amount of alms, Father Pietro was taken aback by the extent of Francis's generosity on this day. Seeing the priest's expression, Francis assured him.

"When this is spent, I will give you as much as you need," he said, slapping his now nearly empty purse.

The priest watched as Francis walked up the path back toward Assisi. He looked at the handful of money in amazement. "He is struggling to be good," the priest thought.

Father Pietro walked into the sacristy of the decrepit church, took some oil that he had been saving, and poured it into the small lamp. Lighting it, the old priest looked with tired, yet shining eyes on the image that had grown to be his closest friend. It was beginning to get dark, but the light from the lamp allowed the priest to stay a while longer. He was grateful to the son of Pietro Bernardone, and he prayed for him.

In the morning, Francis appeared in the Bernardone store full of energy. The hired hand working the counter wondered what was wrong.

"Francis, why are you here so early?" he asked.

"It's a beautiful morning. Why would one want to spend it sleeping?" Francis cheerfully replied. "I'm going to Foligno today. I'll be back by nightfall."

Francis pulled out various bolts of cloth from the cupboard, and asked the hired hand to cut them according to his prescribed measurements.

"You must have a very good customer," the workman speculated.

"I have several," Francis replied.

Francis handed the hired hand a gorgeous brocade. The hired hand hesitated, but Francis waved him off, asking him to measure double that which he had cut off of the other bolts. With a variety of precious imported fabrics wrapped securely in a bundle, Francis left the store. The hired hand held the precious package as Francis saddled his horse.

"You will be making a good sale today?" the nobleman Bernard asked, as he came upon Francis and the workman.

"A very good sale, Bernard. Would you like to see some of the most beautiful fabric in all the world?" Francis responded.

Bernard thought that Francis was joking. "Seriously, Francis, where are you going today with such an impressive bundle?" Bernard asked.

"Foligno," Francis responded, but did not volunteer more.

"Who is the customer interested in such a large purchase?" The hired hand was still uneasy.

Francis smiled, waved at Bernard and the hired hand, and rode off. "If I do not return tonight, do not worry about me," he called back to the hired hand.

The hired hand looked at Bernard with alarm. "He has never before taken this much cloth to anyone in Foligno. He's giving money to poor people all over this commune. He wouldn't drape imported cloth over beggars, would he?"

"Oh, you under-estimate Francis," Bernard assured the hired hand. "If a Foligno nobleman has money, Francis can help him spend it," Bernard laughed. His ready smile tempered the fears of the workman.

"If he clothes the lepers of L'Arce with silk, his father will kill him," the hired hand warned Bernard. "He has already given away too much money there, and he visits the lepers himself."

"If he clothes the lepers with silk," Bernard reasoned, "the news will reach Assisi before Francis is able to unburden himself of the last piece. Besides, the priest of L'Arce would never take such a gift without full assurance that Pietro approved."

"You're right," admitted the hired hand, and he waved good-bye to Francis's friend.

Francis rode hard, careful not to crush the precious material carefully packed in his bag. He was well known in Foligno and felt sure that he would be able to sell his goods. He was right. By early afternoon, he wished that he had brought more to sell. He found himself a place to sit in the piazza and carefully calculated both the money he had gathered and the stones that he would need to rebuild the tiny church. Originally, he had thought about beginning only with the repair of the apse. Thinking further, however, he began to contemplate the wrath that would come to him when his father realized that he was giving money to an obscure church, one that was not worthy of the patronage of a rich and powerful family.

"Lord, it's a bad investment," Francis admitted, looking up into the sky.

He realized that his original plan of liquidating cloth in order to repair the church in stages was perhaps not the best one.

"My father will be enraged when he finds out," Francis admitted. "I should have brought more to sell now," he realized.

He looked hard at his cherished stallion, but tried to dismiss the thought from his mind. He couldn't. Francis stood up and stroked the nose of his precious animal. It took the afternoon, but by Vespers that evening, Francis had sold his horse.

The next morning, Francis began the journey back to Assisi. As he walked, the merchant's son reflected on what he had done.

"There is enough money here to finance the rebuilding of San Damiano," he thought with a sense of profound satisfaction. He held his purse tightly.

Assisians traveling the road from Foligno to Assisi were surprised to see Francis Bernardone walking.

"What happened to your horse?" asked Lord Marescotto di Bernardo Dodici.

"Walking does a soul good," Francis replied good-naturedly. "Walking does a pair of soles bad," responded Marescotto.

Marescotto could not imagine traveling any distance without his horse. Alone again, Francis continued his thoughts. "What have I done?" he wondered, and abruptly came to a halt. "I am a dead man," he realized.

Francis was not overreacting. His actions would make his father the laughingstock of the Assisi commune. He hadn't thought through the consequences. He was only obeying the desire of his Master.

"Surely my father will understand …" Francis stopped short and paused, realizing that it would be impossible to justify his actions to his father.

He went off the road and found a secluded place for himself behind the brambles in a small gully.

"I am a dead man," Francis repeated again, trying to comprehend the repercussions of what he had done. "I have brought dishonor to my father, and I have brought dishonor to the Bernardone name." He trembled at this realization and felt sweat run down his brow and into his eyes, momentarily blinding him.

Surely there was some way to lessen the impact of his actions. He put his head in his hands, tried to slow his breathing, and attempted to think things through rationally. It was no use. He had to give the money back. Yet, if he gave the money back, how could he fulfill the command of his Master?

"Then why do you leave the Master for the servant, the rich Lord for the poor man?" Francis repeated the message of his dream over and over.

He had to obey the Master. He needed to fulfill his Master's desire of rebuilding the small church. If needed, he would give up everything to do what was noble.

"Who do you think can best reward you, the Master or the servant?" The words were Francis's only hope. He could not disregard them.

"I must obey the Master," Francis decided.

He left the gully and headed back toward the road. It was time to make the change. He had been contemplating it for a long time, but had never had the courage. Now, he had to make a choice. He either had to disobey his Master's orders, or separate himself from his family.

Since his youth, Francis had admired the old priest of San Damiano. Lately, whenever he left the old priest, he had the strange desire to stay.

"Perhaps I could repair the old church myself," Francis wondered. He thought about the oblates who worked at the leper hospital in return for their keep.

"I will give the priest the money," Francis thought. "I will put myself under his service. I will no longer be a Bernardone."

The plan seemed like a good one. Exhausted, Francis picked up his pace, knowing exactly where he was headed. He would go to San Damiano, give the priest the money, and never go home again.

The thought of not returning to his father's store filled Francis with a sense of liberation. The priest at San Damiano would be a good guide for his soul. He would have time for prayer; he would no longer need to listen to people speak of war, intrigue, scandals, and other distractions. He would be removed from the gossip of Assisi. He would be poor, but he would have enough. He would have bread, and he would be happy.

When Francis arrived at San Damiano, it was almost dusk. Pausing at the bottom of the mountain, Francis looked toward his new home. He was exhausted, but relieved. He had made his decision. The church was dilapidated and poor now, but he would rebuild it, and in the process, he would learn from the old priest how to find peace. It was the right decision. Francis climbed the slope with a light step.

Father Pietro was kneeling in prayer inside the church. Francis ran up to him and kissed his hands. He hadn't thought through how he would formulate his request. It was all happening so quickly, and yet, on the other hand, the decision had been long in process. The old priest's gentle eyes understood that Francis was trying to say something important. He put his hand on Francis's shoulder.

"I've missed you the last two days," the old priest was kind enough to start. "Where have you been, Francis?"

"I've been doing business in Foligno," Francis replied, and showed the priest his bulging purse.

The priest's eyes widened. "You worked hard, Francis. You must have had many rich customers."

Father Pietro looked toward the open door of the decrepit and neglected church. He had not heard Francis ride up. "Where is your horse? Surely, you did not go to Foligno on foot?" he asked.

"I returned on foot," Francis mumbled, blushing and feeling a bit foolish.

The brow of the old priest tightened. "What happened to your horse, Francis? Did someone try to hurt you?" the priest asked.

"Hurt the son of Pietro Bernardone? Hurt Francis, the knight and prince of all Assisi?" Francis asked in a tone of mock astonishment. Both men chuckled, and then Francis admitted. "Father, I sold my horse. The money is here. The money is yours."

Francis felt relieved that he had finally found the words. He looked at the old priest expecting that he would respond exuberantly Instead, Father Pietro looked pensive. "Pietro Bernardone cannot be interested in supporting the church of San Damiano. Francis, does your father know about this?" the old priest asked.

"Your church needs to be rebuilt," Francis responded, avoiding the priest's question. "I want to help you do this. Please receive me as a guest here, and I will offer my service to you," Francis begged.

Father Pietro knew that Francis was trying to make a formal request. To become a penitent of the church, one needed to give over one's patrimony to it and dedicate oneself to service. The old priest was not surprised by Francis's request, but he was taken aback by its timing. He had listened with sympathy and understanding to Francis's prayers and dreams. The men of Assisi were weary of war. They wanted to dedicate their lives to something that was meaningful and lasting. He could understand Francis's need to escape his life and to take refuge in the church.

"God knows that this place could use some work," the old priest smiled. "Tell me more about this sack of money. Exactly how did you acquire this much money? Tell me everything, Francis." The priest's face was stone serious.

"I sold some cloth and my horse to customers in Foligno," Francis responded. "There is not much more to tell."

The old priest knew that there was more. "Does your father know of this business venture of yours?" the priest asked.

"No," Francis replied reluctantly.

The old priest did not want to shame Francis by reminding him of the laws of the commune. Although Francis was an adult and a businessman in his own right, his father was the legal guardian of the family fortune. Francis had given family money away in public without the knowledge or the blessing of his father. Once Francis's actions became known, there could be irreparable legal consequences. Pietro would have to do something. His reputation as a businessman was progressively being undermined by the eccentric behavior of his son.

"Francis, only a week ago you came here a bit woozy from a night of partying with your friends. Now, you wish to become a penitent?" the old priest asked gently.

The priest had to test Francis's sincerity. He could not use the church as a means to escape the wrath of his father. The priest of San Damiano could not protect or provide for him. "Francis, if you're looking for asylum, perhaps it would be better to consider either San Giacomo or San Rufino. These churches are well fortified and would have the resources to care for you," the old priest suggested.

"I have the resources." Francis again showed the priest his bulging purse. "Please," he continued, "I beg you to receive me as a guest for the love of God."

The old priest hesitated. It was late. The gates of Assisi were already closed, and Francis needed a place to stay. "You may stay for the night," Father Pietro said reluctantly. "Francis, your family is a powerful one. It would not be wise for me to accept your money. I really do not want it in the house."

Understanding the priest's dilemma and yet not wanting to be burdened with the coins any longer, Francis threw his purse through a high, narrow-slit window of the church. It lodged deep inside the stone sill. The old priest wasn't completely happy with this solution, but it was late.

The next morning, all Assisi knew of Francis Bernardone's outrageous conduct.

The usual voices chattered as the gossips argued about what had happened and what was to become of Francis.

"Pietro Bernardone claims there has been a robbery in his store," shouted Muzio.

"There is no robbery. Francis took the cloth that is missing. The Bernardone hired hand said so," Angelo, Francis's half-brother, responded.

"Even so, Pietro had no knowledge of Francis's business venture. The money Francis earned is missing," Tancredi sneered in disgust.

"Not only the money, but Francis is missing too," Bernard said in a worried tone.

"Have they checked the leper hospital?" Galbasia di Peccio wondered.

"The son of Pietro Bernardone, the prince of princes, the knight of knights, the troubadour of troubadours, spends his time washing lepers," a disgusted Lady Peppone exclaimed.

"He never recovered after Collestrada," fretted Lady Marangone, who was still trying to atone for her offense against Pica.

"There were many of us who suffered at the hands of Perugia. Francis has no excuse," the usually more compassionate Carlo retorted. The dark circles around his eyes betrayed how deeply he missed his son.

"Francis has had it too easy. Riches make a character soft," Canon Silvester scoffed.

"Francis is kind," replied Giacomo. "He is not like his father."

"There is no question that he is not like his father, but honor is due one's father," Tancredi insisted.

"I'd kick the hell out of him if I were Bernardone," Monaldo Offreduccio said in a voice filled with anger and contempt.

"I heard he's staying with Father Pietro at the church of San Damiano," Muzio remarked.

"No, Father Pietro would know better than to get in the middle of this," the aged schoolmaster Giovanni di Sasso stated firmly.

A door slammed, and Pietro Bernardone stormed down Via Portica, swearing and making his way to speak with his neighbors Marangone di Cristiano and Marangone's brother Benvegnate. They would help Pietro round up plenty of friends and neighbors, assist him in bringing Francis home, and force Francis to account for his outrageous behavior.

Marangone's son, Bongiovanni, alarmed by all he had overheard, quickly rode off toward San Damiano, hoping Muzio was right about Francis's whereabouts.

"Father Pietro," Bongiovanni kissed the hands of the old priest when he arrived at the church.

"Father Pietro, there is going to be trouble. Francis Bernardone has sold cloth belonging to his father and has not produced the money. There is a rumor that he is staying with you. Is he here, Father?" Bongiovanni asked.

Without replying the old priest put his arm over Bongiovanni's shoulder and led him into the house.

"Francis, what are you doing?" asked Bongiovanni. "They say you stole a large amount of money from your father. Your father has given you everything. You could be disinherited for this. What are you thinking?" Bongiovanni's voice was trembling.

"You must leave here, Francis. They know where you are. You will get Father Pietro in trouble. Your father is gathering friends and neighbors at this moment to bring you to justice. They are talking about banning you from the city. You must hide, Francis. Now!" Bongiovanni exclaimed.

Francis knew that both Bongiovanni and Father Pietro were risking their own well-being in order to protect him.

"Do you have a place to go?" Bongiovanni asked. "I have a place," Francis answered.

"Bongiovanni," the old priest said. "Go immediately to Bishop Guido. Tell him that Francis is thinking of becoming a penitent, but needs time in order to ponder his decision. When things settle down, we will need the bishop's help in negotiating the appropriate legal settlement."

Too frightened to argue, Bongiovanni mounted his horse and took the low road back to Assisi. The merchant's son, deeply grateful to the old priest, quickly gathered his belongings, and knelt for Father Pietro's blessing.

"Have faith, Francis," the priest assured him. "I will meet with the bishop and work out a plan. Meanwhile, hide yourself and decide before God what you truly want to do."

Francis knew that the old priest was right. He needed time to reflect on his actions and his desires. He was used to an elegant lifestyle. Would he be satisfied with the simple life of San Damiano?

"God reward you," the son of Bernardone said to the priest.

Francis knew that he needed to be more prudent. His impulsive actions had placed many good people in jeopardy. The old priest went back into the church, and Francis hid himself in a secret cave that he had used before as a refuge. The caretaker of the family country house in Stradette, a friend of Francis since childhood, provided him with food. During the month that Francis spent in hiding, he prayed constantly that he might be saved from Pietro Bernardone's dreaded rage.

"If I become like my father, I will be forced to devote my life to making money and struggling for power and influence. If I am a servant of the church, I will have my work, prayer, and enough bread to survive. I could be happy with this. I am not happy as a businessman — as the son of Pietro Bernardone," Francis tried to reassure himself.

Francis's spirit fluctuated between apprehension about the life he was choosing, and relief at finally being able to be alone. He loved the silence, and his soul found peace in seclusion.

He had two alternatives. He could appeal to the city consuls admitting that he was wrong and, if mercy was shown him, return to the Bernardone household. Certainly now, however, he would not be trusted and given the privileges of a son. His father would probably confine him to the store. Francis grew anxious thinking about it. It would be impossible for his spirit to sustain such a life.

Or, he could confirm his decision to become a penitent and trust Bishop Guido to work out the necessary legal arrangements. This would mean that he would no longer enjoy the benefits of the family fortune, and there would be no turning back.

*C*hristmas drew closer and the choice, for Francis, became clear — he would become a penitent. He spent long hours meditating upon the Lord of heaven and earth who chose to come into the world as a helpless baby with no shelter and only rags to serve as his covering. For the sake of peace, Francis would learn how to love these rags. For the sake of peace, Francis finally made a firm decision.

Francis emerged from his shelter on a cold January day. It had been snowing heavily, making travel down the steep Subasio slope difficult. Knowing that the old priest of San Damiano would be alone, Francis appeared in the little church just before dawn.

"Father Pietro," Francis met the priest as he came in to say his morning prayers. "Father Pietro, I have made my decision."

The old priest, never knowing exactly what to expect from Francis Bernardone, sat down.

"Tomorrow, I will return to Assisi," Francis announced. "There I will face my father and tell him that I wish to become a penitent."

"You may not survive the process," Father Pietro warned.

Francis was well aware of the dangers of his decision.

"It is safe for you to stay here in the church, Francis, until the snow stops. There will be no travelers coming here today," the old priest assured him.

Francis was grateful for the invitation and accepted Father Pietro's hospitality. The old priest fed him well. Father Pietro did not need to warn Francis about the consequences of his decision, for he could see that the month of solitude had changed him into a different, stronger man: Father Pietro was confident that Francis could survive the shame that would be heaped upon him. He only hoped that he would also survive the physical abuse that his father most certainly would inflict.

The sun glistened on the new blanket of snow. Francis, well rested and well fed, was ready for the short distance back to Assisi. He hardly passed the town gate when the insults began.

"Francis, Francis Bernardone, Francis Bernardone is back." Muzio could hardly hide his glee in being the first to be able to shout out the news.

"He is no son of Assisi; he is a thief. Hang the thief!" cried Lord Marangone. He had spent many days helping Pietro search for his son on the cold Subasio mountain.

"How are the lepers doing, Francis?" mocked a disgusted Lady Peppone. She laughed cruelly, her breasts flopping unevenly up and down.

"The son of Bernardone steals from his father under the guise of religion. Despicable!" Silvester sneered contemptuously.

"Are you going to fight another war, Francis? Maybe you could go to the Holy Land this time and spend your father's money there!" Lord Marangone continued to jeer.

"Where's the money, Francis? Where did you put the money?" taunted Galbasia.

"They say that Bishop Guido has it. Are you going to be buying drinks on the bishop, Francis?" Angelo, Francis's half-brother, jested.

The wrath against Francis seemed boundless. Stones were hurled and mud was flung at him; he was spit on and pushed from one angry person to another. Assisi could not tolerate the criminal behavior of the son of Bernardone. The crowd feared that the behavior that brought dishonor upon Pietro Bernardone's family might infect more of Assisi's sons. Francis would be made an example; order must be kept.

The uproar could be heard in the Bernardone counting room. Pietro stopped his work to take a look at what was going on. He had barely stepped outside the door when Muzio told him the news that Francis was back. Livid with anger, Pietro shoved his way into the crowd. Grabbing Francis by the neck, he shook him violently.

"You goddamn horse's ass!" he screamed. "What the hell do you think you are doing?" He threw his son to the ground and, throwing moderation and discretion to the wind, fell on him like a wolf on a lamb. His eyes glaring, he seized him, hitting him over and over. Dragging him home, he locked him in the basement cellar.

"The commune prison is too good for you, Francis. You have had it too good your whole life. This is the problem. I have given you too much! This is how you treat your father? You goddamn thief" Pietro's voice cracked with rage.

"You will stay here and rot, and when I'm ready, I will put you to work," Pietro said as he slammed the locking bar down on the thick oak door to the cellar.

"Do you know what they are saying about us, Francis?" his father continued. "Tancredi says that Bernardone is more interested in building churches than he is in protecting his land. They say we cannot be trusted. They say we have a weak link in our chain. You are putting the family in danger. Who can respect the Bernardone name when the gossip in town is filled with news of your latest stupidity?"

Pausing only to catch his breath, Pietro continued to yell in the direction of the locked door. "I tolerated the gossip when you decided to give away Bernardone money to beggars. The next thing I hear is that my son spends his time with lepers rather than with cloth. Who the hell wants to buy luxury fabric from a man who touches lepers? Do you ever think, Francis?" A note of pity found its way into the tirade. "Your poor mama, she cries every day for you, and what do you do? I buy you expensive armor and you strut around Assisi with it, saying shit like 'I'm going to become a great knight, a great prince.' Instead of going to war, you come back expecting us to believe that you had a dream. Then, you steal from your father. You make him the laughing stock of Umbria. I cannot show my face. Our profits have fallen through the floor. Customers come not to buy, but to fish for the latest goddamn gossip. What the hell are you thinking of, Francis?"

Pietro feared that if he didn't leave, he might open the door and kill his son. He pounded his way up the stairs, leaving Francis locked in the dark, cold, and cramped cellar. Francis knew that he would receive no mercy from his father. It would be a matter of waiting it out. His only hope was his mother. He hoped that Pietro would need to leave on a business trip soon.

As each day of her son's confinement passed, Pica grew more anguished, fearing that her son would not survive long in the January cold and damp. When Pietro finally left on business, Pica unlocked the cellar and attempted to reason with her son.

"Francis," she pleaded, "return the money to your father. Where did you put it? Somehow we will work this out. You cannot stay here like this."

"Mama, I can no longer be the son of Pietro Bernardone. If you do not let me go, I will die here," Francis responded.

"No, Francis, we have a little time. We can work something out. I will appeal to your father," pleaded Pica.

"Mama, look," Francis said, in a kind but firm tone. "I cannot stay. I can no longer be a Bernardone. If you do not let me go, I will die."

Pica knew the stubbornness of both son and father and feared what would happen on Pietro's return. She gave Francis a large loaf of fresh bread, some cheese, and a flask of wine wrapped in a cloth.

"Run, Francis," she exclaimed. "Run for your life."

Escaping from the cellar, Francis ran out of the San Rufino gate, back to San Damiano. Pietro came home a few days later. After he returned, Pica did not appear in the piazza for an entire week. When she did, she walked slowly and tried to hide the bruises on her face.

6
Disowned

The proud Pietro Bernardone hung his head that cold January of 1206. His wife's bruises reminded him of his sorry state. She avoided him, while the household servants gave him respectful but cold stares. The gossip in the piazza was merciless.

"Francis is back at San Damiano. He is helping the old priest there," Muzio reported. "He will never last. Remember when he went off to be the grand knight?" Tancredi said, with a cynical smile on his face. "Yes, the son of Bernardone is as changeable as the wind," Canon Silvester announced.

"He's sick in the head is what he is," Muzio shot back. "Pietro coddled him. It's Pietro's own fault. Francis always had it too easy," Tancredi said, his voice full of scorn.

"Pietro deserves everything he gets. He's been robbing from those of us suffering hard times for years. I say 'the hell with Pietro Bernardone!'" Raccorro di Ugolino shouted. Raccorro had gone broke under one of Pietro's usurious business ploys.

"Have you seen Pica? She's been badly beaten. Pietro can't control his son and so he takes it out on his wife," Giacomo stated, finding it hard to believe that a man could beat his wife so badly that her bruises would be obvious to anyone who saw her.

"These low-born rabble have dreams about running the commune. They have money, but no sense of nobility. They are low-born scum," Monaldo di Offreduccio growled.

"Is Pica all right?" asked the old humpbacked woman.

"I saw her going into the home of Marangone di Cristiano. Lady Marangone is tending to her injuries," Giacomo explained.

"Lady Marangone said that Pica was beat up badly. She said that she has never seen a woman so black and blue as Pica," Galbasia di Peccio remarked in a sad voice.

"Why doesn't he go out to San Damiano and beat the hell out of Francis? The merchants have no sense of order, no understanding of honor. They do not know how to control their own families. How can they expect to be leaders of the commune? We have chaos now, but it will get much worse," Monaldo di Offreduccio warned.

"They push and push. 'More money, more money,' they say. Where does this money lead us? We send our sons to war and they either die or come back sick in the head," Simone della Rocca lamented.

"Francis is delinquent because Pietro Bernardone does not know how to run his family. He raised him soft. Francis had everything and never learned to obey," Raccorro di Ugolino agreed with Tancredi.

"The son of Bernardone understands nothing of family honor," Tancredi added.

"He understands nothing of being a man. He dresses in the latest fashions and cares only about wine, women, and song. When there is fighting to be done, he's got the fever. I say 'piss on Francis Bernardone.' I say 'piss on everything Bernardone!'" Monaldo di Offreduccio sneered.

The entire population seemed obsessed with the tribulations of the Bernardone household. Pietro stood outside the store and listened to the voices up the street discussing his family business, his sense of humiliation deepening.

The very survival of the Bernardone family was at stake. Francis was taking down the family, and why? There was no revenge gained; there was no profit; there was no honor. White with anger, Pietro stalked back into the counting room and paced up and down, unable to believe what his own son had done to him. Francis had always done crazy things, but before he did these things for honor, glory, or power. He had done them, even though at times he had been a bit misguided, for the family. But this, this was for nothing. All this sadness, all this devastation, this betrayal was for nothing. Pietro slammed his fists on the table. "I am going to the civil authorities. Francis will no longer bring dishonor to the Bernardone name."

The elder merchant had often walked the short distance to the palace of the consuls, but this morning the walk seemed to take forever. The snow-covered streets made negotiating the hill slow and treacherous. The taunts, jeers, and, worst of all, the sympathy of the Assisi people made Pietro even more convinced that he had to take drastic action. He had suffered humiliation long enough. It would end today.

Upon reaching the consuls' offices, Pietro set forth the charges. "My son, Francis, has rebelled against my authority and has stolen a great deal of money from me. He refuses to return this money," Pietro stated.

"These are serious charges, Pietro," the judge Egidio explained. "If found guilty, Francis could be banished from the commune."

"My son is a goddamn robber, swindler, gambler, and pre-tender," Pietro replied. "He is not my son. It is his choice to live like a dog."

The judge repositioned himself in his chair. Bernardone had a point. Francis's transgressions were well known.

"The honor of my family is in jeopardy," Bernardone shouted. "Something needs to be done."

"Exactly what are your grievances?" Egidio asked, try-ing to calm the angry and distraught man who stood before him.

"He refuses to obey," Bernardone responded. "He has turned my name into a laughingstock. All of Assisi ridicules me. I gave my son everything, but my son gives his father no respect. I want to cut him off now! He is no longer a Bernardone."

Pietro was trying to remain in control of himself, but his anger seethed out of every pore. The judge repositioned himself again.

"Under the laws of the commune, you can imprison Francis yourself," he reminded Pietro. "You know where he is. Take some men and go and get him," the judge advised.

"I have done this," explained Bernardone. "My wife pitied him, and she released him. He cannot stay in my house. He causes trouble."

A crowd was gathering outside the judge's office; Bernardone's angry words could be clearly heard, despite the closed door.

"What did he steal, Pietro?" Egidio asked for the record.

"Pieces of scarlet, silks, embroidered brocades, and one of my best horses," Pietro enumerated. "When I was away, he went to Foligno and sold these goods. He purposefully stole the money. He will not give it back."

"It is a lot of money," Egidio agreed, "but it is not an impossible loss for Pietro Bernardone. What does Francis intend to do with this money?"

The merchant was so angry he could hardly get out the words. "He wants to rebuild the church of San Damiano," Pietro choked.

The judge had all he could do to repress a smile. He could understand Pietro's fury, and yet, at the same time, he could not help but find the litigious Bernardone's situation a bit humorous. There were fine churches around Assisi to which a man who wanted to dedicate himself to religion could attach himself. San Damiano was a poor church; it had no power, no protection, and no prestige. Yes, Egidio understood Bernardone's fury, but the penalty for a son's disobedience and defiance of paternal authority was a serious one. In this case, the punishment seemed to outweigh the crime.

"Pietro, if charged with the crimes of insubordination and stealing, Francis would receive the same penalty as a murderer, or as a traitor to the commune. Surely Francis is misguided, but perhaps this penalty is a bit severe," the judge reasoned.

Egidio did not want to prosecute Francis; he preferred that Bernardone take care of his family's business himself. Although

Francis had compromised the reputation of the Bernardone family, the situation would most probably correct itself over time. Bernardone was rich; he would survive. Francis had squandered large amounts of the family fortune before. The difference was that this time the money was to be used for a church that no one in their right mind would want to patronize.

Unaffected by Egidio's hesitation, Pietro repeatedly insisted on his right to a trial. In the end, Egidio had to capitulate.

"Pietro Bernardone," Egidio formally stated, "is it your desire to bring your son to trial on the charges of rebellion and unauthorized use of funds?"

"Yes, because ..."

The judge interrupted Bernardone. He had heard enough. He turned to the notary Giovanni.

"Send a messenger to San Damiano," Egidio instructed. "Tell the messenger to notify Francis di Pietro Bernardone that he is to present himself in three days before the consuls. At this time, he will respond to the accusations of his father, Pietro Bernardone, in order to defend himself according to the statutes of Assisi. If he does not do this, he will be found guilty and will be prosecuted according to the statutes."

Giovanni, the notary, wrote up the summons and gave it to the messenger, Rainuccio di Palmerio. The messenger made his way down the snow-crested hill to San Damiano. The gnarled oak trees glistened, laden with snow, and the air, despite the warm sun, was still cool and crisp. The old priest and the penitent were spending time in quiet prayer when the cry of the messenger echoed in the icy stillness.

"Francis di Pietro Bernardone," the messenger cried out. "Be it known to everyone that Francis di Pietro Bernardone is to be accused and tried by order of the consuls of Assisi."

Francis looked up from his prayer and gazed into the eyes of the old priest. He suspected that his father might pursue legal action, but the reality of the summons was still disconcerting. Francis swallowed hard and vowed to himself that he would maintain his resolve.

"Francis di Pietro Bernardone," the messenger repeated a second time. "Be it known to everyone that Francis di Pietro Bernardone is to be accused and tried by order of the consuls of Assisi."

Francis remained immobile, kneeling before the crucifix to which he was so devoted. Gently, the old priest placed his hand around Francis's arm and helped him to his feet. They walked out of the tiny church and appeared on the threshold together.

Upon seeing Francis, the messenger repeated the third time. "Be it known to everyone that Francis di Pietro Bernardone is to be accused and tried by order of the consuls of Assisi."

He handed the summons to Francis, and Francis opened and quickly read it. The merchant's son had rehearsed his response. "This summons does not apply to me," Francis stated. "By the grace of God, I have been for some time a servant of God, and thus am free from the jurisdiction of civil authority."

Francis handed the summons back to the messenger.

The messenger knew that Francis was making a legitimate, legal protest. He withdrew the summons and made his way up the slippery path back to Assisi where he informed Egidio of the merchant son's response.

The judge was grateful for the opportunity to rid himself of the case. The legislation of the Third Lateran Council specified that a lay man who was living on church property could not be prosecuted by civil authorities without the consent of the bishop. The penalty for disobeying this law was excommunication. If Francis claimed that he was under the authority of the bishop, Egidio was not going to interfere.

Upon receiving the word of Francis's evasion, Pietro was livid. He was not going to be denied justice because Francis had used clever legal tactics. Throwing the judge's message on the money table, Pietro stormed down the hill to the church of Santa Maria Maggiore. Disobeying one's father and stealing from him were also offenses in the eyes of the church. If Francis wanted to be tried in ecclesial court, so be it. One way or the other, Pietro would make sure that he was punished.

A few days later, a second messenger trudged through the ever-deepening snow and arrived at San Damiano. The bishop's messenger entered the San Damiano enclosure and gave Francis the summons. Francis was to appear before the bishop on Monday after Terce at the church of Santa Maria Maggiore. Francis, more composed after successfully responding to the first summons, accepted the summons peacefully. "I will willingly appear before the Lord Bishop who is the father and lord of souls," Francis replied.

Both the old priest and the messenger placed their hands on Francis's shoulder. He was grateful for their support and happy that the issue would finally be resolved. Retreating into the church, he found solace as he gazed into the eyes of the crucified Christ.

The snow was still falling lightly on that February day in 1206. Francis begged the prayers of the old priest and made his way with difficulty up the slippery path toward Assisi. The town's usual hum of activity had been replaced by an eerie silence. Spectators, anxious to witness the well-publicized trial, gathered in the piazza of Santa Maria Maggiore.

The bishop's fortified palace, which was built into the very wall of the commune, was located down the slope from the central piazza, near the Gate of Moiano. It stood next to the church of Santa Maria Maggiore, which had been erected near the ruins of a Roman temple dedicated to the god, Janus. The episcopal residence and church was an imposing complex that boasted a high tower, a loggia with battlements, and a narrow rectangular piazza, and was attached to the palaces of nobles who were faithful supporters of the prelate.

At about 9:00 A.M., the bishop emerged from his palace. He was dressed in a full, blue velvet mantle with large clasps of gold. On his head was an episcopal mitre embroidered in gold. Servants placed the cathedra, the chair from which Guido conducted the official business of the diocese, on the landing of the portico. As the bells rang, the crowd waited in silence.

The bishop addressed the outraged father, who seemed to have aged considerably in the last weeks. "Pietro Bernardone, what are the charges you bring against the accused?"

Pietro came forward with determination. He looked directly at the bishop, averting his eyes from the crowd of spectators who were, he was sure, gloating over his family's tragedy. The hearing was a public admission of his inability to control his son, to take care of his family affairs, and was a devastating disgrace. Pietro had carefully weighed the personal and economic disadvantages of proceeding with the trial, and had concluded that he had no choice. Francis's behavior had to stop. He needed to disown his son for the ultimate good, the ultimate survival of his family.

"Francis is no longer my son, Lord Bishop," Bernardone announced. "He stole from me, when I was away on business. The sum he stole was substantial and has cost me both revenue and honor. Although I have given him everything, I cannot trust my own flesh and blood. For the good of my family, for the honor of my family, he must be cut off. He has committed one outrage after another. The entire commune knows of these things. He is an insubordinate and a thief. He is a goddamn ..." Pietro could hold his anger no longer. He raised his fist and lunged toward Francis.

A knight of the bishop's palace, Tommaso di Raniero, restrained him, holding his arm in a vice-like grip. Pica stood behind her husband in silence.

The bishop proceeded as though nothing had happened. "Francis Bernardone," he addressed Francis. "Your father is greatly incensed and scandalized by your conduct. If you wish to serve God, you must first return your father's money, which he well may have dishonestly acquired in the first place."

Pietro Bernardone's face blackened with rage. He never trusted Bishop Guido, and here in public, the bishop was questioning the integrity of his business dealings. Pietro felt Tommasso di Raniero's grip tighten.

"Francis," the bishop continued, still ignoring Bernardone, "God would not want you to be the cause of such anger in your father, anger which places his soul in grave danger. And God would also not want you to use money obtained dishonestly for restoring the church of San Damiano." The bishop looked up at the crowds and paused, leaving the townspeople wondering if he was referring to Francis's "dishonesty" or Pietro's.

Francis knew that the bishop was right. Throughout his life, he had suffered when Pietro's anger toward himself and his mother raged out of control. Anger was often a source of sin for Pietro. On the other hand, if the bishop did not let him keep the money, how could he fulfill the Lord's command?

The bishop could see that Francis was struggling with confusion, but remained firm. "Francis, your father's anger will abate when he gets his money back." The bishop looked at Pietro as though he were giving him an order.

Then wrinkling his forehead in a kind of tender sternness, the bishop addressed Francis. "Give him his money, Francis, and trust in the Lord, my son. Be strong and fear nothing. God will help you and will provide you with all that is necessary for repairing the church."

Francis thought there was going to be more. Was this his sentence? He looked at the bishop. No, the bishop was finished. He was awaiting a response from Francis.

Though confused as to how he could fulfill the Lord's command, Francis understood that he must obey the bishop. It would be the Lord who would help him repair the church. Francis needed to trust in God. He rose joyfully and addressed Guido.

"My Lord Bishop," Francis replied, "not only will I return my father's money, but his clothes as well."

Before the bishop could respond, Francis leapt past him into the open door of the palace. Within minutes, he appeared naked, holding his clothes in a bundle with the moneybag on top. The crowd gasped. Francis positioned himself in the center of the portico and turned to the crowd.

"Until today, I have called Pietro Bernardone my father. Now, because I am resolved to serve God, I am returning to him the money that has made him so angry. I also give him back the clothes that are his. From now on, I will not call Pietro Bernardone my father, but I will say 'Our Father who art in heaven.' "

The crowd, the bishop, and even Pietro were shocked. Pietro rose from his place, and Francis handed him the clothes and the money. Burning with grief and rage, Pietro grabbed Pica by the arm, left the assembly, and went home. Seeing the naked Francis shivering with cold, and sympathizing with Pica, his poor mother, some of the women in the crowd wept openly for him.

The bishop, admiring Francis's courage, gathered him into his arms and covered him with his voluptuous blue velvet mantle. "Bring some clothes for him," the bishop told his servants.

The servants went into the episcopal palace and, within minutes, brought an old, ragged tunic and a coat that had once belonged to one of the bishop's farmhands. As Francis slipped into the tunic, the bishop continued to shield him. The crowd disbursed. Francis asked for the bishop's blessing and then quietly left. The bishop watched him walk into the distance.

On the way back to San Damiano, Francis met a poor child who had no covering. Taking off the coat given to him by the bishop, Francis insisted that the child take it and put it on. The young boy watched, astonished, as his benefactor walked down the road, clad only in a thin tunic to protect him from the cold and biting wind.

The snow kept falling and provisions at the small church of San Damiano were scarce. The oil lamp below the crucifix was nearly empty. Francis needed to beg for food and oil.

"I did not mean to be a burden to you, Father. I thought that the money would provide for us both," Francis said, feeling ashamed. "I will need to beg so that we can survive."

"Returning to Assisi, Francis, is not a good idea," the old priest cautioned.

Francis knew that the priest was right. The merchant's son had made a radical decision. It would take the citizens of Assisi time to accept this extraordinary transformation of the young man they thought they had known so well.

"Go to the Benedictine monks at Valfabbrica," the old priest suggested. "They are bound to hospitality by their rule. If you work for them, they will feed you."

Driven by hunger and not wanting to deplete further the scant resources of the old priest, Francis made his way north toward Gubbio. The mud and slush made traveling difficult, and Francis was chilled to the bone. The sun shone brightly on the melting snow, but the wind was freezing. After traveling for a good half day, Francis found himself in a dense oak forest near the Chiagio river. Singing praises to God in French, Francis gathered up his courage. The area he was crossing was in a region hotly contested in the skirmishes between Assisi and Perugia. It was infested with roving gangs of marauders from both sides.

Just when Francis thought he was safe, a gang of robbers surrounded him. "Who are you?" they demanded.

Francis looked up at them. They were thugs from Perugia. A shiver of cold spiked up his back.

"I am no longer the son of Bernardone," he thought. "I no longer have a home in this world. I have no reason to fear."

Confident, Francis replied, "I am the herald of the Great King. What is it to you?" he asked.

The man in tattered clothes who was foolish enough to walk unarmed into these forests was obviously mad. The robbers, having nothing to take from Francis and no reason to hate him, struck him and threw him into a ditch filled with deep snow. Wretched as they were, it gave them satisfaction to torment someone who was even more wretched and defenseless.

"Lie there, you stupid herald of God!" one of them shouted.

Francis waited in the ditch until the sound of their horses was well in the distance. When they had left, he shook off the snow and, realizing the freedom of having no family or city, began to sing God's praises. "If I would have said, 'I am Francis di Pietro Bernardone of Assisi,'" he thought, "I would have been taken to Perugia as a prisoner."

He sang the joy of his freedom all the way to the great monastery of Santa Maria di Valfabbrica. Valfabbrica was struggling to survive hard times. Its monks had fought on the side of Assisi in the battle of Collestrada and had suffered great losses to Perugia. Francis knocked at the monastery gate. There was no answer. He knocked a second time, and then a third time.

Seeing before him a homeless beggar, the gatekeeper, without a word of welcome, opened the gate and led Francis to the monastery's guest quarters. The next morning, after being introduced to Prior Ugo, Francis was assigned to work in the guest kitchen washing dishes, splitting wood, cutting vegetables, scrubbing the floor, and tending the fire. He was not offered another tunic or mantle even though it was miserably cold, and he was given only broth to eat. After a week, he was forced by cold and hunger to leave the place. He hoped that his friend Federico Spadalunga in Gubbio would receive him kindly.

"Federico, Federico Spadalunga," Francis shouted.

His old friend recognized the voice, but found no resemblance between the man he remembered so clearly and the person who stood before him.

"Federico, it's Francis," Francis shouted again.

Federico looked down at the tattered, miserable beggar. It must be a joke.

"Francis Bernardone, is that you?" Federico asked in a tone of disbelief.

"It is me, Federico, and I'm starving. Can you help me?"

Overcoming his initial hesitation, Federico dismounted his horse and embraced his old friend. Francis was sick, emaciated, and cold. Federico brought him into the house, warmed him, fed him some soup, bread, and vegetables, and put him to bed. He would listen to Francis's story later. He laid out for him one of his own tunics and a mantle.

In the days that followed, Federico told everyone he knew about the astonishing transformation of his friend and the word spread quickly. Francis was welcomed in the city of Gubbio. When he left the Spadalunga household, he took refuge in the

leper hospital of Gubbio. There he washed the lepers' feet and
bound up their stumps, drawing off the pus and wiping their
sores clean. He felt oddly at home among the lepers; though
their flesh was disfigured, putrid, and bleeding, they still managed to summon the courage to survive. Among them, Francis
gradually became free of his former obsessions — money, honor,
and power. He felt a strange serenity among those who were
discarded by society. Amid their selfish demands and desperate
loneliness, Francis found the peace he had so long sought.

The months away from Assisi were good ones. Francis
was slowly recovering his self-confidence and was growing in
his new identity. As summer approached, Francis returned to
Assisi in order to begin the rebuilding of San Damiano.

The old priest could hardly believe his eyes as he saw
Francis, dressed in the hermit's garb of tunic, belt, and sandals,
descend the path toward the little church. The two embraced,
and the priest immediately brought out some bread and wine.
The cold, hungry days of winter seemed long gone now, and
the warmth of summer brought new hope.

"I have come back to begin rebuilding the church," Francis
promised the old priest.

Father Pietro smiled. He had lived too long to set his hope
in anyone but God. If God wanted the church to be rebuilt, it
would happen.

"Tomorrow, Father, I will visit construction sites in Assisi
and I will begin to beg for stones," Francis reported.

The old priest smiled again. He was glad Francis had
returned. He had missed him.

"Place your trust in the Lord," Francis remembered the bishop
saying. "Be strong and fear nothing. God will help you and provide you with all that is necessary for repairing the church."

The next day, Francis borrowed an old hand cart from the
priest and returned to Assisi, praising God loudly in the streets
and in the piazzas.

"Peace be to you," Francis shouted. "Peace and all good!"

"Fear the Lord and give God honor," Francis preached.

"The Lord is worthy to receive praise and honor."

"All you who fear the Lord, praise the Lord. Hail Mary, full of grace, the Lord is with you," Francis's footsteps almost danced to the words of the angel's greeting.

The townspeople did not know how to respond to such a spectacle.

"Francis has gone mad," sneered Monaldo di Offreduccio.

"Crazy, crazy, crazy," the children cheered and threw pebbles.

"He was never right after the war," Muzio insisted.

Francis faced this incomprehension with serene confidence. In the course of his street preaching, he came to the cathedral of San Rufino. There he found Canon Silvester supervising a small construction project. Francis seized the opportunity.

"Whoever gives me one stone, will have one reward. Whoever gives me two stones, will have two rewards. Whoever gives me three stones, will have a triple reward. Please, I beg you, Canon Silvester, for stones to rebuild the church of San Damiano," Francis pleaded.

The ill-tempered canon was caught off guard. What was going on? Francis Bernardone was a crazy man, there was no doubt about that. If he had gone about it in the right way, he could have had all the money in the world to rebuild the church of San Damiano. Silvester wasn't going to waste the cathedral's good stones on Francis Bernardone's foolishness.

On the other hand, there were people watching. Francis might well be a madman, but he was attracting a crowd.

"Here," Silvester handed Francis one small, cut stone. "Now go away," he ordered.

Grateful, but not totally satisfied, Francis continued.

"Whoever gives me one stone, will have one reward. Whoever gives me two stones, will have two rewards. Whoever gives me three stones, will have a triple reward," Francis repeated.

The townspeople were beginning to snicker. Silvester immediately saw the game that Francis was playing. He could hear
the remarks of those who were delighting in the unmasking of
the grumpy canon's stinginess.

"Here," said Silvester. "Here are two more stones, and I
expect you to pay for them!" Silvester's generosity was reserved
for the worthy poor.

"God reward you, Canon Silvester," Francis responded.

He put the three stones in his cart and hurried off before the
avaricious canon had time to change his mind. Arriving at San
Damiano, Francis knew that his work had begun. God would
provide. The next morning, he would shore up a piece of the
disintegrating building with three new stones.

The old priest could do little to help, but watched Francis
do the work of reconstruction day after day. He also noticed
how fervently Francis applied himself to prayer. Knowing that
in his father's house he had been brought up delicately, had
eaten only the most excellent food, and had been particular
about what he would eat, the old priest did what he could to
procure special delicacies for Francis.

One afternoon, Francis became aware of the priest's efforts.
"Wherever you may happen to go, do you suppose that you will
find another priest who will treat you this kindly?" he asked
himself.

"This is not the life of the poor that you have chosen. You
need to go out, bowl in hand, from door to door and, driven by
hunger, you need to collect the various morsels you may be given.
It is only in this way that you can live voluntarily poor for love
of Jesus Christ who was born poor, lived poor in this world, and
remained naked and poor on the cross," Francis told himself.

The next day, with great fervor, he took his bowl and went
into the streets of Assisi. "The Lord's peace be with you. Peace
and all good," Francis began. "For the love of Jesus Christ,
alms for the poor." Francis held out his bowl.

The townspeople dropped a variety of scraps into Francis's
bowl. Some people, knowing what Francis's former life had

been, were kind enough to give him decent food. Others gave him the garbage that they would have tossed into the sewer.

When he returned to San Damiano, Francis examined the contents of his bowl. His stomach turned. He had never seen such a mess, let alone tried to eat it. Making a great effort, he held his breath and started to gulp it down. He was so hungry that his meal seemed almost delicious.

"The bitter will become sweet; the sweet will become bitter," he prayed.

Francis's heart realized that, although he was weak and often ill with fever, he was able to endure everything, no matter how difficult, for the love of God. His heart was full of words of praise.

"All you nations clap your hands," he shouted. "Shout to God with cries of gladness. For the Lord, the Most High, the awesome, is the great King of all the earth."

"God has made the bitter sweet, and the sweet bitter!" Francis exclaimed. "God has made the bitter sweet, and the sweet bitter!" He closed his eyes to ponder the wonders of the day and fell fast asleep.

Finding new freedom in the fact that he could now procure his own food, Francis appeared daily in Assisi with his alms bowl.

"For the love of Jesus Christ, alms for the poor," Francis begged.

The Assisi townspeople were perplexed. They pitied Francis. After all, his father did leave him in the cold with nothing. On the other hand, Francis had asked for this treatment. He had disobeyed his father. Even the bishop admitted that he had stolen from his father. Was the man who had spent years leeching off of Pietro Bernardone, now going to leach off of them?

"For the love of Jesus Christ, alms for the poor," Francis wailed.

Pietro Bernardone heard the beautiful voice of his impoverished son. It was such a tragedy. He desperately missed Francis in the shop. Business had fallen off; he did not have his son's ability to win the confidence of his buyers. He missed the excite-

ment of Francis's parties, his escapades, and his intoxicating
love of life. Pica was sad. The house was quiet. The Bernardone
family would never be the same. Pietro was grief-stricken and
ashamed to lose his son and to have him appear penniless and,
to all appearances, happy on the streets of Assisi. He responded
in the only way he knew how.

"Goddamn lazy lout." He could not even look at his son.

"Pietro, it is Francis, your son," Lord Tancredi reminded
him.

"He's a goddamn beggar ass," Pietro insisted. "Goddamn
fool leeches off the world instead of working."

Francis regretted being the cause of his father's still escalating anger. Knowing that it was impossible for him to persuade
his father to give up his swearing, Francis devised a plan to at
least reduce its impact.

"Come with me, and I will give you the alms I receive," Francis
promised Albert, his beggar friend. "When I hear my father cursing me, I will turn to you and say, 'Bless me, father.' Then you will
sign me with the cross and bless me," Francis demonstrated.

Albert did as Francis asked. It was a comical sight. When old
Bernardone raged out of control, the half-witted Albert jumped
at the chance to bless Francis over and over again with a big
sign of the cross that he made in the air over Francis, across his
chest, or on his forehead. The simple Albert and Francis became
good friends. Bernardone, seeing that his efforts to discredit his
son were fruitless, did the best he could to avoid him.

*M*eanwhile, Francis kept visiting construction sites in
search of donations. "Whoever gives me one stone, will have
one reward. Whoever gives me two stones, will have two
rewards. Whoever gives me three stones, will have a triple
reward," Francis cried.

He was becoming a familiar sight — just one more of the
many beggars supported by the townspeople of Assisi. Daily
he gathered a stone here and another there. Daily he took his
stones back to San Damiano. Little by little the work was pro-

gressing. The townspeople were stopping by the old church to observe its progress, to contribute stones, to offer food, or to lend a hand. Francis recruited whoever was willing. One day, even his half-brother Angelo stopped by the church. Francis was praying when he heard him ride up with a companion.

"Tell Francis to sell you a penny's worth of sweat," Angelo said scornfully to his friend.

Francis remained kneeling in the back of the church, but responded in French, just loud enough for Angelo and his companion to hear. "I will get a better price for my sweat from God."

Angelo and his companion laughed at him and his construction project, and rode off. Meanwhile, Francis noticed that the oil in the lamp before the crucifix was running low. He finished his prayers, and walked to Assisi to beg for more.

It was late afternoon, and he had not yet been given any oil. Francis had always avoided begging on Via Portica in order to elude meeting family and neighbors. Today, he was desperate.

"My friend Bongiovanni will give me oil," Francis thought.

Quietly, he approached the Marangone household. He was about to knock, when he looked through a window and saw Bongiovanni, Bernard, and Peter di Catania busy gambling. At the sight of his former friends, he turned away, ashamed to beg from them. As he walked down Via Portica toward the piazza, Francis recognized his cowardice. He returned to the Marangone house, knocked, and waited for a reply.

Bongiovanni answered the door and was delighted to find Francis. Francis immediately confessed his fault.

"I was walking by," Francis explained, "and I saw you playing, but I was too embarrassed to come in. Then I realized that I was a coward in God's service, so I had to turn back. In the name of God," Francis said in French, "I beg you for some oil for the poor church of San Damiano."

Francis's friends welcomed him kindly, gave him the oil, and asked him to sit down and eat with them. Out of respect for his new lifestyle, they immediately put away their dice and money. Francis left the house with his flask full of oil and his stomach full of good food. In addition Bongiovanni, Peter, and Bernard promised to help him rebuild San Damiano. They were distressed when they realized that Francis had been avoiding them, and they were happy to have their old friend back.

A week later Bongiovanni, Peter, and Bernard appeared at San Damiano with a wagon load of supplies and tools. They set to work immediately under Francis's direction. Lady Ortolano and her daughters Clare and Catherine regularly brought provisions to the site. Francis watched the three women pray before his beloved crucifix, and he particularly noted the depth of Clare's piety. "Lady Clare is also in love with the poor Christ," Francis realized. He began to pray for her.

Meanwhile, more and more people were walking the short distance from Assisi to see the spectacle. Francis called out loudly to them in French hoping for more recruits and supplies. "Come and help us rebuild the church of San Damiano," Francis invited. "It will become a monastery of women whose life and fame will bring universal glory to our heavenly Father."

The men helping Francis did not have a clue as to what the merchant's son was talking about. Hearing Francis's words, Lady Clare, who was on the path back to Assisi with her mother and sister, stopped to look back.

7
The Gospel

With the help of his friends, Francis finished the renovation of the church of San Damiano. He then started to work on a little church called San Pietro della Spina near his family's estates in San Petrignano about three kilometers from San Damiano. Thanks to the willing assistance of his friends, it didn't take Francis long to repair this church.

Next, Francis started rebuilding the derelict church of Saint Mary of the Angels, known by the locals as the Portiuncula or "little portion." It was located near the leper hospital of San Lazzaro L'Arce. Saint Mary of the Angels was surrounded by thick oaks and belonged to the Benedictine monks of San Paolo who were neighbors to the Bernardones. Francis had no trouble convincing the abbot to give him permission to repair this church. More and more of Francis's former friends came to lend a hand including Bernard, Peter di Catania, and a simple, devout peasant named Giles.

In early 1208, a Benedictine monk had come to celebrate Mass at the Portiuncula for Francis, Bernard, Peter di Catania, Giles, and a few others who had gathered at the tiny, newly rebuilt Saint Mary of the Angels. For two years, Francis had been praying and repairing churches. He continued to wear a hermit's garb, a tunic girded with a belt, shoes, and a walking stick.

The Benedictine read the Gospel in Latin. Relying on his childhood education, Francis struggled to understand the words. The Gospel captivated him, but he didn't fully comprehend it. When the Mass ended, Francis asked the priest to explain the Gospel to him.

"The Gospel describes how the Lord sent his disciples out to preach," the Benedictine monk explicated. "Jesus asked his disciples to go out without gold, silver, money, purse, bread, or staff. He said that they should not have shoes or a second tunic. He told them to preach the kingdom of God and penance."

The words hit Francis like a flash of lightning. "This is what I wish, this is what I seek, this is what I long to do with all my heart!" Francis exclaimed.

Immediately, Francis put into practice the Gospel that he had heard. He took off his shoes, put his staff aside, kept only one tunic, and exchanged his leather belt for a piece of rope. From that day forward, he would no longer dress as a hermit. Instead of taking on another construction project, he spent his time speaking in public with simple words about a life of penance and evangelical perfection. He would begin his sermon with, "The Lord give you peace!" and then would speak simply about converting one's life to Jesus Christ.

The changes in Francis mystified Bernard, Francis's boyhood friend and former neighbor. In his spare time, Bernard helped Francis rebuild three churches, and had admired his dedication and faith. When Francis preached in the piazza of San Gregorio just outside the window of his home, Bernard was intrigued by his words.

"Peace and all good," Francis started. "The Lord give you peace."

"What do we need to do to be converted to the Lord Jesus Christ?" Francis asked the gathered crowd. "The Lord God tells us that we must love the Lord with our whole heart, with our whole soul and mind, and with all our strength. We must love our neighbors as ourselves. We must deny the vices and sins our bodies crave. We must receive the body and blood of our Lord Jesus Christ. In this way we will be converted. In this way we will have peace! In this way we will have peace and all good!"

The crowd loved this simple preaching, spoken in their own language, and outlining a return to basic Christian values. So many longed for the peace that Francis promised.

Francis's words were a welcome respite from the violence which plagued the commune. Assisi mothers wept over their sons who continued to lose their lives in Perugian ambushes. Those who had betrayed Assisi were tied to the tails of horses, dragged through the town, quartered, and hung in pieces above the gates of Assisi. Men were blinded, their tongues cut out, their hands and feet amputated for various crimes. People were hung and mocked in the town's square. The canons of San Rufino publicly argued with Bishop Guido over civil and ecclesiastical privileges. Merchants plotted against nobles, and nobles settled vendettas against merchants. Rape, adultery, incest, and murder were prevalent. Assisi was numb; it was losing its soul.

The church failed to preach effectively against the violence. The Word of God was muddled by illiterate clerics, and hungered after by an ever more educated laity who was becoming cynical of incompetent ecclesiastical leadership. Francis's message, although simple, was a welcomed one. It soothed Bernard's troubled soul. It called him back to honest, unadulterated values. It was a call to sanity in a crazed world.

As Francis finished, the lawyer, Peter di Catanio, engaged him in an animated conversation. Bernard knew that Peter was thinking about joining Francis in his new and radical lifestyle. Bernard was having similar thoughts.

When Francis returned to the Portiuncula, Bernard was waiting for him.

"Bernard, what are you doing here?" Francis asked.

"I am convinced by your preaching, Francis. I want to join you in your way of life. Please come to my home this evening so that we may talk," Bernard asked.

Francis was thrilled; he had so hoped for a renewed companionship with Bernard. Bernard had always been a soulmate. Francis promised that he would return to Assisi as soon as he finished his prayers.

Kneeling alone in the church of Saint Mary of the Angels, Francis expressed his gratitude. "Good and gracious God," Francis could hardly hold back his excitement. "For two years I have lived without companions. Master Bernard is a virtuous and good man. I pray that you guide our conversation this evening."

That evening Bernard, the lawyer, set his case before Francis. "If a person receives from God a few or many possessions, and having enjoyed them for a number of years, no longer wishes to keep them, what would be the best thing for that person to do?" Bernard wondered.

"In this case it would seem, Bernard, that it would be best for that person to give back to God what he had received from God," Francis reasoned.

"Then, Brother, I will give all my worldly goods to the poor for the love of God who gave them to me. What would be the best way for me to do this?" Bernard asked.

"Early tomorrow morning we will go to the church of San Nicolo and, as the Lord taught his disciples, we will learn from the Gospel what we ought to do," Francis responded. "Peter di Catanio will join us too."

The birds were just barely awake and singing when Francis and Bernard walked toward the Cathedral of San Rufino to join Peter.

Together, Francis, Bernard, and Peter made their way into the central square of Assisi to the church of San Nicolo. They went in to pray; but not being clerics, they did not know how to find the passage in the Gospel telling them of the renunciation of the world.

Francis approached the priest of that church. "Father," asked Francis, "would you explain for us the Gospel of our Lord Jesus Christ?"

The priest, always happy to see former students of San Giorgio interested in understanding the Gospel, was delighted to accommodate the strange threesome.

"Brothers," said Francis, "let us open the book of the Gospel and seek counsel from the Lord."

They knelt before the missal in humble prayer.

"Lord, God," Francis prayed, "Father of glory, we beg you in your mercy to show us what we ought to do."

Kneeling before the altar, Francis took the book, opened it, and pointed to a passage.

"If you wish to be perfect, go, and sell all that you have and give it to the poor. Then you shall have treasure in heaven (Matthew 19:21)," the priest translated.

Francis, Bernard, and Peter could hardly believe their ears.

"Thank you, God," Francis exclaimed.

"Brothers," replied Francis, "let us open the book three times in honor of the Blessed Trinity."

Peter and Bernard agreed. Francis again led the group in prayer.

"We thank you most merciful God for your guidance. Lord, Jesus Christ," Francis prayed, "we beg you in your mercy to show us what we ought to do."

Francis opened the book again and pointed to a passage.

"Take nothing for your journey (Luke 9:3)," the priest read.

"Thank you, Lord Jesus," Francis prayed.

"Spirit of God," Francis continued, "we beg you in your mercy to show us what we ought to do."

Francis opened the book.

"If anyone wishes to come after me, let him deny himself (Matthew 16:24)," the priest read.

The three were in awe. The Gospel passages confirmed Francis's preaching. To become poor, to leave the world of intrigue, greed, and war behind, this was the way to peace.

"Thank you, Father, Son, and Holy Spirit for showing us how to live according to the holy Gospel," Francis prayed.

He paused and turned to Peter and Bernard. "Brothers, this is our life and rule. It is the life and rule of all those who may wish to join us. Now we must go and do what we have heard," Francis commanded. "The Lord himself has shown us that we should live according to the holy Gospel."

The next morning the news began to spread throughout the various levels of town clinging to and descending down the slopes of Subasio, even down to the miserable huts of the poor huddled below Assisi's walls. Here lived the unfortunate poor. More than half of the citizens of the commune lived in poverty, the most wretched — those among the lower classes, who had been wounded in wars like the one on the field of Collestrada or ravaged by sickness — lay helpless on the steps of monasteries and churches or wandered in the forests begging for alms and taking shelter wherever they could find it. What they made of the remarkable change in the behavior of Francis Bernardone they kept to themselves.

Word of Peter and Bernard's joining with Francis in his unsanctioned lifestyle penetrated the white and pink stone walls of each and every palace of the nobility clustered near the Cathedral of San Rufino. The Offreduccio palace, one of the grandest, extended from the left side of the cathedral and faced the small piazza that stood before it. The rich and proud canons of San Rufino, men like Silvester, ministered to the spiritual needs of the urban nobility. The canons did not regard the preaching of Francis with enthusiasm, and inside the houses of the nobles, the opinions voiced were harshly unfavorable. Francis was regarded as nothing less than a troublemaker and quite possibly a serious threat to the fragile social order.

Similar sentiments were being voiced as citizens of all classes gathered in the commune's Roman forum and its focal point, the Temple of Minerva with its Corinthian columns and steep stone steps. These steps served as a kind of natural theater from which town politicians could harangue their audiences. Entertainers would play music and put on various types of shows. And preachers, like Francis, could persuade people to lay aside their earthly preoccupation for the sake of the Gospel. Once converted from its ancient pagan uses to the church of San Donato, the former temple had been given to the commune by Abbot Maccabeo, whose monks from the

Monastery of San Benedetto on Mount Subasio served it until 1212, when the commune decided to convert it into a prison.

The commune's forum was filled with small shops and by day served as a marketplace for sellers of produce, pottery, olive oil, and cloth. The Bernardone house and shop, once home to the man who was the cause of the controversy raging everywhere that morning, stood to the left of the temple and behind the small church of San Nicolo. Near it were the homes of the nobles, some of whom had made common cause with rising merchants like Bernardone. Inside those houses, there were also some who derived a secret satisfaction from the humiliations inflicted by Francis's behavior on his father.

On the upper floors of the Bernardone residence, a heavy silence prevailed. No fires had been lit that morning in the kitchen fireplace or the larger one that backed up to it and warmed the adjacent dining room. Motes of dust danced in the golden morning light that made the coffered, wood ceilings and brightly polished tile floors glow. Alone, Pietro Bernardone sat in a chair and stared at the floor. In the large bedroom on the third floor, the bed, with its large wooden headboard, was surrounded by heavy woolen drapes, closed that morning to keep out sound and light. The evening before, Pica had tried to defend her son's name from the harsh criticism of his father, and had suffered the consequences. Now she lay in bed, her body aching and her spirit heavy with sadness. Closed also that morning was the shop, its shuttered front cutting it off from the voices raised in argument as small groups of people gathered in the center of the town.

"Bernard di Quintavalle and Peter di Catanio are joining Francis," Elias di Bonbarone announced.

"They are both lawyers. They know better," Judge Egidio objected, his voice full of disbelief.

"No, really. They are signing papers and selling their properties," Tancredi di Ugone assured him.

"Master Bernard is very rich. Why would he do this?" Egidio was perplexed.

"You have to admit that Francis is a good preacher," Lord Celino stated.

"He's a jackass," Francis's half-brother, Angelo, exclaimed.

"He's a good preacher," Lord Celino insisted.

"Getting a little religion is one thing," replied Angelo, "but living with Francis's whims and stupid ideas, that's another."

"I could imagine doing it," a peasant named Giles said, almost in a whisper.

"You can?" shouted Lord Monaldo Offreduccio in disgusted disbelief. "All of Assisi is going mad!"

"No," insisted the knight Angelo, Tancredi's son. "Assisi is mad. We have nothing except death and violence. There is no future for us, or for our children. Francis is right. We must change our behavior. We must seek peace."

"You sound like you will be the next to join the crazies, Lord Angelo," Francis's brother, Angelo, said scornfully.

"Who are the real crazies?" Giles asked. His question brought an uneasy end to the conversation.

A few days later, Wednesday, April 16, one week before the feast of Saint George, crowds gathered in the piazza of San Giorgio in front of the church of San Giorgio which was annexed to the hospital of San Rufino. Word was out; Bernard was giving away all his money to the sick in the hospital of San Rufino.

When Francis, Bernard, and Peter appeared and met with the hospital's inmates, many of whom were sitting or lying in the warm sun in the San Giorgio piazza in front of the hospital, Bernard's pockets were nearly bursting from the weight of many gold coins. The poor of the hospital were bewildered. They had experienced Francis's kindness to them, but the generosity of Bernard was totally unprecedented. After hesitating, trying to grasp whether all this was real or just a dream, the cripple Broccardo stepped forward, and Bernard poured into his hands as many coins as they would hold. One by one, Bernard and Peter comforted each inmate, heaping their hands and laps full of coins. When the inmates could hold no more, Peter, whose money was gone, helped Bernard throw the rest of his coins into the crowd of Assisi's residents, who were now demanding that some of this largess be shared with them. The townspeople were shouting the reasons why they felt they deserved to receive the benefits of such unprecedented generosity.

"My child suffers from a crooked foot," cried one mother. "My husband has a tumor. He is not able to work," another woman wept.

"My son was wounded in the war," a peasant shouted.

The sorrows of all of Assisi, usually kept private because of family pride, were shared in that brief moment. Francis knew that the gold would bring peace to no one, but he hoped that it might alleviate some suffering.

"You did not pay for those stones you bought from me!" a voice protested.

Francis was taken aback by the accusation. It was Father Silvester, the crusty, penurious canon of San Rufino.

"You did not pay for those stones you bought from me!" Silvester shouted again, shaking his finger at Francis.

The cantankerous canon obviously intended to spoil this moment of utter generosity. Francis could not let this happen. He took a handful of coins from Bernard's treasure and threw them at the disgruntled priest.

"Are you fully paid now, Master Priest?" Francis asked.

Silvester bent over with a grunt and picked up the coins scattered over the cobblestones of the piazza. He left with a grimly self-satisfied expression on his face.

"He made you look like a fool," Silvester mumbled to himself, "but at least you got your money."

The three companions, each dressed in a simple tunic with a rope around his waist, walked in the direction of the valley, through the woods, to the tiny church of Saint Mary of the Angels. There they repaired a small hut near the church to serve as their shelter.

In the following days, news about the extraordinary events that took place in the San Giorgio piazza spread throughout the commune. Upon hearing the reports, Giles decided that if Bernard and Peter, who had more money than he, could risk accepting such a life, so could he. On Thursday morning, April 23, 1208, he attended Mass in celebration of the feast of Saint George in San Giorgio church. During the liturgy, the priest Guido, the rector of both the church of San Giorgio and the hospital of San Rufino, preached on the familiar story of the great knight, Saint George.

"Today we celebrate the saintly nobility of the knight, Saint George," the priest of San Giorgio began. "Why was Saint George noble? Not because he slew the dragon, not because he saved the king's daughter, but because, when he saw persecution and violence, he responded by giving away all of his possessions, laying aside his arms and armor, and putting on the simple garb of the Christians. He proved himself a valiant, noble knight because he gave his life totally to the following of Jesus Christ, who was despised, rejected, and persecuted on this earth. In this, he was utterly generous, utterly obedient, and utterly noble," Father Guido exhorted.

All of his life, Giles had aspired to be a knight. Because he was only a humble peasant, his dream had seemed unrealistic.

"Why was Saint George a noble knight?" Giles could still hear Father Guido's sermon ringing in his ears.

He had been in the San Giorgio piazza and watched Francis, Bernard, and Peter give their money away. Through his devoutness and piety, Giles saw that the three men were indeed knights for Jesus Christ, just like Saint George. Giles resolved to join them. He walked into the valley toward the church of Saint Mary of the Angels where Francis, Bernard, and Peter were staying. The leper colony, with its small chapel surrounded by the wooden huts of its poor outcasts, was located in this valley, quite close to the church. It was well known that Francis continued to nurse and comfort the inmates there. Because Giles did not know the area, when he came to the crossroads near the leprosarium, he began to pray.

"Dear Lord," he asked, "please help me find Francis without any trouble."

Just then, Francis emerged from the woods where he had been praying. When Giles saw him, he prostrated himself at his feet.

"Giles," Francis said. He tried to help the peasant up but to no avail. Giles had obviously put on his best clothes for the feastday. Francis had to smile at their odd combination of colors. "Giles, get up. What do you want me to do for you?" Francis asked.

Giles got up from the ground and knelt before Francis like a knight, with arms crossed, asking for investiture. It was a bizarre sight, a peasant asking investiture from a beggar, but Giles decided that on this day, the feast of Saint George, his longing for the honors of knighthood would be satisfied.

"I want to stay with you, for the love of God," Giles requested. Francis smiled tenderly.

"Giles, the Lord has given you a great gift," he said. "Suppose the emperor came to Assisi and wished to select some citizen of the town to be his knight or chamberlain. There would be many that would strive for such an honor. How much greater should you consider the gift that the Lord has chosen you for his court!"

Giles was completely convinced. Taking his hand and helping him up, Francis led Giles to the Portiuncula. Bernard was busy finishing the small hut.

"Bernard," Francis called out, "the Lord has sent us another brother!" Peter peeked his head out of the little hut. He had been working on the inside.

"We have some bread to celebrate, Francis," Peter suggested.

"Yes," said Francis. "Let us eat to celebrate Giles's coming. Then we will go to Assisi to beg for a tunic for Giles."

As the four made their way to Assisi, a beggar woman approached them. "Alms for the poor," she cried. "For the love of Christ, alms for the poor."

Francis realized that he had nothing to give her. In his sorrow, he said nothing.

"Alms for the poor, for the love of Christ, alms for the poor," the desperate woman persisted.

Francis remained silent, wondering how he might help her. "Alms for the poor, for the love of Christ, alms for the poor," the woman pleaded.

Each time she cried out, Francis's heart anguished because he knew that her need was great. Finally, he had an idea.

"For the love of Jesus Christ, let's give her your cloak," Francis suggested to Giles. He looked at Giles's cloak. It wasn't beautiful, but it was warm.

Immediately, Giles took off his prized but ragged cloak. It was the feast of Saint George. For the love of Jesus Christ, he would sacrifice anything to bring comfort to this poor woman.

"I am a knight of Jesus Christ, and I will give away all of my possessions in order to serve Jesus Christ, who is the true Lord," Giles smiled.

Francis broke out in a boyhood song that celebrated the words of the Legend of Saint George. "I am a knight of Jesus Christ. I have left riches and worldly pomp in order to serve the God of heaven more freely," Francis sang.

That night at Saint Mary of the Angels, the four brothers in Christ, following the direction that the Lord had given them at the church of San Nicolo, planned the course of their future life together. Now that they were four, they could literally go out two by two just as the Lord had sent his apostles. They decided that Giles and Francis would go to the Marches of Ancona, while Bernard and Peter would continue to work and preach around Assisi.

"Peace be with you!" Francis proclaimed. "Peace and all good be with you!"

"Repent, change your lives. Give up bloodshed and take on the ways of peace," Francis chanted.

Giles, the new and simple knight of God, was learning from his Master. He played the role of the ever-obedient squire.

"He is giving some very good advice, trust him," Giles would assure people they encountered as they went forth to preach. Meanwhile the crowds had their own opinions about these vagabonds who wandered into their towns.

"These fools are drunk," one nobleman jeered. "They're not talking like fools," a notary admitted.

"They are either clinging to the Lord and are living a radical life of disciplined holiness   or else they are completely crazy," one priest told his parishioners.

"The way they abuse their bodies seems reckless," a doctor complained. They go around barefoot, in shabby clothes, and they eat very little."

"Be sure to keep the young people away from them," warned a town consul. "We don't want our entire town to be infected with this stupidity."

Francis and Giles returned to the Portiuncula in the middle of August, 1208. Upon their arrival, three more men from Assisi wanted to enter the small group — Sabbatino, Morico, and John della Cappella. A few days later, Philip di Lungo also joined them.

The people of Assisi were not supportive. "They sell their own possessions, and then they expect to eat at our expense," they complained.

The brothers found it difficult to find enough provisions to survive. Their friends, relatives, and nearly all of the citizens of Assisi persecuted them. The people of Assisi, both rich and poor, derided them as madmen and fools.

"They give away their goods in order to beg from door to door — we will not have this!" the consuls complained to Bishop Guido.

Seeing that the brothers were hungry and left without enough to live on, Bishop Guido sent for Francis.

"Francis," the bishop reasoned, "it seems to me that it is very hard and difficult to possess nothing in this world."

"My Lord," Francis replied, "if we had possessions, we would also be forced to have arms to protect them. Possessions are the cause of disputes and strife, and in many ways hinder people from loving God and neighbor. We are determined, Bishop Guido, to have no temporal possessions. We want to live in peace."

The bishop was deeply moved, but the practical reality still needed to be addressed. "It will take time for the families of the brothers to get used to the idea that their relatives have joined your group," the bishop insisted.

"Perhaps it would be best for us to leave Assisi for some time," Francis suggested. Thanking the bishop for his guidance and kindness, Francis returned to the Portiuncula.

That night he addressed the others. "Brothers, let us consider our vocation, and how in God's great mercy, we are called not only for our salvation, but for the salvation of every man and woman. We need to go throughout the whole world exhorting all men and women by our example, as well as by our words, to do what is needed to change their sinful habits and to live moral Christian lives."

"Amen, Brother Francis," Morico exclaimed.

"Do not be afraid to tell people that they need to change their sinful habits, even though people might wonder why brothers who appear ignorant and powerless should tell them what to do," Francis continued. "Put your trust in God who overcame the world. Hope steadfastly in God who, by the Holy Spirit, speaks through you. Exhort all to be converted to God and to observe God's commandments."

Giles cleared his throat nervously. "Francis, I am not much of a preacher. I cannot sing and dance as you can."

"Giles," Francis responded in a kind and reassuring voice, "you will find that some people will be faithful and kind, and they will receive you gladly. You will also find that many are unfaithful, proud, and blasphemous. They will swear at you and try to hurt you. Prepare your heart to suffer everything humbly and patiently."

"I was hoping that I could stay here in the valley and work at the leper hospital," John della Cappella pleaded.

"Do not be afraid," Francis assured his brothers. "It is best for Assisi and for us if we leave for a little while."

Francis divided them into groups of two and sent them off to preach in different towns. Always attentive to the needs of their souls, he taught them the prayer that Pica had given him as a boy.

"On the road," Francis exhorted, "whenever you come upon a wayside cross or church, bow in prayer and say, 'We adore you, most holy Lord Jesus Christ. Here and in all the churches that are in the whole world, and we bless you. Because by your holy cross, you have redeemed the world.'"

The brothers repeated the prayer, and Francis watched them go off in all directions.

"Come, Brother Peter, we must go too," he said.

*P*eople now began to see how these brothers rejoiced in the midst of trials and tribulation. They noticed how zealous they were in prayer. They marveled at the fact that the brothers did not accept money. Most of all, they noticed how the brothers loved and cared for each other.

Gradually, in the towns around Assisi, many became convinced that the brothers were true disciples of Jesus Christ. With remorse in their hearts, they came to ask pardon of the brothers for having previously injured and insulted them. The response of the brothers to their apologies was a simple one. "The Lord forgive you," they said, and they gently encouraged the people to reform their lives.

The brothers stayed on the road for about two months and returned home early in 1209. Francis and Peter returned first, because Francis was eager to welcome the others. He hoped that they had all survived the mission. Francis and Peter were making a small fire outside the hut of the Portiuncula when

Bernard and Giles and Philip and John emerged from the dense oaks.

"Bernard, Giles, John, Philip." Francis did not know which of them to embrace first.

"Brothers, peace, welcome home. How are you? Are you hungry? Tell me everything!"

Francis passed out bread to the hungry and weary brothers. Bernard put his feet up on a small rock.

"We have sore feet, Francis, but happy hearts," Bernard assured him, smiling broadly.

Just as they were settled, Sabbatino and Morico arrived. Francis welcomed them and gave them bread. Sabbatino was bursting at the seams with news of their journey.

"Francis," Sabbatino said, "Morico and I went out and did what you told us to do. We started singing songs of praise to God in the piazza, although Morico has a really bad voice," he said, nudging Morico with his elbow. "When people came to see what was going on, we went up to them and said to each one, 'The Lord's peace be with you!' Then we encouraged the people to change their lives, to live simply, to pray fervently, and to behave morally."

"And what did the people say?" Francis asked.

"Other than telling me I had a beautiful voice?" Morico interjected.

"Some said, 'They are fools,'" Sabbatino mimicked.

"They must be drunk," added Morico.

"They said those things about us too," John reported, "and other things like, 'These young men could have made something of themselves. They could have had a good life. And here they are. They threw it all away and now they want to beg from us. To hell with them!'"

"As if dying from worry over whether you can accumulate a massive amount of money and property is a sane way to live," Peter commented.

"Did the women run away from you?" John asked the others.

"Yes, they were afraid," Peter admitted. "Well, look at us. We are a little scary looking!" The group laughed.

"When you came to a wayside cross or church, did you remember to say the prayer that I taught you?" Francis asked.

The group immediately bowed their heads and, like schoolboys, dutifully recited. "We adore you, most holy Lord Jesus Christ. Here and in all your churches throughout the whole world, and we bless you. Because by your holy cross you have redeemed the world."

As they were praying, a rustling sound came from the oaks. Within minutes, men came out of the woods from three directions. From one side came Giovanni di San Costanzo, and from another, Barbaro. From the direction of the leper hospital came Bernardo, the son of Vigilante di Bernardo di Bellettone, and with him the knight Angelo Tancredi. Francis was busy greeting Giovanni di San Costanzo and Barbaro when he looked up and saw Angelo. For a moment, he stood still — stunned. Angelo had to be the first to speak.

"Francis, we heard about your return," Tancredi's son said. "Bernardo and I have been talking together, and we wish to join your way of life."

Uncharacteristically, Francis was still struggling to find words. Giles noticed this and responded.

"God is doing great things for us! God be praised!" Giles exclaimed. "God be praised!"

"Welcome, brothers," Francis finally got the words out. "You are most welcome! Please join us. We were just sharing stories about what has happened to us the past months."

"We missed you in Assisi," Angelo said.

"We want to hear your stories," Giovanni di San Costanzo replied. "What is it like to live in poverty and to preach to the people?" Barbaro asked.

"Our life is hard, but God always takes care of us," Giles began. "I have a good story about Brother Bernard's and my trip to Florence. You don't mind if I tell it, Bernard?"

"What story are you thinking of?" Bernard wondered.

"Well," Giles said, looking at the new recruits, "Brother Bernard and I went begging through the city of Florence, but

no one would take us in. It was very cold. Finally we saw a
portico that had an oven used for baking, so I said to Bernard,
'Maybe we could stay here for tonight.' Bernard went up to the
lady of the house and asked her whether she would let us stay
for the love of God. She told us that we could not stay in the
house, but when we suggested that we would like to sleep near
the oven, she saw no problem with that."

"But then," Bernard continued, "her husband came home.
'Why did you let those good-for-nothings stay in the portico?'"
Bernard imitated the husband's outrage.

"The woman told him that there was nothing to steal on the
portico other than some wood, and that it was very cold. She
tried to bring us some blankets, but her husband forbade it,"
Giles continued.

"'They are lousy thieves and vagabonds. It's bad enough
that you let them stay,'" Bernard imitated the husband again.

"We froze that night," Giles went on. "The next morning,
Bernard and I went early to the church to pray."

"And to try to get warm," Bernard added.

"A good man of the city, whose name was Guido, started
giving alms to all who were in church, but we refused his alms
because we still had plenty of time to earn our bread by working," Giles reported. Bernardo di Vigilante's eyes widened.

"This man, Guido, said to us: 'Why will you not accept
money like other poor people?'" Bernard said.

"Bernard then explained to him," Giles went on, "that
while it is true that we are poor, our poverty is not a burden
to us as it often is to other poor people. We have become poor
voluntarily by the grace of God, because we wish to follow in
Christ's footsteps."

Giles nudged Bernard to continue. He looked at Bernardo
and Angelo.

"Then the man asked if we had ever possessed worldly
goods," Bernard reported. "I told him that I was noble, that I
was once a rich man, and that I had sold everything, giving it
all to the poor for the love of God."

"The lady who had allowed us to sleep in the portico was so taken by Bernard's story that she told us that she would gladly receive us into her house as guests for the love of God," Giles continued. "But the man, Guido, insisted that we stay at his house. Here we were. One night we nearly froze to death, and the next day we had two offers! God is good! God is good!" Giles chanted.

Bernard couldn't help but crack a smile at Giles's exhuberance. "The man let us stay with him until we moved on. How long were we there?" Bernard asked.

"Ah ... maybe four or five days," replied Giles. "For quite awhile before this, we had a hard time finding hospitality and food. We needed a good rest, and this man, Guido, was very kind to us. I hope that we were also good company for him."

Seeing that Giovanni, Barbaro, Bernardo, and the knight Angelo were absorbed by Bernard and Giles's story, Francis seized the opportunity to offer them some preliminary instructions.

"Our life is a simple one," Francis said. "We sell all that we have and give the proceeds to the poor. After this, we spend our time in prayer, working for our daily food, and in encouraging people to live their lives according to the holy Gospel."

The tiny hut that stood next to the Portiuncula chapel was too small. Some of the brothers had to sleep in the church. The next days, the new recruits gave away their property and money to the poor. After celebrating their arrival, Francis spent time in prayer, asking God what he should do next.

8
Innocent III

The brothers lived a simple, prayerful life at the Portiuncula. During the day, they did manual labor in the town of Assisi, in the fields and olive groves of the commune, and at the leper hospital. If an employer failed to provide them with enough to eat for the day, they begged. Each one confidently made his needs known to the other. Unlike monastics, they ate whatever was given to them, some days eating well and other days eating little. As they worked with their hands, they prayed for all. At midnight they rose to praise God together.

One day, Brothers Morico and Sabbatino were walking up the road to Assisi. They encountered a beggar man who began to throw stones at them. Seeing the stones coming in their direction, Morico jumped in front of Sabbatino to shield him from the stones. Such was the force of their love, one for another.

Gradually, through such example, the people of Assisi began to trust the brothers. Many, in fact, held them in high regard and wanted to promote them to more responsible positions at places where they worked as laborers.

"Brother Angelo is not a bad worker," a manager of an estate reported. "It's amazing, considering that he had never done real work."

"I'm not much for that sloppy tunic they wear and all that religious mumbo jumbo at the Portiuncula," commented Scipione di Offreduccio, "but there is no doubt about it, the followers of Francis are among the best workers in Assisi." The knight

Scipione was the brother of Monaldo, but his temperament inclined him to be a bit more discreet than his brother and he was more open to new ideas. Since his return from exile in Perugia, he had involved himself in the affairs of the commune.

"The problem is that when you have a good worker, you want to give him more responsibility. Francis's brothers do not understand that. All they want to do is the most menial work. I offer them opportunities, and they do not take them," complained Marangone di Cristiano, now head of the Assisi consuls.

"A good example is Francis himself. He was working at the leper hospital, cleaning sores, draining pus, washing the putrid skin of the lepers, and jumping to their every damn demand. The priest, who isn't much good at paperwork, thought he'd give Francis a break and himself too, so he asked the son of Bernardone if he would keep the hospital accounts. Francis turned him down, and said that he preferred to work directly with the lepers," complained Cristiano di Paride, another of Assisi's consuls.

"The man is crazy!" Monaldo di Offreduccio exclaimed.

"It is hard to figure them out," Scipione admitted. "The consuls thought that it might be good for them to entrust Brother Bernard with the responsibility of distributing public funds dedicated to charities for the commune of Assisi. Brother Bernard, with all his fancy education, turned them down and now he's working on some building project."

Everyone agreed that it was a shame. Men with so much talent seemed to be throwing their lives away. Yet, on the other hand, the honest work of the men from Saint Mary of the Angels was sought after and deeply respected.

As Francis was praying, he realized that the men who had dedicated themselves to leaving the world were — despite their poor garb and pious habits or maybe because of them — in danger of being sucked back in. Francis searched for an answer from the Crucified, who had no place to lay his head.

"The Lord Jesus Christ was derided and scorned," Francis thought. "More and more we are thought well of and praised.

We are only useless servants, useless servants." Francis pondered
the words over and over. "We are only useless servants."

"Repair my house." Francis could still hear the words coming from the cross. They burned in him now like a fire.

It was obvious to Francis that more direction was needed
for the group of brothers; their fellowship was growing by leaps
and bounds. There were many apostolic groups who dedicated
themselves to poverty and spoke against clerical corruption,
but Francis did not care for their separatist agendas. He wanted
to dedicate himself to poverty without engaging in argument,
without struggling for power, and without making judgments
or discriminating against anyone. Those who wished to hear
the holy Gospel, he would counsel. Those who did not, he
would pray for.

"It is time for us to request the guidance and support of the
pope," Francis reasoned. "But how could I, a simple, obscure
layman, ever receive an audience with the Holy Pontiff?"

Exhausted and still confused after his prayer, Francis
returned to the Portiuncula for the night. As he was sleeping,
he dreamt that he was walking on a path. Near to the path
was a tall, large, beautiful, strong tree. Francis stood beneath
the tree and was amazed at its height and splendor. Suddenly,
he saw himself being lifted up so that his hand touched the
top of the tree. With Francis's touch, the tree gently bent its
lofty branches to the ground.

The following morning, Francis prayed with the images of
his dream. He realized that the great tree symbolized the pope
himself and concluded that he must go to Rome.

In the spring of 1209, when the brothers had gathered for
the evening meal at the Portiuncula amid the aromatic sweetness of the greening oaks, Francis stood up and addressed
them.

"I see, brothers, that God, in God's mercy, wants to increase
our community. Let us go to our holy mother the church and
tell the pope what our Lord has begun to work through us.

Then, with his consent and direction, we may continue what we have begun. Bishop Guido is in Rome," Francis explained, "he will help us."

The brothers knew that Francis was right. Their numbers were increasing, and they needed more formal direction. Bishop Guido was a strong supporter; he would most certainly help them.

"Let us take one among us as our guide, and let us consider him to be the representative of Jesus Christ for us," Francis suggested. "Let us follow him wherever he leads, and make him responsible for choosing our places of lodging along the way."

Agreeing with Francis, the brothers unanimously elected Brother Bernard as the one responsible for helping the group find lodging and provisions. The brothers knew that Bernard's educated way of speaking and courteous manner would help them obtain the little that they needed to live on.

As they walked down the road to Rome, Francis sang, prayed, and instructed his brothers.

"Hail, Queen Wisdom, may the Lord protect you," Francis sang in his strong, clear voice.

"With your sister, holy pure Simplicity," the brothers responded. "Lady, holy Poverty," Francis continued, "may the Lord protect you." "With your sister, holy Humility," sang the brothers. "Lady, holy Charity," Francis's voice rang through the air, "may the Lord protect you."

"With your sister, holy Obedience," the brothers answered.

The journey was a happy one, filled with the energy and spirit of a fervent beginning. These new apostles would put themselves at the service of the church and, by their preaching and simple example, would proclaim the Gospel in a troubled world. They would accomplish what war, tolls, intrigues, manipulations, and vengeance had not. They would bring Christ's peace into the world.

Bishop Guido was staying with his close friend Cardinal John of Saint Paul, the bishop of Santa Sabina. The brothers announced themselves at the gate of Santa Sabina. A messenger was sent to the bishop's room, and Bishop Guido appeared shortly after. He couldn't believe his eyes as he stared at the growing group of brothers and tried to conceal his shock at the sight of Brother Angelo.

"Francis," the bishop asked, "what are you doing here? You're not thinking about leaving Assisi?"

The bishop knew that the brothers had enjoyed some success in their preaching mission outside of Assisi, and he also knew that a prophet is better accepted outside of his own town. On the other hand, the brothers had done very good work in Assisi. He loved having such men in his diocese, whose life and conduct provided powerful examples, and he could depend on them to do the work of the church. When a church needed cleaning or repair, when the poor needed to be cared for, when there was work to be done, the brothers were willing and available. They did the most disagreeable work without complaint and without demands. Bishop Guido did not want to lose them.

"No, Lord Bishop," Francis explained. "We are not planning to leave Assisi. Rather, because there are more in our number, we have written a simple rule that we would like to present to the Lord Pope for his approval."

Guido was greatly relieved, and promised to give the small group his advice and help. At that moment, Cardinal John of Saint Paul, who was the bishop of Santa Sabina, entered the room hoping to meet Guido's visitors. Trusting in Bishop Guido's good sense, the kind cardinal overlooked the strange appearance of the group of men from Assisi and graciously welcomed them.

In the days that followed, Bishop Guido and Cardinal John of Saint Paul met with Francis and the brothers. Cardinal John was quite impressed with Francis. When Bishop Guido had first explained Francis's purpose in coming to Rome, the cardinal had listened unenthusiastically. As the week progressed, the cardinal began to understand Bishop Guido's respect for these brothers. They did simple and needed work; they did not criticize authority. Francis had a spirit that could touch the hearts of common people.

"The church is losing the people," the good cardinal thought. "The church needs a man like this who can preach effectively to the masses."

"Giuseppi," the cardinal called out to a servant. "Go and find the brothers who are the guests of Bishop Guido and tell them that the bishop and I would like to meet with them before Vespers tomorrow afternoon."

As the brothers were entering the cardinal's office, the cardinal could not help but smile at Guido, who was obviously taken with this Francis. It was an odd picture, this stingy, avaricious bishop and this simple, barely literate brother.

"Francis," the cardinal asked, "have you been comfortable? Is there anything at all that your brothers need?"

"Oh no," replied Francis. "Brother Bernard has found us accommodations well suited to our needs." Francis looked at Brother Bernard who responded with a shy smile.

"Why did you come to Rome? What is your desire, Brother Francis?" the cardinal asked.

"We wish to live, Lord Cardinal, according to the words of the holy Gospel," Francis explained.

The brothers then joined Francis in repeating the precious words given to Francis, Bernard, and Peter from the Gospel in the church of San Nicolo. "If you wish to be perfect, go, sell what you have, and give it to the poor, and you shall have treasure in heaven. Take nothing for your journey. If anyone will come after me, let him deny himself."

The cardinal could see the joy that radiated from these men, dressed in such humble clothing but rich in spirit and faith. "I can see that you are living these words of the Gospel, brothers, but you can do this in Assisi. Why come to Rome?" he asked.

"We wish approval and direction from the Lord Pope for our way of life," replied Francis. His direct, candid response took even the experienced cardinal off guard.

"The church already has many approved ways by which you may follow the holy Gospel. Why not live as monks or as hermits?" the cardinal inquired.

"We wish to exhort all people to reform their lives according to the holy Gospel," Bernard explained. "We wish to do this as poor men, since our Lord Jesus Christ came into this world and had no place to lay his head."

The cardinal was impressed; these men were obviously sincere, and they practiced what they proposed. Their fervor was great, but he feared that with time, and given the realities of the human condition, they might regret choosing such a difficult lifestyle.

"It is better to promise less and do more, than to promise more, collapse under the burden, and, in the end, be a cause for scandal," the cardinal warned them in a kindly way.

The cardinal did not want to extinguish the innocent fervor of the brothers, but he did feel that they needed to be prudent as well as enthusiastic. Francis carefully considered his response. He knew that the cardinal was a good and holy man. Francis was just a beginner; he was not only making decisions for his life, but had taken on the responsibility to lead eleven others. Sensing the cardinal's reservation, Francis closed his eyes for a moment, and imagined the eyes of the Crucified at San Damiano, and then opened his eyes again, knowing that he had regained his perspective.

"Lord Cardinal," Francis asserted humbly but confidently, "the Lord Jesus Christ gave us the holy Gospel so that we might live it. We believe that we can live the Gospel not by our own strength but by the grace of God." His face was radiant with conviction.

It was an eloquent argument from a humble man. Now it was the cardinal's turn to pause. If he insisted that the brother's life was too difficult, then he would be saying that living the Gospel was too difficult. Yet, on the other hand, the brothers would someday grow old and infirmed. Who would take care of them?

The cardinal tried again. "When attempting to discern God's will, one must pay attention to practicalities," the cardinal said gently. "Human beings, good intentioned as they might be, cannot live like angels."

"My Lord Cardinal," Francis replied, "people lose everything they leave behind in this world, but they take with them the rewards of charity. For their charity, God rewards them a hundredfold."

That afternoon the cardinal made no promises, but inwardly he began to sense the power of faith that shone forth from Francis and his brothers.

A few days later, the cardinal had business with Pope Innocent III at the Lateran Palace.

"My Lord Pope," the cardinal began, "I have found a most excellent man who desires to live according to the Gospel. I am convinced that through this man our Lord wills to renew the faith of the Holy Church in the entire world."

Knowing that Cardinal John of Saint Paul was a very astute judge of character and a realist, who was not at all prone to flattery, Pope Innocent III was impressed, even startled by this recommendation.

"Cardinal John," said the pope, "you seem to be quite taken with this man."

"Yes, your Holiness, I am," the cardinal replied cautiously. "I can assure you, he would be an excellent instrument of the Roman church. He is obedient and simple, not complex, a pure spirit whose words inspire, and whose lifestyle is most edifying. He is from Assisi, and Bishop Guido is equally impressed with him."

There was a pause. The pope knew that Bishop Guido was committed to keeping all strains of heresy out of his diocese. "Bring him to me tomorrow," the pope asked, "so that I might meet him."

The next morning, April 16, 1209, the ragged band of brothers from Assisi, accompanied by Bishop Guido and Cardinal John of Saint Paul, were led into the Lateran. The pope received them in a great chamber, a room decorated with a richness and splendor intended to awe those who sought an audience with Peter's successor. Somewhat shocked by their appearance, Pope Innocent gave Cardinal John a questioning glance. Bishop Guido nervously twisted the large episcopal ring on his finger, and kept his eyes fixed on Francis and his companions.

During Innocent III's tenure as pope, he had been inundated with requests from men and women who wanted to live the Gospel literally. Many of the laity were restless; they wanted to read the Gospels for themselves and put them into action. Innocent was eager to take every opportunity to encourage apostolic movements that were loyal and submissive to the institutional church. The church needed to create a more positive image with its lay members. Innocent's policy was to suppress antipapal movements, while attempting to incorporate any groups that were submissive to ecclesiastical authority, but offered prospects for spiritual renewal.

The sight of these men from Assisi, however, made him apprehensive; what did they really want? He glanced at Guido, who gave him a reassuring nod. He knew that he could trust the bishop, who had become rich from exploiting the privileges of the medieval church and would gain nothing by fostering heresy.

"There must be something about these men that serves Guido's interests," the pope thought. He found it amusing to see the worldly, rich, and contentious Guido bringing before him this collection of tattered, apostolic vagabonds.

"Lord Pope Innocent," Cardinal John announced, "this is Brother Francis, a penitent from Assisi, and his followers."

Francis and his brothers bowed low to honor the pope.

"You may get up now," the pope said gently, impressed by the simplicity and sincerity of their reverence. "What do you wish us to do for you?"

"We wish your consent and direction in following the holy Gospel of our Lord Jesus Christ so that we might continue to encourage men and women along the path of conversion to a lifestyle of Gospel values," replied Francis.

"Bishop Guido," the pope had to smile, "these men are from your diocese?"

"Yes, my Lord," the bishop responded.

"You can vouch for their orthodoxy and for their obedience?" the pope asked.

"Yes, your Excellency, I can," replied the bishop, sounding somewhat more confident than he actually felt.

The pope turned his attention back to Francis.

"What is this 'form of life' that you are proposing?" the pontiff asked.

Bernard and Peter di Catania approached the pope and gave him a piece of parchment with a carefully written presentation of the short "form of life" which Francis had composed with their help. As the pope glanced at it, Francis summarized his vision.

"We wish, Lord Pope, to follow the holy Gospel of our Lord Jesus Christ which tells us: 'If you wish to be perfect, go, sell what you have, and give it to the poor, and you shall have treasure in heaven. Take nothing for your journey, and if anyone will come after me, let him deny himself.'"

The pope listened to Francis carefully, wondering if there was any deviousness behind these simple and pious words.

"You wish to preach conversion of life to all?" the pope asked, looking at Guido. Guido once again began to unconsciously work his big jeweled ring up and down his finger.

"Yes," replied Francis, not even noticing Guido's nervousness. "We preach to people, 'Love the Lord with your whole heart, with your whole soul, with your whole mind, with all your strength.' 'Love your neighbor as yourself.' 'Do not follow in the ways of wicked concupiscence and the desires of the flesh.' 'Receive the body and blood of our Lord Jesus Christ.' 'Change your lives, repent, and do penance ...'"

"Yes, Francis, thank you," the pope said, cutting Francis off but still smiling.

Innocent had heard this kind of preaching before, yet this man was somewhat different from the other apostolic preachers. This apparently was a man content not only with physical poverty, but also with the poverty of powerlessness.

This was a man who appeared to have no other ambition than to preach the holy Gospel where he was invited. He might well prove an asset to the church and pose no threat to papal authority or official Church teaching in faith and morals.

Innocent III knew Guido well and was certain that he would carefully supervise Francis. This movement would not get out of hand. Francis was zealous, but basically uneducated in matters of theology. He seemed to accept the direction of authority and yet, at the same time, had a clear vision. Innocent admired that. Keeping the masses loyal to the authority of the Holy See was crucial to Innocent's war against separatist movements. Francis and his eleven brothers might well serve to bolster Innocent's authority and, under Guido's direction, they would probably not be dangerous.

There was also something inspiring about this modest little man standing before him. Innocent couldn't help but like him. Francis was eloquent in his own way, and had a contagiously cheerful way of reaching out to people. Perhaps it was his voice; it had undeniable beauty and clarity. He was easy to listen to, even when he spoke of conversion and repentance. Never had the pope heard the words of the Gospel spoken with such charm and sincerity. Perhaps because he had nothing to lose, Francis was bold in proclaiming the need for repentance.

"One cannot help but like this man," Innocent thought to himself. "Yes, he can be an asset to the church, if properly guided and supervised."

He nodded his assent to Cardinal John of Saint Paul and Bishop Guido. Cardinal John seemed unaffected, as if he had expected the pope's approval, but Bishop Guido expelled an audible sigh of relief. Presenting Francis to the Lord Pope had been a definite gamble for him.

"Go, Brothers, with the Lord," the pope began, "and according to how God might inspire you, preach conversion to all with our sanction and blessing. When God multiplies your numbers and increases grace in you, come and report this to us. We will then concede more to you, and entrust you with greater tasks."

The brothers could hardly believe their ears. Francis had done it, yet what did this permission really mean? They would ask Bernard later to explain what it meant in practice. Now was the time for celebration.

The pope had no doubt that his experienced and apostolic advice would be passionately heeded. If the brothers proved unworthy, the permission to preach could easily be revoked. Although comfortable with permitting the brothers to exhort the people to repentance, Innocent was still concerned by the strange and difficult lifestyle of the brothers.

"My sons, your plan of life seems too hard and rough. We are convinced of your fervor, but we have to consider those who will follow you in the future."

Francis had heard this objection before, both from Guido and from Cardinal John of Saint Paul. He looked at his brothers. They were good men; they now had permission from the pope to exhort the people to follow the holy Gospel. Perhaps the lifestyle of utter poverty could not be successfully followed by all who wished to join him.

"How can I distinguish my personal vocation from the common vocation of this brotherhood?" Francis wondered to himself.

The pope noticed Francis's hesitancy and interrupted his thoughts, saying firmly, "My son, go and pray to God that God may reveal whether what you ask is indeed the will of God. Do this so that we may be assured that, in granting your desire, we will also be doing God's will."

Cardinal John of Saint Paul was pleased with the pope's response, for he knew that Francis was a man of prayer. God would surely hear his prayers and show him how to guide his small band of followers.

"God reward you, Lord Pope, for your kind attention," the cardinal said, and then escorted Francis and the brothers out of the magnificent hall. The audience was over, and Bishop Guido silently followed Francis and his brothers.

In the days that followed, Francis spent long hours in prayer.
The prayer, which he had said at the beginning of his conversion,
was now a prayer not only for himself, but also for his brothers.

Most High, glorious God,
Illumine the darkness of my heart.
Give me right faith, certain hope, and perfect charity.
Lord, give me sense and knowledge
so I might always do your holy and true command.

In the late hours of the night, Francis continued to pray.

Most High, glorious God,
Illumine the darkness of my heart.
Give me right faith, certain hope, and perfect charity.
right faith, certain hope, and perfect charity ...
right faith, certain hope ...

Francis paused.

"Lord," he said, "we wish to live poorly because we want
to follow you, to live as you lived, to be united with you in
your birth, life, and passion. The Lord Pope is worried that this
poverty is too harsh. He is right; it is very hard. My brothers
may not persevere. Is it right for me to demand of my brothers
what may be good and holy only for myself?"

"Give me right faith, certain hope, and perfect charity,"
Francis begged. As he struggled, the answer became clear.

A few days later, Francis and his brothers returned for their
second audience with the pope.

"I was praying," Francis addressed the pope, "as you had
asked me to do, and God spoke to me in a parable."

The pope blinked, marveling at the self-possession of this
simple man. His black eyes held everyone spellbound. Rather
than standing still, he seemed to do a sort of dance with his
feet as he spoke.

"A poor and beautiful maiden lived in a desert," Francis
began, "and a king, seeing her beauty, took her as his bride. He

was sure that she would bear him splendid sons. The marriage contract was drawn up, the marriage was consummated, and many sons were born. When they grew up, their mother said to them: 'My children, do not be fearful and diffident, for your father is a king. Go, therefore, to his court, and he will give you everything that you need.' When the king saw these children, he marveled at their beauty, and recognizing their resemblance to him, said: 'Whose sons are you?' They answered that they were the children of a poor woman who lived in the desert."

Innocent grew impatient. Where was this story leading? What was Francis's point?

"The king," Francis went on, "embraced them joyfully, saying: 'Fear nothing, for you are my children. Seeing that there are many strangers who eat at my table, you, who are my lawful sons, will surely do so with far greater right.' He embraced them joyfully and decreed that all his children by the woman of the desert should be summoned to his court, and be cared for there."

Finishing his story, Francis looked at the pope, who was frowning and obviously still perplexed. He didn't understand the meaning of the parable.

"Lord Pope," explained Francis, "1 am that poor woman who in God's mercy is loved and honored. God has begotten legitimate children through me, and will provide for all those who are raised up through me. God's providence toward all of humankind gives so many good things of the earth to the unworthy and to sinners. In a far greater measure will God provide for those who commit themselves to conversion through the holy Gospel."

The pope was impressed; the brothers would thrive not just on Francis's own example and virtue, but because of the providence and power of God. Though a simple man, Francis's words carried the wisdom of God. His inspiration bore the mark of orthodoxy. Innocent relaxed; Francis's argument was strong and persuasive.

"A few days before you first came to see me," the pope admitted, "I had a dream. The church of Saint John Lateran was saved from falling by being propped up on the shoulder of a small, insignificant man."

Innocent turned to Cardinal John of Saint Paul. "This is surely a holy and good man who will support and uphold the church of God." He raised his hand and made a gesture of blessing. "You have my permission to preach penance to all, and my approval to live the 'form of life' you have proposed," Innocent announced.

With this, Francis and his brothers thanked God and knelt down. It was now Cardinal John who stepped forward; it was his turn to speak.

"Do you, Brother Francis, promise obedience and reverence to the Lord Pope Innocent III?"

I do, with all my heart," Francis promised.

"Those who follow you, Francis, are, in like manner, to promise obedience and reverence to you," the pope declared solemnly. He raised his hand and made the sign of the cross, saying, "Go with our blessing, in the name of the Father, and of the Son, and of the Holy Spirit. Amen."

After being escorted from the papal chambers, the ragged band ran joyfully to the tomb of Saint Peter to offer thanksgiving. That evening, Cardinal John of Saint Paul tonsured the brothers with his own hands, cutting their hair to make a small ring on the crown of their heads to mark them as men in the service of the church able to exhort the people. Then each of the brothers promised obedience to Francis, just as Francis had promised obedience to the pope.

The following morning, Francis and the brothers thanked Bishop Guido and Cardinal John of Saint Paul for their kindness and left, eager to begin their work anew. They walked briskly, their spirits full of joy and their hearts and voices praising God's overwhelming goodness.

9
Clare

Two weeks later on Sunday morning, Bishop Guido announced the news from the San Rufino pulpit.

"Pope Innocent III has given Francis and his brothers permission to preach," the bishop reported.

The reaction in the San Rufino piazza was mixed.

"How did Francis and his brothers make their way into the chambers of the pope?" Elias di Bonbarone wondered.

"Oh, you can be sure that Guido saw to that," Lord Marescotto replied.

"It's all political," Angelo, Francis's half-brother, complained. "The bishop wants to keep the commune under control. It's better to keep people thinking about their souls than their stomachs and purses."

"Francis's brothers are good workers," Scipione di Offreduccio said, winking playfully at Angelo. "They work for next to nothing, which has helped my revenues considerably."

"I do like listening to Francis preach," Rufino, Scipione's son, admitted. "He has a true gift for making the Gospel come to life."

"That's because he doesn't know what he's talking about!" snorted a disgruntled canon from San Rufino. "The son of Bernardone doesn't know theology; he barely understands basic Latin. Now he wants to preach to those of us who are educated, and the pope not only puts up with this nonsense, but officially approves of it. It is all a damn mess. You know that Silvester has gone to the valley too."

"Silvester!" Lord Marescotto exclaimed. "Canon Silvester?"

"Maybe we're all doomed to live in the valley," Elias remarked pensively.

"I don't think there is much danger of that," Marescotto grinned.

"Francis sends the brothers out two by two to preach all over the place. It's not such a bad life," Rufino, son of Scipione, continued.

"If you want to starve," shouted Monaldo di Offreduccio indignantly. He gave all of them a look of disgust and left in a huff. He had better things to do with his time than engage in discussions concerning the apostolic scum living in the valley.

"Yes, not a bad life after all, if you want to live with lepers," Monaldo's brother, Hugolino di Offreduccio, added, looking directly at Rufino.

"It's just like anything else," Elias replied, "if you work, you eat."

Month after month, Francis and his brothers provided the town gossips with plenty of news. Since Perugia and Assisi were enjoying relative peace at the moment, talk about the brothers filled the time once devoted to discussions of revenge on Perugia.

"They've moved again, you know," Muzio reported.

"Where are they now?" asked Raccorro di Ugolino.

"They moved from the Portiuncula to the shack at Rivo Torto," the knight Celino reported.

"All of them?" Raccorro wondered. "There wouldn't be enough room in that hovel for the brothers to sit, much less to lie down and sleep."

"I rode by the other day," Celino said. "I had some bread, so I thought I'd give it to them. I knocked at the door and there they were right on top of each other. Francis carved each brother's name on a beam so that they would all know their spot. They seemed happy enough, but I could never live like that."

"Did you hear how Francis greeted Emperor Otto when he made his way past Rivo Torto?" asked Cristiano di Paride. "He made all the brothers stay in the hovel except Brother Masseo. He sent Brother Masseo out to see the emperor with all his pomp and to cry out, 'Your glory will last only a short time! Your glory will last only a short time!'"

The crowd roared with laughter at Cristiano's all-too-accurate imitation of Masseo.

"What did the emperor do to Masseo?" Celino asked.

"Ah, nothing," replied Cristiano di Paride. "I guess they figured that Masseo was a crazy, runaway leper and didn't want to get near him." "And did you hear about Rufino, Scipione's son?" asked Elias di Bonbarone.

"You mean Lord Rufino of Assisi?" replied Celino.

"Yes," answered Elias, "he has joined Francis too." "What did Scipione say about that?" wondered Celino.

"Oh, you know old man Scipione," laughed Cristiano di Paride.

"He's calm and diplomatic about everything. He just said, 'If Rufino wants to wear sackcloth,' Cristiano mimicked Scipione, 'well that is not such a bad life.'"

"The real question is, what does Rufino's uncle Monaldo think about it?" asked Lord Ranieri di Bernardo. Lord Ranieri had begun negotiating with the Offreduccio uncles hoping to win the hand of their niece, Clare, in marriage.

"Monaldo, well, of course, he's all hot about it, but when all is said and done, Rufino is Scipione's son. Monaldo can't say much," replied Cristiano di Paride.

"I fail to understand how the pope can give his approval to a group of good-for-nothings who destroy family honor, run away from their responsibilities, and then leech off the rest of us." Monaldo di Offreduccio had overheard his name and joined the conversation.

"They only beg when you cheat them out of an honest day's pay," Elias di Bonbarone defended the brothers. "Everyone needs enough to eat."

"Yesterday they moved from Rivo Torto back to the Portiuncula," Filippo di Giacomo informed the group. The knight, Filippo, owned the land adjacent to Saint Mary of the Angels. "A peasant came along driving his donkey and saw the hut at Rivo Torto with the brothers in it," Filippo reported. "He thought to himself, 'These men had everything and they gave it all up, why should I, a poor person, have to respect their claim to have this place. Besides, these are men of the church who will build a big monastery and will eventually take over the entire valley.' The peasant opened the door of the hovel and drove the donkey in saying, 'In with you! In with you! This place will be just fine for us!'"

"All those brothers and a donkey in that little space," laughed Hugolino di Offreduccio. "What did Francis and the brothers do?"

"Well, I heard this story from Brother John della Cappella, who has always been a friend of mine. He said that Francis was pretty annoyed at the peasant because he showed no respect for the brothers who were praying ..." Filippo di Giacomo laughed.

"What the hell kind of respect does he think he should have?" Monaldi di Offreduccio sneered.

Ignoring Monaldo, Filippo continued. "John della Cappella said that Francis turned to his brothers and said, 'Brothers, I know that God has not called me to entertain donkeys and live in the company of men, but to show all people the way of salvation by preaching and wise counsel. We must, above all, make sure of being able to pray and give thanks for the graces received.'"

"So where did they go?" asked Celino.

"I just told you, they moved back to Saint Mary of the Angels," Filippo di Giacomo repeated patiently. "The abbot of the Benedictine monastery on Mount Subasio is allowing them to stay at the Portiuncula; they shouldn't have to worry about donkeys now."

Filippo was still talking when Lady Ortolana, her daughter Clare, and their neighbors Pacifica and Bona di Guelfuccio walked out of the cathedral of San Rufino. Bona's coal black eyes flashed with impishness as she stole a glance at the group of men idling in the piazza.

"That Bona di Guelfuccio is growing up to be quite a handful," Celino commented.

"Yes, she doesn't miss a thing," Hugolino di Offreduccio admitted. "But Clare, hasn't she grown into a beautiful woman?"

"Beautiful, yes, inside and out," Lord Ranieri di Bernardo stated. "She is tender and compassionate."

"They say she saves the food off her plate to feed the poor," Celino said in amazement.

"What man is going to want a woman who starves herself to feed the poor?" Muzio sneered.

"It would be the highest honor for any man to have Clare." Lord Ranieri was quick to defend Clare's honor.

"Everyone knows that you are sweet on Clare, Ranieri," Lord Hugolino di Offreduccio smiled.

"Yes, Ranieri, marry Clare and you'll spend your life strolling through the commune passing out alms to the poor," Muzio said in a tone of contempt.

Elias di Bonbarone did not appreciate Muzio's depreciation of Lady Clare and, aware that both Monaldo and Ranieri were getting angry at Muzio, he changed the subject.

"They say that Francis is going to preach at San Rufino this afternoon. Are you going?" Elias asked.

"Hell, no," replied Muzio, clearly annoyed that Elias should ask such a foolish question. He turned away and headed down the street.

"Francis's preaching always draws a crowd. Lady Clare attends all of his sermons. You can bet on me being there," Lord Ranieri said emphatically and went on his way.

"He certainly has his heart set on Clare," Hugolino di Offreduccio remarked.

"I just hope that Clare doesn't break his heart," Celino said, clearly concerned for his friend.

"Why would Clare want to marry any of them?" Elias di Bonbarone wondered. "The nobles live by war, violence, and cruelty. Lady Clare is looking for peace."

*C*lare's virtue and the strength of her resolve commanded admiration. Far from allowing her beauty to attract prospective suitors, Clare stayed in her house away from the windows. When she went to church, she hid her gorgeous blonde curls behind a veil. Unlike other marriageable women, Clare did not cast her eyes about. When she attended church, it was obvious that she was praying and not just making a public appearance. Her piety and modesty definitely set her apart from other young women in the commune.

That afternoon, Bona and Pacifica di Guelfuccio, Ortolana, and her two older daughters, Catherine and Clare, sat in the front row of the cathedral of San Rufino, as Francis preached about conversion to Jesus Christ.

"All those who love the Lord with their whole heart, with their whole soul and mind, with their whole strength, and love their neighbors as themselves, and receive the body and blood of our Lord Jesus Christ, and produce worthy fruits of penance ..." Francis stared directly at Sister Clare. He was addressing her. "... Oh, how happy and blessed," Francis continued, "are these men and women when they do these things and persevere in doing them because the Spirit of the Lord will rest upon them. They are the children of the heavenly Father whose works they do, and they are the spouses, brothers, and mothers of our Lord Jesus Christ."

Still looking at Lady Clare, Francis went on. "We are spouses when the faithful soul is joined by the Holy Spirit to our Lord Jesus Christ."

Then Francis looked over at Lord Ranieri. "We are brothers to him, when we carry him in our heart and body through divine love and a pure and sincere conscience, and when we give birth to him through his holy manner of working which shines before others as an example."

Bishop Guido peered out from the sacristy, listening to Francis's sermon and studying the face of Lady Clare. Should he even consider what Clare was asking of him? Guido pondered Clare's quiet resolve and determined faith.

"She is a beautiful woman," he thought, "but she is unwilling to be married. Perhaps she is making the right decision."

Still, he was not convinced. Lord Ranieri was a good man. He was courteous, strong, and had more than adequate resources. On the other hand, Bishop Guido could understand Clare's perspective. All her life, she had known only war, and she was tired of talk about revenge. She was learning from Francis, and Francis was convincing her to follow the Gospel of Jesus Christ more radically.

"And who," Guido thought, "wouldn't be convinced by Francis."

He considered his own hard heart and smiled. There was absolutely no danger that he would end up living in the valley. Clare, however, was different. She was young, vibrant, and open to conversion. Guido knew that she had a depth of faith that he would never know.

During the two years which had followed the papal approval of the brothers' "form of life," Francis sent his rapidly growing brotherhood all over Italy to preach. After making arrangements through her cousin, Brother Rufino, Clare had taken Bona with her to speak to Francis and Brother Filippo on a number of occasions. She had approached the bishop asking for permission to allow Francis to receive her as a penitent under the "form of life" that the pope had approved. Guido was cautious. The pope had only given an oral, tentative agreement. Guido knew that Innocent was interested in Francis and the brothers because of their ability and willingness to preach to the masses. Women would not be useful to that purpose.

Two years later, Guido was still spying from the sacristy of the Cathedral of San Rufino, and Francis was still preaching. Bishop Guido looked at the face of Lord Ranieri, Clare's would-be suitor, who knew nothing about Clare's real desires. He also studied the face of Clare. Her unshakeable resolve astounded the bishop. He thought about Clare's uncle, Monaldo, who was becoming more and more impatient with Clare's reluctance to consider marriage.

"It is going to come to a head soon," the bishop feared as he silently moved away from the doorway of the sacristy.

In fact, Clare's uncle Monaldo had made concerted, determined plans. That evening, Lord Ranieri was a guest at the Offreduccio dinner table along with Lord Pietro de Damiano, a neighbor of the Offreduccios. Clare's uncles, Monaldo, Scipione, and Hugolino, swapped stories with their guests concerning exploits in battle, and the wounds they had inflicted upon their enemies. They bragged about the torture of enemy women and children and drank more and more wine to numb their consciences. Enough wine, and one could boast about doing atrocious things.

Just as the servants were putting the finished touches on the table, Lady Ortolana and her daughters, Clare, Catherine, and young Beatrice, entered the room. The men, eyes already glassy with wine, stood to show their respects, and followed the women to the table. The overly generous servings of meats, fruits, and pastries seemed to rise from one level of excess to another. The banquet was intended to display noble hospitality; its effect was to encourage gluttony. There was more wine.

As the food was served, Clare helped herself to a variety of the dishes that the servants had prepared, but it became obvious as the meal progressed that Clare ate very little. Lord Ranieri attempted to follow her example, but soon gave in to his voracious appetite. Lady Otolana observed that Monaldo was becoming frustrated with Clare's remote and unencouraging attitude.

"Sister Clare always tries to leave a considerable portion on her plate for the poor," Otolana explained nervously, but her attempt to ease the tension in the room was not successful. Monaldo was angry; his face was red from frustration and wine. Attempting to focus attention back to the original purpose of the evening, Scipione intervened.

"With two such beautiful women before us," Scipione said, smiling at Clare and Catherine, "Monaldo, Hugolino, and I would be remiss if we did not bring up the topic of marriage."

Lord Ranieri looked longingly at Clare. She was beautiful, virtuous, and gentle. She knew how to control her tongue and how to be both gentle and firm with the servants. She was wise and discreet, and so lovely..

Clare felt Ranieri's gaze and squirmed, but maintained her composure, while seeking a way out of the awkward situation. Catherine, on the other hand, was flustered. She began to cough, and, in an effort to cover her mouth, brushed a cup of wine with her hand, spilling it on the table. Hugolino smiled when he noticed Catherine's nervousness; he, like the rest of the Offreduccio uncles, were really concerned about Clare at the moment, but it was good for Catherine to begin to accept the inevitability of marriage.

The family's exile in Perugia had disrupted the normal order of things. Both Clare and Catherine had shown little interest in marriage, and the Offreduccio uncles had waited until the economic situation of the noble families within Assisi stabilized before beginning to negotiate marriages for their nieces. Few women as beautiful as Clare would be so indifferent to the effects of their charms on prospective suitors. In some ways, this reticence made Clare all the more attractive, and her character and beauty was celebrated throughout the Umbrian countryside.

Monaldo gave little thought to Clare's virtues. To him, Clare was less the virtuous beauty of the Offreduccio household than she was an unmarried niece, an important asset for the alliance of the Offreduccio family with another influential noble family of the commune. The security and prosperity of any noble family depended on the alliances made through marriage. It was Monaldo's duty to see that Clare was properly married, and that both the honor and fortune of the Offreduccio household would be enhanced by this marriage.

Taking advantage of the momentary lull in conversation that followed Catherine's awkwardness, Clare handed her plate to a servant and excused herself from the table. Catherine, embarrassed by her clumsiness, nodded to the guests and followed Clare. Rounding up Beatrice, who had been nibbling on a piece of fruit, Otolana excused herself and followed Catherine. The men found themselves alone.

"Clare is beautiful, Lord Ranieri," Hugolino began.

"She is most beautiful," Lord Ranieri blushed.

"We of course will provide her with an ample dowry," Scipione promised.

Lord Ranieri hesitated. He was truly pleased with Clare, and knew that the Offreduccio uncles would consent to the marriage, but he had asked Clare many times if she would marry him, only to be gently but firmly rejected. Lord Ranieri prided himself on being a gentleman; he did not want to marry Clare against her will. He would not be satisfied with gaining a bride's dowry but not her heart.

The next day, Clare walked the short distance from her home to the bishop's palace. As she entered the office, Guido knew that this was no ordinary visit. Her expression was one of determination and confident self-possession. The bishop had heard rumors that Monaldo was intent on marrying Clare to Lord Ranieri, and that this marriage would take place soon.

"Good morning, Clare," the bishop greeted her, trying to keep the apprehension he felt out of his voice.

Clare fell on her knees and received the bishop's blessing. He then reached down and gently raised her to her feet.

"Clare, we know that God's will is revealed to us in the ordinary circumstances of our life. God has given you great beauty, Clare. It is said that Lord Ranieri is very interested in marrying you. He is a good man, Clare; you will be happy with him."

"Lord Bishop," Clare responded, with some impatience, "you and I have been meeting for over two years. You know that I am not interested in marriage."

"Yes, Clare," replied the bishop in kindly but almost parental fashion, "but we must be reasonable. Your uncle Monaldo is a very powerful man. He has already tolerated many delays. I do not think you can tempt his patience any longer."

"Lord Bishop," Clare insisted, "I will not marry Lord Ranieri."

"But Lord Ranieri is a good man, and a gentle man. He will make a most excellent husband." The bishop was becoming adamant; it was time for Clare to accept the inevitable.

"If I marry Lord Ranieri, what will become of me?" Clare asked. "I will have a husband who murders children and rapes the women of his enemies. I will go to bed with a man who has blood on his hands, and who has no real faith or piety. I will raise sons who, in turn, will also kill, steal, and rape. I will weep over my husband and sons when they are maimed or butchered in the city of their enemies. You cannot condemn me to this life, Lord Bishop."

"Clare, what do you want?" the bishop asked, exasperated by Clare's stubbornness.

"You know what I want, Lord Bishop," Clare replied. "I wish to follow Francis Bernardone in his 'form of life' that has been approved by the pope."

"We have been through this, Clare." The bishop tried to keep his patience. "The pope did not approve this 'form of life' for women. The pope saw the brothers and approved their life because they were preachers. You could give your obedience to Francis, but you cannot be on the road preaching. The pope's permission does not include women."

Clare would not be put off so easily. "The pope said that the brothers were to give their obedience to Francis. I am willing to do this," she insisted. "As for preaching, I can live an eremitical life and preach to anyone who comes seeking the love of God."

"It isn't practical, Clare." The bishop decided to try another approach. "If you wish to dedicate yourself to the service of God, then we should approach the nuns at San Paolo; they can make proper arrangements for you."

"Lord Bishop," Clare was adamant, "if I join the Benedictine nuns at San Paolo, I will spend my life in litigation, property disputes, and war. I have lived my whole life in war. Please, I want to choose peace; I must choose peace."

The bishop paused. Clare was a nineteen-year-old, mature woman who knew her own mind, and her request was valid. Indeed, she was right — her entire life had been colored by war and violence. Bishop Guido had heard the same story again and again from the men of Assisi who had joined Francis. Certainly, it should not be surprising that a woman as refined and sensitive as Clare would have the same yearnings for peace.

"Clare," he said quietly, "do you know what you are asking? For the rest of your life you will live in poverty. You will be cold, and you will have little to eat. You will need a place to stay. You cannot live alone."

"Catherine will join me," Clare declared.

"God, no!" the bishop exclaimed. "Two Offreduccio women choosing abject poverty at the same time. Clare, you cannot be serious."

"I am serious," Clare responded. "Catherine and I are doomed to a life of violence, greed, and misery. Please, dear Bishop," she implored, her voice breaking under the strain of powerful emotions, "the knights in my family are not powerful enough to oppose you. Please, for the good of my soul, Reverend Bishop, allow me to join Francis."

"You freely choose poverty over temporal wealth?" the bishop questioned, making sure that she understood the full implications of her request.

"I choose poverty — so that I may have eternal riches," replied Clare. "You choose celibacy over married life," he asked. "I choose marriage to my Lord Jesus Christ," Clare responded. "You choose the contempt of the world, and the contempt of your family over honor?"

"Dear Bishop," replied Clare, "I choose contempt of the world over honors, poverty over earthly riches, and peace over hatred and war."

The bishop hesitated. Clare knew what she wanted, and he had no argument to the contrary that would serve the good of her soul. Yet, her idea was entirely impractical.

"Where will you live?" the bishop asked.

"San Damiano!" Clare answered without any hesitation.

"San Damiano!" The bishop was surprised. "San Damiano is my church." The bishop thought it over. "That could be arranged," he admitted.

Guido imagined Clare leaving town on the road leading into the valley toward Foligno, walking past the ancient Roman funerary monuments, and heading downhill to the church of San Damiano. This church, so beloved of Francis, was a cave-like structure, made of dark, almost black stones with high slit windows that let in only a limited amount of light even on the brightest day. Before Francis had undertaken repairs and replaced its crumbling stonework, falling walls, and rotting beams, the church had been virtually unsafe to use and was usually empty, even on holy days and religious festivals. Only the old, frail priest was there to watch over it and tend to it — until Francis and his friends had transformed it into a sound structure, lovingly restored to a condition worthy of the magnificent crucifix over its altar — the cross that had played a decisive role in Francis's conversion.

It was possible for Guido to imagine what life would be like for a young woman in a small church situated outside the city walls. There were many other women who were living in small churches similar to San Damiano all over the commune. Father Pietro was old and ill, and would welcome an invitation from Guido to live the rest of his days at the bishop's palace in order to make room for Clare. The dowries of Clare and Catherine would bring the small church a modest endowment to provide for their needs.

Yet, the bishop hesitated. The flight of both Clare and Catherine to the lifestyle of Francis Bernardone would bring unspeakable dishonor and considerably weaken the Offreduccio family. The bishop knew Clare's uncle Monaldo very well; he would go after Clare and Catherine. There would be no protection for them at San Damiano.

"You could go into the valley," the bishop said, thinking out loud. "Francis and the brothers could cut your hair, and you could promise your obedience to God and Francis. Then you must go to the Benedictine monastery of San Paolo for sanctuary. I will speak to the abbess myself; she will make sure that you are protected. Once your uncles see that you are tonsured, they will know that you are worthless as a bride." He looked at her with a deeply concerned, almost anguished expression on his face. "You will be disowned, Clare. If you do this, there will be no turning back."

"What about Catherine?" Clare asked.

"You will need a companion," replied the bishop. "Ask Catherine to see me so that I can be sure of her intention."

"I know that Francis agrees to your plan," the bishop continued. "He talked with me yesterday about it. Clare, I can offer you no guarantees. I will not promise to support you."

"Francis has promised me that he and the brothers will care for us," Clare replied.

Bishop Guido winced. Francis and his brothers were preaching all over Italy, and he worried that their commitment to provide for Clare and Catherine would soon be forgotten as they became more and more absorbed with their preaching.

"There are no guarantees, Clare," the bishop admonished her, "even from Francis and his brothers. People will curse you for the dishonor you have brought to your family. No, Clare, I really can't allow it," the bishop said, reversing himself. The thought of Clare and Catherine joining Francis made him actually tremble.

"If you do not permit me to follow in the footsteps of Francis," Clare replied, "I will be forced to be complicit in corruption, violence, and evil. Dear bishop, you are the shepherd of my soul," Clare pleaded. "Please allow me to live in happiness and peace."

At that moment, a servant came to the door. The bishop quickly facilitated the servant's question, and then decided to take advantage of the interruption to withdraw and take a few minutes to collect himself in the cloister walk. He took his responsibility for Clare's soul seriously. From the perspective of eternity, her choice was valid. Guido tried to picture Clare suffering from hunger at San Damiano; then he tried to picture her happy as the wife of Lord Ranieri. Lord Ranieri was really not such a bad choice for Clare.

The bishop stopped pacing and reassured himself; Clare was a strong and determined woman. She had already shown herself capable of undertaking practices of fasting and penance far beyond those done by any other woman that he knew. Her thoughts were quick and clear, and her reputation was spotless. If Clare could overcome the initial opposition of her family, there was a chance that she could have a happy life at San Damiano.

"Clare is right," the bishop thought. "This is what she needs to do."

He paused again, nervously twirling his ring and wishing he could come up with an alternative plan.

"She could go to the Benedictine monastery of San Paolo," Guido thought. The Benedictine monastery was extremely rich, well endowed, well defended, and constantly entangled in litigation. Clare was searching for peace.

Finding no good alternative to Clare's proposal, the bishop returned to find Clare still resolute.

"Clare, I am the pastor of your soul. I agree with you that you cannot marry Lord Ranieri. I will speak to Francis about making arrangements for you."

"You will make arrangements so that I may join Francis in his 'form of life'?" Clare asked.

"I will do what I can," the bishop replied.

10
The Sisters

The dust from the hooves of the seven horses spread out in a dark cloud as the Offreduccio knights galloped toward the Moiano gate. All of Assisi was scandalized by the news coming from the Offreduccio household.

"Clare is missing," Muzio gasped, as he ran up to the others standing in the central piazza.

"She has escaped to the valley to join Francis Bernardone," Celino announced.

"No, a woman cannot live as the brothers do. Clare cannot stay at the Portiuncula," Alduccio objected.

"Clare is not living with the brothers," Filippo di Giacomo replied. He kept himself well informed of the comings and goings of the brothers who lived near his property at Saint Mary of the Angels and was becoming a very good friend of Francis and the brothers. "She is staying at the monastery of San Paolo delle Abbadesse."

"She will become a Benedictine," Lady Marangone nodded knowingly. She knew many young noble women who had made this choice. "San Paolo is the monastery that most noble women join. What is the fuss?"

"Clare is not going to become a Benedictine. She wants to become a penitent and follow in the footsteps of Francis Bernardone," Filippo di Giacomo answered.

"Did you notice that on Palm Sunday, when the bishop passed out the palms, that Clare waited in her place? She did not go up with the rest to receive a palm. The bishop came down the steps and placed a palm in her hands. This was some sort of a sign; Bishop Guido is involved in this." Lord Marescotto conjectured.

"I didn't notice," Lord Ranieri admitted. "All I saw was Clare's loveliness. Her dress, jewels, and gorgeous blonde hair were exquisite."

"The bishop is most certainly involved," Lord Marescotto repeated. "How else could a noble woman disappear from a guarded home in the middle of the night, exit the walls without being seen, and find herself protected in a monastery able to give her sanctuary? The bishop is responsible for this outrage."

"They say that she left the house through the 'door of death,' " Galbasia di Peccio reported. She was referring to the seldom-used door found in every noble household of the commune, one that was stoutly fastened and used only for funerals, for brides on the day of their weddings, and for emergency escapes.

"The Offreduccio household is secure. The doors are either guarded or barricaded," Joanni di Ventura, a nightwatchman of the Offreduccio household, stated.

"God is with Clare," insisted Galbasia. "Clare escaped through the door of death."

"Clare escaped through the Moiano gate," Lord Marescotto retorted. "Bishop Guido is behind this."

"No," insisted Galbasia. "They say that Clare escaped through the door of death."

At the Benedictine monastery of San Paolo, Clare was cleaning vegetables and reviewing the events of the night before. She remembered running from Assisi in the darkness, making her way through the fields, and seeing the torches of Brothers Francis, Bernard, Filippo, and Clare's cousin, Rufino, who were waiting for her in the thick oaks near the Portiuncula.

The Holy Week moon shone full and bright, and the spring air was warm and pure. The brothers walked with her through the woods in silence. Clare's heart was pounding.

The wind rustled the leaves of the tall oaks, which seemed to spread their branches in a protective cover over Clare and the brothers. The light of the moon glistened off the newly budding green leaves, lighting the path to the small church of Saint Mary of the Angels. There the brothers had gathered to recite the office of Matins, which was said during the warm months in the middle of the night. Francis, Bernard, Rufino, Filippo, and Clare waited outside the tiny chapel while Brother Leo read the evening's reading taken from a homily of Saint Augustine.

"Which of you wishes to be a faithful soul?" the lector asked. "Join Mary in anointing the feet of Jesus with precious ointment. Mary's ointment is a symbol of justice. There is said to have been a pound of ointment because a pound is a weight used in the scales of justice. The word *pisticum* might be the name of the place from which this costly perfume was imported. This name is not meaningless for us, since *pistis* is the Greek word which means 'faith.' Whoever does justice knows that 'the just shall live by faith.' "

Leo took a deep breath and continued reading. "Follow in the Lord's footsteps by living a good life, and anoint the feet of Jesus. Wipe the feet of Jesus with your hair. If you give your surplus goods to the poor — and hair, which is a needless outgrowth of the body, is a surplus good — then you will have wiped the feet of Jesus with your hair. To you, they are surplus goods, but they are goods needed for the Lord's feet. The feet of the Lord on earth, those who endure poverty, are terribly needy and suffer want."

The brothers remained silent, reflecting on what Leo had read. After a few moments, Brother Angelo raised his voice in the responsory.

"I have become a reproach to my enemies. They look upon me and shake their heads. Help me, O Lord my God!"

The brothers repeated the leader's words in unison.

"Help me, O Lord my God!"

"They have spoken against me with lying tongue. They encompass me with words of hatred," Angelo continued. Again the brothers responded.

"Help me, O Lord my God."

Brother Leo, aware of the profound significance of this moment, looked at Clare and continued reading the sermon of Saint Augustine's homily.

"To whom will Jesus say on the last day, 'As long as you have done it to one of the least of my brothers and sisters, you have done it to me? You have spent nothing other than that which you did not need, but in doing this, you ministered to my feet.'

"And the house was filled with the fragrance of the ointment. The ointment is the fragrance of your good example filling the world. The fragrance symbolizes your reputation. Those who live evil lives and are called Christians cast a slur on Christ. Of these Saint Paul says, 'The name of God is blasphemed.' If through these, the name of God is blasphemed, through those who justly give what they do not need to the poor and, in this way, wipe the feet of Jesus, the name of God is praised."

Clare felt profound comfort in the appropriateness of the reading. It was as if Augustine had written these words to give her strength and fortitude on this very night. She appreciated the solicitude that Francis had shown in picking this night for her to join the brothers in their "form of life."

Francis, Bernard, Rufino, and Filippo escorted Clare into the small Portiuncula chapel. Clare knelt down and proceeded to take off her jewelry and place it on the altar of the Virgin Mary. While Brothers Bernard and Filippo shielded Clare, Francis slipped the crude tunic worn by the brothers over Clare's shoulders. Under cover of the tunic, she took off her beautiful dress and placed it with her jewels upon the altar.

When Clare was kneeling again, Francis, Bernard, Rufino, and Filippo gathered around her. Taking scissors, Francis wrapped a tress of Clare's hair around his hand and cut off her beautiful, blonde curls at the nape of her neck. Bernard followed, cutting off some more, and Rufino and Filippo completed the work. Angelo led the responsory, while the brothers responded to each click of the scissors.

"As for me, I counted myself dead upon the earth," Angelo prayed.

Clare's heart raced with excitement. As her golden tresses fell, her joyful voice joined the chorus of brothers. "As for me, I counted myself dead upon the earth."

Clare thus gave herself heart, soul, body, and goods to Jesus Christ, by receiving the tonsure from the hands of Francis, and by donning the tunic of penance. Once this was done, Rufino and Francis accompanied her to the monastery of San Paolo, while the brothers continued to pray silently in the tiny Portiuncula chapel. Clare would wait at San Paolo for the fury that would surely follow.

"Help me, O Lord, my God," Clare was still repeating the morning after her escape. The abbess had assigned her to the monastery kitchen where she worked scrubbing and chopping vegetables. "Help me, O Lord, my God."

The granddaughter of Offreduccio prepared her heart for the inevitable confrontation with her family. Days before her flight, Bishop Guido had explained to her the necessity of staying at San Paolo at least for a time. The monastery was rich, noble, and protected by armed men and papal privileges. The pope had given the nuns the right to receive women who had not yet committed their lives by vow, but who wished to live the Benedictine Rule. Anyone who attempted to cause bodily harm to these women was threatened with interdict and anathema.

The nun in charge of the kitchen treated the new servant woman gruffly. Clare did not intend to embrace the Benedictine way of life, and yet she was exposing the nuns to the wrath of the Offreduccios. The supervisor of the kitchen added more vegetables to Clare's already generous pile and frowned. Clare returned a smile. She was grateful to the Benedictines for their hospitality and appreciated the fact that she was not being given any preferential treatment.

Feeling a soft touch on her shoulder, Clare turned. Mother Abbess motioned for Clare to follow her. They entered the monastery chapel where Clare was given leave to pray. Clare's tired but happy heart reveled in the few precious moments of silence.

Sounds of heavy boots and clinking swords soon could be heard coming from the monastery courtyard, breaking the silence of the chapel. Clare did not need to turn around. She knew the Offreduccio knights had come for her. Rising and moving into the aisle, Clare turned and stood before the altar, her arms outstretched in a gesture of acceptance of God's will.

For a moment, the knights recoiled in shock. Their beautiful Clare was dressed not in rich brocades, rare silks, and embroidered linens, but in the poor, dun-colored wool of the poor. Eyeing her opponents in silence, Clare noticed a flash of rage spreading over the face of her uncle Monaldo. Scipione, sensing the approaching trouble, broke the perilous silence.

"Clare, what are you doing?" he shouted. "You are not a beggar. The knights of your family have risked their lives to protect you." Getting control of his temper, he spoke more quietly. "Come home with us. We will take care of you," Scipione pleaded.

"I have decided to enter the service of Jesus Christ," Clare responded. "I no longer belong to you. I am no longer an Offreduccio."

"Nonsense, Clare," Hugolino responded. "You are too beautiful to be a nun. There are good offers for your marriage."

"I have already been married to our Lord Jesus Christ," Clare told him, her voice clear and strong.

Hugolino looked at the abbess who nodded in agreement with Clare's statement. He frowned his perplexity. How could Clare have professed vows after staying but one night in a monastery? It didn't make sense.

The abbess offered no further explanation, and Hugolino became irritated.

"What is going on here?" he demanded.

Scipione tried to intervene, but it was too late. Monaldo, whose face was red hot with anger, lunged toward Clare.

"We want to know what the hell is going on here!" Monaldo shouted. Instinctively, Clare grabbed hold of the altar cloth with one hand and with the other partially removed the veil from her head. The sight of Clare's uneven stubbles of hair stopped Monaldo cold.

"I will not permit myself to be separated from God's service. I am already joined to Jesus Christ," Clare insisted.

Hugolino again cast a puzzled glance at the abbess; an explanation was in order.

"Clare has taken the habit of penance," the abbess explained. "She is not under the authority of the monastery, but under the authority of Bishop Guido. She is no longer an Offreduccio."

Monaldo was now scarlet with rage and choking on his anger. Hugolino stepped forward and put his hand on Monaldo's shoulder. This angered Monaldo all the more.

"I will not allow you to dishonor the Offreduccio family, Clare," he roared. "You are throwing your life away. This clothing you are wearing mocks your noble blood. No one in our family has ever behaved in this way. You will come back with us." Monaldo raised his fist and lunged at Clare.

Scipione grabbed Monaldo's arm and, tightening his grasp, stared into the eyes of his older brother.

"Control yourself," he whispered. "You are in the church of San Paolo."

"Your hair," Monaldo wailed. "What have you done? You are ruined, Clare! No one will marry you now! You are ruined!"

"I am given in marriage to Jesus Christ," Clare said firmly.

Clare could feel her heart pounding. She grabbed a larger piece of the altar cloth, but continued to stand her ground.

"There is nothing that can be done," the abbess said to the Offreduccio knights. "Go home and forget Clare; she is lost to you."

As the knights left the church, Monaldo had the last word. He turned around and looked at her, his face suffused with anger and his expression resolute.

"We will be back for you, Clare."

*T*wo days later, Monaldo and Hugolino returned, demanding to see Clare. The abbess and two of her assistants met them at the gate. "We have come for Clare," they announced. The abbess was annoyed at their obstinacy.

"Clare has chosen to live as a penitent," the abbess responded. "She is dead to you. She is no longer an Offreduccio. You must accept this."

"Clare cannot claim sanctuary here. This monastery can only offer sanctuary to those who accept the Rule of Saint Benedict. Clare does not intend to become a Benedictine nun," Monaldo retorted.

"Clare does not need sanctuary," the abbess insisted. "She has taken the habit and tonsure of penance. She has the protection of the church. There is nothing more that can be done. Now go home and take care of your affairs."

Hugolino, red with rage, turned, mounted his horse, and rode off. Monaldo, frustrated that his legal argument was so easily reputed by a woman, glared at the abbess, who remained unaffected. She was right; there was nothing more that could be done.

"The dishonor is Clare's. She is no longer an Offreduccio. She can starve for all we care. She will never be remembered in our house again," Monaldo shouted and rode away.

The abbess sighed; the ordeal was over. Clare had been publicly disowned before the abbess and two of her assistants. The abbess asked one of her assistants to summon Clare.

"Your trial is over, Clare. Your family has disowned you before three witnesses. Under the law, they cannot again claim authority over you. You are now free, Clare, to decide your future. Do you wish to remain here as a servant?" the abbess asked.

"Mother Abbess," replied Clare, "I am grateful for your protection and your kindness, but my desire is to be poor like the poor Christ. Here, even as a servant, I am warm and well fed. I am surrounded by great buildings and protected by armed men. The poor of this world do not have all this."

"You do not wish to become a nun, Clare?" the abbess asked.

"I wish to serve Jesus Christ," Clare replied, "but I need to do this in a new way. Here I have everything that I gave up and more. I wish to choose with my whole heart a life of holy poverty and physical deprivation. I want to be poor like the poor Christ."

The abbess studied Clare and admired her fervor, if not her wisdom. Since Clare did not intend to follow the Benedictine way of life, or to serve the nuns of the monastery, she could not stay.

Knowing Clare's intent, the abbess sent for one of the monastery servants. "Go to the Portiuncula," the abbess told the messenger, "and ask Francis to come for Clare." Then she turned to the young woman whom Guido had placed in her care.

"Go in peace, Clare," the abbess said kindly, still admiring the zealous purity of Clare's intention.

"God reward you, Mother Abbess, for your kindness," Clare responded, and knelt to receive the abbess's blessing.

The next morning, Francis, Bernard, and Filippo came to the monastery to speak with Clare.

"Where do you wish to do penance?" Francis asked Clare gently.

"It is not good for me to remain here," Clare replied. "Here, even as a servant I have so much and am surrounded by so many riches. I wish to follow the footsteps of the poor Christ."

"There are penitents at the church of Sant'Angelo di Panzo," Filippo offered. "There you can pray and do simple work in peace."

"Brother Francis," Clare replied, "I wish to follow the 'form of life' of your brothers."

"You cannot do this alone, Clare," Francis replied. "For now, be patient and pray. When others join you, God will show us the next step."

Clare could accept this advice from Francis; she knew that before Bernard and Peter joined him, Francis himself had lived alone for over two years. In emulation of him, Clare would go to Sant'Angelo di Panzo and pray.

Within days after Clare arrived at Sant'Angelo di Panzo, Catherine escaped from the Offreduccio palazzo. Clare had hoped that her sister would join her, but could hardly believe that she would arrive so soon.

"Clare," Catherine sobbed, "I have missed you terribly. I, too, wish to serve God completely. Do not let me be separated from you."

Clare could hardly contain her joy.

"I thank God, my dear sister, for answering my prayers and bringing you here," Clare said as she joyfully embraced her sister.

The two sat down and Clare immediately began to teach her sister the way of penance just as Francis had taught her. Meanwhile, the Offreduccio knights, whose attention had been focused on Clare, were completely unprepared for Catherine's escape. After hearing that she had left to be with Clare, they rounded up some neighbors and, in a desperate attempt to save Offreduccio honor, Monaldo led a posse of twelve men to the church of Sant'Angelo.

Entering the church peacefully, they found both Clare and Catherine at prayer.

"Catherine," Monaldo said, refusing to acknowledge Clare's presence, "why have you come to this place? Get ready to return immediately with us."

"I will not leave Clare," Catherine responded, her eyes glowing with spiritual resolve.

Monaldo's rage overwhelmed him. Without speaking, he shoved Clare out of the way, and ran toward Catherine. Clare spun from the force of the impact, fell, and banged her head on the hard floor. Catherine resisted, but Monaldo kicked and struck Catherine in an attempt to restrain her.

"Goddamn it," Monaldo shouted. "I am in charge of the Offreduccio family. The women in this family need to understand who is the boss."

Catherine continued to struggle and almost freed herself from Monaldo's grasp. Furious at her obstinacy, Monaldo grabbed Catherine's long, beautiful hair and dragged her from the church. Hugolino and Scipione, fearing for Catherine's life, tried to shield Catherine from Monaldo's blows, but then joined Monaldo in dragging the still kicking Catherine out of the church. Clare, stunned by the blow that she had received, could do nothing.

"Clare, help me!" Catherine screamed. "Do not let me be taken from Christ the Lord."

The knights mercilessly dragged Catherine down the mountain, ripping her clothes and strewing the path with hanks of hair they had torn out. Still dizzy, Clare prostrated herself before the altar in tears.

"Dear God, help me," Clare prayed. "What can I do?" Still stunned and shaken by her fall, Clare prayed. "Dear God, help me," she cried.

Catherine's cries of protest suddenly stopped, and Clare's fear for the life of her sister mobilized her. She stood up and ran out the door of the small church. On the path in front of Sant'Angelo, the Offreduccio knights stood around Catherine's limp body. People from the surrounding fields and vineyards were gathering to see the spectacle. Monaldo was out of control and about to strike the obviously unconscious Catherine again. Screaming, Clare ran toward them.

"Leave her alone!" Clare demanded. Monaldo dropped his hand.

"Leave her alone!" Clare repeated, and looked defiantly at Monaldo.

"She is dead," replied Hugolino.

Scipione gazed sadly at Clare. He put three fingers on Catherine's neck.

"She is still alive," he announced.

"I will take care of her. Leave us," Clare demanded. "Leave us now!" Hugolino pushed the still enraged Monaldo into the woods and forced him to sit down.

"You damn fool," Hugolino retorted. "We cannot take Catherine back like this. You almost killed her. She may never recover. Look at what you did to her face! You damn fool!"

Hugolino kicked Monaldo in the shins in disgust.

"Stop it," Scipione said to Hugolino. "The Offreduccio family has suffered enough disgrace for one day."

"We are not leaving Catherine here," Monaldo insisted.

"We are," Scipione responded angrily. "You almost killed her, Monaldo. What excuse will you give for bringing her back looking like this? Everyone has seen how the Offreduccio men protect the Offreduccio women. Such a disgrace! We are leaving, Monaldo, now! Clare will take care of Catherine."

Full of confusion and regret, the knights rode away.

The women of Sant'Angelo helped Clare put Catherine to bed. They gathered cool water from the spring and used it to keep the swelling from Catherine's bruises under control. Others prepared tea and salves. For the next few days, Clare never left her sister's side. As Catherine slowly recovered, Clare continued to soothe her soul by reminding her of the freedom that would come from the embrace of poverty.

Word of the assault on Catherine soon reached the brothers at the Portiuncula. Francis and Rufino went immediately to see her. Seeing Catherine's swollen and bruised face, the brothers wept. Putting her hand on his shoulder, Clare reassured Francis that her sister was going to recover, and begged him to console their souls by preaching to them about the poor Christ.

Astonished at the courage both Clare and Catherine displayed in the face of such hardship, Francis respected their desires to join his community. During the weeks that followed, he came often to Sant'Angelo di Panzo to preach to Clare and Catherine. He also went to Bishop Guido to petition on their behalf.

Since Clare now had a companion, the bishop agreed to allow them to live in the little monastery and church of San Damiano that Francis had repaired. The sisters could hardly contain their joy when they realized that they would be living in the place where Francis himself began his penitential journey. Gazing at the cross, Clare knew that she had finally found her true home.

Francis arrived at San Damiano with the rest of the brothers who were living around Assisi. At Vespers, they all crowded into the church. The brothers sang as Clare accompanied Catherine down the aisle. Catherine wore a white dress that a poor woman had let her borrow for the occasion. Her beautiful blonde hair, although still showing signs of her ordeal, was draped across her shoulders. Clare took her place beside Brothers Bernard and Filippo. Before cutting Catherine's hair, Francis addressed the congregation.

"Catherine, you have chosen to follow in the footsteps of the poor Christ. You have shown great courage in doing this. Your courage reminds me of the story of the young Saint Agnes of Rome who also showed unswerving determination in her desire to give herself totally to God. When she was being forced by a Roman official to marry, Agnes stood firm in her faith and in her choice of Jesus Christ. You, Catherine, have proved yourself to be another Agnes in our time. From today onward, in memory of your courage, we shall call you Agnes."

A tear ran down Clare's face. She had been so busy worrying about Catherine and caring for her, that she had hardly noticed how very tired she was. Even now she hardly noticed, but simply rejoiced in the honor Francis was showing to her sister. Francis was right. Catherine had behaved in a way reminiscent of Saint Agnes.

Catherine knelt before the altar, as Francis gently wound a tress of hair around his fingers and cut it off at her neck. Strand after strand fell before San Damiano's crucifix. Clare and the brothers took their turns cutting Catherine's hair in awed silence. This was a defining moment; they were forming a true society of men and women that was based on peace rather than on profit. Not content to be benefactors of the poor, these brothers and sisters were following Christ by living in the world without property or privilege.

Clare closed her eyes for a moment and remembered the night of her tonsure. There she saw the strands of the newly renamed Agnes's hair fall, and knew that God would see her sister's sacrifice as a gift of all that was superfluous, given in love. Clare imagined her sister in that moment wiping the feet of the poor Christ with the locks of hair that fell at every snip. Catherine was Agnes; Catherine was Magdalene. At this moment, Catherine was the embodiment of all holy women.

The brothers shielded Agnes while Clare helped her change into the tunic of penance and placed a veil on her head. No longer able to restrain her emotion, Agnes wept. Clare wiped her face gently with her hand as she presented her sister to the brothers. Agnes's tears brought out the fading traces of her bruises. Clare also wept, grateful for the moment and grateful that her sister was alive and well.

Francis joined Clare and Agnes beneath the cross and addressed them.

"Clare and Agnes," Francis said, "you have shown all of us gathered here that you have no fear of poverty, hard work, trial, shame, or contempt of the world. Instead, because through them you can better follow the poor Christ, you regard these things as great delights. Therefore, moved with compassion for you, we have written for you this 'form of life.'"

Brother Leo came up the aisle and handed a tiny piece of parchment to Francis. Francis opened the parchment and read it to the assembly.

"Clare and Agnes, because by divine inspiration you have made yourselves daughters and handmaids of the Most High King, the heavenly Father, and have espoused yourselves to the Holy Spirit, choosing to live according to the perfection of the holy Gospel, I resolve and promise on behalf of myself and of my brothers to always have the same loving care and solicitude for you as I have for them."

"Tomorrow, Clare," Francis continued, "I will send you brothers to care for you. Your courage has been a noble example for us. We are honored that you have chosen to join us."

The entire church was filled with tears of joy and happiness. Clare had risked everything for this moment. Not knowing how to express the joy that all were feeling, Brother Leo began the Te Deum. Brothers and sisters sang together their joyful thanks to God.

> *You are God, we praise you.*
> *You are Lord, we acclaim you.*
> *You are the eternal Father,*
> *All the earth worships you.*
> *To you all the angels,*
> *All the heavens and powers of the universe,*
> *Cherubim and Seraphim,*
> *Proclaim in endless praise.*
> *Holy, Holy, Holy, Lord God of Hosts*
> *Heaven and earth are filled with your glory!*

11
Struggle

*B*etween 1212 and 1221, Francis and Clare witnessed rapid
growth in the community of brothers and sisters. In one sense,
the daily life of the sisters and brothers was a common one.
The brothers worked in the fields as day laborers, as preachers,
and as caretakers of poorhouses and leper hospitals. The sisters occupied themselves with housework, gardening, spinning
thread, weaving, dying cloth, and sewing and embroidering
corporals and liturgical vestments for churches.

What distinguished the brothers and sisters from the commune of Assisi and from older religious orders was their
economy. While Assisians and many religious were constantly
struggling to profit from the rising money economy, the brothers and sisters of penance accepted only day wages. Sharing
what they had with each other, the brothers and sisters survived
on these resources and thus developed an alternative society in
which individual persons were treasured over profits.

There were setbacks. In 1215, Francis attended the Fourth
Lateran Council in Rome. After the liberal policies of Innocent
III, many in the curia wished to curb the excessive prolifera-
tion of new religious rules. In 1209, Francis had obtained oral
approval for his "form of life" from Innocent III, and the
preaching and work of the brothers was already becoming an
important element of the ecclesiastical fabric. The sisters were
not yet established in 1209, and it was obvious to Francis that
Clare's claim of living under the "form of life" of the brothers

was not on firm ground. Francis shuddered as he witnessed the Council approve legislation concerning new religious rules.

"So that too many religious orders might not lead to grave confusion in the church of God," the secretary of the Council read, "we strictly forbid anyone from now on to found a new religious order. Whoever desires to become a religious should enter one of the already approved orders. Likewise, whoever wishes to found a new religious house should take the rule and institutes from the already approved religious orders."

After the Council, Bishop Guido and Francis discussed the potential impact of this decree on Clare and her sisters.

"In many ways, Clare's life differs little from that of the nuns of St. Benedict," Guido stated.

"Clare is not a Benedictine," Francis replied. "She has chosen a penitential life following the poor Christ as a poor woman. She is living under our 'form of life.'"

"Your 'form of life' was approved because of the church's need for preachers able to reach the hearts of common people," said Guido.

"If the curia organizes female penitential communities under a common structure, they will not accept Clare's claim to live the 'form of life' of the brothers."

"But Clare specifically experienced her call as the following of the poor Christ," Francis reminded the bishop.

"This is true, but the San Damiano community lacks the basic structures of a religious organization. At the very least," the bishop demanded, "Clare must accept the direction and governance of her sisters."

"Clare has no desire to have authority over her sisters," Francis objected. "The sisters gather and make decisions together."

"The curia cannot understand this way of operating," the bishop insisted. "Following the poor Christ is an admirable spiritual axiom, but the curia intends to organize and regulate groups of women like Clare who have begun nontraditional experiments. Many communities of women will need to accept changes. Clare must accept this."

Francis knew that the bishop was right. He also knew that Clare would not be happy with the bishop's decision. When Francis approached Clare and her sisters with Bishop Guido's order, he faced strong resistance.

"We have promised obedience to you, Francis. If we promise our obedience to Clare, the bond between the brothers and sisters is broken," Agnes objected.

Francis remained quiet. The sisters did not fear being subject to Clare's authority, but they did fear being amalgamated into a generic form of religious life that they had never intended to embrace.

"Clare," Francis pleaded, "the policies of the curia are changing. Bishop Guido has promised to do all he can to protect your commitment to living the most perfect poverty. There is only so much that can be done."

"If I am to accept the direction and governance of my sisters," Clare responded, "then I will follow the example of Jesus Christ who lowered himself to be the servant of all. It will be my responsibility to wash the hands of the sisters, to serve and wait on those at table, to obey orders rather than give them, to clean the mattresses of the sick sisters, and to wash and kiss the feet of the serving sisters."

The sisters gasped at the penitential program that Clare had outlined for herself. Before, the menial work of the monastery was divided with charity and equity. Now, it seemed, a great part of it would belong to Clare. Francis was pleased with Clare's creative evangelical obedience. He could report to Bishop Guido that Clare accepted the direction and governance of the sisters.

Twice a year, on the Feast of Pentecost and on September 29, the Feast of Saint Michael the Archangel, the brothers gathered in Assisi to discuss the issues of their ever-growing community, to organize their missionary efforts, to pray and worship together, and to share stories. As the brothers traveled to regions far from Italy, the community was able to meet only once a year.

In 1217, at the chapter meeting held at the Portiuncula, Francis sent the brothers to preach in France, Germany, Hungary, Spain, and all over Italy. He appointed the diplomatic and able Brother Elias di Bonbarone as leader of the brothers sent to the Holy Land. Since the brothers had more zeal than experience, and since most did not speak the languages of the missionary territories, they encountered many difficulties.

In France, people asked if the brothers were Albigensians. The brothers had never heard about the Albigensian heresy. They replied that they did not know who the Albigensians were. The brothers were brought before the bishop and the university professors who read their "form of life," and who sent a letter questioning their identity to Pope Honorius III. After receiving a letter from the pope declaring that the brothers' rule had been confirmed by the Holy See, the brothers were finally given permission to preach.

The sixty or more brothers who went to Germany were less fortunate. When the people asked if they wished to have shelter or to eat, the brothers simply answered, "ja."

Seeing that when they said the word "ja" they were treated with kindness, they answered "ja" to whatever question they were asked.

"Are you heretics? Have you come to corrupt Germany as you have corrupted Lombardy?" a prominent German asked.

The brothers, oblivious of what was being asked, simply smiled and replied, "ja."

As a result, some of the brothers were imprisoned. Others were stripped naked and made fun of in public. The persecution was so intolerable that all of the brothers returned to Italy.

In Hungary, shepherds set their dogs upon the brothers and struck them with the crook of their staves. The brothers wondered why they were being treated like this.

"Perhaps it is because they wish to have our outer tunics," one speculated.

The brothers gave the shepherds their outer tunics, but the shepherds continued to molest them. Another theory was needed.

"Perhaps they wish to have our under tunics also," one of the brothers suggested.

The brothers gave the shepherds their under tunics, but the shepherds still harassed them.

"Perhaps they want our breeches also," another brother surmised.

The brothers gave away their breeches, and the shepherds stopped their blows and let them go away naked. One brother claimed that he had lost his breeches fifteen times in this way. Since, overcome by shame and modesty, he could not bear losing his breeches again, he soiled them with the dung of oxen. When the shepherds saw his filthy breeches, they wanted no part of them and never harassed that particular friar again. In the end, all of the brothers sent to Hungary also returned to Italy.

In Morocco, Brothers Bernard, Peter, Accursio, Adiuto, and Ottone were martyred. The news of their martyrdom sent shock waves through the new community. It seemed like the generous missionary sacrifices of the brothers were producing little fruit.

During the chapter meetings at the Portiuncula, Francis gave his struggling brothers spiritual admonitions to guide them in their work and preaching. He would begin his admonition with a Gospel verse, and then outline an application of the verse to the brothers' lives.

For the brothers chosen as leaders, Francis remembered the example of Clare.

"I did not come to be served but to serve, says the Lord. Those who are placed over others should glory in such an office only as much as they would were they assigned the task of washing the feet of the brothers," Francis proclaimed.

When, after the martyrdom of the brothers in Morocco, certain brothers were bragging about the fact that they now belonged to a community that had been blessed with the blood of martyrs, Francis put the situation in perspective.

"Let all of us, brothers, look to the Good Shepherd," Francis exhorted, "who suffered the passion of the cross to serve his sheep. The sheep of the Lord followed him in tribulation and persecution, in insult and hunger, in infirmity and temptation, and in everything else, and they received everlasting life from the Lord because of these things. Therefore, it is a great shame for us, servants of God, that, while the saints actually did such things, we wish to receive glory and honor by merely recounting their deeds."

To those who were tempted to brag about their preaching prowess, Francis had this advice.

"The apostle says: 'The letter kills, but the Spirit gives life.' People are killed by the letter who merely wish to know the words alone, so that they may be esteemed as wiser than others and be able to acquire great riches to give to their relatives and friends. In a similar way, those religious are killed by the letter who do not wish to follow the spirit of sacred scripture, but only wish to know what the words are and how to interpret them to others. And those are given life by the spirit of sacred scripture who do not refer to themselves any text which they know or seek to know, but, by word and example, return everything to the Most High Lord God to whom every good belongs."

To brothers who were discouraged from what they had suffered while engaged in missionary work, Francis had words of guidance.

"The Lord says: 'Love your enemies and do good to those that hate you, and pray for those who persecute and blame you.' Those persons truly love their enemies who are not upset at any injury that is done to them, but out of love of God are disturbed at the sin of another's soul. And let them show their love for others by their deeds."

Finally, Francis used his musical talent to teach the brothers how to behave on their journeys as noble knights of the Lord. At the chapter meetings when newcomers joined the brotherhood, he sang of virtue's victory over vice.

Where there is charity and wisdom
    there is neither fear nor ignorance.
Where there is patience and humility,
    there is neither anger nor disturbance.
Where there is poverty with joy,
    there is neither covetousness nor avarice.
Where there is inner peace and meditation,
    there is neither anxiousness nor dissipation.
Where there is fear of the Lord to guard the house,
    there the enemy cannot gain entry.
Where there is mercy and discretion,
    there is neither excess nor hardness of heart.

*F*rancis, himself, had failed in his missionary endeavors. He tried to go to Palestine, but contrary winds blew his ship back to Slavonia. He attempted to go to Morocco, but he became ill and had to return. He tried to go to France, but Cardinal Hugolino prevented him from leaving Italy.

"Brother," the cardinal said, "I do not want you to cross the mountains, for there are a number of prelates and others in the Roman curia who would like to interfere with the interests of your order. The other cardinals and I, who love your order, will be able to protect it and to help it much more effectively if you remain within this province."

"Lord Bishop," Francis replied, "I would be greatly ashamed of myself if I stayed here and sent my brothers to far distant provinces."

"Why did you send your brothers to undergo so many trials so far away and to die of hunger?" the bishop reproached Francis.

"Lord Bishop, do you think and believe that God has sent the brothers for this province alone?" Francis replied. "God has chosen and sent the brothers for the good and salvation of everyone in the entire world. They will be received not only in Christian countries, but also in non-Christian ones. Let the brothers observe what they have promised God, and God will give them everything that they need."

The cardinal was surprised by Francis's response. Francis was zealous, but he lacked a practical understanding of internal church politics.

"We need you to stay here, Francis," the cardinal ordered, "but you may send Brother Pacifico and the others to France."

Francis returned to the valley of Spoleto, and spent the next two years preaching in all parts of Italy. Throughout the provinces, the brothers proclaimed a message that penetrated the hearts of all, especially the young. Unmarried women, having heard the brothers preach, petitioned them.

"What are we to do? We cannot preach on the roads and in the towns as you do. Tell us how we can find peace."

In many towns, the brothers negotiated arrangements for these women. Clare sent her sisters to some of these newcomers to teach them the "form of life" lived at San Damiano. Lay people also wanted to change their lives in response to the teachings of the brothers.

"We have spouses," they said. "We cannot divorce them. Teach us how we can walk in the path of salvation."

For these people, Francis and the brothers organized a lay community of penance. This community provided men and women with the social support they needed to be faithful to a penitential lifestyle. Francis would preach to the crowds summarizing the contents of the penitential program.

We should pray always and never lose heart.
We must confess all our sins to a priest.
Anyone who does not eat the body and blood of the Lord
*   cannot enter the kingdom of God.*
Let us perform worthy fruits of penance.
Let us love our neighbors as ourselves.
*   Let us do good to our neighbors rather than harm.*
Those who have power to judge others should exercise
*   judgment with mercy.*

Let us give alms, for people lose everything they leave
behind in this world, but they carry with them the
rewards of charity and alms which they gave.
We must fast and abstain from vices and sins, and from
excess food and drink.
We must visit churches frequently and show respect for
the clergy.
We must love our enemies and do good to those who
hate us.
We must obey the commands of our Lord Jesus Christ.
We must not be wise and prudent according to the flesh.
Rather, we must be simple, humble, and pure.
We must never desire to rule over others. Rather, we must
be subject to every human creature for God's sake.

In 1219, Francis placed the care of his brothers in the hands of Matthew of Narni and Gregory of Naples, and left Italy to take part in the Fifth Crusade. At the Fourth Lateran Council, Francis had heard Innocent III announce his intention to conquer Islam in battle. The pope had asked Cardinal Hugolino, who had already met and advised Francis in Florence, to preach the crusade in Lombardy and Tuscany. The cardinal did this preaching with great fervor.

"Prepare yourselves, you faithful ones, and be powerful sons," the cardinal boomed from the pulpit, "for the moment has come to wreak vengeance on the nations that occupy and profane the Holy Land, on those who regard the glory of the cross of Christ as folly, and who mock the ignominy of the Lord's passion. To receive the reward of great happiness, let everyone of the faithful hasten to take up his cross and follow the glorious standard of the Supreme King. Let no one excuse himself from the service of Christ."

Francis, who was always willing to serve Jesus Christ, met Brother Elias di Bonbarone in Syria, and taking Brother Illuminato with him, headed toward the great Egyptian city of

Damietta. His aim was to obtain peace not by the sword, but by preaching the word of God.

When Francis and Illuminato came into the Christian camp, they were welcomed by the French bishop, Jacques de Vitry. De Vitry was fascinated with the many varieties of new forms of religious life of his time, and he found Francis particularly interesting.

"This Francis and his brothers are totally detached from temporal things," the bishop reported to the other clerics. "They go among their former friends and say, 'come along,' and so one group brings another."

"What kind of life do they live?" asked a prelate.

"During the day they go into cities and villages, giving themselves over to the active life of the apostolate. At night, they return to their hermitage or withdraw into solitude to live the contemplative life. And there are women also."

"Women?" asked de Vitry's friends. "How can women live such a life?"

"The women live near the cities in various hospices and refuges," the bishop reported. "They live a community life and sustain themselves by the work of their hands, but they accept no regular income."

"I see how the women can gather to pray and to live a religious life," replied another bishop, "but how do the men organize themselves as a community?"

"Once a year, the men of the order assemble to rejoice in the Lord and to eat together. They profit greatly from these gatherings. They seek the counsel of upright and virtuous people. They draw up and promulgate holy laws and submit them for approval to the Holy Father. Then they disband again for the year to preach to all," the bishop explained.

The Christian army was led by Jean de Brienne, the brother of Gautier de Brienne. Francis's heart remembered younger days, when he had been willing to risk everything to go to Apulia to fight under the great Gautier de Brienne. Now, without armor, horse, or sword, he had come dressed in sackcloth and armed only with the word of God.

The city of Damietta was surrounded by rings of walls with twenty-two gates, one-hundred-ten towers, forty-two castles, and a large navigable moat that had thick iron chains installed to impede an enemy crossing. It was well supplied and defended by skilled archers.

The crusaders suffered from bloody defeats, extreme temperatures, desertions, and disease. The Christian army was made up of many nationalities and was a patchwork of many different weapons and uniforms. The crusaders brought with them the same conflicts between nobles and commoners, knights and foot soldiers, rich and poor that they had at home. The unity of this army was constantly undermined by rumors, distrust, and suspicion. Francis had known of war in Assisi, but he had never experienced the evil of war on such a great scale.

Everywhere the blood of Christians mixed with the blood of Moslems. The shadows of dusk revealed severed heads and limbs littering the sands. Young children and old men and women were hacked down without mercy. Brazen vultures and incessant flies attacked the dead as well as the wounded.

In August, Brothers Leonardo di Gislerio, Elias di Bonbarone, and Peter di Catanio joined Francis and Illuminato at Damietta. At the end of August 1219, while Francis and his brothers were spending their time preaching and caring for the sick and wounded, and admonishing the crusaders about their failure to behave as Christians should, Cardinal Pelagius, John de Brienne, and the other Christian leaders planned a new assault on the Moslems.

"The Lord has shown me," Francis reported to Brother Illuminato, "that if the battle takes place as planned, it will not go well for the Christians. If I go to the leaders of the Christian army and tell them this, I will be treated like a fool. If I am silent, I will not escape my conscience. What should I do?"

"You have been called a fool before, Francis," Brother Illuminato chuckled. "This has never stopped you. Do what is right before God, and forget about human judgments."

Francis thanked Brother Illuminato for his sound advice and went to the leaders who, as he expected, dismissed him as a fool. They led their armies in battle on August 29, 1219, the feast of the beheading of Saint John the Baptist. The crusaders advanced toward the Moslem camp. The Moslems pretended to retreat, and Christians followed them into an arid, deserted piece of land between the Nile and Lake Manzalah. Realizing that they had been duped, the Christian leaders argued over strategy, while their troops, in full armor, suffered severely from the intense heat of the August sun. Crazed with heat and thirst, the Christians broke ranks, rushing in desperation without form or discipline against the Saracens, who slaughtered them. The Christian army lost over four thousand men including hundreds of knights and nobles. Francis remained in prayer, while Brother Illuminato kept him informed of the tragic events.

The sultan used the temporary victory as an opportunity to negotiate peace. The Egyptian city of Damietta, with its eighty thousand inhabitants, was surrounded. The crusaders had managed to choke off all access to provisions. John of Brienne favored peace, but Cardinal Pelagius, expecting the arrival of more crusaders, held fast to the dream of conquering Egypt in order to ensure having a base for the eventual conquest of Jerusalem.

Francis, unconvinced that war was the way to obtain peace, approached Cardinal Pelagius with a plan. If the sultan became a Christian, peace could be won without further bloodshed. Francis would end the bloodshed by preaching the Christian faith to the sultan. The cardinal agreed to let Francis proceed on his suicide mission, but not before reminding the crazy man from Assisi that the sultan had decreed that anyone who brought him the head of a Christian would be rewarded with a Byzantine gold piece.

"Though I walk in the shadow of the valley of death, I fear no evil, for you are with me," Francis prayed.

Brother Illuminato accompanied Francis as they passed into Moslem territory. In the field they came upon two bleating lambs. Francis was overjoyed.

"Place all your trust in God, Brother Illuminato, because the words of the Gospel are fulfilled in us: 'Remember, I am sending you out like sheep among wolves.'"

Suddenly a few men from the sultan's army spotted them, attacked them, beat them, put them in chains, and dragged them to the sultan. On entering the sultan's chambers, Francis and Illuminato bowed to give the sultan proper respect. The sultan, wondering if Francis and Illuminato might be holy men because of their strange dress and appearance, welcomed their visit as a welcome respite from the intrigues of his court.

"Are you ambassadors of the Christian army?" asked the sultan, "or have you come wishing to profess the Islamic religion?"

"We have been sent by God, not by men, to show you and your subjects the way of salvation. We are here to proclaim to you the message of the Gospel," Francis proclaimed.

Francis preached with great eloquence to the sultan on the mysteries of the Trinity and Jesus Christ. The sultan was impressed with Francis's enthusiasm and courage.

"You are most welcome to stay in my court," he told Francis.

"If you and your people are willing to believe in Jesus Christ, for love of Christ, I would be only too happy to stay with you," Francis responded.

The sultan, whose throne was surrounded by Islamic clerics and politicians, smiled politely. Francis recognized that the ruler had little freedom to consider Francis's proposal. A different strategy was needed.

"If you are afraid to abandon the law of Mohammed for the sake of Christ," Francis suggested, "then light a big fire and I will go into it with your priests. That will show you which faith is more sure and holy."

The sultan's learned advisers looked at each other apprehensively.

"I do not think that any one of my priests would be willing to expose himself to the flames," the Sultan said thoughtfully. He wondered if this ragged Christian was serious — or sane.

"If you are prepared to promise me that you and your people will embrace the Christian religion, if I come out of the fire unharmed," Francis proposed, "I will enter it alone. If I am burned, you must attribute this to my sins. If I am saved by the power of the Christian God, then you must acknowledge that Jesus Christ is the power and the wisdom of God, the true God and Lord, the Savior of all."

The sultan looked again at his clerics, who seemed quite reluctant to engage in this contest of faiths.

"Your offer is most tempting, Brother Francis," the sultan replied kindly, "but it is not possible. Such a promise would make me a traitor of the Moslem religion. Those of my court would immediately be obliged to kill both you and me. I have enjoyed your company, and would be pleased if you would take as a token of our visit, these precious treasures."

"I do not want gifts," said Francis. "I came only to preach to you the Gospel of the Lord Jesus Christ."

The sultan had never before experienced a Christian who was not eager for gold.

"Brother Francis," replied the sultan, "please take these gifts and give them to the Christian poor or use them for the good of Christian churches."

"I came with empty hands hoping to gain your soul," Brother Francis answered. "If I cannot have your soul, then at least allow me to leave in the poverty of the Lord Jesus Christ."

The sultan had never met such a wise and holy Christian. He ordered his soldiers to provide Francis and Illuminato safe passage back to the Christian camp.

The crusaders continued to tighten their stranglehold on Damietta. At the beginning of November, the Christians climbed over its outer wall and found a plain that had served as a massive burial ground, filled with shallow graves washed out in the recent rains. Inside the city, there were only the dead and a few living dead. Francis and Illuminato wept over the magnitude of this profound human tragedy. Of the eighty thousand inhabitants, only three thousand had survived. Of these three thousand, only one hundred were healthy. Even the undisciplined mob of crusaders was stunned into silence by the magnitude of the horror, but only for a moment. The smell of booty was stronger than the stench of death, and the Christians avariciously looted the city of its gold, silver, precious stones, and silk.

Amid the frenzy of looting, Francis and Illuminato walked back to camp empty-handed. In the camp, the crusaders fought each other over their plunder, arguing over rights to booty and territory. Overwhelmed by the ungodliness of it all, Francis withdrew for prayer, while Illuminato kept watch.

"Francis," Illuminato whispered. "Francis, Brother Stephen is here to see you."

"Brother Stephen?" Francis questioned.

"Yes," said Illuminato, "he has crossed the sea to see you. He has important news, and he begs that you might listen to him."

Francis finished his prayer and followed Illuminato to receive Brother Stephen.

"What could be so important that a simple lay brother would need to come all the way from Italy to see me?" Francis wondered.

Brother Stephen carried a piece of parchment that he hurriedly gave to Francis.

"I humbly beg your pardon, Brother Francis, because I have made this journey without the permission of my superiors," Brother Stephen admitted.

"What prompted you to this disobedience, Stephen?" Francis asked.

"Certain brothers have met, and they have changed your rule," Stephen complained. "They wish to limit even further the brothers' access to meat and milk products, and they want us to fast four days a week instead of two. Under them, we are becoming monks, not apostles."

Francis skimmed the document that Stephen had brought with him. "These new laws have caused grave divisions among the brothers," Stephen reported.

"Come, Brother Stephen," Francis said, putting his hand on Stephen's shoulder. "You have come a long way. Rest for a while and we shall talk about this later."

Francis and Illuminato shared the news of the new legislation with Peter di Catania and Elias di Bonbarone. Later they roused Stephen so that he could eat with them.

Peter passed out the plates of food. Meat was being served. Francis turned to his friend, the former lawyer, with the problem.

"My Lord Peter," Francis asked, "what should we do? There is meat on this plate."

"Ah, my Lord Francis," Peter replied, "do whatever pleases you, for you have the authority."

"Well," Francis said, looking gently at Stephen, "as the Gospel says, let us eat what has been set before us."

Stephen ate heartily, happy to be in the presence of Francis. Peter refilled Stephen's plate with another piece of meat.

"Stephen, what other news do you bring from Assisi?" Elias asked. "There is much division concerning many things," Stephen said, chewing his meat.

"Brother Philip has sought legislation from the pope to defend Clare and her sisters. Brother John della Cappella has gathered together a large group of lepers, both men and women, and has withdrawn from the brotherhood. He has written a rule for them and has set himself up to be their founder. He has gone to the pope to have this rule confirmed."

Brothers Francis, Elias, and Peter were stunned. They had focused on preaching the holy Gospel to the sultan, but meanwhile at home, the brothers were interpreting the words of the Gospel to suit their own purposes and ambitions.

"It is time for us to return to Italy, brothers," Francis admitted. "We will leave as soon as we can find passage."

Once in Italy, Francis met with other brothers, who confirmed the reports of Brother Stephen. Francis was ill again, and his usual fever was accompanied now with a painful eye disease that he had acquired in the East. The group of twelve that Francis had presented to Pope Innocent III had grown to number nearly five thousand brothers. Francis could no longer personally teach and admonish them. His trusted patron and supporter, Cardinal John of Saint Paul, who had provided Francis and the early brothers with access to the pope and with sound advice, had died.

"We need someone who will take the place of Cardinal John of Saint Paul for us," Francis admitted to Peter di Catania.

Instead of returning directly to Saint Mary of the Angels, Francis went to Orvieto where Pope Honorius III was staying. Pope Innocent III had died of a fever on July 16, 1216, in Perugia, and the old and frail Honorius was elected to succeed him two days later. The papal assistants recognized Francis and led him into the papal offices. The pope was conducting business and, when he came out of his chambers, he found Francis waiting for him. Honorius III had heard much about this man of Assisi and was delighted to have the chance to meet him personally.

"Holy Father," Francis said, "may God give you peace."

"May God bless you, son," the pope answered.

"My Lord," Francis continued, "since you are an important man and continually oppressed with heavy burdens, the poor cannot often gain access to you in order to speak with you when they have needs. Please give me someone to whom I may speak when I have a need — someone who will take your place in listening and making decisions regarding my problems and those of my community."

"Who do you wish me to give you, son?" Honorius asked.

Francis and Peter had prayed about and discussed this issue. They had decided to ask for Cardinal Hugolino, who had given Francis advice when he had intended to go to France.

"The Lord of Ostia, Cardinal Hugolino," Francis requested.

The pope was pleased with Francis's choice. He approved the request, and Francis confided in Cardinal Hugolino. The cardinal immediately revoked the letters of Brother Philip, and dismissed Brother John and his followers from the curia in shame. Satisfied that his Order was again in good hands, Francis, with Brothers Angelo and Leo, took the road back to Assisi.

12
Greccio

*H*earing the sudden uproar, Brothers Masseo and Filippo sprang to their feet, darted out the door of Saint Mary of the Angels, and peered expectantly down the road toward the leper hospital. There had been so many celebrities assembling for the Pentecost chapter meeting on May 30, 1221, that the Portiuncula, once quiet and abandoned, seemed to rival the bustle of Rome itself. Masseo ran ahead and motioned to Filippo. "Get Elias," Masseo shouted. "It's Francis."

Pressing his strong and limber frame through the frenzied crowd, Masseo finally reached the fragile Francis and positioned his body to shield him from the crushing mob. Brothers Angelo and Leo, who had traveled with Francis, nodded to Masseo, grateful for the relief.

"Ah, Brother Masseo," Francis said. His darkened, obviously painful eyes squinted in a valiant attempt to endure the harsh sunlight. Masseo could see that thick mucous oozed from his eyes and formed yellowish crusts on his cheeks, dripping at times to form scaly spots on his habit.

Brother Elias came moments later, running ahead of a party of knights from Assisi who had been assigned to keep order. The knights included Francis's own half-brother, Angelo, who the commune had authorized as the official organizer of the Pentecost event. Horses and armor soon surrounded Francis who walked with Brothers Masseo, Elias, Leo, and Angelo to the church of Saint Mary of the Angels.

Even the great success of the wealthy merchants of Assisi could not rival the prominence and fame that Francis's brothers had brought to the Assisi commune. Bishops and religious dignitaries were arriving, among them Lord Raynerius Capocci, a Cistercian who was the cardinal deacon of Rome's Saint Mary in Cosmedin. The brothers looked forward to hearing Francis's words, and the hoards of Assisians and other lay people from the surrounding communes were also eager to hear him preach. They could be seen coming from all directions bringing cartloads of food and other necessities for the gathering.

The commune fathers had spent months organizing the event. Some of the friars were elderly and could not easily sleep in the tiny, portable shelters made of woven mats of reeds that the brothers assembled for themselves. The only other shelter on the grounds was afforded by the small church of Saint Mary of the Angels, and beside it, the tiny hut that Francis, Peter, and Bernard had repaired long ago. To solve the problem, the commune consuls organized the building of a large, stone hall, on the other side of the church of Saint Mary of the Angels, to serve as a gathering place and shelter.

Francis blinked hard, thinking that his eyes were deceiving him. He leaned toward Masseo, and Masseo stooped so that Francis could whisper in his ear. "Foxes have holes, and the birds of the air have nests, but the Son of Man has nowhere to lay his head," Francis said. Masseo peered sorrowfully into Francis's diseased eyes. He had feared that Francis would not be happy about the new addition to the Portiuncula grounds. "I am worried," Francis said aloud to his friends, "that if Saint Mary of the Angels has such large and comfortable accommodations, that the brothers will go back to their provinces with ideas to build what they have seen here."

On Sunday, May 30, 1221, the bells of Assisi rang out to announce the feast of Pentecost. Thousands of brothers from near and far celebrated the feast with all those who had gathered from the commune, and then spent the next days debating various elements of their rule. Brother Caesar had inserted biblical texts into the still-evolving document, and Francis had made some revisions, composing a sermon and a song for its end.

Francis was ill, but determined to preach and admonish his brothers. He waited for the right moment. On Tuesday morning, he took the podium that stood next to the new hall. "Foxes have holes, and the birds of the air have nests," he shouted, "but the Son of Man has nowhere to lay his head." Francis cleared his throat, struggling to project his voice that, despite its weakness, retained its youthful clarity. "When the brothers need a house built for them, it should be small, like those of the poor," Francis asserted with all his strength. "The brothers should live in it as strangers and pilgrims for it is a house that is not their own. A pilgrim shelters under another's roof and then passes on peacefully, longing for his heavenly home."

Francis waved his hand and nodded to Brothers Masseo, Filippo, Angelo, Leo, Bernard, Illuminato, and Rufino, who climbed unto the roof of the new hall with Francis. The crowd, anticipating some sort of spiritual performance, stood silent, wondering what would happen next.

Brother Leo ripped off the first tile and sent it crashing down to the ground. Brother Masseo came to Francis's aid as he and the brothers started tearing tile after tile off the roof of the new building.

"What are they doing?" Lady Marangone exclaimed.

"It's staged. He's not ripping off the real tiles," Lord Marescotto di Bernardo Dodici assured her. "Its part of the sermon. There is a point to this."

"I'm not sure." Lady Marangone had known Francis for a long time, and from the beginning, she had serious doubts that Francis would be happy with the new building.

"Oh God, you are right!" Lord Marescotto exclaimed. "He is pulling the thing apart! Angelo!" Marescotto shouted. "Stop him. He's trying to pull down the building!"

Francis's half-brother, Angelo, sat on his horse, stunned. The men-at-arms were at the Portiuncula to maintain order, not to arrest the celebrity. Angelo rolled his eyes in frustration; even now, Francis could be expected to cause trouble. Shaking his head, Angelo gave the order for the knights to approach. The crowds moved back, both to give the horses room and to avoid the falling debris.

"Francis, stop!" Angelo ordered. "What do you think you are doing?"

"The brothers are to live in simple, small, wooden houses like the poor," Francis insisted. "It is not possible for us to accept this house."

"The house belongs to the commune of Assisi," Angelo shouted. "Stop destroying it. It does not belong to you."

"Oh," Francis smiled impishly. "If the house is yours, then we will no longer touch it."

With that, Masseo and Angelo helped Francis and the others off the roof. Francis wobbled onto the podium, and Elias tentatively asked him if there was anything else he wanted to say. "Yes, Elias," Francis replied in a weak voice. "Tell the brothers that since this house belongs to the commune of Assisi, the brothers are not to take care of its repairs."

Brother Elias stood up and made the announcement. "The Brother says that since this house does not belong to the brothers, but to the commune of Assisi, the commune is responsible for its repairs."

Shaking his head at Elias, and still wondering why Francis would pull such a stunt, Angelo turned his white stallion and faced the people. His strong, stately figure commanded authority. His face, with its warm dark eyes and thin features, bore the elegant refinement of his mother. "Because this house belongs to them, the people of Assisi will come once a year to make the needed repairs," Angelo proclaimed amidst the cheering crowd.

The incident had exhausted Francis. For the rest of the week, he listened to the discussions, and intervened when necessary, but did not take a prominent role in the liturgies or the proceedings. Because of his inability to project his voice, Francis sat at the feet of the competent Brother Elias and tugged at his tunic whenever he had something to say.

*A*s the chapter meeting was drawing to a close, Francis remembered that the brotherhood had not yet been established in Germany. He tugged at Elias's robe, and Elias bent down to listen, while the crowd, though restless after about a week of assembly, waited patiently. "Brothers," Elias finally announced, "thus says the Brother. There is a certain region called Germany. In this region there are devout Christian people who, as you know, often pass through our country. They perspire under the heat of the sun, bear large staves, wear large boots, sing praises to God and the saints, and visit the shrines of the saints."

Throats cleared and bodies shuffled as Elias continued. "Once the brothers who were sent to the Germans were treated badly and because of this they were forced to return to Italy. The Brother does not want to command anyone to go to Germany against his will. However, if any brothers, inspired by zeal for God and for souls, wish to go, let them rise and gather in a group."

There was a pause, then whispers, and then a rumble. Francis squinted, trying to count the rising shadows through his infected eyes. "One ... two ... three ... eight ... nine ... ten ... fifteen ... sixteen ... seventeen ..." Francis squinted again. Surely his eyes were mistaking him.

Jumping off of the platform, Elias counted the brothers off in groups of ten. Hurrying back onto the platform, Elias whispered the news to the ailing Francis. "There are ninety." Francis nodded, smiled, and whispered his instructions.

"The Brother appoints the German brother, Caesar of Speyer, as the minister of Germany. Brother Caesar," Elias announced, "Brother Francis gives you authority to choose whomever you wish from among these brothers."

Brother Caesar stood, and immediately began organizing and interviewing the ninety volunteers. While the mission to Germany was forming itself, men and women from Assisi mingled with the brothers, sharing drinks and sweets with them. Some of the brothers withdrew into the woods for a respite in prayer.

The young Brother Jordan of Giano flitted from one conversation to another, not knowing exactly how he wanted to use his time. He was enjoying the company of the brothers from his province, but was tempted to mingle with the ninety brothers in the German group in order to get to know them. He was sure, given the stories he had heard, that those who went to Germany would immediately be martyred. He regretted that he, unlike many of his older confreres, had not made it his business to get to know the brothers who had been martyred in Morocco. This time, he wanted to make sure that if the brothers were martyred in Germany, he would be able to say to new brothers coming into the order, "I knew this one, and I knew that one."

Not able to resist the temptation, and seeing that some of the other brothers were doing the same, Jordan assumed an air of confidence and made his way over to the German group.

"Who are you and where do you come from?" Jordan asked each brother.

He approached a certain gregarious brother by the name of Palmerio, a deacon, who later would become the guardian who oversaw the brothers in Magdeburg. Palmerio smiled broadly, revealing two teeth stuck in the middle of nowhere. His habit was spotted with the remains of last week's food, but he was a friendly, inclusive fellow, always drawing a crowd of brothers around him.

"Who are you and where do you come from?" Jordan asked Palmerio. "I am called Palmerio," said the brother, looking Jordan over. "And you are … ?" Palmerio asked. "My name is Jordan," the younger brother admitted. He was no longer sure that he should have gotten himself mixed up with this rather raucous crowd.

"You are not strong, but I bet that you are smart. Am I right?" Palmerio asked. Jordan blushed.

"Yes, he is a smart one," Palmerio smiled at his little company. "We will need some smart ones among the Germans."

Jordan panicked. He had told God repeatedly that he would be willing to go anywhere, but not to the Germans. "I am not one of you," Jordan quickly explained. "I am only here because I want to meet you, not because I want to go with you."

"Oh," Brother Palmerio laughed. He placed his huge hand on Jordan's shoulder. "Brothers, Brother Jordan here wants to meet the holy martyrs!" The brothers laughed, as Palmerio made the announcement with mock solemnity.

Jordan stiffened, and tried to appear calm. "Really, I am only here because ..." It was no use. He had been captured, at least for the moment.

"Come, Jordan, stay and talk with us for awhile," Palmerio invited, still laughing, but with a kindly expression in his soft brown eyes. Looking at this tall and burly brother, Jordan instantly knew he could trust him. "You will find that we are wonderful company," Palmerio promised with a broad grin.

Jordan felt trapped. While the brothers going to Germany were certainly a jovial bunch, the frail, young Jordan did not want to be numbered among them. He tried to ignore Palmerio and his friends, and focused on Brother Elias, who was attempting to hold the assembly's attention by announcing the much-anticipated appointments from the podium. Jordan heard Elias call his name for another province.

"Thank you, God," Jordan uttered out loud, barely able to stand under the weight of Palmerio's grasp. "It has been so good meeting all of you, but I must go," Jordan excused himself politely but firmly, looking directly at Palmerio.

"Brother Caesar," Palmerio shouted. "this one is young and smart, let's not let him get away."

Brother Jordan, now even more determined, tried to make his escape. It was too late; Palmerio had gotten Brother Caesar's attention. Jordan pivoted, still in Palmerio's grip, only to find himself face to face with the stout and learned Brother Caesar.

"I am not one of those who volunteered," Jordan protested. "I did not rise with the others. I am only here because ..."

Jordan's "because" was sounding weak, even to him. He knew that he was in serious trouble.

"Do not let this young one get away," Palmerio repeated, winking playfully at Brother Caesar and grinning with his two remaining front teeth.

Brother Jordan broke free of Palmerio's grasp and ran back to his province brothers, hoping that his escape would resolve his predicament. It didn't. When Brother Elias announced the brothers that would go to Germany, Brother Jordan's name was on the list.

"Please," Jordan pleaded with the older brothers of his province, "do something!"

Approaching the platform, three respected elders of Jordan's province objected. "Jordan is not healthy enough to go to Germany. He is weak; Germany is too cold for him. He does not want to go. Brother Francis said that only those who volunteered would go to Germany. Jordan did not volunteer."

Not knowing how the mix-up happened, Elias asked Jordan to come forward. "In holy obedience, Brother, I command you to decide whether you want to go to Germany or return to your province," Elias demanded.

Elias' command under obedience thoroughly befuddled the otherwise intelligent and even-tempered Jordan. What did God want him to do? How was Jordan to know the will of God? "If I stay in my province, am I doing this just because I am afraid of martyrdom?"

Jordan wondered. "Perhaps by staying, I would only be following my own will. There would be no blessing in that. Yet, I am weak and afraid of pain. If the Germans torture me, I might not be strong enough to stand firm in faith."

Jordan's stomach turned sour; he nervously crossed his arms, his fingers plucking at the sleeves of his habit. He needed to speak with a wise and experienced brother. Immediately, he thought of the brother who had lost his breeches fifteen times in Hungary. Looking around at the crowd, Jordan spotted him sitting with the brothers of his own province.

The brother was old. His face was wrinkled like a fig that had been left hanging in the sun too long. "Brother," Jordan asked, "this is what Elias commanded me. Under obedience I must make a choice, and I don't know what to do."

The older brother had learned through the years both how to embrace poverty and how to survive. He understood the impact Jordan's decision would have on his ability to be a faithful follower of Jesus Christ. Placing his hands into the hands of his younger brother, the brother spoke with a gentle kindness the hard words he knew Jordan's troubled soul needed. "Go to Brother Elias," the older brother counseled, "and say to him: 'Brother, I neither wish to go nor to stay behind. Whatever you command me, that I will do.'"

Jordan's gut twisted. He looked directly into the aged, sun-wrinkled face of the wise brother. The old brother squeezed Jordan's hands in an attempt to help him pluck up his courage. Thanking him, Jordan walked apprehensively, yet serenely back to the podium.

"Brother Elias," Jordan quivered. "I neither wish to go nor to stay behind. I will go wherever you send me."

"Brother Caesar has need of you," Brother Elias smiled at Jordan. "You will go to Germany."

The rule that Francis had brought to the 1221 chapter proved to be too wordy for the brothers to commit to memory. It also lacked the juridical sophistication necessary to obtain approval by the Roman curia. Two years later, before the chapter meeting of 1223, Francis; the jurist, Brother Bonizio; and Francis's faithful scribe, Brother Leo, secluded themselves in the Fonte Columbo hermitage in the mountains outside of Rieti. The valley of Rieti was a few days' journey south of Assisi between the lush Reatini and Sabini mountains. The limestone mountains harbored many caves formed from splits in the ancient rocks. In one such narrow cave overlooking a steep, heavily wooded mountain slope of holm oaks, Francis prayed and prepared a revision of the rule for the 1223 chapter.

Brother Leo had been through this exercise before with Francis and, like Francis, was becoming weary of it. Remembering the fiasco that had taken place after Francis's departure to the East, Leo grudgingly understood the value of clear legislation. Francis's health was obviously declining, and Leo had to face the inevitable reality that his friend's ability to guide the brothers personally was coming to an end. On the other hand, the need to legislate what had in the early years of the community been accepted spontaneously and generously, pained Leo's heart. The brothers were preaching the Gospel to nearly every corner of the known world, but, in their desire to receive the respect and support needed to be successful in their preaching mission, they were at times compromising their dedication to the poverty and powerlessness of the Poor Christ.

The June 11, 1223, Pentecost chapter approved with some revisions the work that Francis composed at the hermitage of Fonte Columbo. After the chapter, Francis set out for Rome to obtain Pope Honorius III's definitive confirmation. As soon as they entered Rome, Francis, weary and ill, knocked at the palazzo of Jacopa dei Settesoli, a Roman noblewoman of high rank. Over ten years ago, Francis had come to Rome to report Clare and Agnes's entrance to the Holy See. Jacopa, who had been just twenty-two at that time and recently widowed with two small children, heard Francis preach. Francis's words were balm to her sad, lonely, and desperate heart. Jacopa immediately extended an invitation for Francis and his brothers to stay in her home. This pious woman and the street preacher soon became close friends. Again in Rome, Francis depended upon Lady Jacopa's gracious hospitality while his dealings with the curia dragged on.

In the cold gray of December of 1223, the curia finally accepted Francis's rule. It was nearly Christmas, and Francis, weary of the tedious business of legislation, was eager to rest his mind in meditation on the poor, infant Christ.

*N*ow that he had provided for his brothers' future, Francis focused again on his original desire: to observe the holy Gospel in all things, and to follow the teaching and the footsteps of

Jesus Christ with great zeal and fervor of heart. He decided to spend Christmas in Greccio, a mountain hermitage that sat on a steep cliff a short distance north of Fonte Columbo.

"Francis," a voice resounded off the rugged, wooded cliffs. "Francis, welcome to Greccio!"

Francis interrupted his prayer to greet the familiar voice. "Giovanni," Francis exclaimed. "How good it is to see you! How are you and your wife?" Giovanni was a noble of Greccio who lived in a nearby castle and had a special love for Francis and his brothers.

"We are well, Francis," Giovanni replied, "and since you have last seen me, God has given my wife and me a baby boy." Francis looked at the youthful Giovanni. He was a strong man, but still had the innocence of a boy. Francis loved him like a son.

"What glorious news, Giovanni!" Francis embraced his friend. "You will be a good father. You know what is important in God's eyes."

"You will stay in Greccio for Christmas, won't you, Francis?" Giovanni asked.

"I have just gotten here, Giovanni!" Francis laughed. "I am tired and need time to pray. We can talk about plans for Christmas later."

"All right," said the energetic Giovanni, "but I am assuming that you will not miss the chance to celebrate my son's first Christmas."

Giovanni paused, shocked by how frail and weak Francis had become. "Let me know if you need anything," Giovanni said gently, grasping his friend's arm. Giovanni was off as quickly as he had come. He loved Francis's company, but also respected his need for solitude.

Francis's exhausted spirit found it difficult to settle into prayer. The horrors of Damietta and the brothers' need for detailed legislation haunted him. When he closed his eyes he saw bloodshed, heard the cries of battle, knew the wrenching agony of losses, and remembered the cruelty and rapacity of the victor. At other times he heard his brothers wrangling over this or that particularity, seemingly impervious to the desire to give everything back to God with total generosity. Francis discovered that his spirit was bruised by war and legal wrangling. The demons taunted him, their unholy, negative voices echoing in his weary mind.

"It was all for nothing, Francis. There is no peace. You have no peace. Your brothers cannot live in peace. It is folly to think that Jesus Christ can bring peace to the world. You are a fool, Francis. You are a miserable, sick, stupid fool who is only a burden on his brothers. You have failed, Francis. It was all a dream; it was all a miserable dream."

Each time Francis closed his eyes, the demonic voices tormented him in the darkness. If Francis opened his eyes, the light glaring off the fresh December snow sent piercing pain through his temples. Francis longed to regain the peace of earlier days. He sought to enter into more complete aloneness in order that he might meet again the Savior of his soul.

About fifteen days before Christmas, Francis was finishing a meal at the hermitage with his brothers. "Brother Masseo," Francis said, "please go to Lord Giovanni's castle and ask him if he would be so kind as to come and see me." Brother Masseo immediately left. He and Brother Leo were so worried about Francis. Lord Giovanni was a good friend, and Francis was so happy about his new baby. Surely, a meeting with Giovanni would lift Francis's spirits.

"Brother Francis," Giovanni's young, energetic voice proceeded him. "Brother Francis, I'm here. It's Giovanni!"

Francis came out of the hermitage happy to hear his friend, although not opening his painful eyes until the voice came nearer. "Thank you so much for coming, Giovanni," Francis said.

"Oh, it's a pleasure," Giovanni assured Francis.

"How's your baby boy?" Francis inquired.

"He is good, Francis, and growing so fast. You have to come and see him. My wife and I are hoping that you will stay in Greccio for Christmas, and that you and the brothers will join us for Christmas dinner."

"I've been thinking about Christmas, too," Francis said. "If you want us to stay here for Christmas, Giovanni, we must think about preparing the Christmas liturgy. I have an idea. This year, I would like to see with my own eyes the infant who was born in Bethlehem. I want to see the baby lying in a manger, with his mother and father, shepherds, ox, and ass, just like it is written in the Gospel story."

"This can be done, Francis." Giovanni wrinkled his brow as he began to think through the details. "What should we do about the angels?" Giovanni asked, grinning impishly.

"God will provide the angels." Francis chuckled. "Brother Masseo will gather the brothers from all the surrounding areas for the liturgy."

"Yes, and I will announce the celebration to the people of Greccio." Giovanni's mind was racing. "I will work with Brothers Leo and Masseo to get everything ready. Don't worry about anything!"

Two weeks later, a light snow fell on the Greccio mountain. Francis could make out torches winding up the step slope toward the brothers' hermitage. Giovanni had announced to all that Francis was going to preach the Christmas sermon. A large group of brothers had met in Greccio and were leading the procession of worshipers up the mountain singing hymns of anticipation through the forest of beeches and oaks.

At the hermitage, Giovanni and the brothers had outdone themselves. In a stone grotto they had placed a large pile of straw. As the ceremony began, an ox and ass were led through the crowd of worshipers and tied to posts in the grotto. Giovanni, his wife, and their newborn son followed the animals. Shepherds with some sheep from the valley took their place proudly at the front of the assembly. The brothers mixed with the crowd, their resounding voices leading the congregation in song. Francis held the book of the Gospels high as he squinted through his diseased eyes that ceased to pain him in the gentle flickering light of torches and candles. Incense wafted over the crowd and disappeared quickly into the crisp, mountain air.

"Glory to God in the highest," the congregation sang with the angels, "and on earth peace to all of good will." Francis, clothed in a white linen and silk vestment embroidered in gold that Clare had made for him, sang the Gospel. As he preached, his beautiful voice rang through the snow-laden woods.

"Ring out your joy to God our help," Francis proclaimed. His feet made dancing movements as he spoke. "Shout with cries of gladness to the Lord God living and true! For the Lord, the most high, the awesome, is the great king over all the earth. For the most holy Father of heaven, our King before all ages has sent his beloved Son, Jesus Christ, from on high and he was born of the Blessed Virgin Mary."

"This is the day the Lord has made," Francis cried out.

"Let us rejoice and be glad in it," the congregation joyfully responded.

"For the most holy beloved child is given to us," Francis continued, waving his hand toward Giovanni's child, who was quietly resting in the arms of his mother. "Jesus Christ, the babe of Bethlehem, was born for us along the way!" Francis paused, and then cried out, "He was placed in a manger, because there was no room for him in the inn."

"Glory to God in the highest and on earth peace to all of good will," the congregation, led by Brother Masseo, sang out.

"Let the heavens be glad and the earth rejoice!" Francis continued. "Let the sea and all that is in it be moved! Let the fields and everything that is in them be joyful!"

"Sing a new song to the Lord!" Francis intoned.

"Sing to the Lord all the earth!" the brothers responded.

"For the Lord is great and worthy of all praise," Francis shouted. "God is awesome, beyond all gods," the brothers sang out. "Give to the Lord, you families of nations!" Francis exclaimed. "Give to the Lord glory and praise," the brothers responded. "Jesus Christ was born for us along the way!" Francis continued.

"He was placed in a manger because there was no room for him in the inn."

"Glory to God in the highest and on earth peace to all of good will," the entire congregation sang out, led by Brother Masseo.

Francis remembered a Christmas antiphon that Clare and her sisters had taught him. Exhausted in body, but refreshed in spirit, he intoned the hymn in order to give himself a little time to recover his strength. Brother Masseo's bass voice boomed with joy, and Brother Leo joined him with his light but perfectly pitched baritone voice. Masseo waved his arms through the crowd as the brothers and the people of Greccio caught on to the simple antiphon:

> *O marvelous humility!*
> *O stupendous poverty!*
> *The King of the angels,*
> *The Lord of heaven and earth,*
> *Is laid in a manger!*

The crowd repeated Clare's antiphon over and over. The children of Greccio were gathering around Giovanni and his wife, all hoping to hold or at least touch the baby. Seeing that Francis was ready, Masseo brought the song to a quiet close. Amidst the light snow, Francis's voice bleated gently, like a young lamb.

"Tonight, my dearest people of Greccio, we celebrate the great mystery of our God coming in human form and lying in a manger. Tonight with our own eyes we watch our Lord Jesus Christ taking on human flesh and coming to live among us in the form of a baby wrapped in swaddling clothes."

"Here with us tonight, God comes!" Francis gently took Giovanni's baby boy from his mother's arms and held him high in the air for all to see. "Our God comes as a baby," Francis announced. Moving behind the altar with the baby tucked securely in his left arm, Francis's raised his right hand: "He comes as food for all of us!"

"Look, brothers and sisters, at the humility of God," Francis continued. "Love God with all your heart and hold nothing back. Give yourselves totally to God, because God gives totally to you!"

The people of Greccio talked about the Christmas liturgy at the brothers' hermitage for months. Francis, who loved the piety and faithfulness of the people of Greccio, remained at the hermitage until after Easter. There, during the seasons of Christmas and Lent, he began to recover his sense of peace. He spent hours alone in the woods listening to the prayer of birds, watching the play of animals, and savoring the smells and gentle breezes of early spring.

"Brother Francis!" Francis looked up the path from his cave, but in the bright sunlight he could not make out his visitor.

"Brother Francis," Leo repeated, edging carefully down the acorn-laden path toward the cave that Francis was using for prayer.

"Brother Francis." Leo stood before his friend, breathless and excited.

"Yes, Brother Leo, what is it?" Francis asked.

"I found this rabbit caught in a trap," Leo explained.

Francis took the rabbit from Brother Leo and gently placed it on the ground in front of him. The rabbit stared at Francis with wide, dark eyes, and shivered nervously. Knowing that Francis would give the poor rabbit compassion and comfort, Leo walked back up the hill.

"Brother Rabbit," Francis encouraged the animal, reaching his hand out slowly and then gently patting its backside. "Do not be afraid, Brother Rabbit. You are free to go wherever you please." The rabbit bobbed its head, hopped a few paces, and hesitated. "What is wrong, Brother Rabbit?" Francis asked.

Hearing Francis's gentle voice, the rabbit turned, lifted its ears, twitched its nose, studied Francis's face for a long time, and then made its way back to him. Francis slowly put out his hands. The rabbit paused about an arm's length from Francis, who slowly picked up the rabbit and settled it in his lap. He petted the quivering animal gently.

"Brother Rabbit," Francis cooed. "You do not want to let yourself be trapped again." Not wanting to further frighten the creature, Francis gave the rabbit one last stroke, and placed him tenderly on the ground. "You may go now, Brother Rabbit," Francis said, again gently patting it on its back.

The animal hopped a short distance and then turned to stare as if longing to return to the safety and protection of Francis's lap. "Brother Rabbit, you are so good to me," Francis smiled. "You know that the mountain winds are still cool, and that Brother Francis does not wear fur. You wish me to cuddle you so that I will be able to stay warm."

Francis slowly reached out his hands, and the rabbit willingly allowed him to hold it. He petted the rabbit, calming it by holding it close to his heart. When placing it on his lap, the rabbit settled in, perfectly content to remain there.

"Brother Rabbit," Francis continued, "surely you can go now." Again Francis placed the rabbit on the ground, and gave it one last loving pat. The animal turned around again, looking at Francis with big brown eyes. It twitched its ears and then laid them back again, comforted to be in Francis's presence. Francis picked it up, and the rabbit snuggled in his lap, while Francis prayed.

Later that afternoon, Francis arrived at the hermitage carrying the rabbit.

"Brother Masseo," Francis said. "Brother Rabbit and I have grown very fond of each other, but it is time for him to return to the forest."

"Brother Rabbit," Francis held the animal to his face and twitched his nose playfully against the cold nose of the rabbit, "you know now not to get yourself caught in another trap. Do not be afraid, and let Brother Masseo take you back to the woods."

Brother Masseo disappeared down one path with the rabbit, while Francis took another way back to his cell, his heart full of love for all of God's creation.

*D*uring the final days of Lent, the brothers saw little of Francis. On Easter Sunday, the brothers at the Greccio hermitage set the table with white linens and glassware in honor of the feast. Coming from the woods, Francis, leaning heavily on his walking stick, entered the hermitage and saw that the table had been extravagantly decorated. No one had seen him enter, so he retraced his steps, borrowed the hat of a poor man who was staying with the brothers at the hermitage, and, staff in hand, went back into the woods. He waited there until the brothers began to eat. They were in the habit of not waiting for him when he did not come after the bell for meals rang out.

"For the love of the Lord God," Francis shouted, disguising his voice. "Give alms to this poor, sick wanderer." He had pulled the hat down low on his forehead, so that it obscured most of his face.

"Come in, for the love of God." Brother Angelo mistook him for a beggar and invited him in while chewing a mouthful of vegetables.

Francis entered and refused to sit at the table, so the brothers gave him a dish. Sitting alone, he took off his hat and put the dish in the ashes of the fire. "I am sitting as a Friar Minor should sit," Francis announced. "We should be moved by the example of the poverty and humility of the Son of God even more than other religious. I saw the table prepared and decorated, and I knew that it was not the table of poor people who beg from door to door."

Brother Leo was so ashamed that he could hardly hold back his tears. Brother Masseo immediately took his plate and not only placed it in the ashes, but sprinkled ashes on top of his food as a penance for presuming to eat like the rich. Brothers Leo and Angelo followed, and soon all the brothers joined Francis sitting near the fire. Brother Masseo ran back and forth serving the food, while the brothers enjoyed their Easter meal on the floor, just as they had done in the early days of the order.

After Easter, Francis returned to Saint Mary of the Angels and rested there for a number of months. Seeing that some of the brothers were over-anxious about the success of their ministries, Francis preached to them a passage from their earlier rule.

"Let us be on guard, dear brothers, that we do not turn our minds and hearts away from the Lord under the guise of achieving some reward, or of doing some work, or of providing some help. In the holy love that is God, I beg all of you, my brothers, to overcome every obstacle and to put aside every care and anxiety so that each of you might strive, as best as you can, to serve, love, honor, and adore the Lord God with a clean heart and a pure mind. This is what God desires above all else."

In early August, Francis, with Masseo, Leo, and Angelo, left Saint Mary of the Angels for the mountain hermitage of La Verna, a few days' journey north of Assisi high in the Apennines.

13

La Verna

The business of the Pentecost chapter meeting at the Portiuncula had exhausted Francis. Stooped and ravaged by sickness, it was only the fire in his soul and the solicitude of his brothers that gave Francis the energy to climb Mount La Verna's treacherous slope. Numb with weakness, Francis closed his eyes, happy to be alone in the inconspicuous little hut of branches and mud that the brothers had built for him about a stone's throw from the brothers' hermitage. His shelter was protected by a colossal, winnowing beech tree that overshadowed a little plot of green, while itself clinging tenaciously to the rocky edge of a sheer precipice. Under the tree's outstretched branches, Francis sat in his hut quietly, his worries lulled by the patter of the raindrops on its leaves.

"I will die soon," Francis admitted to Brother Leo. "I need time alone in order to recollect myself and weep over my sins before God. Whenever it seems right to you, Brother Leo, bring me a little bread and water. Do not let anyone other than our brothers come to see me. You can take care of whatever needs anyone else has yourself."

"Blessed aloneness!" Francis sighed as the rhythm of the gentle rain hushed his wearied soul. The mountain lit up in a dazzling flash of lightning and seemed to shudder from the repeated strikes.

"The rocks split," Francis remembered the words from the Lord's Passion. The prayer that had absorbed him in his Lenten days at Greccio returned to him like an old, familiar friend. "All of you who pass by the way, look and see if there is any sorrow like unto my sorrow."

Francis closed his eyes in order to see the blessed eyes of his Master. The pain from his crown of thorns was mirrored in Francis's own swollen temples. Yes, Francis had felt the agony of his sorrow, not over his brothers' missionary zeal, but over their persistent attempts to mitigate the Gospel message under the guise of health, convenience, honor, and success. Francis gazed with compassion into the sorrow of his harrowed, anguished Jesus, and rested there.

"Many dogs have surrounded me. A pack of evildoers has closed in upon me. They looked and gawked at me. They divided my garments among them and for my tunic they cast lots."

Francis fingered his torn, stained tunic. "When I die, they will fight over this." He shook his head and smiled. It was a foolish distraction; his mind returned to the sorrow of his Lord.

"They pierced my hands and my feet. They have numbered all of my bones." One by one, Francis pondered the wounds of his beloved Jesus. He took refuge in those precious hands that healed, and in those feet that made all of the earth God's footstep.

"They looked and gawked at me. They have pierced my hands and my feet. They have counted all of my bones. I am poured out like water, and all my bones have been scattered."

The thunder boomed again. The rain danced, cooling the thirsty August stone.

"My strength is dried up like baked clay," Francis prayed. Truly, he had no more strength. His fever raged and his eyes were nearly blind. In spite of his desire to serve God, Francis feared that he had accomplished nothing during his lifetime. His brothers preached, but they did not love poverty.

"Do they love you, Jesus?" Francis anguished. He pondered again the face and wounds of his beloved Christ. "Do they love you?"

Jesus's eyes returned sorrow for Francis's sorrow. In the silence, Francis gazed with love into those tender eyes.

"Do they love peace? Do they wish to be united to the poor Christ who was scorned, broken, and mocked? Have I been an example? I am a wretched sinner. Oh God, be merciful to me, a sinner," Francis anguished, his tears flowing, like cleansing rain.

"I am an outcast to my brothers and a stranger to the children of my mother."

"No," Francis thought, "I am a stranger to my own children. I have borne children who do not understand their mother's heart."

Francis thought of Pica, his own mother. He remembered her pious deeds, her fine features, her bruises. "What do I know of her?" Francis wondered. Where did she come from? What did she love? What had she thought of her son?

"It is the role of a mother to bear pain, to give birth, to weep, and to remain alone — utterly self-giving in her love," Francis admitted.

"Holy Father, zeal for your house has consumed me and the insults of those who attacked you have fallen on me."

The lightning blitzed across the night sky, dancing wildly amidst the now pouring rain.

"My strength is dried up like baked clay. My tongue cleaves to my jaws."

A cool wind swept through Francis's little cell, while overhead the majestic beech creaked in the squall.

"They have pierced my hands and my feet," Francis repeated. "They have counted all my bones."

It was as if the La Verna mountain, lashed by the storm, reflected the upheaval in Francis's body and soul. Gusts of chilling wind swept hissing doubts, and the purified, oxygenated air calmed the nagging fever of Francis's mind and body.

"Sister Water, so pure and clean," Francis whispered. He put his head outside the hut and blindly turned his face up to receive the full brunt of the storm. He rested in the water and in the love of his Lord.

A stone's throw away, Brother Leo was also awake, pacing in desperate anguish. His mentor and friend would soon die. At the thought, hot tears spilled over Leo's wind-chapped cheeks.

"Will I have the courage to embrace the poverty of Jesus Christ with all my heart without Francis's example?" Leo wondered. "I am not gifted in preaching or in prayer. I am a secretary and a mother hen, but not an exemplary man; there is nothing inside of me that is great or noble." Leo's anguished heart pulsed with scrupulous tears. "I am a lukewarm man — a man who is harsh and critical of others. I am an unloving, parsimonious person."

Given an entrance, the devil's disparaging judgments infiltrated Leo's heart and soul. "I am a small man," Leo fretted. "I have tried to repent of my faults, but my repentance has not borne fruit. I stay near to Francis so that I can walk in his virtue. Without him, I am a dry, uncharitable, uninspiring, and uninspired man."

Morning could not come soon enough for the tortured Brother Leo. At the first rays of dawn, he took a small piece of bread and a little water and hurried to Francis's cell.

"Brother Francis," Leo called gently. "Brother Francis, it is Leo." There was no response. He peered into the cottage and saw Francis deep in prayer.

"Brother Francis," Leo cried out again. "Brother Francis, please, it is Leo."

Francis recognized the troubled voice and slowly emerged from the depths of his prayer. Brother Leo waited.

"What do I really want from Francis?" Leo asked himself. "How can Francis help me? He would give me anything, if I just knew what to ask of him."

Leo paced back and forth. "Brother Francis," Leo shouted more loudly. "Brother Francis, it is your Brother Leo."

"If I had something of his," Leo thought, desperately wondering what that might be. "If I had a piece of writing, a piece of writing that Francis wrote for my soul."

"Brother Francis," Leo continued to call.

Francis hobbled out of the cell and looked, still dazed, toward Brother Leo. "He doesn't even see me," Leo admitted. "Brother Francis," Leo called, "may I come in?"

"Of course, Brother Leo," Francis replied. "You are here early this morning."

As he walked toward his mentor, Leo already felt better. "I worry too much," he thought, but he was still plagued by self-doubt. As Leo approached, he studied the face of his friend. Francis's eyes were partly closed by the residue of a discharge that had not been totally washed away by the tears and rain of the night.

"So many of my brothers seem lost in this world," Francis said, noticing that Leo was staring at his soiled habit. "They suffer with the Crucified, while I can do little other than pray for them."

Instinctively, Leo pulled his habit over his head. "Here, Francis," Leo said, handing Francis his tunic. "Give me your habit so that I can wash it."

Francis nodded and bent over in a painful effort to slip his tunic over his head. Leo, naked except for his breeches, immediately assisted him, replacing Francis's stained habit with his own.

"I'll wash it and bring it back to you right away," Leo said, dutifully wadding Francis's dirty tunic under his arm.

"Thank you, Brother Leo," Francis replied weakly. The pain in his abdomen was becoming so severe that he could no longer stand up straight. There were so many things that he could no longer do, and depending on his brothers for these things was difficult. "Brother Leo," Francis asked as Leo turned to go back, "could you bring me an inkhorn, pen, and parchment?"

Brother Leo froze in his tracks; did Francis perceive the anguish of his soul and know the comfort a parchment written for him in Francis's own hand would bring? No, Francis must have other business. His request had nothing to do with Leo.

Suddenly remembering that he was carrying Francis's bread and water, Leo handed them to him and then hurried back to his cell. Throwing Francis's tunic on a stool, he gathered ink-horn, pen, and parchment, and ran back.

"You are a good man, Brother Leo." Francis took the writing materials and sat on the ground, using a flat ledge of rock as a desk. He wrote quickly and intently as though his pen could not write fast enough to capture the outflowing sentiments of his soul. At the bottom of the page, Leo saw him draw the Tau cross, begging God for the salvation of all.

"Take this parchment, dear Brother, and keep it carefully until you die," Francis admonished Leo. "May God bless you and protect you from all temptation. Do not be troubled because you are tempted. The more you have temptations, the more I consider you a servant and friend of God, and the more I love you. Truly I tell you that no one should consider himself a perfect friend of God until he has passed through many temptations and tribulations."

Leo could not hold back his tears. How did Francis know the torment of his soul? Leo's doubts and temptations fell away in the presence of Francis's unconditional love. With Francis's grace perhaps he, too, could be a great lover of God.

Not knowing what else to do, Leo kissed Francis's hands. Francis smiled kindly and waved for him to go. Safe inside his cell, Leo sat on the floor, eager to read Francis's words to him.

"Brother Leo," the letter said. "Brother Francis wishes you health and peace! I speak to you, my son, as a mother. I place all the words that we spoke on the road in this phrase briefly, and as advice for you. If it is necessary for you to come to me for counsel, I say this to you. In whatever way it seems best for you to please the Lord God and to follow in his footsteps and his poverty, do this with the blessing of God and with my obedience. And if you believe it necessary for the well-being of your soul, or to find comfort, and you wish to come to me, Leo, come!"

Brother Leo put the letter on the floor safely in front of him, placed his head in his hands, and sobbed. There were brothers in Germany, England, Spain, France, Italy, Hungary, and the East. There were now thousands of brothers. Many of these brothers regarded Francis as a holy man, but only Brother Leo held in his hands an invitation to approach Francis day or night for the good of his soul. Leo gazed at the tiny birds fluttering in the brushes outside of his little window. The sun was warm and the puddles left by last night's rain were evaporating in hazy mists of purified mountain air.

"I am a sinner," Leo admitted, "a sinner who is loved. A sinner who is loved by both God and Brother Francis."

Francis, both touched by Leo's visit and recognizing Leo's need for his compassion and teaching, felt a deep concern for all his brothers. "Lord God, when I am gone, what will happen to your poor little family that you have entrusted to this sinner?

Who will console them? Who will correct them? Who will pray to you for them?"

Francis knew that God understood the anguish of his heart. In the quiet, words of consolation rose within him. "Do not grieve if you see some brothers who are not good and who do not observe the rule as they should. Do not think that, because of them, your community is declining. There will always be many who will observe perfectly the Gospel life of Christ."

Francis placed his hand on the trunk of the mighty beech tree. Protected by its shade, Francis could see clouds of mist rising from the precipice.

The Feast of the Assumption of the Virgin Mary on August 15 marked the beginning of Francis's annual fast in honor of Saint Michael. He wished to be more secluded during this time, so he and Brother Leo searched for a remote spot to set up another hermitage. On the south side of the mountain, they spotted an area that was isolated and perfectly suited for this purpose, but it could not be reached, because in front of it there was a very deep chasm in the rock. Leo gathered the brothers who hoisted a log across the chasm to serve as a bridge and built Francis a small hut.

"Go back to your place and leave me here alone," Francis said to his brothers, "because with the Lord's help I intend to spend this time without distraction or disturbance of mind. None of you must come to me."

Brother Leo began to panic. How would Francis eat? What would happen if Leo needed him for the good of his soul?

"Brother Leo," Francis smiled, sensing Leo's anxiety, "you may come once a day with a little bread and water, and once again late at night for the hour of Matins. When it is time for Matins come quietly, and when you reach the end of the bridge say: 'Lord, open my lips.' If you hear me answer, 'and my mouth shall declare your praise,' come into my cell, and we will say Matins together. If I do not reply, then go right back and do not disturb me."

Francis was usually awake when Leo called him. A falcon, who had its nest near Francis's cell, woke him up every night before Matins by crying out and beating its wings against the side of the hermitage. It would not leave until Francis arose. Sometimes, when Francis was very weak or ill, the falcon would awaken him somewhat later. Francis took a great liking to this holy "bell" because the falcon helped him drive away all laziness and aided him in his prayer. Sometimes it kept him company during the daytime as well.

One night, just before the Feast of the Exaltation of the Holy Cross in September, Leo crossed the bridge to pray with Francis. "Lord, open my lips," Leo called out.

There was no response.

"Lord, open my lips," Leo tried again. Again there was silence.

Brother Leo did not return as Francis had instructed, but because he wanted with all his heart to learn from Francis, he entered his cell. The moon shone brightly through the open door. Francis wasn't there.

Leo tried not to panic. "Perhaps he is praying in the woods," he reasoned.

By the light of the moon, Leo made his way through the forest searching for Francis. Soon, he heard Francis's voice.

"Who are you, my dearest God, and what am I, but your vilest little worm and useless servant?" Francis prayed.

Leo paused, trying to hide behind a tree.

"Who are you, my dearest God, and what am I, but your vilest little worm and useless servant?" Francis repeated.

Francis chanted the prayer over and over. Leo stayed well hidden. As he peered once around the trunk of the tree, he saw Francis bathed in light. Filled with awe, Leo realized that he should not be there and decided to make his escape. Francis heard the sound of his feet across the twigs.

"Whoever you are, I command you, in the name of our Lord Jesus Christ, to stay where you are. Don't move from that spot!" Francis commanded.

Brother Leo froze and waited. "I have ruined everything," he thought. "I have betrayed the trust of my friend through blatant disobedience."

"Who are you?" Francis asked.

"I am Brother Leo, Father," Leo admitted, wiping his hands down the sides of his habit.

"Why did you come here, little Brother Lamb?" Francis asked. "Did I not tell you many times not to eavesdrop on me? Tell me, under holy obedience, what you saw or heard."

Brother Leo was shaking. He grasped the letter that Francis had written for him that he had sewn in a little pocket over his heart. His heart pounded wildly. "Father," Leo sobbed, "I heard you praying and saying with great wonder, 'Who are you, my dearest God, and what am I, but your vilest little worm and useless servant.' I also saw you bathed in light."

Leo fell to his knees and begged Francis to forgive his disobedience. Francis put his hands on Leo's shoulders. Leo knew that he was forgiven, but he still had many questions. He tried to summon his courage. Time was running out. "Father

Francis," Leo ventured, "please explain to me the experience of prayer that I saw you having this night."

While usually very private about the intimacy of his prayer, Francis was open to sharing with Leo because of his purity and meekness. Since God had already allowed Leo to witness his prayer, it would be unkind to leave him with only questions.

"Little Brother Lamb of Jesus Christ," Francis gently addressed the weeping Leo. "Tonight God showed me two truths. One was of knowledge and understanding of the Creator, and the other was of knowledge of myself. When I prayed, 'Who are you, my dearest God,' I contemplated the depths of the infinite goodness, wisdom, and power of God. When I said, 'What am I?' I saw the depths of my vileness and misery. So I prayed, 'Who are you, the Lord of infinite wisdom and goodness and mercy, that you visit me, a vile and contemptible worm?'"

Leo's eyes were wide open, trying to memorize Francis's every word. Francis paused and studied the face of his simple brother.

"Be careful, Brother Leo, not to go watching me anymore. Now go back to your cell with the blessing of God. I am grateful to you for taking such good care of me," Francis assured him, placing his hand on Leo's arm.

The mid-September Feast of the Holy Cross was only a few days away. "Leo," Francis said, "bring to me the book of the Gospels." Leo crossed the log bridge, went back to the brothers' hermitage, and returned with the Gospel book. Francis knelt with Leo in prayer and both remained silent for a long time. Finally, Leo opened one eye; Francis was still praying. Leo closed his eye again, holding the book tightly to his chest. After waiting for an extended period of time, Leo opened his eyes and wiped his hand on his habit.

"Brother Leo," Francis said noticing Leo's restlessness. "Let us open the Gospels three times to see what the Lord will tell us."

Leo handed the book to the almost blind Francis. Francis remembered the morning that he and Brothers Peter and Bernard sought direction from the Lord at the little church of San Nicolo. Everything had been so simple, so exciting then.

Francis pointed, and Leo began to read. Each time Francis opened the book a reading from the passion of Christ appeared. Francis understood; he was approaching the moment of his martyrdom.

He had given away his clothes so that he might become one with the poor Christ. He had followed the wandering Christ, and had been called "crazy" by his family. Like him, he had preached to the crowds, and had cared for the sick. Now, he would follow the crucified Christ, enduring the passion of God's unconditional love in a sinful world.

As Leo expected, Francis did not answer his call the next few days, but retreated even more deeply into prayer. "My Lord Jesus Christ," Francis prayed. "I pray that you grant me two graces before I die. The first is that during my life, I may feel in my soul and in my body as much as possible, the pain which you, dear Jesus, sustained in the hour of your most bitter passion. The second is that I may feel in my heart as much as possible that excessive love with which you, O Son of God, were inflamed in willingly enduring such suffering for us sinners."

With this prayer, Francis contemplated with intense devotion the passages from the passion of Christ that Brother Leo had read. He pondered the infinite and unconditional love of God and the poverty of his own love. He gazed again into the eyes of his Master.

"The bitter will become sweet, and the sweet will become bitter." The words of Jesus played as a mantra in Francis's wearied soul.

"I wish to be united to both your anguish and your love," Francis uttered. "I wish to be united to both your anguish and your love."

Francis prayed throughout the night. In the morning, Leo announced, "O Lord, open my lips." Francis did not reply.

The following night, shepherds in the area saw the mountain aflame with intense light. In the village of Romagna, a short distance from La Verna, the light came through the windows of an inn, and the muleteers, confused and thinking that the sun had risen, saddled and loaded their animals. They were already on their way when they saw the light extinguished and the real sun rise.

Francis woke from his contemplation of the glorious crucified Christ with both joyous consolation and sheering pain. There began to appear on his hands and feet the marks of nails as if he had been crucified with his beloved Jesus. The nails extended through the back of his hands and the soles of his feet and seemed to be bent and beaten back. The heads of the nails were round and black. On Francis's right side a wound appeared, an incision from a spear; it was open and inflamed. Blood often flowed from it, staining his habit and breeches.

Masseo, Angelo, Illuminato, and Leo noticed that Francis did not let anyone see his hands or feet, and that he could not put the soles of his feet on the ground. They also noticed, when they washed his clothes, that his habit and breeches were bloody. Francis realized that he could not hide what had happened to him, but he was perplexed because he had always been careful not to flaunt God's intimacy with him. Uncertain about what to do, Francis conferred with the discreet Brother Illuminato, who was able to help Francis settle his conscience.

"Brother Francis," Illuminato said, "you know that God sometimes shows us divine mysteries not only for ourselves but also for the sake of others. You should greatly fear being judged guilty of concealing something that God has shown you for the sake of many."

Convinced by Illuminato's argument, Francis described what he had experienced in the recent months of his solitude. Although his wounds gave him great joy of heart, they also caused him almost unbearable pain. Francis needed someone to help him care for his wounds, so Brother Leo solicitously applied ointments and bandages. Francis allowed Leo to change the bandages every day except from Thursday evening until Saturday morning. During this time, he did not want to temper the pain of Christ's passion with any remedy. For the love of Christ, he wished to experience in his own body the sufferings Christ felt on the cross.

*A*fter the Feast of Saint Michael at the end of September, Francis bade farewell to his brothers and started the journey southward toward Assisi with Brother Leo. Brothers Masseo, Angelo, and Illuminato wept profusely, thinking that they might never see him again. A devout peasant accompanied Leo and Francis. Francis rode on the peasant's donkey because, given the wounds in his feet, he could barely walk.

The shepherds had reported throughout the valley what they had seen. When the people of the district heard that Francis was passing by, all of them, rich and poor, noble and commoner, came out to see him. With devotion and desire they wanted to touch him and kiss his hands. Francis had Leo bind his hands in double bandages, and he covered his palms with his sleeves, leaving bare only his fingers for the people to kiss.

As Francis was riding near a village on the border of the commune of Arezzo, a woman came to him, weeping and carrying her eight-year-old son in her arms. The boy had had dropsy for four years, and his stomach was so swollen that when he stood up, he could not see his legs or his feet. The woman placed her boy before Francis and begged him to pray to God for him. Francis dismounted the donkey, prayed over the little boy, and put his hands over the boy's stomach. As he did this, the swelling disappeared, and the boy was cured. Francis gave him back to his mother, who proclaimed throughout the region what Francis had done for her child.

That same day, Francis passed through Borgo San Sepolcro. Before he came near the town, crowds from the city and the fields ran to meet him. Many of them went before him with olive branches crying out loudly, "Here comes the saint! Here comes the saint!"

The crowd pressed around Francis, but although he was touched and pulled in all directions, Francis stayed calm. He had seen on La Verna a vision of the next world, and even with the pressing throngs, Francis remained rapt in the peaceful contemplation of God.

That evening, Francis arrived at the brothers' house at Monte Casale. There was a brother in this house who was tormented by seizures. When Francis, sitting at table, heard the friars tell about the serious and incurable sickness of this brother, he felt compassion for him. He took a piece of bread that he was eating, made the sign of the cross over it, and sent it to the sick friar. As soon as the brother had eaten the bread, he was healed and never again suffered from seizures.

Francis rested at Monte Casale for several days, and then made the short journey south toward Perugia to Città di Castello. He sent two brothers from Monte Casale to escort the peasant and his donkey back home to La Verna. At Città di Castello, the citizens brought a deranged woman to Francis who was disturbing the whole neighborhood with mournful howling and piercing shrieks. Francis prayed, made the sign of the cross over her, and commanded the devil to leave her. The devil immediately departed, leaving her sound in mind and body.

As the news of this miracle spread among the people, another woman brought to him her young son who was seriously ill with a terrible ulcer. With great faith, she asked Francis to make the sign of the cross over her little boy. Francis took the child, raised the bandage over the sore, and made the sign of the cross three times over the ulcer. He then bound it up again with his own hands and gave the child back to his mother. Since it was evening, the mother immediately put her son to bed. The next morning when she went to take him from the bed, she found that the bandage had fallen off and, looking at the ulcer, she saw that her son was completely healed.

Francis stayed at Città di Castello for one month. During that time, he healed many. He then left to journey southward to Saint Mary of the Angels with Brother Leo and with a good man who loaned him a donkey.

It was a bitterly cold day. Francis rode the donkey, led by the peasant, while Leo walked a little ahead of them. In the early days of the brotherhood, Francis would often instruct and admonish his brothers during these long trips. Now Leo and Francis went in silence. Leo missed the early days.

"Brother Leo," Francis called.

Thinking that something was wrong, Brother Leo immediately stopped to attend to Francis.

"Brother Leo," Francis continued. "If the brothers in every country gave perfect examples of holiness and integrity, Brother Leo, write it down and note carefully that perfect joy is not in that."

Brother Leo began to grope in his pocket for inkhorn, pen, and parchment. Francis smiled at the sight of his brother's frantic search for writing implements. He was glad to stop for a moment; he needed the rest. Brother Leo scratched furiously, writing down Francis's words. Francis nodded to him. Leo blew the ink dry and folded the parchment into his pocket.

When they had walked on a bit, Francis called, "Brother Leo." Leo stopped and again attended to his charge.

"Even if a brother gives sight to the blind, heals the paralyzed, drives out devils, gives hearing to the deaf, makes the lame walk, restores speech to the dumb, and brings back to life a person who has been dead for four days, write that perfect joy is not in that."

Leo again pulled out his ink, pen, and parchment. "Can you repeat what you just said again, Francis?" Leo asked. Francis repeated, and Leo wrote. Leo dried the ink, put the parchment in his pocket, and the three continued their journey.

"Brother Leo," Francis cried out strongly after they had gone just a little further. This time, Leo immediately reached for his writing supplies. "Brother Leo, if a brother knew all languages, all sciences, and scripture, and if he knew how to prophesy and reveal not only the future but also the secrets of the consciences

and the minds of others, write down and note carefully that
perfect joy is not in that."

Leo looked up at Francis who had ceased speaking and
was clinging weakly to his seat on the donkey. Leo wrote, blew
on the ink to dry it, and again placed the parchment in his
pocket.

They walked a little further, when Francis called out force-
fully. "Brother Leo, little lamb of God, even if a brother could
speak with the voice of an angel, and if he knew all the courses
of the stars and the powers of herbs, and if he knew all about
the treasures of the earth, and the qualities of birds and fishes,
animals, humans, roots, trees, rocks, and waters, write down
and note carefully that true joy is not in that."

They went on a bit further. Leo now kept the pen and
parchment in his hand and was leading the donkey, while
the peasant walked ahead. Francis called out. "Brother Leo,
even if a brother could preach so well that he could convert all
the infidels to the faith of Christ, write that perfect joy is not
there." Leo remembered Damietta, and the torrents of tears
that Francis had wept over the fallen city. He faithfully wrote
down Francis's words.

Francis kept this pattern up for a distance of two miles.
Finally, unable to contain his impatience and curiosity, Brother
Leo cried out: "Father, I beg you in God's name, to tell me
where perfect joy is."

Francis had been waiting for that question.

"When we come to Saint Mary of the Angels," Francis
explained, "soaked by the rain and frozen by the cold, all soiled
with mud and suffering from hunger, and we ring at the gate
and the Brother Porter comes out and says angrily: 'Who are
you?' We say, 'We are two of your brothers.' He contradicts us,
saying: 'You are not telling the truth. Rather you are two thieves
who go around deceiving people and stealing what is meant to
be given to the poor. Go away!' The Brother Porter does not
open for us, but makes us stand outside in the snow and rain,
cold and hungry, until night falls. If we endure all those insults

and cruel rebuffs patiently, without being troubled and without complaining, and if we reflect humbly and charitably that the porter really knows us, and that God makes him speak against us — Brother Leo, write that perfect joy is there!"

Brother Leo looked at Francis. There was a spark in his eye, a light that was obviously coming from a place far beyond his frail and ailing body.

"If we continue to knock," Francis continued, "and the porter comes out in anger, and drives us away with curses and hard blows like bothersome scoundrels, saying: 'Get away from here, you dirty thieves — go to the hospice! Who do you think you are? You certainly won't eat or sleep here!' If we bear this patiently and take the insults with joy and love in our hearts, oh, Brother Leo, write, this is perfect joy!"

Brother Leo could hardly write quickly enough to keep up with Francis's dictation. Without a pause, Francis continued.

"If later, suffering intensely from hunger and painful cold with night falling, we knock, call again, and loudly beg them to open for us for the love of God, and the porter grows even more angry and says: 'Those fellows are bold and shameless ruffians. I'll give them what they deserve!' And he comes out with a club and beats us, covering our bodies with wounds — if we endure all those evils, insults, and blows with joy and patience, reflecting that we must accept and bear the suffering of Jesus Christ patiently for love of him — Oh, Brother Leo, write, this is perfect joy!"

Brother Leo's mind was racing with objections. Surely it would not be good for every soul to hear this advice. He looked carefully at Francis's blind eyes and torn feet and hands. The depths of Christ's poverty had given Francis a freedom that few others would understand.

Francis was still on fire with his story. "Here is the conclusion, Brother Leo. Above all the graces and gifts of the Holy Spirit that Christ gives to his friends, the one of conquering oneself and willingly enduring sufferings, insults, humiliations, and hardships for the love of Christ is the greatest. For we cannot glory in any of the marvelous gifts of God. These gifts are not our own but God's, as the apostle says: 'What do you have, that you have not received?' We can, however, glory in the cross of tribulations and afflictions, because they are ours. As the apostle says: 'I will not glory except in the cross of our Lord Jesus Christ.'"

Leo knew that Francis had just confided his deepest secret. For so many years, he had wanted to know the depths of Francis's heart, and Francis had never confided this to him. Now, on the road in the middle of nowhere, Francis, without warning, shared the fruit of years of prayer and poverty with Brother Leo. Leo folded the parchment and placed it carefully in his pocket, not sure that he had been ready to hear these difficult words.

14
Assisi

It was December 1224, and a cold wind swept down from Mount Subasio into the Spoleto valley. Feeling out of place in the morning bustle of the brothers' house, Francis slowly hobbled outside, but soon sought shelter in the church of Saint Mary of the Angels. He pulled open the creaking wooden door and found the tiny church empty. Happy to be alone, Francis slowly worked his way toward the front of the church, nostalgically fingering the cold stone wall as he passed. He had repaired these very walls. He remembered the tonsure ceremonies of Bernard and Peter, and smiled when he recalled Clare's radiant loveliness the night he cut her hair before this very altar. He relived the many chapter meetings at the Portiuncula. He felt proud of the generosity of his brothers in traveling great distances to preach the Gospel. He remembered the disagreements, the legislative wrangling, and the pettiness that sometimes occurred. Placing his hands squarely on the cold stone, he recalled the many hours he had prayed and sought direction in this tiny church.

Francis longed for days past when he served the lepers and was held in contempt. He feared that his days of mountain solitude were over. He was now known as a holy man and a miracle worker. "It was better when I was ridiculed and thought of as a fool," Francis admitted to himself.

The friars were eager to attend to their famous, suffering brother, and vied with each other for the opportunity to care for him. Francis longed for solitude and for peace. It was also becoming obvious that the cold foggy dampness of the valley aggravated his symptoms. Seeing Francis's need, Leo and Bernard searched for a place nearby where he could enjoy greater solitude in a less damp location. San Damiano was the obvious answer.

Four brothers, who begged and served as chaplains for Clare and her sisters, stayed in the small quarters attached to the San Damiano monastery that had once been occupied by the now deceased Father Pietro. The sisters' monastery consisted of a cloister, choir, and refectory on the ground floor, and a dormitory, oratory, and infirmary on the second floor, while the brothers lived in rooms attached to the front of the church, with sleeping quarters on a lower level that was built into the hill. Francis asked the brothers to build him a little hut of mats anchored onto a wall of this lower level. San Damiano was quiet, and the brothers positioned Francis's hermitage so that it was both sheltered from the wind and exposed to the warmth of the afternoon sun. Francis's eyes could no longer tolerate even the light of a fire, and for two months he remained in the hut in total darkness. His eyes caused him so much pain, he could neither lie down nor sleep.

Just above in the dormitory of San Damiano, Sister Clare was also ill and confined to bed. Her sisters tried their best to ease Clare's concern over Francis by preparing food that they hoped Francis's ailing stomach could digest.

Day and night, there were mice running around the hermitage that would boldly scamper right over Francis, so that he could neither sleep nor pray. One night, weary of his tribulations, Francis felt sorry for himself. "Lord, help me in my troubles so that I may have the strength to bear them patiently!" he pleaded.

"Tell me, Brother," the Lord answered. "If, in compensation for your sufferings, you were given an immense and precious treasure, the whole earth changed into pure gold, pebbles into precious stones, and the waters of the rivers into perfume, would you not regard the pebbles and the waters as nothing compared to such a treasure? Would you not rejoice?"

"Lord," Francis answered, "that would be a very great, precious, and inestimable treasure!"

"Well, Brother," the Lord continued, "be glad and rejoice in the midst of your infirmities. Right now, live in peace as though you were already sharing my kingdom."

Francis closed his weary and painful eyes. He knew from experience that the Lord's love was worth far more than gold and precious stones. "Live in peace as though you were already sharing my kingdom," the Lord had said. Subjecting himself to the power of his Master's unconditional love, Francis imagined himself in the midst of the angels and saints before the throne of God.

A mouse ran over his face, pouncing on his swollen eyes. "Are you playing in praise of God, Brother Mouse?" Francis addressed the creature that had long since escaped into a corner.

Francis could hear another mouse approach, pause, and then scamper off. "The creatures of the earth praise God and minister to our needs," Francis reflected. "Without them, we cannot live. So often, we use the gifts of the earth to offend God, or we are angry at God's creatures for praising God as they were made to do."

Francis dozed, and the mice continued to play. Francis pictured himself before the throne of God, together with the mice who praised God as only they can do. The rhythm of the mice's patter and the heavenly music of the angels refreshed his weariness.

"Most high, all powerful, good Lord," Francis sat up. It had been a long time since he had had the inspiration to compose a song.

Most High, all-powerful, good Lord!
Praise, glory, honor, and every blessing are yours.
To you alone, Most High, do they belong,
And no one is worthy to pronounce your name!

In his near blindness, Francis pictured the colors and sounds of the heavenly chorus. The angels sang "Holy, Holy, Holy" while the saints joined the angels in voices high and low. There was a playful, lightheartedness about the heaven he imagined. He pictured Saint Peter booming with energetic zeal, but untrained voice. He imagined Saint George sitting upright in proud attention upon a pure white stallion. He imagined Saint Agnes, Saint Catherine of Alexandria, and the other radiant virgin martyrs singing with clear voices that almost matched the purity of the angelic overtones. His mother, who had died long ago, was there, her face beautiful and her footsteps light and free. All were surrounded by the all-powerful majesty and love of God. All sang "Holy, holy, holy" for no one could pronounce the name of God. God was beyond every name, every category, and every description.

As Francis continued to compose, a mouse stirred, but snuggled back into its corner.

> *Praise be to you, my Lord, with all your creatures,*
> *Especially Lord Brother Sun.*
> *He is the day. You illuminate us through him.*
> *He is beautiful and radiant with magnificent splendor*
> *Of you, Most High, he is a sign.*

Francis placed his hand on the wall of his hut. The warmth of the morning sun rivaled the heat of Francis's own fevered body, and mirrored the loving energy of God. "At sunrise all the earth praises God for life, for another day, for the light to see the good things of earth and the good things of God," Francis thought.

> *Praise be to you, my Lord, for Sister Moon and Stars,*
> *In heaven you have created them clear, precious,*
>   *and lovely.*

Francis pondered the radiant beauty of Clare's smile. When the brothers were weary and tired, sick, and ready to compromise the rigors of poverty, Clare was the light that illumined, consoled, and gave them new direction. Like the moon and stars, Clare was clear, precious, and lovely. Like the moon and stars, she offered light, peace, and direction.

> *Praise be to you, my Lord, for Brother Wind,*
> *and for air, clouds, stillness, and every season,*
> *by which you give your creatures food.*

> *Praise be to you, my Lord, for Sister Water,*
> *She is useful, humble, precious, and chaste.*

Francis had spent half of his life in the mountains. He knew the wind and its every mood. Francis recalled the pounding rain on La Verna's crags. He remembered the sound of its pelting rhythms, and the glorious freshness of the water-purified air. Francis breathed deeply, wishing that the memory would clear the stuffy dampness of his cell.

> *Praise be to you, my Lord, for Brother Fire,*
> *By whom you illumine the night.*
> *He is beautiful, jovial, robust, and strong.*

Francis imagined the brothers' voices around the evening fire. Over the years, they had prayed, danced, sang, and told stories around Brother Fire. The fire leapt with the freedom of spirit that Francis had so desired to share with his brothers — it had strength, it had heat, it had light, and it had joy. The fire of love still burned in Francis's heart, even though his body was reduced to ashes, still ardent, but without the energy of youth.

> *Praise be to you, My Lord, for our Sister, Mother Earth*
> *She sustains and governs us,*
> *And produces diverse herbs and fruits with colored flowers.*

The poppies would bloom again. Francis loved their vibrant color and fragrance. The oaks at the Portiuncula would be green again. The winter would pass, and Mother Earth would renew herself. Mother Earth would obey her own laws and respect those who did not abuse her. She thrived in peace, and was made barren by the salt of war and violence.

> *Praise and bless my Lord,*
> *Give him thanks,*
> *And serve him with great humility.*

"The role of human beings is to praise God, just as you are doing, Brother Mouse," Francis said as a little creature whizzed over his foot. It was all coming together. "All speak the wonder of God," Francis prayed. "God, you have made all things to praise, worship, and celebrate the splendor of your glory!"

"O Lord, open my lips," Leo's voice sounded outside Francis's door.

"And my mouth shall declare your praise," Francis answered.

Leo stooped to enter the tiny hut and found Francis radiant and eager to sing his *Canticle of Creation* for Brother Leo. Surprised, but happy at Francis's uplifted spirit, Brother Leo, with characteristic simplicity, wrote down Francis's song, repeating each line after Francis.

"Please find Brother Pacifico for me," Francis asked Leo. His heart was joyful, and for the moment, he felt young again. "Before he joined us," Francis explained, "Pacifico was a great poet and a master of courtly song. He could help me now. I want him to go through the world with a few other friars to preach and sing the praises of God. It can be done, Leo!" he exclaimed. Francis's heart raced with his new idea for a way to preach the Gospel.

"A preacher can first deliver the sermon," Francis imagined, "and then the brothers can sing the *Canticle of Creation* as true troubadours of the Lord. After the Canticle, the preacher can announce to the people, 'We are troubadours of God. The only reward we want is to see you live a truly penitential life.'

Isn't this who we are, Brother Leo?" Francis exclaimed. "We are troubadours of God who strive to move people's hearts in order to lead them to the joys of the spirit."

Hesitant to dampen Francis's excitement, Brother Leo cleared his throat, trying to find a way to tell Francis about a new conflict between Assisi and Perugia. The people of Perugia had revolted against their nobility and defeated them in battle. The Roman church had ordered the commune of Assisi to support the nobility and, as expected, Bishop Guido readily complied. The podestà, the leader of the commune of Assisi, Oportulo di Bernardo, sided with the people against the wishes of Pope Honorius III. In response to this disobedience, Bishop Guido excommunicated him. Oportulo responded by having the commune boycott the bishop. Criers and trumpeters went through the city forbidding Assisi's citizens to have commerce, deal with, or communicate with Guido. Families were divided, people were robbed and killed, women were violated.

Francis's heart sank. The movement of brothers and sisters came into existence because of the wisdom and direction of Bishop Guido. Oportulo was a good friend of Francis. His daughter, Agnese, had joined Clare five years ago and was living at the monastery of San Damiano. It grieved Francis that no one, religious or lay, was able to mediate peace between his two good friends.

Brother Leo knew that the news would deeply distress Francis. He silently began unwrapping one of Francis's bandages in order to apply a clean dressing. "Brother Leo," Francis sat up with a start. "Brother Leo, please, go right now and find Brother Masseo and Brother Pacifico. Go at once, Brother Leo."

Brother Leo dropped the bandage and ran to the Portiuncula to find Brothers Masseo and Pacifico. Brother Masseo ran ahead of the others and ducked into Francis's cell.

"Brother Francis," Masseo announced, "it is Brother Masseo."

"Ah, Masseo," Francis sighed, "please do this for me. Go to the podestà and tell him for me that he should go to the bishop's palace with the important men of the commune, and ask him to gather all the people."

Masseo left immediately. A few minutes later, Brother Pacifico arrived with Brother Leo, who trailed breathlessly after him.

"Brother Pacifico," Francis smiled. "I have written a Canticle in praise of God. You must learn it quickly, for Brother Masseo is already in Assisi gathering a crowd." Francis sang the hymn swaying his weary body to the dance-like rhythm. Before the last stanza, he added a verse for the benefit of the bishop and the podestà.

Praise be to you, my Lord,
Through those who grant pardon for love of you,
And sustain infirmity and tribulation.
Blessed are those who endure in peace,
For they will be crowned by you, Most High.

Pacifico listened first and then sang the Canticle twice, with Francis. "Take Brother Angelo and go to the palace of the bishop," Francis ordered Pacifico. "In the presence of the bishop, the podestà, and all the people who have assembled, sing the Canticle. I have confidence that the Lord will put humility and peace in their hearts."

Brother Pacifico taught Angelo and Masseo the Canticle, and the three brothers stood on the steps of the bishop's palace. In a loud, clear voice, Brother Pacifico announced, "Despite his sufferings, Brother Francis has composed this *Canticle of Creation* to praise God and to edify all of you. He asks you to listen with faith and devotion."

The brothers began to sing. Greatly respecting Francis, the podestà folded his hands as if he were listening to the Gospel. Soon, because of his great love and respect for Francis, tears flowed from his eyes. When the brothers finished, Oportulo cried out before the entire gathering, "In truth, not only do I forgive the Lord Bishop who I ought to recognize as my master, but I would even pardon my brother's and my own son's murderer." The podestà threw himself at the feet of Bishop Guido and said to him, "For the love of our Lord Jesus Christ and of Brother Francis, his servant, I am ready to make any atonement you wish." Hanging his head with shame and helping Oportulo to his feet, the bishop responded, "My office demands humility of me, but by nature I am quick to anger. You must forgive me!"

The two embraced and went into the bishop's palace to discuss how they could work as agents of peace in the dispute. The crowd gasped. "Oportulo and Guido are reconciled. This is a miracle!" they shouted.

During that winter, both Cardinal Hugolino and Brother Elias had ordered Francis to go to the Rieti valley to see a doctor who had a reputation for healing diseases of the eye, but Francis was too weak to travel in the cold weather. In June, with the coming of temperate weather, Elias, who was observing Francis's growing weakness, assigned brothers to accompany him on his journey. Before he left, Francis visited Clare and her sisters who wept, fearful that they might never see him again. Eager to console them and knowing that his illness had burdened them, Francis decided to write a song for Clare's sisters that would encourage them in their particular form of life.

Lying in his little hermitage, Francis heard the voices of Brothers Pacifico, Angelo, Masseo, and Leo sing his new song to Clare and her sisters in the church of San Damiano.

Listen, little poor ones, called by the Lord,
From many parts and provinces.
Live always in the truth,
That you might die in obedience.
Do not look to the life outside,
For that of the Spirit is better.
I pray you out of great love,
That you use the alms given to you by the Lord
*   with discretion.*
Those who are weighed down by sickness
And the others who are wearied because of them,
All of you, bear it in peace.

For you will sell this fatigue at a very good price,
And each of you will be crowned queen in heaven
With the Virgin Mary.

The sisters loved their song, and sang it often for their consolation. As he was leaving, Francis visited Clare briefly and wept with her. Both were grateful for the time Francis had spent at San Damiano. Both knew that this precious gift of time would not be repeated.

For nearly a year, Francis went through treatments for his eyes, first in Rieti and then in Siena. His temple and cheek on one side of his face were cauterized, his ears were pierced with red-hot irons, he was prescribed countless salves and ointments. After months of agony with no cure, Francis convinced Elias to allow him to return to the Portiuncula but again the summer's heat took a toll on Francis's health, so the brothers took Francis to the mountain town of Bagnara. There his health took a turn for the worse. In early September, knights from Assisi entered Bagnara to take Francis home. He was too weak to ride, so the knights took turns carrying Francis's limp body like a child through the mountains, back to the bishop's palace in Assisi. Since the Assisians were afraid that he might die and that thieves might steal his body, they posted knights around the palace.

To comfort his soul and ward off discouragement in the midst of his sickness, Francis asked the brothers to sing the *Canticle of Creation*. He especially liked the Canticle sung at night for the edification of the knights who were guarding the palace. When a doctor from Arezzo came to visit him, Francis asked him for an honest prognosis. "You will die in late September or early October," the doctor predicted. Francis raised his arms and said, "Welcome, Sister Death!" Knowing that he was to die soon, Francis begged his brothers to carry him back to Saint Mary of the Angels.

During the final days of September, Brother Elias came to Saint Mary of the Angels to visit the ailing Francis. "Francis," Elias began, "you know that unless God grants a miracle, your sickness is incurable.

"According to the doctors, you do not have much longer to live. I am reminding you of this to comfort your spirit, so that your brothers and others who come to visit you might find you joyful in the Lord. Your life and conduct have already been an example. The way you die will also be a witness."

Francis smiled. "Since I will soon die," Francis whispered, "have Brother Angelo and Brother Leo come and praise our Sister Death for me." Angelo and Leo arrived and, forcing back their tears, they sang Francis's Canticle. Before the final chorus, Francis interrupted them, tagging another verse onto the hymn.

Praise be to you, my Lord, for Sister Bodily Death,
Whom no living person can evade.
Woe to those who die in mortal sin.
Happy are those whom she finds in your holy will,
Because the second death will not harm them.

The next day, Francis called Leo. "You know how much Lady Jacopa di Settesoli from Rome has always loved our community. I think that she would greatly appreciate it, if she were informed of my condition." "Leo," Francis addressed his faithful scribe, "please write to Lady Jacopa and ask her to send us some of that gray monastic cloth, which the Cistercians make, for a tunic. Ask her also to send us some of that cake that she prepared for us many times when we were in Rome."

Leo produced ink, pen, and parchment. Just as he finished writing the letter, Brother Angelo entered with the news that Lady Jacopa had come from Rome and was at the gate asking to visit Francis. "What shall we do, Brother Francis?" asked Angelo. "Shall we allow her to enter and come to your bedside?"

The solution was obvious to Francis. "The rule concerning women is not applicable to Lady Jacopa whose great faith and devotion brought her from so great a distance," Francis responded. Angelo returned with Jacopa who had brought with her a bolt of course gray Cistercian fabric, ingredients for an almond cake Francis loved, a large quantity of wax, and some incense.

"Brothers," Lady Jacopa said softly, trying to speak through her tears, "I began to pray and in my heart I heard a voice say to me, 'Go and visit your Father Francis. Hurry, for if you delay, you will not find him alive.'"

With the fabric that Jacopa brought, the brothers made Francis a tunic for his funeral. Lady Jacopa made Francis his cake, but Francis was so ill that he could hardly touch it. "Brother Bernard would love this cake," Francis smiled, hoping to console his dear Jacopa. He turned to Masseo and said, "Go and tell Brother Bernard to come right away." When Brother Bernard arrived, he sat at the foot of Francis's bed. "Father Francis," Bernard asked, "I beg you to bless me and to give me a sign of your affection." Francis stretched out his hand and mistakenly placed it on Brother Giles who was sitting next to Bernard. "This is not Brother Bernard," Francis said. Then Bernard came closer and Francis put his hand on his head and blessed him. "Brother Leo, write this down," Francis asked. "Brother Bernard was the first brother the Lord gave me. He was the first one who fulfilled the Gospel to the letter by distributing all his goods to the poor. For this and for all his merits, I am obliged to love him more than any other brother. I wish and order, to the extent that lies in my power, that the minister who is responsible for the order, whoever he is, cherish Brother Bernard and honor him as taking my place."

"Now," Francis declared in a weak voice, but with an impish twinkle in his eye, "let us eat cake to celebrate Brother Bernard!" Jacopa was dishing out cake to the brothers, when Brother Filippo arrived with the news that Clare also appeared to be near death. On hearing the report, Francis's heart was filled with anguish. He could not go to see Clare to comfort her in her agony. "Brother Leo," Francis said, "we must write to Sister Clare."

Leo produced his ever-ready writing materials and wrote as Francis dictated. Clare had so struggled to remain faithful to the choice of poverty, despite the fact that she received little support from some of the brothers and had even at times been second-guessed by the well-intentioned Cardinal Hugolino. Francis's countenance had been joyful until now, but as he wrote to his dear Clare, a tear fell from his blind eyes.

"I, little brother Francis," Francis dictated, "wish to follow the life and poverty of our most high Lord Jesus Christ and of his holy mother and to persevere in this until the end. I ask and counsel you, my Ladies, to live always in this most holy life and poverty. Keep a most careful watch so that you never depart from it because of the teaching or advice of anyone."

Brother Leo, who also deeply loved and respected Clare, handed the letter to Francis. "Brother Filippo," Francis called, holding the letter in the air. "Take this letter to Sister Clare. Let her know that before she dies, she and all her sisters will see me again and will receive great consolation from me." Filippo took the letter but then paused, torn whether he should stay with Francis, or go to Sister Clare. "Go, Brother," Francis ordered. "Brother Filippo, go!"

The next morning, Francis asked to see all the brothers staying at the Portiuncula. Speaking with them, as a father to his sons, Francis begged them to love God with all their hearts. He exhorted them to cling patiently to poverty, and to observe the Gospel of Jesus Christ. He placed his right hand on the head of each one and blessed them. When he had finished, he extended his hand over all of them. "Farewell, all you my sons, in the fear of the Lord," he said. "May you remain in God always! Happy are those who persevere in the things they have begun. I am going to the Lord, to whose grace I commend all of you."

The brothers gathered around Francis's bed, some openly sobbing, some holding back tears, and others needing to be near to touch their dying father. As the hours dragged on, Elias brought loaves of bread to Francis so that he might bless them.

He was too weak to break the bread himself, so Brothers Bernard and Elias broke it for him. Francis gave a piece to each of his brothers, and, because he suspected that some might be tempted to keep their bread as a relic, he asked the brothers to eat their entire piece.

Surrounded by his brothers, Francis died during the night of October 3, 1226. Since in Francis's time the days were measured from sunset to sunset, the commemoration of his death was celebrated on October 4. The news spread quickly, and in the morning, the people of Assisi hurried to the Portiuncula. Waving palms in their hands, singing hymns and Francis's *Canticle of Creation*, the priests from the city, the brothers, and all the people escorted Francis's body to Sister Clare. When they reached the church of San Damiano, Brother Elias opened the iron grate through which the sisters received Holy Communion. The brothers lifted the body of Francis from the stretcher and held him in their arms before the opening.

Sister Agnes supported her ailing sister, Clare, who approached the window. Her dark ringed eyes, emaciated face, and weakened limbs reflected the inconsolable anguish of her soul. As she viewed Francis's body, Sister Clare sobbed, and her head fell on the breast of her spiritual father. Agnes, weeping profusely herself, supported her sister, gently comforting her. The other sisters slowly took their turns approaching the window, kissing Francis's hands that the brothers had folded over his body, and bathing Francis's body with their tears. When they finished, Agnes gently lifted the inconsolable Clare, and Elias replaced the grate.

Wishing with all his heart to comfort Sister Clare, Brother Leo swallowed his tears and began to sing as loudly as he could. The brothers and the people joined him.

"Most high, all-powerful, good Lord!
Praise, glory, honor, and every blessing are yours.
To you alone, Most High, do they belong,
And no one is worthy to pronounce your name!"

Praise be to you, my Lord, with all your creatures,
Especially Lord Brother Sun.
He is the day. You illuminate us through him.
He is beautiful and radiant with magnificent splendor
Of you, Most High, he is a sign.

Praise be to you, my Lord, for Sister Moon and Stars,
In heaven you have created them clear, precious, and lovely.

Praise be to you, my Lord, for Brother Wind,
And for air, clouds, stillness, and every season,
By which you give your creatures food.

Praise be to you, my Lord, for Sister Water,
She is useful, humble, precious, and chaste.

Praise be to you, my Lord, for Brother Fire,
By whom you illumine the night.
He is beautiful, jovial, robust, and strong.

Praise be to you, my Lord, for our Sister, Mother Earth.
She sustains and governs us,
And produces diverse herbs and fruits with colored flowers.

Praise be to you, my Lord,
Through those who grant pardon for love of you,
And sustain infirmity and tribulation.
Blessed are those who endure in peace,
For they will be crowned by you, Most High.

Praise be to you, my Lord, for Sister Bodily Death,
Whom no living person can evade.
Woe to those who die in mortal sin.
Happy are those whom she finds in your holy will,
Because the second death will not harm them.

Praise and bless my Lord,
Give him thanks,
And serve him with great humility.

Epilogue

*O*n Sunday, July 16, 1228, the streets of Assisi, festively decked out with flowers and banners, were filled with a throng of brothers, cardinals, bishops, abbots, prelates, secular rulers including John of Brienne, the King of Jerusalem, and hundreds of ordinary, devout people. The trumpeters sounded the arrival of Pope Gregory IX, who, surrounded by cardinals and prelates of the papal court, rode into Assisi for Francis's canonization ceremony. Cardinal Hugolino had become pope, taking the name of Gregory IX, on March 19, 1227, and was honored to celebrate the canonization of his friend. The people met him waving olive branches.

The pope, in vestments richly sewn with gold threads and covered with precious stones, presided over the ceremony held in the piazza in front of the church of San Giorgio. "He shone in his days as the morning star in the midst of a cloud, and as the moon at the full. As the sun when it shines, so did Francis shine in the temple of God," Gregory praised his friend during his sermon.

After the sermon, Pope Gregory IX lifted his hands to heaven and proclaimed in a loud voice: "To the praise and glory of Almighty God, the Father, Son, and Holy Spirit, and of the glorious Virgin Mary and of the blessed apostles Peter and Paul, and to the honor of the glorious Roman Church, at the advice of our brothers and of the other prelates, we decree that the most blessed father Francis, whom the Lord has glorified in heaven and whom we venerate on earth, shall be enrolled in the catalog of saints. His feast shall be celebrated on October 4, the day of his death."

The piazza erupted into cheers, and the cardinals intoned the *Te Deum*. As the churchmen continued their song of praise, a lone humpbacked woman began singing the *Canticle of Creation*. The people joined her in waves and the song rang out in counterpoint to the *Te Deum* and the cheers.

The next day, Monday, July 17, 1228, Pope Gregory IX laid the foundation stone for the Basilica of San Francesco that was to house the remains of Francis and to serve as the destination for the many pilgrims who wished to visit his grave. Brother Elias supervised the building of this grand edifice. Wishing to be close to the grave of his friend, Pope Gregory IX built a magnificent papal palace next to the basilica to serve as his residence when he was in Assisi.

As for the other characters in this story, it is thought that Francis's half-brother, Angelo, died in 1228, and that Pietro and Pica died well before. In the missal that Francis opened to consult the holy Gospel in the church of San Nicolo, there is an obituary note that says that Bishop Guido died shortly after the canonization ceremony in 1228.

Brother Angelo died about 1258. He is buried near Francis's tomb. Brother Bernard spent much of his time in prayer on mountain hermitages, and was sought out by brothers who wished to hear his stories about the early days of the Order. He died at the church of San Francesco between 1241–1246, and is buried in the lower church of San Francesco. Lady Jacopa is buried near the tomb of Saint Francis.

Brother Giles retired to the Monteripido hermitage near Perugia in 1234. Like Bernard, he was visited by Pope Gregory IX, Brother Bonaventure, who wrote an official history of Saint Francis, and others who wished to listen to his early memories of the Order. Giles became a renown mystic and died at Monteripido on April 22, 1262.

Brother Illuminato provided Bonaventure with valuable information concerning Francis's audience with the sultan and about the stigmata. He died about 1266. Brother Leo lived to be an old man, dying about 1278 in Assisi. He was also sought out for his memories of Francis, and he is buried with Angelo near Francis's tomb. Brother Masseo spent his remaining years in the Carceri hermitage above Assisi on Mount Subasio and later at the hermitage of Cibotola west of Perugia. He died in Assisi in 1280, and is also buried near the tomb of Francis.

Brother Pacifico died in Lens, Belgium, about 1230. Brother Jordan stayed in Germany his whole life, became a well-respected leader in the German province, and wrote a chronicle of the early German mission. He died after 1262. Brother Filippo served as visitator of the sisters of San Damiano from 1228–1246. He died in Perugia about 1259. Brother Rufino died about 1278, and is buried near Francis's tomb. Brother Silvester, who also became known for his mysticism, died in Assisi about 1240. His tomb is in the lower church of San Francesco.

Clare spent her life struggling to secure for her sisters the privilege to live without property and privileges. Francis's friends Leo, Giles, Filippo, Elias, and Angelo supported her in this struggle. After much hardship, she received canonical approval for her Rule, the first rule written by a woman to receive this approval, as she lay on her deathbed on August 9, 1253. Two days later, on August 11, 1253, surrounded by the sisters of San Damiano, her blood sister Agnes, and Brothers Angelo and Leo, Clare died. Agnes died in November 1253, soon after her sister. In 1255, Pope Alexander IV canonized Clare.

Historical Note

$\mathcal{S}$ince the thirteen-century, no other time in history has provided those interested in Saint Francis with so much information
on the saint. During the past two hundred years, scholars have
discovered new manuscripts of thirteenth-century Franciscan
writings, have produced critical editions of Franciscan texts, and
have continued to uncover ecclesiastical, civil, sociological, and
archeological information about thirteenth-century medieval
Umbria.

To construct a historical creative project, one must determine the historical value of the given sources. This use of the
historical-critical method in Franciscan sources is called the
"Franciscan Question." Such a process presupposes a number
of complex considerations. One must determine the social,
political, and cultural contexts — *Sitz im Leben* — of a particular
writing, identify the proximity and understanding of the author
to the events narrated, and use philological-literary tools to
determine manuscript genealogies, literary genres, and textual
comparisons.

Those who wish to read further concerning the state of the
"Franciscan Question" might want to study Luigi Pelligrini's "A
Century Reading the Sources for the Life of Francis of Assisi,"
in *Greyfriars Review*, 7:3 (1993): 323–46. Franciscan sources
in their original languages can be found in Enrico Menestb
and Stefano Brufani, eds., Fontes Franciscani (S. Maria degli
Angeli, Assisi: Edizioni Porziuncola, 1995).

While earlier work on the "Franciscan Question" was often
founded on the assumption that earlier materials are the best,
work from the 1960s to the present has emphasized the contex-

tual over the chronological. Certainly, the writings of Francis and Clare are of inestimable value, although even these must be classified as handwritten relics, pieces that were dictated literally, and summarized dictations, i.e., The Admonitions.

In choosing source material for the early life of Francis, I gave primary place to *The Legend of the Three Companions (1246)*. In this, I followed the lead of Thomas of Celano who used *The Legend of the Three Companions,* or at least the oral and written stories behind this text, as a primary source for his *Second Life of Saint Francis,* and more recently of Raoul Manselli in his work *St. Francis of Assisi* (Chicago: Franciscan Herald Press, 1988).

Most Franciscan biographical material, including *The Legend of the Three Companions* and *The Legend of Perugia,* can be found in Marion A. Habig, ed., *St. Francis of Assisi: Omnibus of Sources* (Chicago: Franciscan Herald Press, 1973). The three-volume translation by Regis Armstrong, J. Hellmann, and William Short, *Francis of Assisi: Early Documents* (New City Press, Hyde Park, NY), updates and expands the *Omnibus.* The first volume of this text includes the writings of St. Francis, *Celano's First Life,* and *The Life of St. Francis* by Julian of Speyer. I used some details for Francis's early life from *The Anonymous of Perugia,* trans. Eric Kahn, in Damien Isabell, *Workbook for Franciscan Studies* (Chicago: Franciscan Herald Press, 1979).

I am indebted to the archival work of Arnaldo Fortini in *Francis of Assisi* (New York: Crossroad, 1992), and have based all of my characters on real Assisi people. Although I gave due consideration to Fortini's critics and tried to avoid his tendency to use historical sources in a noncritical way and to stretch at times the limitations of archival sources, his meticulous archival research was critical to the earlier chapters of this novel.

Throughout the book, dreams, visions, the lives of other saints, and prayer experiences play an essential role. My own twenty years as a Franciscan and as a scholar have convinced me of the need to write Christian biography from a Christian perspective. Francis's experience in meeting and falling in love with Jesus Christ was a real experience, and I present it as such. In doing so, I have tried to illustrate Francis's path as an authentic Gospel journey — a journey that is possible for people in our time to adapt and to follow.

In addition to *The Legend of the Three Companions,* I used Francis's own account of the meeting with the leper found in the first three verses of Francis's *Testament.* I consulted Bonaventure's *The Major Legend* as well as *The Legend of Perugia* for source material on the last days of Francis's life. Presently, the best English translation of Bonaventure's *Major Legend is* found in Ewert Cousins, *Bonaventure* (New York: Paulist Press, 1978).

Francis: The Saint of Assisi interprets the early Franciscan movement as a movement of people, men and women, vowed religious and lay. I tried to avoid projecting onto the earliest years the formal legal complexities and polemics that plagued the later First and Second Orders. In the same way, in dealing with the large crowds of lay people that followed Francis, I did not speculate on the formalization of the Third Order. In short, I focused less on Orders and more on the broad Franciscan movement. I have learned this from my study of Clare who, the sources seem to suggest, also had this understanding. Clare saw herself as under the umbrella of Francis's 1209 *Rule* and resisted juridical efforts to separate the brothers from the sisters. While the precedent of the First, Second, and Third Order structure was already established with the Humiliati, Francis, Clare, Giovanni, and Jacopa were less interested in founding canonical Orders as they were in following in the footsteps of Jesus Christ.

For an excellent review of the relationship between Francis and Clare as found in Franciscan sources see Margaret Carney, "Francis and Clare: A Critical Examination of the Sources," in *Greyfriars Review* 3:3 (1989): 315–43. Marco Bartoli's *Clare of Assisi* (Quincy, IL: Franciscan Press, 1993) is also helpful. Raffaele Pazzelli outlines a history of the Third Order in *St. Francis and the Third Order* (Chicago: Franciscan Herald

Press, 1982). The study of the formalization of the Secular Franciscan Order is found in Robert M. Stewart's *De Illis Qui Faciunt Penitentiam — The Rule of the Secular Franciscan Order: Origins, Development, Interpretation* (Roma: Istituto Storico Dei Cappuccini, 1991). Those interested in the Third Order sisters might consult Raffaele Pazzelli, *The Franciscan Sisters* (Steubenville, OH: Franciscan University Press, 1993).

Clare's *Process of Canonization* and to a much lesser extent *The Legend of Clare* are key documents in developing Clare's portrait. Bona di Guelfuccio, Pietro di Damiano, and Lord Ranieri di Bernardo were witnesses in Clare's *Process.* The writings of Francis to Clare are taken from the biographical sixth chapter of Clare's *Rule.* For all sources concerning Saint Clare, see Regis Armstrong, *Clare of Assisi: The Lady* (New York: New City Press, 2006).

Fortini's genealogical work constructing Clare's family tree was very helpful — see Arnaldo Fortini, "New Information about Saint Clare of Assisi," *Greyfriars Review 7:1* (1993): 27–69. Also helpful in developing the Bernardone family portrait was Richard C. Trexler, *Naked Before the Father: The Renunciation of Francis of Assisi* (New York: Peter Lang, 1989). On Clare's tonsure and escape from her home, see an article by Bertulf van Leeuwen entitled, "Clare, Abbess of Penitents," in *Greyfriars Review 4:2* (1990): 73–81. The decrees of the Fourth Lateran Council can be found in Norman P Tanner, ed., *Decrees of the Ecumenical Councils, vol. 1* (Washington, D.C.: Georgetown University Press, 1990): 227–71.

For the creative reconstruction of the journey to the sultan, *The Chronicle of Jordan of Giano* in Placid Hermann's *XIIIth Century Chronicles* (Chicago: Franciscan Herald Press, 1961) has some value. Bonaventure's *Major Legend* gives colorful details. Sections of Jacques de Vitry's Letter of 1220, and chapter 32 of his *History of the Orient* (see *Francis of Assisi: Early Documents,* pages 580–85), are also helpful.

Jordan of Giano's assignment to Germany is an autobiographical account found in *The Chronicle of Jordan of Giano.* I included it, not only because of its historical solidity, but also because it beautifully captures the mood and spirituality of the early brothers.

The texts for the sermon at Greccio are adopted from Francis's "Vespers for Christmas" from the *Office of the Passion,* from Francis's *Letter to the Entire Order,* and from Clare's *Fourth Letter to Agnes of Prague.* Details of the Greccio stories, the Christmas story, and the rabbit who became the companion of Francis, were based on accounts found in Celano's *First Life.*

While the second part of *The Little Flowers of Saint Francis,* "The Considerations on the Holy Stigmata," has questionable historical value, its persistent popularity and proven ability to convert lives establishes it as an important spiritual source. "The Considerations on the Holy Stigmata," better than any biographical account, develops Francis's spiritual journey toward the stigmata, beginning with the dynamic of his prayerful desire, his persistent prayer and deepening need for solitude, and ending with the desired grace. While the hagiographic pattern of the holy person is certainly the framework of *The Little Flowers* account, the hagiographic stylistics, accompanied by the stark reality of Francis's impatience with his long and painful illness, helps one to understand Francis's identification with the crucified Christ. Using this same rationale, I have included the story of perfect joy, also from *The Little Flowers,* because of its proven spiritual value. See Raphael Brown, *The Little Flowers of Saint Francis* (New York: Doubleday, 1958). I relied upon *The Legend of Peruga as* my primary source for the last years of Francis's life.

Clare's lament upon the death of Francis is stylized by Celano. Although I did not quote his hagiographic rhetoric, I feel that Celano did not exaggerate the depths of sorrow Clare felt at the death of Francis. Clare's desperate struggle to remain faithful to her dream of living without personal or communal property or privileges becomes the story of her life after Francis's death. For Clare's story in full see Joan Mueller

The Provilege of Poverty (University Park, PA: The Pennsylvania State university Press, 2006).

We do not possess a formal canonization process for Francis as we do for Clare. Details of Francis's canonization can be found in *The Legend of the Three Companions* and in *The First Life of Celano.*

Finally, a historical novel is ultimately a creative work. While I have tried rigorously to follow the lead of the historical sources in both fact and spirit, the color needed to make a historical sketch come to life, i.e., clothes people wore, personalities they had, transitional scenes, the appearance of places, were often my own invention. Other than this color, I tried to keep the work simple, or perhaps one might say complex, in that I did my best to abstain from placing a contemporary slant on the story. It seemed to me that the early Franciscan story in and of itself was far more powerful than any point of view I might impose upon it. If there is any personal bias, it is my emphasis on the Franciscan struggle for peace, which seems to be consistent with the spirit of both Francis and Clare.